TROL

In the center of the s
between the two comba
are you certain you w
by combat to the death.

"*I* would," Zoli said. "It's not combat, it's bloody murder. I've eaten seafood that had more hope of killing me than *this* idiot." She gestured scornfully at Goodwife Eyebright.

"*Will* you withdraw?" Duke Janifer turned to Goodwife Eyebright, entreating her with his eyes. "Pleeease?"

Eyebright stood herself up a bit taller and held the sword she'd been given as though it were a carpet beater. "I'd sooner die."

"I was afraid you'd say that." The duke sighed, shrugged, and tossed a bright orange kerchief high into the air. As he dashed from the arena he called back over one shoulder. "When it hits the ground, start fighting."

The audience gasped and held its breath. Zoli went into her preferred fighting stance, grim and silent, eyes fixed on the floating kerchief. Goodwife Eyebright, on the other hand, began jabbering the instant the bit of cloth left the duke's hand.

"My gracious, aren't you in a hurry? I'm sure it's not going to take you long to kill me, but don't you worry about that. Nor about all my poor little lambkins that'll be left orphaned and helpless, oh no, don't you give any of them a second thought. You've done your duty, you don't have to bother your head about whether they'll be decently clothed and fed and who'll tuck them into their cold, lonesome little beds of a winter's night with not ever the comfort of a loving mother's kiss on their tiny tear-stained faces, no. Don't you concern yourself over their bitter tears or their heartbreaking sobs or their—"

Under Goodwife Eyebright's verbal barrage, Zoli's shoulder trembled and her sword drooped by degrees, leaving a hole in her defensive posture fit to drive an oxcart through. . . .

—from "Troll by Jury"

The Chick is in the Mail

EDITED BY

Esther Friesner

A Baen Books Original

Baen Publishing Enterprises
P.O. Box 1403
Riverdale, NY 10471
www.baen.com

ISBN: 0-671-31950-7

Cover art by Larry Elmore

First printing, October 2000

Distributed by Simon & Schuster
1230 Avenue of the Americas
New York, NY 10020

Production by Windhaven Press, Auburn, NH
Printed in the United States of America

Contents

Introduction

Esther Friesner

Tradition is a wonderful thing. It gives us a sense of history, of belonging to something greater than ourselves, but it most of all gives us someone and/or something other than ourselves to blame for the embarrassing stuff we feel compelled to do. Yes sir, every time you find yourself serving the fruitcake-that-tastes-like-a-doorstop at Christmas, or saying, "Prithee, my comely wench, but mightst thou servest me an hotte dogge with ye workes?" at a local Ren Faire, or fighting the neighborhood raccoons for property rights to a swiftly rotting jack-o'-lantern at Hallowe'en, or singing the Whiffenpoof Song at the big Harvard–Yale game when you wouldn't know a whiffen if it poofed all over you, you can always defend your actions with the proud and clarion cry: "It's a *tradition!*"

(You can also try blaming it on your kids, if you prefer, but that won't work with the Whiffenpoof Song. Even kids aren't *that* gullible.)

1

Now here at the *Chicks in Chainmail* series of hard-hitting and culturally enriched anthologies, we've got a little tradition of our own. We call it Blaming Someone for the Title of the Current Book. Your humble and obedient editor took full responsibility—and rightly so—for the series concept as well as for the title of the first book, but since then, although the concept has remained true and fixed as the pole star, the blame for the titles of individual volumes in the series has gone skipping merrily hither, thither, and yon.

So let it be known, now and for all time, that the person who came up with the title for *this* one is Mr. Robin Wayne Bailey of Kansas City, Missouri, a fine writer and a great American. (He also has a story in this anthology, but please note that there is *no connection* between coming up with a title for our fourth *Chicks* book and getting a story accepted. None. So don't go getting any erroneous ideas. Thank you.)

Now that we've settled that, I'd like to share with you one of the joys of Editorhood. Recently, along with the rest of the *Chicks* series fanmail, I received a rather . . . unique missive from a gentleman by the name of Jeffrey Tolliver who resides in the great state of Ohio. With Mr. Tolliver's consent, I now share with you a brief description of the contents of his letter:

Chicks in chain mail.

Yes, that's right, your eyes have not betrayed you: Mr. Tolliver is a talented and creative maker of chain mail armor and so, inspired no doubt by the literary splendors of this august series, he crafted chain mail for five (count 'em, five) stuffed chickens. Of the *toy* stuffed chicken variety. Chain mail on a *roast* stuffed chicken is just *sick*.

I have photographic proof of this chicken bechainmailing in my possession. He named them after the

Dionne quintuplets and, in my opinion, they are darned cute. He also crafted two wonderful sets of chain mail for a pair of teddybears, Leif Bearicson and Bearic the Red and encourages us all to support our right to arm bears.

None of this is my fault either. I've got witnesses.

With stuff like that happening in the so-called Real World, you would think that the contributors to this volume of *Chicks* might be hard-pressed to outdo it on the strange-and-wonderful scale, but they did. You'll find tales here by some Repeat Offenders as well as by some First-Timers. You'll also find characters who have appeared in previous *Chicks* books cheek-by-jowl with new creations. Think of it as opening a box of chocolates, only without anyone doing a bad Forrest Gump imitation. Make it a nice, *big* box of chocolates, while you're at it, Godiva for preference, and go heavy on the cherry cordials. I hope you'll be pleased.

Now before I free you to romp barefoot through the rest of this volume, I'd like to take a moment of your time for something serious: This book is dedicated to the memory of my mother, Beatrice Friesner, who passed away in the autumn of 1999. She went through the Depression, World War II, taught in a one-room schoolhouse in upstate New York before serving in the New York City public schools—junior and senior high—for over thirty years, and raised me. (Her own mother insisted that her daughter as well as her sons get a college education even when most people scoffed, saying that higher education was wasted on a girl. Ha!) She faced plenty of trials and adversity in her life, but she never backed down and she always put up a good, honorable fight. I consider her and her mother before her to be true Warrior Women.

I also consider this to be one tradition that is well worth carrying on.

To His
Iron-Clad Mistress

Kent Patterson

You don't need no chain mail bra, dear.
You don't need no brass pants, too.
You don't need to dress in armor
When I'm snuggled close to you.

Don't think that you can charm me,
Or prove our love more real,
By buying all your underwear
From the boutique at U.S. Steel.

So what say we drop the hardware,
The swords and shields and toys,
And make love less like Sherman tanks,
And more like girls and boys.

Sweet Charity

Elizabeth Moon

Krystal Winterborn eyed her lumpish fellow members of the Ladies Aid & Armor Society, and sighed. There they were: the brave, the bold, the strong . . . the plain.

She was tired of being the butt of their jokes, just because she paid extra on her health-care plan for a complexion spell to keep her peach-blossom cheeks and pearly teeth. They laughed at her herbal shampoos, the protective grease she wore on summer maneuvers. They rolled their eyes at her fringed leather outfits, her spike-heeled dress boots.

Well, this year's Charity Ball would show them. No more laughing, when she was Queen of the Ball, and raised many times more for the orphaned daughters of soldiers killed in the line of duty. She would never have to hear their condescending "Shut up, Krystal" again.

When the chair asked for volunteers, Krystal surprised everyone by signing up for Invitations.

Harald Redbeard had come to the city in the character of an honest merchant. Downriver, on the coast, everyone knew he was a Fish Islands pirate. The coast patrol had almost trapped him in Hunport, but instead of making a break for the sea, he'd come upriver with his crew, until things quieted down.

It was nigh on midwinter when he reached the kingdom known to its downstream neighbors as the Swordladies' Domain. He grinned at that—most of the mountain kingdoms had a reputation for fierce warrior women. But the only warrior women he'd seen had been bouncers at Gully Blue's tavern in Hunport. He'd tossed both of them into the harbor.

An icy wind blew from the mountains, and lowering clouds promised snow as the crew offloaded their cargo; Harald sent old Boris One-eye off to find them an inn. One-eye reported that he'd found rooms at the Green Cat, and he'd seen some warrior women.

"Like soldiers, they are, in uniform."

"Not a problem," Harald said. "If they're part of the city guard, that'll make it all the easier for us."

"How?"

"City guards are city guards the world over," Harald said, rubbing fingers and thumb.

That night in the Green Cat's bar, Harald kept eyes and ears open. One particular corner table caught his interest. A cute perky blonde wearing fringed black leather and polished brass pouted at the louts around her, who were all clearly ready to do anything for another glance down her cleavage.

If that was an example of local women warriors, he and his men had nothing to worry about. She was too pretty, too smooth-skinned and full-lipped, to know what to do with the fancy little dagger at her belt, let alone a real sword. Her followers, big and muscular enough, wore fashions he'd seen only in the grittier port brothels, but no visible weapons.

When the blonde pushed back from the table, he saw that she actually had cute little muscles in her arms. She glanced over at him, and he grinned, raising his mug appreciatively. She stuck out her adorable lower lip; one of her followers turned to glower at him. Harald shrugged, unperturbed. He watched as she undulated across the room. Every part of her— many visible through the long black fringe—suggested unspeakable delights.

Harald turned back to his ale, as she flounced out the door, to find that the burly fellow with the bits of metal through his ears and nose was now beside him. "She's beautiful," Harald said. Under the table, his hand slid down to the hilt of his boot knife. "You can't blame a man for looking."

"S'long as you're respectful," the man said.

"Oh, I am," Harald said. "But such beauty cannot be denied."

The burly man grinned. "Since you appreciate her many qualities, perhaps you'd like to make her acquaintance a little closer?"

What was this? Was the woman a high-priced whore, and this her pimp? Did they think he'd been born under a rhubarb leaf, and still had the dew on his backside?

Harald brought the knife up in one smooth motion, and laid the tip in an appropriate place. To his surprise, the burly man neither flinched nor changed expression.

"No need for that," he said. "I just wanted to invite you to the Ladies' Aid and Armor Society Charity Ball. Being as it's midwinter, and cruel dull for a stranger in town otherwise, with all the taverns closed for three days—I thought you might enjoy it."

"The Ladies' Aid and Armor Society? What's that,

a bunch of women in bronze bras and fringe playing with toy swords?"

The man laughed. "Not exactly. But they clean up nicer than usual, for the Charity Ball for the Orphans' Fund. There's this contest, for queen; everybody who goes can vote. Thing is, the other cats pack the place with their supporters, so although our Krystal is far and away the most beautiful, she never wins. This year, we're changing that. All I want from you is a vote for her. We'll pay the donation and everything."

These upriver barbarians had strange customs. Collecting money to support girl orphans, when girl orphans properly managed could support him? Taverns closed three days? His crew would go crazy and start breaking open barrels on their own; he couldn't afford that. This ball now—fancy dress, jewels, money—looked like fun and profit combined.

"Tell you what," Harald said, slipping the knife back into his boot. "My friends wouldn't like it if I went and they had to stay here with nothing to drink. If you can get us all in, that's more votes. How about it?"

"Great. My name's Gordamish Ringwearer, by the way; you can call me Gordy. I'll need all your names for the invitations—nobody gets in without one."

Mirabel Stonefist scowled at the stacks of invitations. Every year, she tried to argue the Planning Committee into hiring a real scribe to address them, and every year the Committee insisted it was too expensive. They had to have money for decorations, for the orchestra, for the food, and of course the drink. Which meant that each member of the LA&AS had to address a stack of envelopes herself, in whatever scrawly, scribbly, crabbed and illegible handwriting she possessed.

Primula Hardaxe, chair of the Committee, always made some remark about Mirabel's handwriting. *I never claimed to be an artist*, Mirabel thought, stabbing the tip of the quill into the ink-bowl. *Not with anything but a sword, that is*. She looked at the list she'd been given. Naturally she was not entrusted with the invitations to important persons. She hadn't been since the time her version of "Lord Pondicherry and Lady Cordelia" was misread as "Lard Pound and Laid Coldeels" and delivered to the butcher's.

She was halfway through the list when her old resentment cleared and she noticed the names. Harald Redbeard? She'd heard that name before, surely. She shook her head and copied it as carefully as she could. Skyver Twoswords? Again, something tickled her memory then withdrew. Gordamish Ringwearer? Probably the cavalry units; they recruited all sorts of people, not just the solid peasants and smalltraders' children who ended up in the *real* army.

She realized she'd just left the "g" out of Ringwearer, and muttered an oath. That's what thinking did for you, caused mistakes. It wasn't up to her to decide who got invitations; all she had to do was address the blasted things. She struggled through Piktush Drakbar, Zertin Dioth, Badaxe Oferbyte, and the rest.

At last, she had her stack finished—smudged with sweaty thumbprints, slightly rumpled, but finished. She put them in the basket (noting that it was now half full) and stirred them around. With luck, Primula wouldn't know who had done which. She hoped that every year.

Three days before the ball, Mirabel tugged at the bodice of her green ball gown. Her armor still fit; what was the matter with this thing?

Of course she could wear a corset. She hated corsets. Just something else to take off, the way she looked at it. She tugged again, and something ripped. Perhaps she could get through the ball without raising her arms. No. She liked to dance, and she liked to dance fast. She pawed through her trunk. The old copper silk still had that chocolate stain down the front where she'd jogged someone's elbow, and the midnight blue had moth all up the front center panel.

Time for a new gown, then; after all, she'd worn this one four years.

Strictly speaking, it was not a costume ball. But it had become customary for guests to dress up in whatever fanciful outfits they chose. Thus the appearance of a crew of pirates (striped loose trousers, bucket boots, eye patches), several barechested barbarians, and someone clad mostly in chains and other bits of uncomfortable-looking metal attachments provoked little comment. They had invitations, surrendered at the door to a little girl wearing the red cloak of a Ladies' Aid & Armor Society ward, and that was all that mattered.

Sergeants Gorse, Covet, Biersley, Dogwood, Ellis, and Slays, all resplendent in dress blue, were not so lucky. They had attended the ball for years; the Ladies' Aid & Armor Society knew better than to exclude sergeants. This meant nothing to the stubborn nine-year-old who had been told to let no one through without a card. Last year she'd been banished to bed after singing "Sweet Sword of Mine" with the orphan chorus, and she was determined to prove she was old enough for the responsibility.

"They just forgot to send ours, or it got lost," Sergeant Gorse said. "We're *sergeants*, Missy. Sergeants are always invited."

"Miss Primula said no one can go in without an invitation, no matter what they say." The nine-year-old tossed her butter-colored braids and glared up at them. The sergeants shuffled their feet. Any one of them could have tucked her under one arm and

had room for a barrel of beer, but she was an orphan.
A soldier's orphan.

"Suppose you call Miss Primula, then."

"She said don't bother her," the nine-year-old said.
"She's busy."

Sergeant Heath strolled up behind the other sergeants, also resplendent in dress blue. "What's going
on here? Why are you fellows blocking the door?"

"They don't have invitations!" clashed with "This
child won't let us in, and we're *sergeants*."

"Decided not to invite you lot this year, eh?"
Sergeant Heath smiled unctuously at the child, and
reached past Sergeant Gorse to hand over his card.
"Remember your antics last year, do they? That bit
with the tropical fruit surprise not quite so funny on
second thought?" He strolled through, exuding vir-
tue. The others glared after him, then at Sergeant
Gorse.

"It wasn't my fault," Sergeant Gorse said. "It was
really Corporal Nitley, and I know *he* got an invitation." He looked around and spotted a familiar figure hurrying along the street.

"She'll take care of this," he said confidently. She
was, after all, in his unit.

Mirabel Stonefist discovered that no one had time
to make her a gown, or even repair the old one. She
tried the plastic wizard the Ladies' Aid & Armor
Society had on retainer, but he was overbooked,
without even a spare six-hour reweaving or banish-
stain spell.

She couldn't possibly mend it herself. She was even
clumsier with needle and thread than with a pen. That
left only one possibility, her sister Monica. The
Monica who was still angry with her for not rescuing Cavernous Dire from a dragon. Hoping for the
best, Mirabel knocked on her sister's door and
explained her problem.

"You have a lot of nerve," Monica said. "You didn't even invite us this year."

"I put your name on the list," Mirabel said. "I always do."

"I'm sure," Monica said, in the tone that meant she didn't believe it. "But when you need something—at the last minute I notice, never mind my convenience—here you are. I'll fix it for you all right!" Monica grabbed the dress, and ripped the bodice all the way to the waist. "There!" Then she slammed the door in Mirabel's face.

Mirabel turned away from the door. That was it, then. She would just have to go in uniform, and be laughed at. As she trudged down Sweet Street, someone hailed her.

"Why so gloomy?" Dorcas Doublejoints asked. Dorcas, an exotic dancer, had maintained her friendship with the LA&AS ever since they'd solved the mystery of her missing belly.

Mirabel explained, and displayed the torn bodice.

"Oh, that's not a problem." Dorcas eyed her. "You won't fit my clothes, but we have lots of clothes in my house. Come along with me."

Mirabel stood in Dorcas's suite, with a flutter of lovely girls around her, all offering their best gowns. She noticed that they all called Dorcas "Miss Dorcas, dear" and drew her own conclusions. Somewhat to her surprise, she found that the strumpets' best gowns were fine silk of the first quality.

Her fashion advisors settled on an apricot-shot silk with shimmering highlights. It hugged her body to the hips, then flared into a wide rippling skirt. Three-puff sleeves ended in a drape of ivory lace. A small scrap of the same lace peeked from the depths of the decolletage in front. Mirabel had always liked low-cut gowns, but this one—she peered at herself in the mirror, wondering if she dared.

"Of course you do," Dorcas said, and the girls murmured agreement and admiration. "You have a beautiful back, and quite sufficient cleavage. Enjoy it while you can." Mirabel grinned at her image, thinking what her sister would say. No one had mentioned "corset," either.

The girls put up her hair, sprinkled it with something glittery, then painted her face. Ordinarily Mirabel didn't use cosmetics, but she liked what she saw in the mirror. A shy redhead offered her dangling emerald earrings, and a luscious brunette contributed an emerald necklace so spectacular that Mirabel knew it must be a fake. At last Dorcas handed her a fluffy shawl, refused her offer of payment for the loan of all this finery ("Don't be silly, dear; we're friends") and ushered her out the back door.

So, in the gathering gloom, Mirabel Stonefist found herself going to the ball in the most gorgeous outfit she'd ever worn. Although it was a cold evening, and so much exposed flesh should have chilled her, she felt warm through with excitement. She would be careful with her borrowed glamour, she told herself. No jogging elbows, no tripping, no catching the lace on someone's belt buckle. She'd take everything back the next day, safe and sound.

"Hey—Stonefist!"

She looked up, and there were the sergeants—six of them anyway—in their dress blues.

"Yessir?" Even on Ball Night, she couldn't avoid calling them "sir," at least once.

"Did you write the invitations this year?"

"Some of them," Mirabel said cautiously. "Why?"

"We didn't get ours," Sergeant Gorse said. "Didn't you notice we weren't on the list?"

"I didn't do all of them," Mirabel said. "Everybody helps. Are you sure they didn't just get lost? What did Primula say?"

"We can't ask Primula," Sergeant Gorse said, "because that child at the door won't let us in without an invitation, and she won't call Primula to the door. Get this straightened out."

"Of course," Mirabel said. She paused. "Are you sure it didn't have anything to do with the tropical fruit surprise?"

"Yes!" they all said. Mirabel shrugged, and turned away to the door.

"Good evening, Miss Mirabel," said the child. The flaps of her red felt cap liner almost reached her shoulders; the little bronze cap with its tiny spike glittered in the torchlight. "I'm being really careful about the cards."

"Good for you," Mirabel said absently, looking around for Primula. Stalls offering the orphans' handiwork filled every alcove; guests were expected to buy patchwork pigs, lopsided clay bowls, and other useless items to swell the Orphans' Fund. Primula—wearing the same stiff black bombazine trimmed in purple bobbles that she'd worn for the past millennium—leaned over the piecework table. Mirabel threaded her way through the crowd, nodding to acquaintances, and heard the last of the lecture.

"—Now remember—you curtsey and say 'Thank you, kind sir' or 'kind missus' as the case may be, and hand them the purchase first, then the change. Is that clear?"

"Yes, Miss Primula." The freckled girl in charge of this stall was older than the doorkeeper—old enough to be allowed to handle money. Primula turned away, and caught sight of Mirabel.

"My dear! A new dress after all?"

"In a manner of speaking." Mirabel let the shawl drop, and Primula blinked.

"Is it that low in back?"

Mirabel twirled, to a chorus of wolf whistles.

"Well," Primula said. "I must say I'm surprised. I thought you'd be wearing that old green gown forever."

Mirabel ignored this. "Did you leave the sergeants off the list on purpose?"

"The list?"

"Invitations. Sergeant Gorse didn't get one. Or Sergeants Covet, Biersley, Dogwood, Ellis, and Slays. They're all outside—they were sure you'd *meant* to invite them—but little Sarajane at the door wouldn't let them in, or call you."

"But of course they're invited," Primula said. "Though I did think that tropical fruit surprise trick wasn't funny. Now who was it, who should have had their names . . . ?" She closed her eyes, evidently trying to remember. Mirabel touched her arm.

"Thing is, they're out there in the cold now. Don't you want to let them in?"

"Oh. Of course." She bustled away. Mirabel let the shawl drop again and looked around for people she knew. An eye-patched pirate with a red beard and moustache appeared in front of her, his visible eye twinkling.

"My dear, I am tempted to live up to my costume and carry you away into tropical captivity—you are delectable."

She didn't recognize his accent, or his face, but what did that matter? "Sirrah, I fear you admire only my jewels, and not my face—"

"T'would be useless to deny the beauty of your jewels, but you—" His eye raked her up and down, and his hand stroked his moustache. "You are the pearl beyond price, compared to which your emeralds are mere baubles of colored glass."

Mirabel blinked. With that glib tongue, he ought to be a horse trader, but she knew all the horse traders in town. "I fear, sir, I know you not."

"I'm Harald Redbeard," he said.

"I wrote your invitation," Mirabel said. "I've been wondering who you are. Shall we dance?"

"With a will," he said, and offered his arm.

In the course of the first two dances, Mirabel discovered that Harald suited her perfectly as a dance partner. Tireless, nimble, quick-witted, familiar with all the standard dance patterns and variations . . . and with unflagging appreciation of her charms, which he described in terms that made her fantasize about the latter half of the ball.

She would happily have danced more with Harald Redbeard, but Nuttin Broadaxe tapped her firmly on the shoulder at the end of the second, and she remembered that she'd promised him a dance last week.

"Excuse me," she said, giving Harald a last squeeze of the hand and significant glance from under her lashes. He bowed.

Nutty was, after Harald, a letdown. A competent enough dancer, he felt no obligation to flatter someone he already knew beyond, "Gosh, Mirabel, this dress doesn't have any back at all!" and "Good thing that necklace isn't real; some thief would have it off you in no time." Instead, he regaled her with a description of the Queen's emerald necklace: "a lot like that paste thing you're wearing, actually, but of course hers is real." The last thing Mirabel wanted to hear about was the Queen; the Queen didn't like women soldiers in general, and Mirabel in particular.

Mirabel parted from Nutty at the end of that dance, pleading a need for something to drink, and went in search of Harald. Before she was halfway to the drinks table, Primula had caught her by the arm. "Mirabel, didn't you have Sergeant Gorse in your list of names?"

It took a moment to think what Primula was talking about, and then she shook her head. "No—I'd have remembered. At least half mine were people I'd never heard of."

"Oh." Primula let go and wandered off. Mirabel made her way to the drinks table, handed in her chit for a free drink, and spotted the chancellor, Sophora Segundiflora, chatting with two ministers of state, and a banker. Mirabel edged that way, keeping an eye out for Harald.

"Mirabel . . . what a lovely gown," Sophora said. "And necklace, too. So like the Queen's, did you know that?" Her voice had the slightest edge.

"No . . . it's borrowed."

"Ah. I'm glad you didn't wear it just to annoy her. It's amazingly good—it hardly looks like paste at all."

No one ignored Sophora's hints. "Do you think I should take it off?"

"Perhaps—oh, dear." Sophora looked past Mirabel and then murmured, very fast. "It's too late, be sure you tell her it's a cheap imitation and that you borrowed it." Then, in her usual ringing tone, "Good evening, Your Majesties. What an honor to have you at the ball."

Mirabel turned. The Queen's face squinched up as she recognized Mirabel—then paled in fury as she recognized the necklace.

"Where did you get that!?" the Queen demanded. "What are you playing at?"

Mirabel looked at the Queen's necklace—as like her borrowed one as if it were spell-doubled, except that the emeralds seemed somehow diluted of their rich green color. Perhaps that was because of the taupe gown the Queen wore, perhaps the colors cancelled out or something. "I'm—I'm sorry, Your Majesty," she said, attempting a curtsey. "I just borrowed this—I didn't know—"

"Borrowed! From whom, may I ask?"

"A—a friend." Instinct, racing ahead of thought, warned her not to give a name. "A—a dancer. It's only paste, Your Majesty, and I didn't know it was a copy of yours—"

"A likely story," the Queen sniffed. She turned to the King. "You promised me mine was unique. No other like it, you said, an exclusive design. And now I see it around the neck of a muscle-bound swordswoman who got it from some bawd. What do you say to that, eh? I demand that you take this up with the Royal Jeweler; if he's selling copies on the sly—"

Mirabel glanced at the King, who looked paler than the Queen. He patted the Queen's arm. "It's not like that—" he began.

"Not like what?" the Queen asked. Her brow furrowed. "Did you *know* about this? Did you intend for me to be humiliated in front of everyone?"

Mirabel edged away from what promised to be a royal spat of epic proportions, and bumped into a large well-muscled man in barbarian costume of fur and leather, who leered straight down her cleavage. She vaguely recalled seeing him with Krystal, but couldn't think of his name.

"You're . . . stunning," he said, dragging his gaze back up to her face, but only momentarily.

"Who are you?" Mirabel asked.

"Skyver Twoswords," he said.

Another one whose invitation she'd addressed, and wondered about. "You're a friend of Krystal's, aren't you?" she asked.

He gulped, blushed, and said, "Well, sort of. More than, actually."

Mirabel eyed him with more interest. "Sort of?"

"Well, she's . . . you know . . . she's different."

Different was not the adjective Mirabel would have chosen. Just then the band struck up "Granny Morely's Wedding," one of her favorite pattern dances, and she smiled at Skyver. "Want to dance?"

"Er . . . I'm sorry . . . Krystal told me to stay here."

"Do you always do what Krystal says?" *It was on*

a bright May morning . . . when Granny Morely came . . . Her foot tapped the rhythm.

"Well . . . er . . . yes. I'm supposed to . . . "

. . . With all her friends and relatives . . . to change her maiden name . . . Skyver looked glum and embarrassed all at once, and Mirabel didn't want to miss the dance. She looked around for another partner.

"There you are!" Sergeant Gorse said. He beamed at her, not his usual expression. "May I have the honor?"

They set off into the pattern: *She had pink ribbons in her hair . . . she had them on her shoe . . .* and Sergeant Gorse inserted his words where he could. "I wanted to thank you . . . for getting us in. Some mistake . . . just as we thought . . . "

"My pleasure," Mirabel said, ducking under his upraised arm twice for *She turned herself about again, as shy maids often do*, and caught sight of Krystal in the middle of the next row. She was dancing with Harald, and Mirabel almost tripped to see the same look given to Krystal that he had given to her. Then she shrugged—what did she expect from a smooth-tongued stranger at the ball? She continued the figure with her usual enthusiasm, all the way to *And so you see, dear children, was never such a sight, as Gramps and Granny Morely, upon their wedding night*, which ended with a whirling embrace.

"You dance as well as you . . . er . . . look," Sergeant Gorse said.

"My turn, Quill," said Sergeant Dogwood. He bowed to Mirabel. "If I might have the honor."

Mirabel spent the next five dances with the sergeants, one after the other; by then she wanted a rest. Though the sales booths hid the alcoves, she managed to squeeze in behind the patchwork animals, where she lounged sideways on the bench with her feet up. The freckled girl looked at her.

"I don't know if you're supposed to be here. Miss Primula said—"

"Miss Primula hasn't been dancing with six sergeants, child; my feet hurt."

From her vantage point, she could peek over the pile of patchwork animals and see the dancers. At one side of the ballroom, the King and Queen sat on a dais, pointedly not looking at each other. Sophora had collected another two ministers and the Duke of Mandergash. Then she spotted Harald by his red beard, and next to him Krystal.

Krystal leaned gracefully against a pillar, her followers around her . . . two barbarians, a man dressed in leather straps and chains, half a dozen pirates, and someone wearing a long plaid skirt with his face painted green and a green target painted on his naked chest. Krystal herself wore a gown like nothing Mirabel had ever seen—it might have been painted on, glittering silver mesh slit up the side to reveal her tall dress boots. She was, Mirabel had to admit, incredibly beautiful.

"Mirabel Stonefist, what *are* you doing back there lounging at your ease while the rest of us—" Primula glared over the stack of stuffed animals.

"I tried to tell her, Miss Primula," bleated the freckled girl. "She wouldn't listen."

"She never does," Primula said to the girl. Then to Mirabel, "Come right out of there; I need to talk to you."

"My feet hurt," Mirabel muttered, but she knew it would do no good. She got up and squeezed back past the corner post of the booth.

"I had to go to the office for my master lists," Primula said, "I have them here." She waved a sheaf of papers.

"*And now, majesties, lords and ladies, gentlemen and women of quality, it's time to vote for the Queen of the Ball—*" That was Lord Mander Thunderblatt.

"We honor the Ladies' Aid and Armor Society, by choosing one among them to reign as queen for a night—meaning no disrespect to Your Majesty, of course . . . "

"Will you pay attention, Mirabel! Quickly now— you say you didn't have Sergeant Gorse on your list?"

"No, I told you."

"Do you remember who you did have?"

Mirabel thought about it. "Corporal Venturi, Corporal Dobbs, Granish the greengrocer, Stebbins the headgroom of the royal stables . . ." She noticed Primula ticking these off on the master list. "Er . . . Harald Redbeard, Skyver Twoswords, Gordamish Ringwearer, Piktush somebody . . . I can't remember anymore. Someone named Overbite or something like that."

"Just as I thought!" Primula looked simultaneously triumphant and furious. "Those are not on my list at all."

"All of them?"

"No, the last four. Who gave you your list?"

Mirabel blinked. "Krystal, of course."

"Now you remember the rules," Lord Mander said. *"Nominators contribute a gold piece to the Fund; voters contribute ten silvers. Ladies of the Society may not nominate themselves—not that any of our hostesses would—but may nominate another Member, as well as vote . . . "*

"That scheming little tramp!" Primula said. "I see it all now—"

"I nominate Krystal Winterborn!" someone called.

"She's wanted to be Queen for years," Primula said. "And now she's cheated—"

"Huh?"

"She stacked the lists," Primula said. "Erased some of the names she knew would vote against her and added her friends." Primula tapped her own sheaf of papers. "I'll soon put a stop to this nonsense—"

"*I nominate Cabella Ironhand!*" called someone else. Cabella had been Queen of the Ball for the past three years; as a sergeant herself, she could count on the sergeants and corporals to vote for her.

"*I nominate Sophora Segundiflora*," yelled another.

"I refuse the nomination," Sophora said. "But thank you."

Across the floor, Harald Redbeard met Mirabel's eyes and grinned; then he winked. "*I nominate Mirabel Stonefist*," he said loudly. Krystal whirled and glared at him; Mirabel felt as if she'd just had the wind knocked out of her. What did he mean? She'd never been a candidate for Queen of the Ball.

"What are you up to?" asked Primula.

"Nothing," Mirabel said. "I had nothing to do with it."

Primula glared at her, but apparently decided Krystal was the bigger game, and started across the floor.

"Nominators, make your way to the Donations Table," Lord Mander said. "Voters, you may begin lining up to vote when the nominations have been verified. Nominees, come join me at the front of the room."

"Go on, silly," said the freckle-faced girl when Mirabel hesitated. "I didn't realize you were important—imagine being nominated for Queen of the Ball."

Mirabel made her way through the crowd, accepting congratulations and wolf whistles, until she joined Krystal and Cabella at Lord Mander's side. The room seemed full of eyes; she had never been shy, but she'd also never stood on a dais being stared at by a roomful of people while wearing a whore's dress and a necklace that annoyed the Queen. She could see over the heads of the others to the Donations Table, where Harald was just then handing over a gold piece to one of the clerks.

"Look 'em over, folks," Lord Mander bellowed past her ear. "Here they are, three lovely and talented Members of the Ladies' Aid and Armor Society. For those who don't know them well, let me introduce . . . Krystal Winterborn." Krystal twirled; her gown glittered in the light. Enthusiastic cheers from part of the crowd, including her barbarian followers. "Cabella Ironhand." Cabella, in a handsome rose brocade, smiled and waved at the crowd, to similar cheers from her supporters.

Mirabel felt like a stray cow at auction, not a candidate for Queen of the Ball. As far as she knew, she had only one supporter, and he had his back turned, leaning over the Donations Table. "Mirabel Stonefist," Lord Mander said, and she struck an attitude and did a swirling dance step. To her surprise, another storm of wolf whistles and cheers broke out.

Lord Mander looked at the Donations Table, got the wave he was waiting for. "All right, folks—all the nominations have been verified. You vote with your silver . . . form three lines, have your coins ready . . . you know the rules." He nodded, and the band began to play "Stillwater Faire" to cover the shuffling and talking.

Cabella turned to Mirabel. "Do you know what Primula's upset about? She cornered me to ask about the list of people I'd addressed invitations to . . . she's never complained before."

Past Cabella's shoulder, Mirabel saw Krystal's tense face. "I'm not sure," she said. It wasn't her place to embarrass Krystal in front of the whole group. "I thought it was just me; she complains about my handwriting every year."

"Well, whatever it is, she thinks it's serious. She's talking to our Chancellor—" Cabella nodded to the far corner, where Primula, gesturing and waving papers, had trapped Sophora Segundiflora.

"She thinks everything is serious," Krystal said, with an edge to her voice.

Harald Redbeard was relieved to find that aside from a few unarmed sergeants in dress uniforms the ball consisted of civilians in fancy outfits. Some costumes required weapons, to be sure—the barbarians had fake spears, and Gordamish Ringwearer had a peculiar looking knife that couldn't possibly work in a fight—but nothing he need worry about. No one had tried to relieve him or his crew of their pirate cutlasses, which were not fake at all, and with which he intended to make a clean sweep of the gathering's jewels and gold.

His nomination of Mirabel Stonefist—whom he did intend to steal away for later enjoyment—would generate more cash in easily-snatched piles. He'd explained to Gordamish that it took fewer votes overall to win in a three-way split than a two-way split.

Now Harald leaned against the wall, arms crossed, waiting for his moment and wondering where the city guard was. He hadn't seen a guardsman all day. He imagined they were all carousing in some illegally open tavern barred to the public. This crowd now—he eyed them professionally. From royalty obviously self-indulgent to citizens full of good food and strong drink . . . easy marks, every one.

The only problem he foresaw was that necklace. Which one was real? Maybe he'd better snatch both. As the lines of voters thinned out, Harald glanced around and signalled his crew.

"And the winner is . . . " Lord Mander bellowed. Silence fell; the woman at the Donations Table pointed to one of the piles. "Krystal Winterborn!"

Cheers and groans from the crowd, a shriek of glee from Krystal, then a booming, "No, she's not!"

"Am *too*," Krystal said, stamping her foot. The crowd roared.

"No." Sophora Segundiflora made her way to the nominees' stand. "Some voters were not invited guests; Primula has explained how the misunderstanding occurred." She scowled at Krystal, who pouted back. "We are going to expel the wrongfully invited guests, and vote again." In a low voice that Mirabel could barely hear over the hubbub, Sophora said, "You're lucky, Krystal, that we care more about the reputation of the Society than you do, you naughty girl. Otherwise we'd expose you publicly."

"But Chancellor—"

"Shut up, Krystal," Sophora said. Then, more loudly, "As your names are called, please line up over there—" She pointed toward the band. "If your name is not called by the end of the list, you can simply leave and no questions will be asked."

"Oh, we'll leave now, if it's all the same to you!" Mirabel recognized that voice, but it took her a moment to realize that Harald Redbeard and the other pirates had surrounded the Donations Table, and the cutlasses laid to the clerks' necks were not decorative accessories. Two pirates were already scooping the piles of coin into the Society's brass-bound money chest. Another pirate was creeping up behind the Queen.

Even as she stared, Mirabel felt a sharp steel point at her back. "I'd come along if I was you," said someone behind her. "Cap'n's got a fancy for you, as well as them pretties you're wearing. Be a good girl now."

Mirabel's years of training took over, and she threw herself forward off the dais, tucked and came upright; she heard the pirate curse, the boom of his foot as he leaped after her, then the louder thud of his body as he hit the floor near Krystal. Sophora stood over him, his cutlass in her hand. "Here, dear—you're quicker." She tossed the cutlass to Mirabel. "Go save the Queen."

"I'll get you!" the pirate snarled at Sophora, reaching for the long dagger in his boot, but Krystal's accurate kick made him grab something else instead. Krystal took the knife and his life before he could move.

Mirabel whirled. The Queen screeched, hands to her neck, as the pirate tugged at her necklace one-handed, while fending off the King with his cutlass. Mirabel charged across the floor, but before she could intervene, the necklace broke. The pirate thrust it into his belt, and ran for the door. Mirabel followed.

Behind her, sergeants bellowed and corporals cursed. A good dozen of the members ran for the armory, where they could find weapons enough to deal with a mere handful of pirates, no matter how vicious, but in the meantime—Harald snatched one of the wards from her booth, and held a blade to her neck. His men did the same; one even had the child who had guarded the door, holding her by her braids, with the cutlass over her head.

"Now, now—you don't want me to hurt this sweet child, do you?"

The uproar sank to a growl, and Mirabel skidded to a stop just out of reach of Harald Redbeard. He winked at her. "Come on along, sweetheart—I'll teach you how to use that thing properly. I like a girl with spirit."

"Do you?" Mirabel said, and signalled.

The nine-year-old dropped abruptly to the length of her braids, then bounced up between her captor's legs. Her little bronze cap hit his pelvic arch with an audible crunch. He shrieked and fell; she grabbed his cutlass and hamstrung the pirate next in line. As Harald turned to look, the girl he was holding sank her teeth into his thumb; Mirabel stepped to one side and ran her blade up under his ribs.

"I already know how to use this thing," she said, wincing as blood spattered her borrowed gown. The girl grabbed his cutlass, and passed it to another adult. Two of the other pirates dropped the children they held, only to find that the girls were more dangerous loose, and all the guests knew how to use a cutlass when they had one.

"But you aren't *real* warriors," moaned the last survivor, cowering from the blows of three energetic orphans pelting him with misshapen pottery from the pottery stall. "Cap'n said so—"

"Your Cap'n might say something different now," Krystal said. "If he could." Her blade, already bloody, swung once more.

In the aftermath of the brawl, in the flurry of cleaning up, no one could find the Queen's necklace. Not until they stripped the pirates' bodies, and the shattered remnants were found in the codpiece of the pirate who'd been felled by Sarajane. "So the Queen was wearing paste . . ." Sophora said, and looked at Mirabel. Mirabel sighed. She knew where her duty lay, but how she would explain to Dorcas . . . first blood on the gown, then this . . .

"Here." She unhooked the clasp and handed it over. "Tell her you found it, and mine was crushed."

Sophora smiled at her. "Mirabel, you're finally growing up. I'm proud of you."

When the crowd settled down, Lord Mander collected Cabella and Mirabel and tried to call for a second vote, but a loud yell of "We already *paid*!" drowned him out.

Cabella took Sophora aside. "Look—I've been Queen before, and you don't want to give it to Krystal. Why not Mirabel? She's decorative enough, she fought the pirates, and she gave up the necklace."

Sophora looked at Mirabel.

"But I—but I never imagined—"

"Sounds like a Queen to me," Sophora said. She gave Mirabel's name; cheers rang out. Lord Mander put the tinsel crown on Mirabel's head, and a score of men stood in line to dance with her, bring her drinks, fetch her snacks, anything she wanted.

She could get used to this Queen business.

The King himself took her hand for the last dance of the evening. The King danced better than Mirabel expected, though his gloved hand wandered along her spine.

"About that necklace," he murmured in her ear.

"I borrowed it," she said.

"From a gorgeous brunette in Dorcas's house?" he asked.

"Yes . . ." She worked it out—if he knew that, then—for the first time she felt a pang of sympathy for the Queen. Over his shoulder she saw Corporal Nitley lurking near the wine punch, only to be collared by Sergeants Gorse and Dogwood. No tropical fruit surprise this year, then. Over his other shoulder, she saw Primula herding a sulky Krystal and her followers, loaded with dirty dishes, toward the kitchen.

"Thank you, my dear," the King said, "for getting me out of a very sticky situation. I will, of course, explain to the . . . er . . . young woman who had been . . . er . . . taking care of it. But is there anything I can do for you?" His hand wandered lower.

"No, thank you," Mirabel said, surprised to realize that what he could give, she didn't want. Not from him, anyway. "Only a donation to help our poor defenseless orphans."

A resounding crash came from the kitchen passage; Krystal stormed back into the ballroom. "It's not *fair*," she said. "Why should I have to do all the work? I killed *two* pirates."

"Shut up, Krystal," Mirabel said, in chorus with others.

The Catcher
in the Rhine

Harry Turtledove

I don't know how I got here. Wait. That's not quite
right. What I mean to say is, I know how I got to
Europe and everything, for Chrissake. They sent me
over here to find myself or something after that
trouble I had. I'm sure you know about that. I'm
certain you know about it. Practically *every*body knows
about it. Some of the biggest phonies in the world
think they know more about it than I do. They really
think so. It's like they read it in English class or
something.

So like I say, I know how I got to Europe. I don't
know about this finding myself business, though. I
swear to God, if you can't find yourself, you've gotta
be some kind of psycho. I mean, you're right *there*,
for crying out loud. If you weren't right there, where
the hell would you be?

And sending somebody to Europe to find himself

has got to be the stupidest thing in the world. You have to be a lousy moron to come up with something like that, you really do. You can't find *any*thing in Europe. Honest to God, it's the truth. You really can't. All the streets go every which way, and they change names every other block, or sometimes in the middle of the block.

Besides, the people don't speak English. Try to have an intellectual conversation with somebody who doesn't know what the hell you're talking about. Go ahead and try. It's a goddam waste of time, that's what it is.

Anyway, I went through France, and some of that was pretty neat, it really was, and all of it was historical as hell—not that I was ever any good at history. What I mean is, every single stinking bit of it happened a long time ago—some of it happened a goddam long time ago—so how am I supposed to get all excited when some phony moron of a teacher stands there and goes on and on about it? It's not easy, I tell you.

After I was done with old France, I went over to Germany because it's next door, you know—and I took this boat trip up the Rhine. I don't know what the hell "Rhine" means in German, but it looks like it oughta mean "sewer." The whole river smells like somebody laid a big old fart, too. It really does. I won't ever complain about the Hudson when I get home, and you can walk across the Hudson, practically.

When I get home. *If* I get home. The boat stopped at this place called Isenstein. It's a real dump, I tell you, but back of it there's a kind of a crag thing with a castle on top. I wasn't gonna get off the boat—I'd paid the fare all the way up to Düsseldorf, wherever that is—but the river just smelled so bad I couldn't stand it any more, so I left. Maybe they'd let me back on the next one. And

if they didn't, who cares? I had piles of money and
traveler's checks and stuff.

Well, let me tell you, the streets in old Isenstein
didn't smell so good, either. That was partly because
it was still right *next* to the Rhine, and it was partly
because the people there had the most disgusting
personal habits in the world. I saw this one guy standing in the street taking a leak against the side of a
crumby old dirty brick building, and it wasn't even
like he was drunk or anything. He was just *doing* it.
And then he went on his way happy as you please.
I wouldn't've believed it if I hadn't seen it with my
own eyes, and that's the truth.

They had a church there, so I went inside and
looked around. I always tried to look at those cul-
tural things, because who knows when I was ever
coming back again? Coming back to Europe, I
mean—I wouldn't've come back to Isenstein if you
paid me, you can bet your bottom dollar on that. But
the church was pretty dirty and crumby, too. By the
time I got done looking at it, I was feeling pretty
goddam depressed. I really was. So I got the hell out
of there.

I was feeling pretty goddam *hungry*, too. I was
feeling hungry as a sonuvabitch, if you want to know
the truth. I didn't exactly want to eat in Isenstein—
it really was a filthy place. You have no idea how filthy
it was. But I was *there*. Where else was I gonna eat,
is what I want to know.

Getting something to eat when you don't speak the
language is a royal pain in the ass. If you're not
careful, they're liable to give you horse manure on
a bun. I'm not kidding. I'm really not. When I was
in France, I got a plateful of *snails*, for crying out
loud. Real snails, like you step on in a garden somewhere and they go crunch under your shoe. With
butter. If you think I ate 'em, you're crazy. I sent 'em
back pretty toot sweet. That means goddam fast in

French. But whatever they gave me instead didn't look much better, so I got the hell out of *that* place toot sweet myself.

Over across the street from the church in old Isenstein was this joint where you could get beer and food. Nobody in Germany cares if you're twenty-one. They don't give a damn, swear to God they don't. They'd give beer to a *nine*-year-old, they really would. If he asked for it, I mean.

So I got a beer, and the guy sitting next to me at the bar was eating a sandwich that didn't look too lousy—it had some kind of sausage and pickles in it—so I pointed to that and told the bartender, "Give me one of those, too." Maybe it was really chopped-up pigs' ears or something, but I didn't *know* it was, so it was all right if I didn't think about it too much. The guy behind the bar figured out what I meant and started making one for me.

I'd just taken a big old bite—it wasn't terrific but I could stand it, pigs' ears or not—when the fellow sitting next to me on the *other* side spoke up and said to me in English, "You are an American, yes?"

If you want to know the truth, it made me kind of angry. Here I was *starv*ing to death, and this guy wanted to strike up a conversation. I didn't want to talk. I wanted to eat, even if it didn't taste so good. So with my mouth full, rude as anything, I said "Yeah" and then I took another bite, even bigger than the first one.

He didn't get mad. I'd hoped he would, I really had, but no such luck. He was a very smooth, very polite guy. He was a little flitty-looking, as a matter of fact—not too, but a little. Enough to make you wonder, anyhow. He said, "We do not often Americans in Isenstein have." He talked that way on account of he was foreign, I guess. I took another bite out of this sandwich—it probably *was* pigs' ears, it sure tasted like what you'd think pigs' ears'd taste like—and he asked me, "What is your name?"

So I told him, and he damn near—I mean *damn* near—fell off his chair. "Hagen Kriemhild?" he said. Boy, he must've had cabbages in his ears or something, even if I was still kind of talking with my mouth full. "Hagen *Kriemhild*?"

"No," I said, and told him again, this time after I'd swallowed and everything, so he couldn't foul it up even if he tried.

"Ah," he said. "*Ach so*," which I guess is like "okay" in German. "Never mind. It is close enough."

"Close enough for what?" I said, but he didn't answer me right away. He just sat there looking at me. He looked very *intense*, if you know what I mean, like he was thinking a mile a minute. I couldn't very well ask him what the hell he was thinking about, either, because people always lie to you when you do that, or else they get mad. So instead I said, "What's *your* name?" You can't go wrong with that, hardly.

He blinked. He really did—his eyes went blink, blink. It was like he'd forgotten I was there, he'd been thinking so goddam hard. He'd been thinking like a madman, I swear to God he had. Blink, blink—he did it again. It was crumby to watch, honest. I didn't think he was going to tell me his lousy old name, but he did. He said, "I am called Regin Fafnirsbruder."

Well, Jesus Christ, if you think I even *tried* to say that like he said it, you're crazy. I just said "Pleased to meetcha" and I stuck out my hand. I'm too polite for my own good sometimes, I really am.

Old Regin Fafnirsbruder shook hands with me. He didn't shake hands like a flit, I have to admit it. He said, "Come with me. I will you things in Isenstein show that no American has ever seen."

"Can't I finish my sandwich first?" I said—and I didn't even want that crumby old sandwich any more. Isn't that a hell of a thing?

He shook his head like he would drop dead if I took one more bite. So I went bottoms-up with my beer—they make *good* beer in Germany, and I wasn't about to let *that* go to waste—and out of there we went.

"Whaddaya got?" I said. "Is it—a girl?" Could you be a pimp and a flit at the same time? Would you have any fun if you were? I always wonder about crazy stuff like that. If you're gonna wonder about crazy stuff, you might as well wonder about *sexy* crazy stuff, you know what I mean?

"A girl, *ja*. Like none you have ever met." Old Regin Fafnirsbruder's head went up and down like it was on a spring. "And also other things." He looked back over his shoulder at me, to make sure I was still following him, I guess. His eyes were big and round as silver dollars. I'm not making things up, they honest to God were. So help me.

"Listen," I said, "it's been nice knowing you and everything, but I think I ought to get back to my boat now."

He didn't listen to a word I said. He just kept going, out of Isenstein—which wasn't very hard, because it's not a real big town or anything—and toward that tumbledown castle on the crag I already told you about. And I kept walking along after him. To tell you the truth, I didn't *want* to go back to the boat, or to the smelly old Rhine. The farther away from there I got the better, you bet.

All of a sudden, these really thick gray clouds started rolling in, just covering up the whole goddam sky. It hadn't been any too gorgeous out before, but *these* clouds looked like they meant business, no kidding. "Hey," I said, kind of loud so old Regin Fafnirsbruder would be sure to hear me. "You got an umbrella? It looks like it's gonna pour."

"*Ja*," he said over his shoulder. Yeah it was gonna pour or yeah he had an umbrella? It wasn't like he *told* me, for crying out loud, the stupid moron. I'll tell you, *I* didn't have any umbrella. Jesus Christ, I didn't even have a crumby *hat*. And my crew cut is so short, it's like I don't have any hair at all up there, and when it rains the water that hits on top of my head all runs down right into my face, and that's very annoying, it really is. It's annoying as hell.

But old Regin Fafnirsbruder started up this crag toward the tumbledown old crumby ruin of a castle, and I kept on following him. By then I was feeling kind of like a goddam moron myself. I was also panting like anything. I haven't got any wind at all, on account of I smoke like a madman. I smoke like a goddam *chim*ney, if you want to know the truth.

Sure as hell, it started to rain. I knew it would. I *told* old Regin Fafnirsbruder it would, but did he listen to me? Nobody listens to you, I swear to God it's the truth. This big old raindrop hit me right square in the eye, so I couldn't see anything for a second or two, and I almost fell off this lousy little path we were walking on, and I would've broken my damn neck if I had, too, because it was a *crag*, remember, and steeper than hell every which way.

"Hey!" I yelled. "Slow down!"

That's when the biggest goddam lightning bolt you ever imagined smashed into me and everything went black, like they say in the movies.

When I woke up, there was old Regin Fafnirsbruder leaning over me, almost close enough to give me a kiss. "You are all right, Hagen Kriemhild?" he asked, all anxious like I was his son or something. I think I'd kill myself if I was, I really do.

"I told you, that's not my name." I was pretty mad that he'd taken me all this way and he couldn't even bother to remember my crumby old name. It's not like it's Joe Doakes or John Smith so you'd forget it in a hurry. I sat up. I didn't want to keep laying there

on account of he might try something flitty if he
thought I couldn't do anything about it or anything.
"What the hell happened?"

Right then was when I noticed things had started
turning crazy. Old Regin Fafnirsbruder had asked me
how I was in this language that wasn't English, and
I hadn't just understood him, I'd *answered* him in
it, for Chrissake. Isn't that gorgeous? I figured the
lightning had fried my brains but good or something.

Then I realized it wasn't raining any more. There
wasn't a cloud in the goddam *sky*, as a matter of fact.
Not even one. It was about as sunny a day as old
Isenstein ever gets, I bet.

I took a deep breath. I was gonna say "What the
hell happened?" again—old Regin Fafnirsbruder
hadn't told me or anything—but I didn't. And the
reason I didn't is that the breath I took didn't stink.
With the nasty old Rhine running right by it, the air
in Isenstein always smelled like somebody just laid
the biggest fart in the world right under your nose.

But it didn't, not any more. It smelled like grass
and water—*clean* water—and pine trees, almost like
one of those little air freshener things, if you know
what I mean. Too good to be true. It wasn't one of
those, though, on account of I could smell cows and
pigs and horses, too, somewhere way the hell off in
the distance. It was like I wasn't by a town any more,
like I'd gone off into the country. But I was still sitting
right where that old lightning bolt had clobbered me.

Old Regin Fafnirsbruder started dancing around.
I'm not kidding, he really did. He had this grin on
his face like he was drunk, and he was kind of halfway
between doing an Indian war dance and jitterbugging.
Watching the old sonuvabitch shake his can like that
was pretty damn funny, it really was.

"I did it!" he yelled, not keeping time with his feet
or anything. "My magic worked!" He still wasn't
speaking English, but I understood him okay.

"Crap," I said. Actually, I didn't say "crap," actually, but what I said meant the same thing as crap, so that was all right. "What do you mean, your magic?"

He still didn't answer me. He was too busy dancing and hollering and having a high old time. He was a very self-centered guy, old Regin Fafnirsbruder was, egocentric as hell. It made him a real pain in the ass to talk to, to tell you the truth.

"What do you *mean*, your crumby magic?" I said again. I hate it when I have to repeat myself, I really do.

Finally, he remembered I was there. "Look!" he said, and he gave this wave like he was in the lousiest, corniest movie ever made. I swear to God, this wave was so goddam big that he almost fell off the side of the mountain himself.

So I looked. I didn't want to give him the satisfaction, but I finally went and did. I looked back over my shoulder, and I almost felt like the lightning plowed into me all over again. There was the Rhine, all right, like it was supposed to be, only it was blue, blue as the sky, blu*er* than the goddam sky, not the color the water in a toilet bowl is when somebody gets there *just* in the nick of time. No wonder it didn't stink any more.

And somebody'd taken old Isenstein and stuck it in his back pocket. Instead of a real town, there were these maybe ten houses by the riverside, and they all had roofs made out of straw or something. So maybe old Regin Fafnirsbruder *had* worked magic. If he hadn't, what the hell had he done? I didn't know then and I still don't know now.

When I got done gawking at Isenstein—it took me a while, believe me—I looked up to the crumby old tumbledown castle at the top of the crag. There it was, all right, big as life, but it wasn't crumby or old or tumbledown any more. What it looked like was, it looked like somebody built it day before yesterday. There wasn't a single stone missing—not even a pebble, I swear—and all the edges were so sharp you could've cut yourself on 'em. Maybe not even day before yesterday. Maybe yesterday, and I mean yesterday after*noon*.

Oh, and there was this ring of fire all the way around the castle. I didn't see anything burning up, but I sure as hell saw the flames. I heard 'em, too—they crackled like the ones in your fireplace do, only these were ten or twenty times as big. When I was a little kid, I had this book about Paul Bunyan and Babe the giant Blue Ox. It was a pretty crumby book with really stupid pictures, but I remembered it right then anyway on account of if old Babe had tried to walk through those flames, he'd've been short ribs and steaks in nothing flat, and I mean well-done.

"Now shall you your destiny fulfill." I already told you old Regin Fafnirsbruder talked like that sometimes. He did it even when he wasn't speaking English. He wasn't much of a conversationalist, old Regin Fafnirsbruder wasn't.

"What the hell are you talking about?" I said. "And where the hell did Isenstein go, anyway?"

"That is Isenstein, Isenstein as it is now," he said, and then a whole lot of weird stuff I didn't understand at all, and what language he was talking in didn't matter a goddam bit. Time flows and sorceries and I don't know what. It all sounded pretty much like a bunch of crap to me. It would've sounded even more like a bunch of crap if I hadn't kept looking back at that little handful of houses where old Isenstein used to be. Then he pointed up the hill. "You shall to the castle go. You shall through the flames pass. You shall the shield-maiden Brunhild asleep there find. You shall with a kiss her awaken, and you shall with her happily ever after live."

"Oh, yeah?" I said, and he nodded. Just like before,

his head bobbed up and down, up and down, like it was on a spring. If he wasn't the biggest madman in the world, I don't know who was. But he was calling the shots, too. I may not apply myself too much—people always go on and on that I'm not *apply*ing my goddam self till I'm about ready to puke sometimes—but I'm not stupid. I'm really not. Old Regin Fafnirsbruder knew what he was doing here, and I didn't have the faintest idea. So I figured I'd better play along for a while, anyway, till I could figure out what the hell was going on.

"Go to the castle up," he said. "You will it is all as I have said see."

I went on up. Now he followed me. Like I said before, the old castle looked so new, it might've just come out of its box or something. Sure as hell, the fire went all the way around the goddam place. The closer I got, the more it felt like fire, too. I pointed to it. I made damn sure I didn't touch it or anything, though, you bet. "How the hell am I supposed to get through that, huh?"

"Just walk through. You will not harmed be. My magic assures it."

"Oh, yeah?" I said. Old Regin Fafnirsbruder's head bobbed up and down some more. He looked pretty stupid, he really did. "Oh, *yeah*?" I said. He kept right on nodding. "Prove it," I said to him. "You're such a madman of a wizard and everything, let's see *you* go on through there without ending up charbroiled."

All of a sudden, he wasn't nodding so much any more. "The spell is not for me. The spell cannot for me be," he said. "The spell is for you and for you alone."

I laughed at him. "I think you're yellow, is what I think." I figured that'd make him mad. If somebody's a coward, what's he gonna hate more than somebody else coming out and *tell*ing him he's a coward, right?

I guess it worked. I guess it worked a little too

goddam well, if you want to know the truth. Because what happened was, old Regin Fafnirsbruder came up and gave me a push, and he *pushed* me right into those old flames.

I screamed. I screamed like hell, as a matter of fact. But I didn't burn up or anything—he was right about that. The fire felt hot, but hot like sunshine, not hot like fire. It hurt a lot more when I fell on my ass from the push, it honestly did.

"What'd you go and do *that* for, you goddam moron?" I yelled, and then I started to go on *out* through the fire. I didn't get very goddam far, though. It wasn't just hot like sunshine any more, let me tell you. It burned the tip of my shoe when I stuck it in there, and it would've burned the rest enough, too, if I'd been dumb enough to give it a chance.

Old Regin Fafnirsbruder was laughing his ass off watching me looking at my toasted toe. "You must what I want do," he said. "Then will you what you want get. When you come out with Brunhild, you may through the fire pass. Until then, you must there stay."

"You dirty, filthy, stinking goddam moron," I said. "I hope you drown in the goddam Rhine."

He just ignored me, the lousy sonuvabitch. He had no consideration, old Regin Fafnirsbruder didn't. I started up toward the fire again, but I didn't stick my foot in it this time—you bet I didn't. I sat down on the ground. I felt so depressed, you can't imagine how depressed I felt.

But after a while I stood up again. What can you do when you're just sitting around on your butt and all? I thought I'd get up and look around a little, anyway. So I did that, and I came to this door. I opened it—what the hell? At least old Regin Fafnirsbruder couldn't keep staring at me through the flames any more. And after I went through, I slammed the hell out of that old door. To tell you the truth, I kind of hoped I'd break it right off the hinges, but no such luck.

I thought I'd end up in this big old hall full of guys making pigs of themselves and getting stinking and pinching the serving girls on the butt the way they did back in medieval times, but that isn't what ended up happening. I walked into this little— bedroom, I guess you'd call it, but it wasn't a bed this girl was laying on, it was more like a little sofa or something.

She was kind of cute, as a matter of fact, if you like big husky blondes. But I'd never seen a girl in chainmail before. To tell you the truth, I'd never seen *any*body in chainmail before, and sure as hell not anybody sleeping. It looked uncomfortable, it really did.

She had on a helmet, too, and a sword on a belt around her waist, and this shield was leaning up against the bed or sofa or whatever the hell it was. I stood there for a while like a crumby old moron. In the fairy tales you're supposed to kiss the princess, right, and she'll wake up and you'll both live happily ever after. That was what old Regin Fafnirsbruder had told me would happen, but you'd have to be a real moron not to see he was playing the game for him and nobody else. And if I kissed this girl and she didn't happen to like it or she thought I was trying to get fresh with her or something, she was liable to *mur*der me, for Chrissake.

I wished I could've figured out some other way to get out of there. I hate doing what anybody else tells me to do. I hate it like anything, if you want to know the truth. Even when it's for my own good and everything, I still hate it. It's nobody's goddam business but mine what I do. Not that anybody listens to me. Yeah, fat chance of that. You think old Regin Fafnirsbruder gave a damn about what I thought? Fat chance of that, too.

But I was stuck in this old castle. I was stuck really bad. If Brunhild there couldn't get me the hell out, who could? Nobody. Just nobody. So I leaned down and I gave her this little tiny kiss, just like it *was* a fairy tale or something.

Her eyes opened. I'd expected they would be blue—don't ask me why, except she was a blonde and all—but they were brown. She looked at me like I was dirt and nobody'd invented brooms yet. Then she said, "You are not Siegfried. Where is Siegfried?" She spoke the same language as old Regin Fafnirsbruder, whatever the hell it was.

"I dunno," I said. I bet I sounded really smart. I sounded like a goddam moron, is what I sounded like. "Who's Siegfried?"

Her face went all soft and mushy-like. You wouldn't think anybody who was wearing armor could look so sappy, but old Brunhild did. "He is my love, my husband to be," she said. Then she sort of frowned, like she'd forgotten I was there and was all of a sudden remembering—and she didn't look any too goddam happy about it, either. "Or he was to have been my husband. The man who came through the fire can claim my hand, if he so desires."

I've always been backasswards with girls. Here she was practically saying she'd *let* me give her the time, but did that make me want to do it? Like hell it did. What it did was, it scared the crap out of me. I said, "I don't want to marry *any*body, for crying out loud. I just want to get the hell outa here, if you want to know the truth."

Brunhild thought about that for a couple seconds. Then she sat up. The chainmail made little clink-clank noises when she moved—molding itself to her shape, you know? She had a hell of a shape, too, I have to admit it. A really nice set of knockers.

"What is your name?" she said, so I told her. Just

like old Regin Fafnirsbruder's had, her eyes got big. "Hagen Kriemhild?"

If you really want to know, I was getting pretty goddam tired of that. I said it again, the right way, louder this time, like you would to somebody who was pretty dumb.

But it went right by her. I could tell. Old Brunhild wasn't much for intellectual conversation. She said, "How came you here, Hagen Kriemhild?"

"That's a goddam good question." I explained it as well as I could. It sounded crazy as hell even to *me*, and I'd been through it. She was gonna think I'd gone right off the deep end.

Only she didn't. When I finally got through, old Brunhild said, "Regin Fafnirsbruder is an evil man. How not, when Fafnir his brother is an evil worm? But I shall settle with him. You need have no doubt of that."

She stood up. She was almost as tall as I was, which surprised me, because I have a lot of heighth and she was a girl and everything. But she really was, so help me God. She took out her sword. It went *wheep* when it came out of the old scabbard, and the blade kind of glowed even though the bedroom wasn't what you'd call bright or anything.

"What are you gonna do with that thing?" I said, which has to be one of the stupidest goddam questions of all time. Sometimes I scare myself, I really do. Am I a goddam moron, too, just like everybody else?

But old Brunhild took it just like any other question. "I am going to punish him for what he did to me, for this humiliation. Come with me, Hagen Kriemhild, and guard my back. He has besmirched your honor as well as mine."

I don't know what the hell she thought I was gonna guard her back *with*. I had some German money in my pocket, and my traveler's checks and all, and a little leftover French money I'd forgotten to change, and that was about it. I didn't even have a *pock*et knife, for crying out loud, and I'm not what you'd call the bravest guy in the world anyhow. I'm pretty much of a chicken, if you want to know the truth. But I followed old Brunhild outa there just the same. If she could get out through the fire, maybe I could too. I hoped like hell I could, anyway.

There was old Regin Fafnirsbruder on the other side of the flames. He gave Brunhild the phoniest bow you ever saw in your life. "So good you to see," he said. What he sounded like was, he sounded like the headwaiter at this fancy restaurant where all the rich phonies and all their whory-looking girlfriends go to eat and he has to be nice and suck up to the sonsuvbitches all day long even though he hates their stinking guts. "Does your bridegroom you please?" He laughed this really dirty laugh. Pimps *wish* they could laugh the way old Regin Fafnirsbruder laughed right then, honest to God.

Old Brunhild started yelling and cussing and whooping and hollering like you wouldn't believe. She started waving that goddam sword around, too. She wasn't very *care*ful with it, either—she damn near chopped *me* a couple of times, let me tell you. I had to duck like a madman, or I swear to God she would've punctured me.

All old Regin Fafnirsbruder did was, he kept laughing. He was laughing his ass off, to tell you the truth. He really was.

Well, that just made old Brunhild madder. "You will pay for your insolence!" she said, and so help me if she didn't charge right on out through the fire. I halfway thought she'd cook. But she was hotter than the flames, and they didn't hurt her one bit.

Anyway, I figured I'd better try and get outa there, too. Old Regin Fafnirsbruder had said Brunhild was my only chance of doing that, and *she'd* said I was supposed to guard her back even though I didn't know what the hell I was supposed to do if somebody did go and jump on her. So I ran after her. People always say I never listen to *any*body, practically, but that's a goddam lie. Well, it was this time.

I didn't run all that goddam *hard*, though, on account of I didn't *know* for sure if the fire would let me go the way it did for old Brunhild. But it felt like it did when that goddam sonuvabitch moron bastard Regin Fafnirsbruder pushed me through it going the other way—it was hot but not *hot*, if you know what I mean.

Let me tell you, old Regin Fafnirsbruder didn't look any too happy when Brunhild burst out of the ring of fire with me right behind her—not that he paid all that much attention to *me*, the lousy crumby moron. Actually, when you get down to it, I can't blame him for that, to tell you the truth. Here was this ordinary guy, and here was this goddam *girl* with chainmail and this sword coming after him yelling, "Now you shall get what you deserve!" and swinging that old sword like she wanted to chop his head off—and she *did*, honest to God.

But old Regin Fafnirsbruder was a lot sprier than he looked. He ducked and he dodged and she ran right on by him. The sword went *wheet!* a couple times but it didn't cut anything but air. And old Regin Fafnirsbruder laughed his ass off again and said, "*Your* blade is my life to drink not fated."

Well, old Brunhild was already madder than hell, but that only pissed her off worse. She started swinging that sword like a madman—up, down, sideways, I don't know what all. I swear to God, I don't know how old Regin Fafnirsbruder didn't get himself chopped into dog food, either, I really don't, Hou*di*ni couldn't have gotten out of the way of that sword, but Regin Fafnirsbruder did. He was a bastard, but he was a *slick* bastard, I have to admit it.

Finally, he said, "This grows boring. I shall another surprise for you one day have." Then he was gone. One second he was there, the next second he wasn't. *I* don't know how the hell he did it. I guess maybe he really was a magician, for crying out loud.

Old Brunhild, she needed like half a minute to notice he'd disappeared, she really did. She just kept hacking and slashing away like there was no tomorrow. She'd already hit the ceiling in fourteen different places, and she wasn't anywhere close to ready to calm down. I wanted to keep the hell out of her way, was all I wanted to do right about then, if you want to know the truth.

Only I couldn't. There was this castle with the ring of fire around it, and there was the slope that headed down toward old Isenstein and the Rhine that didn't stink any more, and there were me and old Brunhild. That was it. Talk about no place to hide. If she decided I was in cahoots with old Regin Fafnirsbruder after all, she'd chop me in half. I didn't know how the hell he'd dodged her, but I knew goddam well *I* didn't have a chance.

Anyway, Brunhild *fi*nally figured out old Regin Fafnirsbruder'd flown the coop. She didn't rub her eyes or go "I can't believe it" or anything like that. She just sort of shrugged her shoulders, so the chainmail went clink-clank again, and she said, "Curse his foul sorcery."

Then she remembered I was there. I swear to God, I wouldn't've been sorry if she'd forgotten. She walked over to me, that crazy armor jingling every step she took, and she looked up into my face. Like I said before, she didn't have to look *up* very goddam far, on account of she had almost as much heighth as I did.

"You came through the fire for me," she said. "You

did it unwittingly, I think, and aided by Regin Fafnirsbruder's magecraft, but the wherefores matter only so much. What bears greater weight is that you did it."

"Yeah, I guess I did."

Old Brunhild nodded. The sun shone off her helmet like a spotlight off the bell of a trombone in a nightclub. She took this deep breath. "However it was done, it was done. As I said when first you woke me, if you would claim me for your bride, you may." And she looked at me like if I was crumby enough to do it, she'd spit in my eye, honest to God she did.

Isn't that a bastard? Isn't that a bastard and a half, as a matter of fact? Here's this girl—and she's a *pretty* girl, she really is, especially if you like blondes about the size of football players—and she was saying "Yeah, you can give me the time, all right, and I won't say boo," only I know she'll hate me forever if I do. And when old Brunhild hated somebody, she didn't do it halfway. Ask Regin Fafnirsbruder if you don't believe me, for crying out loud. And she was holding on to that sword so tight, her knuckles were white. They really were.

I said, "When I woke you up back there, in that crazy old castle and all, didn't you tell me you were in there waiting for Sieg—for somebody?" I couldn't even remember what the hell his name was, not to save my life.

"For Siegfried." Old Brunhild's face went all gooey again. I'd kind of like to have a girl look that way when she says *my* name—or else I'd like to puke, one or the other. I'm not sure which, I swear.

"Well," I said, "in that case maybe you'd better go on back in there and wait some more, don'tcha think?"

She swung up that old sword again. I got ready to run like a madman, I'm not kidding. But she didn't

do any chopping—it was some kind of crazy salute
instead. "*Ja,*" she said, just like old Regin
Fafnirsbruder, and then she put the sword back in
the sheath. "I will do that." And then she leaned
forward and stood up on tiptoe—just a little, on
account of she was pretty goddam tall, like I say—
and she kissed me right on the end of the nose.

Girls. They drive you nuts, they really do. I don't
even think they *mean* to sometimes, but they do
anyway.

I wanted to grab her and give her a real kiss, but
I didn't quite have the nerve. I'm always too slow at
that kind of stuff. Old Brunhild, she nodded to me
once, and then she walked on back through the fire
like it wasn't even there. I heard the door close. I
bet she laid down on that old sofa again and fell
asleep waiting for old Sieg-whatever to get done with
whatever he was doing and come around to give her
a call.

As soon as that door closed, I decided I wanted
to kiss her after all. I ran toward the ring of fire, and
I damn near—*damn* near—burned my nose off. I
couldn't go through it, not any more.

No Brunhild. Damn. I shoulda laid her, or at least
kissed her. I'm *always* too goddam slow, for crying
out loud. I swear to God, it's the story of my life.
No Regin Fafnirsbruder, either. I don't know where
the hell he went, or when he's coming back, or if he's
ever coming back.

If he's not, I'm gonna be *awful* goddam late making
that Rhine boat connection to old Düsseldorf.

What's left here? A crumby castle I can't get into
and that little tiny town down there by the river where
Isenstein used to be or will be or whatever the hell
it is. That's it. I wish I'd paid more attention in history
class, I really do.

Well, what the hell? I started toward old—or I
guess I mean new—Isenstein. I wonder if they've

invented scotch yet. I swear, I *really* wish I'd paid more attention in history class.

Jesus Christ, they're *bound* to have beer at least, right?

With the Knight Male

(apologies to Rudyard Kipling)

Charles Sheffield

I received the final payment this morning. To: Burmeister and Carver, Attorneys. Payable by: *Joustin' Time*.

Logically, Waldo should have signed the transfer slip. He deserves the money, far more than I do. But given his contusions, fractures, lacerations, and multiple body casts, he is in no position to sign anything. In fact, all the negotiations, arguments, offers, and counteroffers to *Joustin' Time* had perforce to come from me. But if Waldo learns anything from his experience—doubtful, given his history—my extra effort on his behalf will be well worthwhile.

I ought to have been suspicious at the outset, when Waldo drifted into my office from his next-door one, preened, and said, "Got us a client."

"That's nice. Who is he?"

"She. It's a lady, Helga Svensen."

50

I ought to have stopped it right there. Every man is entitled to his little weakness, but Waldo's track record with women clients has been, to put it mildly, unfortunate.

On the other hand, although the love of money is widely acknowledged to be the root of all evil, the *lack* of money isn't too good either. The legal firm of Burmeister and Carver—Waldo and me—was at the time utterly broke.

I said, "What does this Helga Svensen want us to do?"

"Nothing difficult. Seems she's a major player in the pre-Renaissance tournaments that have been so big recently. There's a royal games next week at the Paladindrome on Vesta, and she wants our help with her performance contract. She also asked me to check out one of the accessories. Wants to know if it can be shipped legally interplanet before she commits to anything."

I nodded. World-to-world tariff laws were a nightmare—or, seen from another point of view, a boon for hungry attorneys.

"What is it this time?" I said. "Bows, swords, tankards? Antique suits of armor? Jousting equipment?"

"None of them." Waldo helped himself to a handful of chocolate malt balls sitting in a jar on my desk. "Mainly, she's interested—mm—in the—mm—blagon."

"The flagons?"

"Naw." He had spoken with his mouth full, and was forced to pause and swallow before he could say, "The dragon. Apparently it's a different model from what they've been using before. I'm going to meet Helga Svensen over at Chimera Labs tomorrow morning and we're going to check it out together. Want to come?"

I did not. The mindless rush of the biolabs to create, through fancy DNA splicing, everything from centaurs to basilisks to gryphons has never made sense to me. On the other hand, there is such a thing as due diligence. If we were going to object to—or press for—import/export restrictions on a dragon, I needed to take a look at one.

"What time?" I said.

"Nine o'clock. Nine o'clock sharp."

"I'll be there."

But I wasn't. An unpleasant conversation with our landlord concerning past-due office rental delayed me and I did not reach the offices of Chimera Labs until nine-thirty. The aged derelict on duty at the desk wore a uniform as wrinkled and faded as he was. He cast one bleary-eyed look at me as I came in and said, "Mister Carver? You're expected. First room on the left. The brute's in there."

"The dragon?"

He stared at me gloomily. "Nah. The dragon's straight ahead, but you can't see it. You're to go into the room on the left."

In twenty years of legal practice I had heard Waldo called many names, but "brute" was not one of them. Puzzled, I opened the indicated door.

The voice that greeted me was not Waldo's. It was a pleasant, musical baritone, half an octave deeper than his. That was fair enough, because its owner was over two meters tall and topped Waldo by a full half-head.

She ignored my arrival and went on reading aloud. "'Article Twelve: Should a competitor fail to appear at the allocated time for his/her/its designated heat, semifinal, or final, he/she/it will lose the right to compete further in the tournament, and will in addition forfeit prior cumulative earnings and/or prize money, unless a claim of force majeure can be substantiated before an arbitration board approved by the tournament officials'—you see, it's this sort of blather that ties my head in knots—'in advance of the participation of said competitor in any tournament event.' Now what the devil does that mean?"

Waldo offered a lawyer's nod of approbation. "Nice. It means that if you don't show up for an event, you lose everything unless you can prove to them *in advance* that you couldn't possibly show up. Which is, practically speaking, impossible." He had noticed my arrival, and turned to me. "Henry, this is Helga Svensen. Helga, this is my partner, Henry Carver. Henry is an absolute master at reading the fine print of a contract. If anyone can beat the written terms by using the contract's own words, he can."

While Helga nodded down at me with what I sensed as a certain rational skepticism, I took my chance for an examination of our new client. She was more than just tall. She wore a scanty halter of Lincoln green that revealed breasts like alpine slopes, shoulders wide enough to support a world, and tattooed arms the size of my thighs. Her matching green skirt, shockingly short, ended high up on thighs as sturdy and powerful as the fabled oaks of Earth. Waldo is a substantial man and his recent dieting efforts had been a disaster, but I have to say that next to Helga Svensen he resembled a sunstarved weed.

Her mind was still on the contract. She flourished the offending document and said, "And this bit is nothing like the usual agreement. 'Article Seventeen. Any bona fide member of a participating team, such representative or representatives to be termed hereinafter collectively *the contestant*, may enter into single combat with the dragon. Should the contestant slay or otherwise defeat the dragon, the contestant will win the Grand Prize; should the dragon slay the contestant, all prize money already won by the contestant will be forfeited. In the event of the simultaneous death of both dragon and contestant, the dragon will be deemed the winner.'"

"Sounds clear enough to me," Waldo said. "You kill the dragon and survive, you win big. What's wrong with that?"

"It's too generous." Helga wore her hair in long, golden plaits. They swayed about her plump pink cheeks as she shook her head. "They offer a Grand Prize at every tournament, and nobody has won one in five years—which is how long *Joustin' Time* has been in business. But the prize has never been for dragon-slaying, which isn't too hard. That's the other reason I'm here. I want a sneak preview of the dragon." She glanced at a massive left wrist seeking a nonexistent watch. "What time is it?"

"Nine-forty-five," Waldo said.

"Then he'll be there. Come on—quietly, now."

She opened a small door at the back of the room, lowered her head, and squeezed through. About to follow her into a dark and narrow corridor, I hesitated and turned to Waldo.

"Is this going to be safe? I mean, a dragon . . ."

"Oh, I'm sure we can trust Helga. Come on." He ducked through.

Was this really Waldo Burmeister, a man nervous in the presence of toy poodles and somnolent cats? I followed him, wondering about his interaction with Helga Svensen before I arrived.

I didn't wonder long because other concerns took center stage. The dark corridor ran for about fifteen meters and ended in a great, dimly-lit chamber. I couldn't see much at first, but a smell like a mixture of ammonia and sulfur made my nostrils wrinkle. I heard a whisper ahead of me, answered in Helga's soft baritone. She handed something to a dark figure who at once slipped away into the gloom.

Helga turned to me and Waldo. "Right, we're promised five minutes. Let's take a peek."

I wasn't sure I wanted to. As my eyes adjusted, a shape was coming into focus by the far wall. It was hunched and enormous, at least seven feet high and thirty feet long. I saw scaled legs like tree trunks ending in feet equipped with gleaming talons, a wrinkled body the size of an upturned rowing boat, a long, barbed tail, and a crocodile head. As I watched, two pairs of batlike wings on each side of the body moved slowly up and down in a breathing rhythm. The whole thing was absolutely terrifying.

"Strange," Helga said in a puzzled voice. "Looks just like the dragon they used in the last tournament. I killed that one myself, with a spear thrust to one of its hearts—but there was no Grand Prize offered for doing it. What game are the crooks at *Joustin' Time* playing now? I wonder if there's something in the contract that says you can't wear armor when you fight the dragon?"

She made no effort to keep her voice down and the dragon heard her. The barrel-sized head with its great jaws turned in our direction. Green eyes blinked open.

Waldo stayed at Helga's side, but I began to back away nervously.

"It's all right," Helga said. "You're quite safe, because it's chained up. You can see the fetters on each leg and around the body."

While she was still speaking, a roaring sound filled the air. Two roiling clouds of blue flame emerged from the dragon's nostrils and streaked in our direction. They narrowly missed Waldo and Helga, came close enough to me to singe my trousers, and incinerated the leather briefcase that I was holding. I dropped the smoking debris as Helga said, "So that's it!"

She sounded delighted as she went on, "It's a real first. They've talked about flame-breathing dragons in the games for years, but they never worked. The last one got the hiccups and blew itself to bits during the opening ceremonies."

"You plan to *fight* that thing?" I said, as I tried to remember what had been in my briefcase. The only thing I was sure of was a sandwich.

"Not me." Helga gave a booming laugh, reached down, and patted out the glowing remnants of my case with one enormous bare hand. "Not now that I know what it can do. I'm not crazy, you know! This time I'll just do the jousting and the hand-to-hand combat. I always do well with those."

I could believe that, even without a survey of the competition. As she bent over, sinews like ship's cables sprang into view in her arms and legs.

"But you'll see for yourself," she went on, "at the tournament. Now, I got what I came for, and I have to be going. Lots to do!" She led the way out of the dragon chamber and dumped a sheaf of papers into my hand as we reentered the front room. "Here's the contract. After what Waldo told me about you and your fine-print reading, I know you'll find a way around all the weasel-wording. See you at the royal games!"

She was gone, with a flash of bare limbs and the swirl of air that denoted the presence of a large moving mass. I turned on Waldo. "At the games? What did you tell her? What did you agree to?"

He wasn't looking at me. He was staring raptly after Helga.

"Isn't she the most gorgeous thing you ever saw in your life?" he said. "Those blue eyes, that perfect complexion. Did you see those cute dimples? On her face, too. It seems a shame to take payment for services from someone so wonderful."

Waldo's little weakness. He was smitten—again. It was time to tear up the contract, give back the fee, find a plausible excuse for non-performance, and make sure that we didn't go within a million miles of Helga Svensen and the *Joustin' Time* tournament.

Why didn't I follow my own sound instincts? Because our landlord had told me that he would wait at our office for payment and if he didn't get it he was going to crack my skull? Because when Waldo was in love, nothing in the known universe could prevent the romance from running its natural or unnatural course? Because Waldo was holding in his hand Helga's check for our services, more money than we had seen in months?

Yes, certainly. All of those.

But also because, after meeting Helga, I could see no way that anyone else in the games had a prayer of beating her. She was a shoo-in, an absolute cert. When we had paid the rent, a fair amount of Helga's fee would be left over. Back her to win at the jousting, take those winnings with reverse odds that she would *decline* to fight the dragon (there is no substitute for inside information), and watch our initial investment compound to the skies. . . .

I could see it, I could feel it, already I could taste the celebratory champagne.

As I was saying, every man has his little weakness.

Until forty years ago, Vesta was a nowhere place. Plenty of volatiles and a few hundred kilometers across, but still with surface gravity so low you could spit at escape velocity.

The gravity generators changed all that. Now Vesta, like much of the Asteroid Belt, was prime real estate. Add in the Vestans' liberal laws toward physical violence, and the Paladindrome had become one of the system's top sports venues.

Waldo, of course, wanted nothing better when we arrived at the 'drome than to seek out the divine Helga. I left him at the competitors' enclosure and set off on my own little excursion. I had called up the general plan of the Paladindrome on our trip from the Moon, and found that during the first half of the royal games the sword fighting, archery, and jousting would be the main attractions. They were all to take place on a central strip of beaten earth within the main oval of the 'drome, a straightway two hundred meters long and about fifty meters wide. All around the interior of the oval, temporary structures were being installed to support special needs. At this end of the strip were the armorers' tents, the stables, the silversmiths, the food concessions, the sideshows, and the competitors' private enclosure. I noticed that the dragon had his own awning and cage just beyond the end of the jousting strip, right next to the competitors.

I also noticed that, although occasionally goaded by employees of *Joustin' Time*, the dragon did not belch fire. It did not, in fact, do much of anything. Someone must be keeping the beast high on tranquilizers and low on methane until the second half of the games.

A deceptive practice, but it was working. Competitors strolled up, examined and occasionally poked the dragon with a mace or the blunt end of a pike, and at once went off to sign up for the great Slay-the-Dragon event.

The scene was colorful and chaotic, and it seemed likely to become more so once the tournament actually started. The competitors might be all female, but the workers and hangers-on were not. I saw a woman arguing furiously with an artificer wearing a cloth apron. As I walked by she ripped off her metal breast plate and threw it to the ground.

"Look at 'em," she screamed. "Look what it's doing to 'em. What do you think you are, a lemon squeezer? How am I supposed to fight for three days inside that thing?"

He growled back, "That's the size you told me."

He reached a blackened hand toward her exposed anatomy. "If I was to hammer the metal out right here—"

"Touch that and you're dead!"

I averted my gaze and walked on. My own interests lay at the other end of the jousting strip, a part of the oval where you would find the seamier side of the tournament.

The first section I reached was home to the drinking tents. Judging from the sounds that came out of them they were already doing a thriving business. Fifty yards farther on, in the Free-For-All, I was accosted half a dozen times by beauties of every sex. I politely refused their service, including that of a woman who somehow realized that I was a lawyer and offered me "a contingency-basis go as a professional courtesy." Their advances were mildly annoying—but not nearly as irritating as what I found when I came to Bettors' Row. There I learned that shopping for odds would not be possible at the tournament. *Joustin' Time* controlled every betting station!

When you have no choice, you do what you have to. I went to one of the terminals and entered the name, *Helga Svensen*. The reply came back, *No such competitor*.

It was preposterous. I knew for a fact that she was competing in the jousting—I had seen, read, and approved her entry form. It took assistance from a cheerful lady bettor wearing a hat with the printed motto, THE WAGES OF SIN IS DEBT, to help me out.

"Helga Svensen," she said. "Oh, she fights in these games as the Warrior Queen. She's very good, but me, I fancy the Iron Maiden. More tricky."

I was already making a complex cascade bet for heats, semifinals, and final on the Warrior Queen, with a double on jousting and a parallel reverse bid for no dragon, so I didn't listen to her very closely. I vaguely pitied the Iron Maiden if she had to face

Helga, and went on with my bet. A bet, I might add, at lousy odds. *Joustin' Time* not only controlled this part of the action, the odds that they offered guaranteed a substantial fraction of the stake for themselves. Also, to limit their possible losses they put a ceiling on bet rollover at eighty percent of winnings.

Even so, when you roll eighty percent of winnings back each time into a new stake, the total return grows fast. I made a note of the final payout and decided that Waldo and I were going to be rich. Of course, Helga had to win, but that was a foregone conclusion.

As I was receiving my bet confirmation, my neighbor nudged me. "Want to change your mind? That's the Iron Maiden over there."

Four terminals down, placing a bet of her own, stood an enormous black-haired woman. Studying her powerful frame I felt a moment of doubt. I stepped closer, made a point-by-point physical comparison from her bare toes to her braided crown, and was reassured. The Iron Maiden was big, no doubt about it; but Helga could take her.

My detailed inspection was unfortunately subject to misinterpretation. The Iron Maiden smiled down at me and clasped my arm in a powerful hand.

"You're new here, aren't you?" she said in a strong Scots accent. "You're a sweet-looking wee man. If you're interested in me you should speak up, an' we could find a private game of our own. I bet you never played 'hide the scepter.' You'd make a fine royal prince."

I made unintelligible gobbling noises, retrieved my arm, and fled to the relative safety of the wild animal show.

A wasted opportunity to play the prince, get close to Helga's top competition, learn her strengths and weaknesses, and adjust my bet accordingly?

You must be joking. It's moments like this that prove I'm not a compulsive gambler.

Joustin' Time may be run by a bunch of mercenary rogues, but one reason for their success is that they attend to details. The opening ceremony was a pageant in itself, flags flying bravely in the (artificial) breeze, heraldic trumpets blaring, false sun high in the 'drome's false blue sky, real hawthorn trees blooming all around the oval, and pipers in full regalia marching up and down. The final event of the opening was a massed parade of the competitors, four hundred brawny women kicking up the dust, strutting along clad in bright metal and little else. Had Waldo not been already in love, I think he would have died of a surfeit. As it was, he and I stood together among the spectators and agreed that even in such company Helga stood out for her size, power and vitality.

The first event was the individual sword fights. I have no taste for combat, and the sight of blood makes me weak at the knees. I took a stroll. I had to go all the way to the outer perimeter of the Paladindrome before the bloodthirsty howls and screams of the warriors behind me faded into the background. When I reached the wall it was a shock to look beyond the 'drome and see the surface of Vesta curving rapidly away, a stark and barren jumble of boulders, shadowed cliffs, and a handful of busy mining robots. The builders of the 'drome had made a wise choice when they decided that the area within would be as flat as the surface of Earth and as little like the Asteroid Belt as possible. I stood for a long time, the scenes in front of and behind me a thousand years apart.

When I returned, the tag-team sword fights were finishing and the dusty surface was being sprayed with water in preparation for the archery contests. I checked the scoreboards, keeping a wary eye open for off-the-mark practice arrows. As I had hoped and anticipated, Helga was performing magnificently. She had ripped through the heats, semifinals, and finals in short order, and stood in first place. Our winnings had already rolled over into her next event. Since Helga scorned all forms of entertainment involving no contact with the adversary, she had skipped the archery. I did the same, heading past the archers toward the tent where Helga should be preparing herself for the jousting.

At the end of the field I found the Iron Maiden in my path, grimy and sweaty and sitting cross-legged on the grass. I would have ignored her, but she was having none of that.

"Now then, my prince," she said, as I was walking past. "I've a bone to pick with you. You led me on before. You didn't tell me that you were sweet on Helga."

I had to stop at that. "Helga Svensen? I'm not sweet on her. Whatever made you think that?"

"I saw you during the parade. You hardly took your eyes off her."

"That's because I put a bet on her." I felt obliged to add, "And you're mixing me up with my partner, Waldo. He has this thing for her, he's the one who watches her all the time."

"No more than natural. She's a beautiful woman an' a very worr-thy opponent, an' she deserves a lot of respect." The Iron Maiden rose to her knees. "So you're not her feller, then. What's your name?"

"Henry. Henry Carver."

"An' I'm Flora McTavish. I think you an' me could be guid friends." She turned and leaned her body forward away from me. "For a start, would you grab my cuirass?"

"I beg your pardon?"

She pointed to a sort of leather breastplate sitting

on the ground a few feet in front of her. "My cuirass. I canna quite reach it from here. Aye, and my
greaves and cuish sitting next to it, if you wouldn't
mind. It's time I got my things together and went over
to the competitors' area."

The bits and pieces she asked for weighed a ton,
and I wished that the designers of Vesta's local gravity
control had cut a few corners. Flora took the armor
from me one-handed and with no sign of effort. "Will
ye be seeing Helga an' your friend, then?"

"I'm on my way there now."

"Then mebbe ye can give her this, as my tribute
to a great competitor." She reached into her generous cleavage and pulled out a silver flask. "Pure malt
whiskey, thirty-five years old an' wi' a taste to make
a dead man dance."

I was more than happy to have a reason to escape.
The flask went into my pocket and I was away. Flora
called something about getting together later, but I
paid little attention. I was looking ahead, seeking
Helga's colors in among hundreds of others.

I didn't see them. What I did see was Waldo,
sitting simpering outside one of the tents.

"Where's Helga?" I said as I came up to him.

He nodded toward the flap. "Inside. She's putting
her armor on—and she promised that after the jousting I can help her to take it off."

"This is from one of her friends." I held out the
flask of whiskey. "I'll just give it to her."

Waldo was having none of that. "*I'll* give it to her.
You wait here."

He tapped on the cloth flap of the tent, waited
about five milliseconds, and disappeared inside. I
heard an exclamation, a giggle, and some whispering.
About a minute later Waldo emerged.

"She says she'll have a drop now, and share any
that's left with us after the jousting. She asked us to
go now and make sure her horse is saddled and ready."

I couldn't tell if a horse saddle was put on backwards or perhaps even upside down, while Waldo makes me appear as an equestrian expert. But apparently Helga's word was law. We headed off together toward the stables.

"She asked who gave you the whiskey," Waldo said when we were halfway there. "But I couldn't tell her."

"I should have gone into the tent. I could have told her who it came from."

"Well, you never told me."

"You never asked."

"You still could have mentioned it."

"I didn't see any reason to." Rather than bickering indefinitely, I added, "The whiskey came from a woman called Flora."

"Never heard of her." Waldo was sulking.

"She doesn't use that name as a competitor. She fights as the Iron Maiden."

Waldo stopped in midstep. "Are you *sure* it came from the Iron Maiden?"

"Positive. She handed the flask to me herself."

"But the Iron Maiden is in second place to Helga. Didn't you see the scoreboard? They're very close, and that means they'll meet as opponents in the jousting."

We stared at each other for a fraction of a second, then set off for Helga's tent at a run.

I arrived four steps ahead of Waldo, barged in without asking, and was relieved to see the giant figure of Helga sitting over by the far wall. She leaned against a tent pole, and her armor was spread on the floor in front of her.

"It's all right," I said to Waldo as he rushed in. "She's—"

Her eyes were closed. She had not moved.

Waldo howled. "She's dead!"

"No." I could see she was breathing. "She's

drugged." I picked up the flask and shook it. Half empty. "Come on, we have to wake her up."

Waldo had subsided to the floor in his relief. "No need for that. She can sleep it off."

Sometimes I wonder which universe Waldo lives in. I glanced at my watch. "In half an hour, Helga has to take part in the jousting. We have all our money on her to win."

"What about the sword fight winnings?"

"Article Twelve: Should a competitor fail to appear at the allocated time, blah-blah-blah—unless Helga fights the Iron Maiden, we lose a fortune."

"She can't fight. Look at her."

Helga was snoring peacefully, her mouth open to reveal pearly and perfect teeth.

"She has to," I said grimly. "Come on."

For the next five minutes we tried shouting, pinching, pouring cold water on her head, burning cloth under her nose. Not a twitch. After we tried and failed to lift her to her feet, so that we could walk her up and down the tent, I realized that Waldo was right. Helga couldn't fight.

We were doomed.

I paced up and down the tent myself. We had twenty minutes. Helga *had* to fight.

But Helga didn't have to *win*. All she had to do was appear. If she fought and lost, we would still have twenty percent of our winnings, the amount they refused to let us roll over into the next bet.

I turned to Waldo. "Come on. We have to do this quickly."

"Do what?"

"Get you into Helga's armor. You have to fight in her place."

"What?!"

"You heard." I handed him the helmet. "You don't have to fight well. It's enough just to show up."

"I can't pretend I'm Helga. I look nothing like her. For heaven's sake, Henry, I have a *mustache*."

"You'll be inside her suit of armor, with a visor covering your face. There won't be an inch of you showing."

"Then why don't you do it?"

"I'm not half her size. I'd rattle around inside her armor like a pea in a can. For you, though, it won't be a bad fit."

"Henry, you've gone mad. I can't do it." He folded his arms. "I won't do it."

Twenty minutes. Fortunes have been made in twenty minutes, empires lost, cities destroyed, whole nations doomed or saved.

I sat down opposite Waldo. After five years in law school and four times that as a practicing attorney, it was time to see how much I had learned of the gentle arts of persuasion.

I began, "Think how grateful Helga will be . . ."

He didn't look bad, not bad at all.

Admittedly—I squinted into the sun—Waldo was close to two hundred meters away at the other end of the straightway, so that the finer details of the way he sat on the horse were probably lost to me. I hoped he had paid attention to my last cautionary words. "Don't say a word to *anyone*, no matter who they are. After the jousting is done, ride this way. I'll take care of the horse, you go back inside the tent and take off the armor. If anyone comes in after that, you tell them Helga needed to sleep after a hard day."

It might work. It *could* work. Waldo just had to ride the length of the field without falling off, then he would be back at the exhibit area where he had started. The competitors' tents were close by, and Helga's was near the front. He could ride the horse right up to it.

I hoped that he could see. Helga's armor had been

made for her, half a head taller. Stretching up as high as he could, Waldo had been able to get one of his eyes level with a nose hole. He had complained about that quite a bit. On the other hand, what did he need to see? The horses had been trained well, and I knew from watching previous contestants that a straight path was the easiest one for the animal.

The Iron Maiden would start from close to where I stood. I wished I could see the expression on the face behind the visor. There had been no more of the "fine sweet prince" talk, and my bet was that she was scowling and wondering where her plan to nobble Helga had failed.

The blue flag was slowly being raised. When it fluttered down, the two contestants would begin to ride toward each other, first at a canter and then at a full gallop.

There was one other detail that I preferred not to think about. Each rider was armed with a lance about twenty-five feet long. Even after watching some of the other jousters, I didn't know how the cumbersome thing was supposed to be supported. I finally lashed Waldo's weapon to the saddle in one place and tucked the rounded haft between his arm and breastplate. The chance that he would hit anything with it was negligible, but at least the point could not drop too far and convert the event to the pole vault.

The chance that the Iron Maiden would damage Waldo was another matter. I had downplayed the risk, telling him that no one in the jousting had been killed. I did not mention that there had been a couple of very violent dismounts. It would only send him off on another tirade of protest.

The blue flag was starting down. That made little difference, because Waldo's horse had decided to use its own best judgment on the matter and started to canter forward a few seconds earlier.

I heard a loud curse from inside the helmet of the

Iron Maiden. She dug her heels into her own horse and it whinnied and jerked forward.

The crowd became silent, the only sound the thundering hooves. It did not take a connoisseur to detect a certain difference of styles between the two contestants. The Iron Maiden sat rock-steady on her horse and the tip of her lance moved as though it was fixed to a straight line parallel to the ground.

By contrast, I could see occasional daylight between Waldo and his saddle. The end of his lance described random motion within a vertical circle twenty-five feet ahead of him. The radius of that circle increased as the horse moved from a canter to a full gallop.

I had never before realized how fast horses can run. The horses that I bet on seldom seem to manage more than an arthritic crawl toward the winning post. But Waldo and the Iron Maiden were approaching each other at an impossible speed.

They were forty meters apart—twenty—a crash of metal—they were somehow past each other, and the spectators were screaming in horror. The tip of the Iron Maiden's lance had struck Waldo squarely in the middle of his helmet, ripping it loose from the rest of his armor. As the helmet rolled away across the dirt, the headless knight galloped on.

Rode toward me. Rode straight at me. As I threw myself out of the way, convinced that the decapitated rider was about to lance Helga as she lay sleeping inside her tent, the horse at the last moment veered off. The lance leading the way, horse and burden missed the competitors' enclosure and plunged into the next one.

I couldn't see behind the awning separating the enclosures, but the noise that reached me was frightful.

It took a couple of weeks to arrange the hearing, long enough for Waldo to be out of the hospital. He claimed that he ought to come to court and present part of our arguments, but I dissuaded him on the grounds that his broken and wired jaw denied him his customary verbal clarity.

The rest of his head was intact. Unable to maintain a high enough position in Helga's suit when on horseback, he had slipped down to peer out through a slit in the neck piece. He had been untouched by the lance that removed the helmet, but the force of his final collision did considerable damage.

I expected to be alone in the court, except for the judge and the team of seven attorneys representing *Joustin' Time*. When I heard another group of people slip into the back as the proceedings began, I was too busy listening to the *Joustin' Time* claims to take notice of new arrivals.

Their list of purported offenses and damages was impressive. The lead attorney, Duncan Whiteside, a man of earnest demeanor and awkward body language, took four and a half hours to deliver it, but I could boil everything down to this:

- Messrs. Burmeister and Carver had illegally taken part in a tournament organized by *Joustin' Time*.
- Messrs. Burmeister and Carver had by their actions forced cancellation of the jousting contest.
- Messrs. Burmeister and Carver, by killing the tournament dragon, had forced the cancellation of the entire second half of the program.

Both compensatory and punitive damages were sought.

When Duncan Whiteside finally dribbled to a halt, Judge Solomon looked at me and said, "You may now respond to these charges."

"Thank you, Your Honor. I will be brief."

I had seen the judge's eyes rolling during the previous presentation. Hubert Solomon was a man of famously few words, and he admired the same trait in others. I figured I had five good minutes and I did not intend to go a second over.

"Your Honor," I said, "I would draw your attention to Exhibit Seven, the contract between Helga Svensen and *Joustin' Time Enterprises*."

"I have it."

"Article Nineteen, paragraph four, clause five. Let me read it aloud, since the print is awfully small. 'The terms and conditions of this contract will apply *in toto* to any designated representative of the contractor.' Your honor, Burmeister and Carver are designated representatives of Helga Svensen. My colleague, Waldo Burmeister, represented Helga Svensen in the jousting tournament. I would simply make the comment that were an attorney *not* deemed to be a designated representative of a client, the entire legal profession would be irreparably damaged."

"Your point is noted. Continue."

"Burmeister and Carver, jointly and severally, had no part in the decision to cancel the jousting tournament. Therefore we cannot be regarded as responsible for such a decision."

"Noted. Continue."

"Now, as to the dragon—"

"Objection!" Naturally, from Duncan Whiteside.

Judge Solomon had an odd frown on his face as he stared at me. "Mr. Carver, this is a serious matter. I hope that you are not proposing to argue that Mr. Burmeister did not kill the dragon."

"Not at all. Your Honor, it is a central point of our argument that Mr. Burmeister's lance undeniably killed the dragon. Now let me draw your attention to Article Seventeen of the contract. Again I quote: 'Any *bona fide* representative of a participating team, such representative or representatives to be termed hereinafter collectively *the contestant*, may enter into single combat with the dragon. Should the contestant slay or otherwise defeat the dragon, the contestant will win the Grand Prize.' Since Mr. Burmeister was a representative of Helga Svensen, and killed the dragon, the Grand Prize should be paid—"

"Objection!" The lead attorney for *Joustin' Time* was on his feet. "Your Honor, the dragon was *asleep* when Mr. Burmeister killed it."

"Mr. Whiteside, you must allow Mr. Carver to finish his sentences, otherwise—"

"Your Honor, the dragon-slaying part of the tournament had not even begun."

"Mr. Whiteside, you must also allow *me* to finish my sentences." Hubert Solomon was enjoying the tussle. Otherwise he would have bitten off Duncan Whiteside's head. He nodded to me. "Mr. Carver, proceed."

"Thank you. Your Honor, I have little to add. Nothing in the contract mentions the time or circumstances in which the dragon must be slain in order for a contestant to win the Grand Prize. Mr. Burmeister slew the dragon, and therefore won the Grand Prize. The amount owed to us is given in Exhibit Two."

"Very good." The judge abruptly stood up. "I now call a ten-minute recess."

He swept out. I knew where he was going—to private chambers for a good laugh.

I felt an urge to do the same. I headed for the exit, carefully avoiding the dismayed eyes of the *Joustin' Time* team. They were not complete fools. They knew they had ten minutes to agree among themselves on the terms of a mediated settlement.

Near the door I came to the group of people who had arrived late. It offered the impression of a group, but actually it was just Helga Svensen and Flora McTavish.

Together! Clad today in light, springtime armor, they sat side by side smiling at the world.

"Mr. Carver." Helga reached out and enveloped my hand in hers. "You were brilliant, totally brilliant."

"You were." Flora beamed at me. "Helga told me you'd do it, but I didn't see how. You're a genius!"

"Not really." I coughed modestly. "It's far from over, you know. And all I did was read the fine print."

"But *how* you read it!" Flora's eyes were shining. "Would you be willing to read *my* fine print?"

While I was pondering the possible implications of that question, Helga stood up. "I'm going to leave the two of you to talk. Is it too soon for me to go and see Waldo?"

I thought of my partner, splinted and swathed from head to toe. In his present condition I didn't think that even Waldo could get into too much trouble. "You can go and see him," I said, "but you won't see much of him."

"I'll tell him things are going well." She thundered out, shaking the floor with her girlish tread.

I turned to Flora. "I don't understand. She brought you here. She's *talking* to you."

"Of course she is. Helga and I are best friends."

"But you drugged her and tried to kill her!"

"Oh, nonsense. Drugged her a wee bit, aye, but that's all in the game. I knew it wasn't Helga, the minute I saw that lance wobbling about. I thought she was snoring in her tent, and somebody had tied a stuffed dummy up there on her horse."

Stuffed, perhaps, and far too frequently for someone on a perennial diet; but Waldo was no dummy.

"There's a big tournament coming up on Ceres," Flora went on. "I'd like you to be there with me."

I could not talk any longer. A buzz of activity at the front of the room announced that Judge Solomon had entered and Duncan Whiteside was already stepping toward him, an anxious expression on his face.

I ran for the steps, calling over my shoulder, "Go there, and do what?"

I *think* that Flora, behind me, said, "Read my fine print." But it sounded an awful lot like, "Be my fine prince."

Patterns in the Chain

Steven Piziks

Knit *one*, purl *two*. Knit *one*, purl *two*.

A shadow drifted across the mouth of Mother Berchte's cave. She waited and rocked, careful to keep her tail away from the stone rockers of her chair. White sparks snapped from her needles.

Knit *one*, purl *two*. Knit *one*, purl *two*.

The shadow drifted closer, and Mother Berchte lost patience. "I see you," she growled. "Get in here."

The shadow froze.

"Yes, I mean you. Move it."

Knit *one*, purl *two*. Knit *one*, purl *two*.

The shadow hesitantly stepped into the light thrown by the fireplace. The girl was young, not yet twenty. She held a short sword before her with a farily competent air, though her grip was so tight Berchte was sure she was leaving permanent fingerprints on the hilt. The girl's red-blond hair had recently been hacked off. Probably with a blunt dagger, if Berchte was any judge.

74

"Well?" Mother Berchte prompted in her harsh voice. "What's your name, girlie?"

Knit *one*, purl *two*. Knit *one*, purl *two*. Berchte's needles glowed like angry volcanos. The girl tried not to recoil, and Mother Berchte grinned. Berchte knew full well she was an imposing sight, almost eight feet tall with horns on her head and fangs in her mouth and claws on her fingertips. And a tail, of course. The latter was a bitch if she wasn't careful with the rocking chair.

"Jeweline," the girl said timidly. "My name is Jeweline."

Of course it is, Mother Berchte thought. "And?" she said aloud. "You didn't climb all the way up here just to tell me your name."

Jeweline took a deep breath. Although the inflation of her chest did nothing for Mother Berchte, it earned an admiring snort from Nassirskaegi in his corner. Jeweline's head snapped around and her eyes widened for a split second before she could school her features back into impassivity. Berchte awarded her silent points for quick recovery. Many people reacted badly to giant goats the size of horses, but few hid their surprise so quickly. Nassirskaegi yawned, revealing yellow teeth.

"Um . . . r-raiders attacked our holding," Jeweline said. "My parents were slain, my brothers murdered. My sisters were taken. I need to rescue them."

"With that?" Mother Berchte pointed scornfully at Jeweline's sword with her chin. Her knitting needles flashed through another row, and the swiftly growing shirt clinked in her lap.

"With your help," Jeweline said. "If you'll give it."

Mother Berchte nodded and rocked, knitting without answering. Jeweline shifted uncomfortably. A drop of sweat trickled down her face.

Knit *one*, purl *two*. Knit *one*, purl *two*.

"Well, why not?" Mother Berchte said at last.

"That's a hell of a climb, and you deserve something for it. Choose one."

Jeweline peered about the dimly-lit cave. "Choose one what?"

Mother Berchte blew at the fireplace. The flames blazed up, throwing the cave into almost painful brightness. Dozens of mail shirts glittered and sparkled from every wall, each with a unique style and design. Different types of wire knitted artfully into the weave created patterns and pictures. This one showed a silvery dragon breathing copper fire. That one portrayed an exquisitely-rendered griffon leaping into a star-flecked sky. Another twisted the eye with a fractal pattern of falling red-gold leaves.

Jeweline gasped and lowered her sword. "You made all these?"

Mother Berchte grinned with crooked teeth and briefly held up the half-finished hauberk in her lap before returning to work. The needles sparked and flashed. Friction and torsion softened the wire, making it easier to work.

Jeweline whistled under her breath, sheathed her sword, and went over to examine the mail shirts. Mother Berchte watched her until the girl's eye fell on a shirt hanging in a corner half hidden by a stout wooden wardrobe. The shirt was old and rusting. It looked like moths had been at it, though what kind of moths would go for solid steel even Mother Berchte didn't care to think about.

Knit *one*, purl *two*. Knit *one*, purl *two*.

Jeweline put out a finger to touch the old hauberk, and a sly smile stole over her face. Mother Berchte narrowed her eyes and kept on knitting. The girl had obviously heard some of the old tales. Either that or she had been down to the river talking to Father Fluss. Slobbery bastard. And Jeweline was just the type to set him slobbering.

"What about this one?" Jeweline asked, holding up the rusty shirt.

"You don't want that one, girl," Mother Berchte replied evenly. "It's old and poorly made."

"I don't want to be greedy," Jeweline said in a modest voice. "I'll take it."

Mother Berchte shrugged without missing a stitch. "It's your life."

Jeweline pulled the hauberk over her head, leaving wide streaks of rust in her hair, and hurried for the cave's entrance. At the last moment she turned back. "Thank you," she said sincerely, and left. Mother Berchte watched her go.

Nassirskaegi bleated once.

"Sunrise, I expect," Berchte answered.

Something clinked and clanked at the mouth of the cave. Jeweline entered, sword at her side, battered mail revealing more than it probably should. She was covered with cuts, scratches, and bruises, and her movements were stiff. Behind her, the sun was chasing the last of the stars away from the pale blue sky.

"Didn't work, did it?" Mother Berchte said mildly. Knit *one,* purl *two.* Knit *one,* purl *two.*

"You tricked me," Jeweline cried. "This shirt is worthless! If Father Fluss hadn't given me flashflowers to blind the bastards, I would have been killed."

"I told you not to take it, girl," Mother Berchte growled. Jeweline opened her mouth to protest, but Berchte cut her off. "Let me guess. You thought that the best shirt in the bunch would be disguised as a rusty piece of junk. You thought this was some stupid fairy tale to put the kiddies to sleep."

Jeweline snapped her mouth shut and set her jaw. "I just want to get my sisters away from those . . . men."

"Then do something sensible," Mother Berchte scoffed. "The first lesson you have to learn is never settle for less than the best."

Jeweline squared her shoulders. "All right." She shrugged out of the rusty mail shirt, marched over to the wall of mail, and chose another, one tightly knitted from the stoutest steel, yet light enough to wear easily. A two-headed eagle glowered defiantly in the design, and the shirt gleamed softly in the firelight as Jeweline pulled it on. Mother Berchte watched with interest.

Knit *one*, purl *two*. Knit *one*, purl *two*.

"Thank you," Jeweline said curtly, and left.

Nassirskaegi bleated a question.

"Sunset," Berchte replied.

"You filthy, lying old bitch," Jeweline spat before Mother Berchte could say a word. Outside, the sun touched the horizon and turned the clouds a brilliant scarlet. "You told me not to settle for less than the best. Now look at me!"

The mail shirt was bloody and torn, and new scratches tore angry lines down both her arms. Mother Berchte bared her teeth and growled low in her throat at Jeweline's tone of voice, but Jeweline stood firm and matched Berchte's glare. After a moment, Berchte nodded approval.

Knit *one*, purl *two*. Knit *one*, purl *two*.

"Let me guess," Mother Berchte said. "Father Fluss gave you blastberries to let you get away this time."

Jeweline stared at her. "How did—?"

"I'm not stupid, girlie," Berchte snapped. "But you are. Start paying attention to the pattern and maybe you'll win."

"What the hell is that supposed to mean?" Jeweline snapped back. "There isn't any pattern."

"Of course there is. It's why you haven't rescued your sisters yet."

"You're crazy as a cat in a violin shop." Despite the angry snarl in her voice, Jeweline had edged forward until she was right next to Mother Berchte's rocking chair. Her head barely reached Berchte's chest, even though Berchte was seated. Nassirskaegi admired her from his corner and nibbled a bit of hay in an extremely suggestive manner.

"Look for the pattern." Mother Berchte's needles clicked faster and faster until her fingers were a blur. "I've already given you the first lesson: never settle for less than the best. The second lesson is that everything happens in threes. You've had your third visit with Father Fluss, if that pouch at your waist is filled with sleepyseed like I think it is. This is your third visit to me. And in a moment you'll be making your third try to rescue your sisters."

"What about the armor?"

"You've already destroyed two sets, girlie," Berchte grumped. "You're on your own there. I don't knit this stuff for free."

"Is it true that you take your goat to bed with you?" Jeweline asked abruptly.

Berchte stopped knitting for a moment and lashed out a hand. It caught Jeweline squarely across the face. She cried out and stumbled backward to the mouth of the cave.

"Don't be rude," Berchte told her mildly. She tried to pick up her knitting, but ended up staring down at her lap in puzzled astonishment instead.

"Over here," Jeweline called.

"Shit," Berchte muttered into her lap.

"You're good at guessing," Jeweline continued. "I'll bet you can guess what I want next."

Berchte glared across the cave to the entrance where Jeweline was brandishing the missing knitting needle. "Maybe I'll take up crocheting."

"Yeah, right. Come on—you know what I want.

Three lessons, three meetings, three rescues. And three shirts."

Berchte met Jeweline's eyes for a long moment. Then she nodded once and jerked her head at the old, rusty hauberk Jeweline had abandoned on the stony floor. It was still rusty, but when Jeweline picked it up, the holes vanished and the rust fell away, revealing glowing chain links that crackled and hummed with power. Jeweline tossed the needle toward Berchte's chair. She snatched it out of mid-air and slid it back into her knitting.

Knit *one*, purl *two*. Knit *one*, purl *two*.

"I'd have given it to you anyway, you know," Berchte said.

"Uh huh." Jeweline shrugged out of the ruined shirt and into the good one.

"Like you said," Mother Berchte told her, ignoring the sarcasm, "three visits, three rescues, three shirts. All part of the pattern. You also have to make a third choice."

Jeweline blinked. "What were my first two?"

"To try rescuing your sisters and to seek the help you needed."

"And my third?"

"Whether you want to stay in the pattern or not," Mother Berchte said. "Whether you really want to rescue your sisters."

Jeweline narrowed her eyes warily. "What makes you think I don't?"

"You're the youngest. You're probably the prettiest. And they picked on you all your life because of it, didn't they? Now you're going to show your sisters once and for all that you're the smartest, the bravest, and the most resourceful. Do you honestly think your sisters will be grateful and pile affection on you? That they'll kiss your fingers and beg forgiveness for all the nasty things they've done?" Mother Berchte spat into the fireplace and the flames flared green. "I guarantee you they won't. They'll blame you for the raid. They'll blame you for your brothers' and parents' deaths. And they'll blame you for not rescuing them earlier. Oh yes, girlie—they will."

"I have to rescue them. They're my sisters," Jeweline said stoutly, though there was doubt in her voice.

"And sisters can be the cruelest of all," Mother Berchte said. "They made fun of you for learning swordwork from your brothers, didn't they? They called you names and gossiped about you and spread rumors that you handled your brothers' blades as well as their swords, didn't they?"

Jeweline flushed and looked away.

"Meanwhile," Berchte continued, knitting needles still clicking on her lap, "you have a man waiting for you in the river at the bottom of this mountain. And maybe if you kiss him, you'll see he isn't as ugly as you thought."

"He isn't ugly," Jeweline said quickly, then blushed again.

Berchte gave a knowing nod. "The fool likes you, girlie. He never gave *me* blastberries and sleepyseed. So choose: your ungrateful sisters or him. Or walk away entirely. No one's forcing you to complete the pattern."

"You're a bitch," Jeweline said. "A horrible old bitch."

"Life's the bitch, girlie," Mother Berchte said affably. "That's your third lesson. You can leave now."

Jeweline gave Mother Berchte once last look, then spun and marched out of the cave. Berchte picked up her knitting again. Knit *one*, purl *two*. Knit *one*, purl *two*.

Nassirskaegi bleated a question.

"She's going to rescue her sisters, of course," Berchte replied gruffly. "But I don't think she's going to stay with them. Not anymore."

Knit *one*, purl *two*. Knit *one*, purl *two*. Wire unwound steadily from Berchte's cable spool and Berchte allowed herself a heavy sigh. She had gotten a young girl to start thinking for herself, and that was nice. But she was really going to miss Father Fluss.

Arms and the Woman

Nancy Kress

The hour after the third-year class in Advanced History of Armor Styles was supposed to be my research time, but a tyro knight had asked to see me, and of course tyros are so sacred that we mere loremasters must drop everything and counsel them, no matter what valuable papers might miss the *Loremaster Quarterly* deadline. To make it worse, the apprentice turned out to be Tyro Marigold. I have little patience with stupid people; it is my only fault. Marigold is the stupidest apprentice that Castle Olansa has ever had. By far.

"Loremaster Gwillam, I'm being *haunted*," she said, sitting on the edge of the wooden bench in my study, her blue eyes perfectly round. The emblem on her breastplate was upside down. I reached over and twisted it to its locked and upright position.

"If you're being haunted, then go get a spell from Father Martin."

"I can't, because—"

"Don't tell me you 'can't.' You know tyros are exempt from hauntings during all of training except vigil week." Although probably she didn't know. Certainly I hadn't been able to teach her much about chivalric lore. Why should Father Martin have been any more successful teaching her about death duty?

"I can't see Father Martin about this because—"

"Don't tell me 'can't,' girl! Just do it!"

"—the ghost is my aunt, First Dame Cecilie of Castle Thlevin!"

That, of course, put a different cast on the situation. I leaned forward and scrutinized Marigold carefully. No, she wasn't lying. Her pop-eyed blue gaze looked genuinely baffled, and genuinely frightened. Besides, she was too stupid to lie.

Which was what made the situation interesting. Ghosts almost never choose relatives to haunt for their tuitions. Obviously an unstilled ghost has to haunt someone to learn whatever lessons it failed to learn in life, but usually relatives are part of the reason they didn't learn the lesson in the first place. Wisdom deficits tend to run in families. Most ghosts need to go outside the family to discover the principles they didn't see illustrated in life. So why was a First Dame haunting her own niece?

And why *Marigold*? What could a tyro this stupid— she was dead last in the lists for jousting, hunting, arcana, military strategy, fencing, astrology, and heraldry—possibly teach anybody? The only award Marigold had ever won, in three years at Castle Olansa, was Miss Congeniality, and I suspect that was a pity vote by the other tyros. The tyromistress is constantly trying to eradicate their sentimentality, but with thirty-three teenage girls in the tyro class alone, it's difficult.

Marigold squirmed under my close inspection, looked away, looked back, nervously fiddled with her armor emblem, which again ended up upside-down. No, she wasn't lying.

"Tyro, when did you last see the ghost of First Dame Cecilie?"

"Last night! At midnight, Loremaster. Oh, she was so aw-ful! She wore full armor—breastplate, tace, tasset, pauldron, all of it—and was smeared with blood! And she had no . . . no right arm!" The young voice was filled with horror. The right arm, the sword arm.

"All right," I said. "You may go."

"G-go? But . . . but what should I do?"

"Nothing, until I send for you again. That will be this evening. I need to think."

At the mention of thinking, Marigold nodded reverently, in homage to a foreign activity. She tiptoed out, so as not to disturb my thinking, her armor clanking on the stone threshold. When she'd clanked out of sight, I closed the door to my study and posted a watchraven. I needed to use everything at my disposal, both scrolls and spells, to learn what I could about First Dame Cecilie of Castle Thlevin.

"What did he say? What did he tell you?" The tyros crowded around Marigold in the Third Bedchamber. They had just come in from strength training and the smell of strong healthy sweat perfumed the summer air. "What's he going to do, Marigold?"

"He's going to think."

The other residents of the Third Bedchamber nodded sagely, but Tyro Anna frowned. She was first bed in the First Bedchamber, top of the lists, and wouldn't have ventured this far near the bottom for anything less momentous than haunting by a relative. Anna was tough, smart, and much resented, although this did not save her from Loremaster Gwillam's sarcasm. Some of the other girls turned to stare at her coldly.

Anna said, "'Think'? That's it? What action is he going to take on your behalf, Marigold?"

"He's going to send for me this evening," Marigold said. She smiled, glad to have been able to produce information for Anna, whom she admired. It was a smile of exceptional sweetness; Marigold possessed neither jealousy nor malice.

Anna said, "That's not action, that's postponement of action. Did he say anything else? Try to remember!"

Obediently Marigold racked her mind. "Nooo . . . that was all."

"Then keep me informed of your next visit to him," Anna ordered, and swept out of the room.

Catherine muttered, "That one will be having to haunt somebody herself, someday. To study humility."

"Oh, never mind her," Elizabeth said. "Tell us again about the ghost, Mar!"

Obligingly Marigold described yet again the terrible armless figure in the long red robe, while the Third Bedchamber shivered and squealed.

After six hours of scrolls and spells so intense that my head hurt, I knew much more about First Dame Cecilie than she would have liked me to know. Or anyone else, either. I poured myself an ale, watched the glory the sinking sun made of my small stained-glass window, and pondered amid the litter of my small library.

First Dame Cecilie had been born into an undistinguished yeoman family—Marigold's family—in West Riding, forty-seven years ago. She had been tested in the usual way at her woman-ceremony, and, astonishingly, had proved to have ability in knighthood, lore, war counsel, *and* barter. Only at childlove and housewifery had she scored low. Several castles had made her a bid, and her proud parents had chosen knighthood at Castle Treffin, very ivy-rank.

Cecilie had easily become first bed in the First Bedchamber, and at class knighting she'd won every honor open to her. She'd left Treffin to join Princess Margaret's army, then invading the Sixth Kingdom, and distinguished herself in several battles. She'd married a beautiful and wealthy landowner, Duke Michael of Kern, and had done such a superb job of reorganizing and leading his household forces that no one had dared challenge the duke's army.

That had apparently been the problem.

Cecilie had had nothing more to do. There was no war to fight. She'd borne Michael twins, beautiful daughters, but she had no talent for housewifery or childlove, and her daughters did not fill her days. The house steward, a woman just as formidable as Cecilie, successfully resisted Cecilie's efforts to take over the household barter. Cecilie grew more idle, more bitter, and more desperate. Michael did not understand. They got separate bedchambers.

Finally Cecilie took to pretending she had a lover. This gave her an excuse to go away for a week at a time. Away from the estate, she disguised herself as a foreign knight and entered second-rate tournaments where credentials weren't checked too closely. Naturally, she won them all. She was too good, and some-one traced her real identity. There was a scandal, and Cecelie was disgraced. Michael divorced her. She was disarmored by the Parfait Gentle Knights Association. Her birth family disowned her.

But there was more. After a few years, Cecilie tried the foreign-disguised-knight routine *again*, and again she was exposed. After that, she holed up for a few months in an abandoned monastery in the wilds of North Riding. Naturally I couldn't summon up what had happened there; even the lingering-spirit-of-a-place was thick with spells. But no one else entered during Cecilie's stay there. I am sure of that. And when she emerged, she had only one arm.

She entered the second-rate lists a third time, was not recognized, fought badly (she had, after all, only one arm), and was killed in her second tournament. She was buried, an anonymous knight, in a greave yard.

I'd brought my watchraven inside my library when I'd finished working. Now I raised my goblet to it.

"The most major scroll of my career, raven. Perhaps of any loremaster career!"

The raven stared at me from his shiny flat black eyes.

"There are only two possibilities, you know. Cecilie was completely unable to bend with fate. Marigold bends with everything anyone asks of her. Marigold is too close a relative for haunting under any but the most extraordinary circumstances, which always means that no one else's actions have ever matched so closely the dead ghost's mistakes, nor ever will. There are hundreds of people that Cecilie could have observed in order to learn ordinary flexibility. No, it's an extraordinary event. And there are only two possibilities, raven!"

It stared at me impassively.

"Either Tyro Marigold, too, will cut off her own arm, in some way that will teach Cecilie her death lesson. Or—listen to this!—we have here an example of the rarest of all death tuitions. There hasn't been even one in the last century. If Marigold doesn't cut off her own arm—then the haunting is a *reversal*! It won't be Cecilie who learns from Marigold, but Marigold who learns from Cecilie! And either way, I can write the scroll before it happens, and have it ready to go! I will be famous, you stupid bird! I will be called to Queen Eleanor's court! I will be revered and consulted and rich and never see this dump of a training castle again! What do you think of *that*?"

A mistake. If I hadn't been so exhausted and jubilant and ale-wild, I would never have asked a raven a direct question. They have a limited vocabulary, all of it irritating.

"Clever bore."

"Oh, shut up. What do you know? You're as stupid as Marigold and the rest of the giggling tyros!"

The raven stared at me, unblinking.

Marigold and her best friend, Tyro Catherine, stood outside the loremaster's chamber, clutching hands. Catherine had come to lend Marigold spiritual support, even though both girls understood that only Marigold would be summoned into the chamber. They awaited that summons now. Both wore full dress armor except for helmets, in honor of the solemnity of the occasion. Their fidgeting clanked on the stone floor.

"What if he tells you to *talk* to the haunt?" Catherine breathed.

"Oh, he wouldn't! I couldn't!"

"But he might. You know how he is."

Marigold nodded. Her chin piece clinked against her gorget, which in turn rattled her breastplate, with its slipped emblem. "I don't—oh, what was that? Around the corner!"

"Not your aunt. Really! I saw the right hand. It was *there*."

"Oh," Marigold said, visibly relaxing. "Who was it?"

"I didn't see. But I guess it was one of those snotty First Chamber girls."

Marigold looked puzzled. "Why would they be here?"

"Oh, Mar, you're so innocent. Don't you know they're all jealous of this?"

"Jealous? Of this? Of *what*?"

"Of all the attention you're getting from the loremaster! Any of them would die for a private conference with him!"

"Ooohhh," Marigold said. Her smooth brow

creased. "But . . . Cathy, I don't think so. They don't like him any better than we do. He's just as mean to them, you know. Even to Anna."

"I know. But she's probably jealous anyway. That whole crowd sucks up to all the teachers."

"But, Cath . . . I don't think they—"

"You don't think it because you're so nice. But everybody else in our chamber can see it. That Anna—oh!"

The door opened to reveal the loremaster. Marigold and Catherine clutched hands harder (clink, rattle). The loremaster frowned.

"You are not needed here, Tyro Catherine. Go away."

"Yes, sir."

"On second thought, stay."

"S-stay?"

"I said so, didn't I? God, you girls are a waste of air. Come in. Sit there. No, not there—*there*."

Marigold and Catherine settled their armor on the edge of the raised stone hearth, empty in the warm summer. They sounded like a tray of dropped kitchenware. Loremaster Gwillam studied them with distaste.

Long miserable moments dragged by for the girls. Just when they could bear it no longer, the loremaster barked, "Tyro Catherine, have *you* seen this haunting?"

"No, sir."

"Are you lying?"

"No, sir!"

"I think you're lying."

"I d-don't lie, sir."

"If you say that, you're lying now. Everybody lies. Isn't that true?"

"Yes . . . no . . . I—"

"Do you think I lie?"

"No, sir."

"You're wrong. I lie. Am I right?"

"Yes . . . no . . . I . . . "

"Stupid as I thought. Both of you. Tyro Marigold, this is what I'm going to do. I'm going to go where you go, do what you do. Everywhere. I will see what you see, and thus gather information on this haunting. I will—"

"Everywhere?" Marigold gasped.

"Everywhere. I will sleep in the Third Bedchamber. The tyromistress has given her permission. Her watchravens will accompany me, for propriety's sake. But I will be with you, and I will get to the bottom of this."

The girls looked at each other, appalled. Catherine, the bolder, finally said, "But, sir . . . "

"But what?"

"What . . . what if the haunt doesn't appear again?"

"It will appear again."

Once more the girls stared at each other.

"However," Loremaster Gwillam said, "I will certainly not tell you what I expect. You are both too stupid to understand. You may go. I will join you as soon as the tyromistress's ravens are delivered to me."

Outside the loremaster's closed door, Marigold burst into tears. Catherine put an arm around her.

"To have him . . . " sob, clank " . . . watch me all the time . . . " clank, sob " . . . *criticizing* the way he does . . . oh, Cath!"

"I know," Catherine soothed. "Old sot!"

"Sshhhh! He'll hear you!"

"I don't care if he does!"

But at a sound behind them, they both scurried away, raw-nerved and rattling.

Tyro Marigold was not lying. The other girl believed her utterly; I examined Catherine specifically to be sure of this. The haunting is real, there is nothing like it in all the modern literature, and I am going to be renowned throughout the Twenty-four Kingdoms.

All I need is for Marigold either to lose her sword arm or to learn something significant from the haunt of her aunt.

For the next five days I stuck to Marigold like a spell on a frog. I watched intently as she jousted; no fall severed her arm. I peered over her shoulder at her lesson scrolls; no writing changed to haunted runes from a tutelary ghost. I sat on the sidelines as she worked out in the ring; no opponent's sword cut through her elbow. I knelt beside her at vigil; no haunt appeared, dressed in bloody armor.

I was not discouraged. But I may have become a touch impatient with the stupid tyros (it is my only fault). Unfortunately, they are all stupid. This is how I know I will have nothing to learn beyond the grave—I am being given all my trials now.

On the sixth day, however, it happened. Everybody saw it, even the watchravens.

Thus is scholarly vigilance rewarded in the worthy.

"I can't stand it," Marigold moaned. "I can't, I can't!"

"Keep your voice down," Tyro Elizabeth said nervously from the pallet beside Marigold. Loremaster Gwillam slept on Marigold's other side. Three watchravens perched on the six-inch-high carved wooden fence between.

"Liz, it's awful. Today in Summa Logicales he screamed at me that I was horse dung. In front of everybody!"

"I know. But quieter, Mar. Shhhhh."

"What does he want from me?"

Elizabeth didn't answer. No one knew. From beyond the symbolic fence came the loremaster's soft snoring. The ravens' black eyes, wide open, gleamed in the moonlight from the open window.

"And tomorrow," Marigold moaned, but very quietly, "we have to—what was that?"

"I didn't hear any—oh!"

Both girls sat up, grabbed each other, and rose to their knees to look out the window. Then they shrieked to raise the dead, although in this case that was unnecessary.

The haunt of First Dame Cecilie of Castle Thlevin stood a hundred yards off, at the edge of the wood. At such a distance she was a small armor-clad figure, but clearly one-armed. She keened despairingly, "Marigold! Marigold of West Riding!"

"Oh! Oh!" Marigold shrieked.

"What? What?" screamed the rest of the Third Bedchamber, now awake.

"Severed yore!" cried the watchravens.

"Go! Go to her, you stupid girl!" Loremaster Gwillam cried, bolt upright on his pallet, clutching the windowsill greedily. His striped nightcap fell over one eye and he shoved it away. "Go! Wait—go alone!"

"Alone?" cried Marigold, aghast.

"Yes, yes! How else can she cut . . . er, how else can she learn whatever she must know from you? Go!"

Marigold was not the brightest young woman in the Twenty-four Kingdoms, but she did not lack bravery. At an order from a loremaster, she started to pull on her armor.

"No, wait—I *will* go with you!" the loremaster cried.

"You go with—no, no, I'll go alone!"

"Are you contradicting me, Tyro?" Loremaster Gwillam pulled himself up to his full height, plus slightly tilted nightcap.

"No," Marigold said miserably.

"Never sore," said a raven.

"Ever on the floor," said another.

But by the time they reached the edge of the wood, the haunt of Dame Cecilie had vanished.

The mistake was mine. I admit it; I am not one such as cannot admit when he is in error. I was impatient (it is my only fault). I should not have tried to go with Marigold the Stupid. I should have instead let her go alone, respecting the sacred privacy of a tuition haunting, and then spied on her with a spell pool. Next time, I will know better. Next time, I will be better prepared.

Next time came two days later.

Although I thought, before those two days had elapsed, that I had my prize. Tyro Marigold fell at sword practice in the armory.

She was matched against Tyro Catherine, who was as inept as she. Oh, I will be glad when I shake the dust of this brackish excuse for a castle from my boots, and leave these stupid girls behind me! Living always among women is itself enough of a curse; living with tyros is a flagellation no loremaster should have to bear.

The practice was held indoors in the armory, a windowless building large enough to hold all thirty-three tyros, only because outside it rained. For an hour the tyros had been set at the pel-quintain, a stake driven upright into the ground, with which they "fenced" with double-weight sword and shield. Each girl wielded forty pounds of metal, so that when it should be changed for regular weaponry, sword and shield would seem light by comparison. Rain drummed steadily on the roof, just above the bannerettes and pennoncels stored in the rafters. A rack against the wall held more shields, swords, and armor, most of it slung over nails and pegs.

"Change now!" called the training mistress. "Hut, hut!"

The weary girls staggered to the wall rack and

switched their double-weight swords and shields for standard-weight. Training Mistress Joan again paired them off, this time without regard for list ranking. Perhaps it was a deliberate attempt to expose them to different competencies. Or perhaps Joan was weary, too, and paired whomever happened to stand beside each other.

Or perhaps—I thought then—it was fate.

Tyro Anna smiled, nastily, at Tyro Marigold, who smiled back, waveringly.

"Begin!"

The girls started whacking away. Tyros, of course, were not allowed to foin; a direct thrust of the point by such beginners might cause serious injury. So they slashed and feinted and whacked, most of them unbalanced by the sudden change in weapon weight, all of them looking as silly as flailing chickens thrown into a pond. And in the midst of the whacking and flailing and lurching, Tyro Marigold tripped.

She slashed at Anna, who moved easily out of the way. The too-hard slash unbalanced Marigold, carrying her sideways until she crashed into a pel-quintain. That caromed her into the wall rack of armor. It was bolted to the wall, but the careless and stupid and exhausted tyros had slung their double-weight weapons on the pegs any which way, and many pieces fell.

A double-weight sharpened sword fell bladeside toward Marigold's right forearm.

The room seemed underwater, so slowly did the sword fall. There was time for me to jump to my feet, to raise my fist halfway to the sky, to cry out.

"Yes! Oh, thank you, Fate!"

The sword turned in the air, as heavy objects sometimes will. And Marigold turned, too, twisting her body away from the falling weapon. With both these turnings, the sword landed flatside on Marigold's arm. It would leave no more than a bruise.

I could not contain myself. "You stupid bitch! Why

did you move? Do you know what you've thwarted, what you've destroyed, you moronic thieving turd, you silly bitch—"

They all looked at me, tyros and teachers alike, mouths gaping open. They did not understand. I stalked from the room, and it was many hours before I could calm myself and return to my usual deep understanding of a complex situation, my usual far-seeing knowledge.

She had not lost her arm. Even though it was the perfect time for it. This, I finally saw, was intended as a sign to me. Marigold would not lose an arm, so the other circumstance must be the truth. This was a reverse haunting, and soon Marigold would learn something from Dame Cecilie instead of the other way around.

Once I realized this, I was no longer disappointed that Marigold had not been maimed. In fact, I could see that her escape was a gift to me. It showed me the broad outlines of the marvelous phenomenon I was chosen to witness, even if the exact details must wait for my later sharp-eyed discovery.

After that, I stuck closer to Marigold than ever. But in my far-seeing mind I began writing my paper, certain that soon the rest of the gift would be given me.

The next night, it was.

"You must try to eat, Mar," Elizabeth whispered. Catherine hovered anxiously on Marigold's other side at the long refectory table.

"I can't," Marigold whispered back. "Not with him watching me like that."

Loremaster Gwillam sat across the table. His attention had been momentarily distracted by a watchraven, which had swooped over his shoulder and stolen a piece of fish from his plate. The loremaster batted away the bird, which mumbled something unintelligible around the fish in its beak—the mumble ended in either "door" or "whore." The loremaster then returned his gaze to Marigold. Under that gaze— steady, intent, cold—the girl felt she couldn't breathe properly, let alone eat.

Or joust.

Or fence.

Or sleep.

"You must try to sleep," Catherine whispered at bedtime, squeezing Marigold's hand. Marigold nodded wanly.

Nonetheless, she was snoring when the voice came from beyond the window. "Maaarrriigggoooollllddd . . ."

"Wake up, you stupid girl! It's her! Dame Cecilie is here!" Loremaster Gwillam shook Marigold until her teeth rattled.

Fearfully, Marigold crawled up from her pallet and peered over the windowsill. As before, the one-armed figure stood at the edge of the woods.

"What on earth is she *wearing*?" said one of the girls clustered behind her.

"Where's her armor?"

"That's a gown like my mother used to wear when . . . when . . . "

"She's pregnant!" Catherine gasped.

"With a horse, at least!"

"Haunts can't get pregnant!"

"No, they . . . can they, Loremaster?"

"Shut up," Loremaster Gwillam said. "Go out there, Marigold."

"Me? Alone? No, I—"

"Go on, you silly bitch! This is it!"

The loremaster pushed Marigold so hard she fell over. An indignant, scared murmur ran over the tyros. Elizabeth started to say quaveringly, "Loremaster, you mustn't—" when the figure by the woods made a quarter turn, and someone cried, "Oh my good heavens! Now she's got *two arms*!"

It was true. The haunt, undeniably dressed in a gown instead of armor, undeniably pregnant, was also undeniably bi-armed.

Loremaster Gwillam appeared to be having a fit of some kind. "Two arms! A restored arm! A reverse haunting! Oh, my paper, oh the ground-breaking, oh the scientific sensation, the—get going, girl! Get out there before the haunt decides not to teach you anything!"

"T-t-teach me . . ."

"Go!"

Marigold went. Shaking, and brave despite her fear, she pulled a cloak over her nightdress and stumbled alone across the dark open expanse between the castle and the wood. The tyros of the Third Bedchamber, watching, huddled together in awed silence.

Closer, closer . . . and then Marigold and her dead unmaimed aunt stood face to face in the gloom.

"Ooohhh," groaned Elizabeth softly, in sympathy.

"She's so *brave*," moaned Catherine.

"Endeavor more," said a raven.

I had it. I had it! Not from that stupid girl, who staggered back from her historical and miraculous meeting and promptly fainted. But who needed her? I went immediately to my chamber and invoked a spell pool. The pool had stood ready for days.

And there, in the inky waters, they appeared clear as morning. Marigold walking toward Dame Cecilie and, as the tyro got closer, a distinct view of the haunt herself. She did indeed have two arms—she held up both to stop her niece from approaching too close. She did indeed wear a house-gown instead of armor, and it did indeed bulge in pregnancy. All was clear except her face, partly hidden by her unbound hair as it swung forward. Yet Marigold was certain of the face. She choked out, "Aunt Cecilie . . ."

"Yes, child. It is I." The voice, coming from my spell pool, was low and sepulchral.

"You look . . . you look so . . . waxy . . . "

"I have been dead these nine years."

"That would explain it," Marigold faltered.

"Child. Learn from me. Don't—"

"Aren't you . . . forgive me, aunt! Aren't you . . . "

"Spit it out, child."

" . . . supposed to learn from . . . from . . ."

The stupid tyro couldn't finish. Well, the idea of anyone learning anything from Marigold was indeed hard to conceive of. Dame Cecile helped her out.

"Learn from me, child. Be willing to change your armor."

Marigold looked innocently down at herself. "But I'm not wearing armor."

"It's metaphorical," the ghostly voice said, a bit impatiently. "If you can no longer do something well, don't do it any longer. Do not go armored in failure. Give yourself to the new life completely. Not like me."

"But . . . I can't do *anything* well," Marigold said.

"Good . . . bye . . ."

Gown fluttering, the haunt of Dame Cecilie waddled backward into the woods, waving with both arms. The gown slipped back from her forearms and I could just make out, inside the right elbow, a tattoo of clasped hands. It was then that jubilance seized me; that is exactly the kind of detail that makes for memorable papers!

In the spell-pool image, Marigold gasped. Quickly Dame Cecilie said, "Say no more! Please!" and that, too, was a good detail for the paper. Dame Cecilie knew how significant her reverse haunting was, how rare, how important. It must have been a terrible strain on her materialization. She could take no more, not even another word.

The haunt disappeared into the night woods.

The pool went dark, and I hurried back to the

Third Bedchamber. I doubted that the stupid girl could tell me any more than I had seen—spell pools, after all, are the exact truth—but it never hurt to be thorough.

The Third Bedchamber was full of girls, more than the eleven that belonged there. They had fluttered in from the first two chambers, clacking and fussing like the geese they were. Marigold sat in the center of this feminine maelstrom, on a chair whose back was topped by two of the tyromistress's watchravens.

"Tyro Marigold! Tell me what happened between you and Dame Cecilie!"

She did. It was precisely as I had seen in the spell pool, of course. I listened to her stumble through the account, as dim-witted in the telling as in all else. And then I was ready for the important question.

"And from your aunt's haunt—did you learn anything?"

Marigold smiled strangely. "Oh, yes."

"And what did you learn?"

She recited, in the same mechanical voice with which she recited her memorized lore in class (when she could remember it at all):

"'Be willing to change your armor. If you can no longer do something well, don't do it any longer. Do not go armored in failure. Give yourself to the new life completely.'"

"But what does it mean to *you*, you stupid child?"

Marigold took a long time to answer. The gaggle of girls stayed quiet, almost holding their breaths. Finally she said slowly, "It means that dung happens, and when it does, you should walk on a different path."

That, of course, I did not put in my paper, which was dignified, important, magnificent. I penned it that night, working feverishly until dawn (of course, I'd already written the "Background" and "Search of the Literature" sections). In the morning I sent it off by

Feudal Express, which guaranteed that it absolutely, positively would be in Queen Eleanor's court by the next day.

The summons from court would probably take a week. Maybe less. And I would be on my way, out of Castle Olansa, free forever of stupid tyros and squires and second-rate faculty.

Maybe it was self-indulgent of me, but I took my imminent escape as reason to no longer treat the girls with kid gloves. Finally, I could speak to them in class as their stupidity deserved. It was a great relief to me.

"No, no, Marigold, not like that," Anna said. "Hold your arm like this, so I can't get under your guard . . . Yes. Much better."

The tyros went at it again in the practice yard, Anna in standard armor, Marigold in double-weight. They circled, feinted, thrust . . . and Marigold scored.

"Well done!" Anna said.

In the circle of watchers, Elizabeth whispered to Catherine, "Mar really is getting better, isn't she?"

"She was never *that* bad," Catherine said loyally.

"Oh, come on, you know she was terrible. But with Anna giving her all these lessons . . . Anna isn't so mean, after all."

"I still don't like her, Liz. But she's tough, I'll give her that. She's out there like a champion even after what the loremaster called her in class today. And she's being very nice to Marigold."

"She should be, after what—"

"Shhh," Catherine said. "Here he comes!"

The girls held their breaths. Carefully the circle shifted, a feminine realignment to shield Marigold and Anna until Loremaster Gwillam had passed. However, he hurried past with no more than a single contemptuous sneer at the practice yard.

"He's going to pack," Elizabeth said. "He got a

summons from Queen Eleanor's court. He leaves tomorrow."

The two girls covered their mouths and giggled.

In the practice circle, steadily improving under Anna's careful tuition, Marigold's eyes were as bright as her armor.

I had nailed the lid of my box and packed the fragile items, such as the spell pool, in barrels lined with hay. The headmistress had given me a cheap cloak pin and a cold speech of farewell, the ungrateful bitch. As I checked under the bed for any forgotten items, I noticed the note pinned to my pillow.

Come to the wood at moonrise
to meet Dame Cecilie.
Methinks you will regret it
if you do not.

My first reaction was outrage. Who would *dare* . . . The writing was large and round and girlish, an inkblot on one corner.

"Ever deplore," said one of those damned ravens, and for some reason, a cold spear pricked my spine.

Bluebells bloomed in the wood, and honeysuckle and loosestrife and violets. Summer light filtered down between the green leaves, dappling the ground with gold. It was two days before graduation. The air was light and warm.

"Lloorrremmmaaassstttterrr Gggwwillaaammm . . . ."

And she was there, First Dame Cecilie of Castle Thlevin . . . dressed in bloody armor, pale as death, one-armed until she moved.

"Hey nonny nonny, Bill," she said, and threw away the carved stump of her severed arm. With both hands she pulled off the waxy death mask, and I was staring at Tyro Anna. A burst of laughter behind me sent me whirling to see the rest of the tyros rising from bushes and dropping from trees.

"What is the meaning of—"

"You can guess the meaning, Bill," Anna said. "Can't you?"

All I could do was stare in stupefaction.

"It was a mummery," Anna said. "Only you never guessed it, did you? We did our research on our classmates' knightly kin—thank you for teaching us how—and we put it to good use. A shame you already wrote your paper and sent it off, isn't it? You're going to look a bit of a fool when the truth comes out."

I opened my mouth, but no words came out, only a bleat. "Marrr—"

"Marigold didn't know it was us," Anna said. "Nor did any of the Third Bedchamber. They couldn't have played their parts so well if they had. Oh, and there's one thing more that you don't know, loremaster. After graduation, I'm not doing my squireship here at Castle Olansa. I'm doing it at court. My cousin has found me a place there. In fact, there'll be a steady supply of us tyros going up to court in the future. You'll probably want to use your new position to make things as comfortable as possible for us, don't you think?"

"Or else," Elizabeth said.

"Don't you have anything to say, Bill? Your mouth is wide open. Don't you want to call us silly bitches or stupid idiots or worthless dung?"

Marigold said, "Maybe that's enough, Anna. He looks sorry."

"Oh, he's sorry, aren't you, Bill? He's sorry he thought we were too stupid and too defenseless to take care of ourselves."

Anna stepped closer. She raised her forearm and I saw, through my numb horror, that the inside of the elbow had a tiny tattoo. Of clasped hands.

Suddenly I remembered that the emblem on Marigold's breastplate, the one that was always coming loose, was two clasped female hands.

"Your lore doesn't include everything," Catherine said to me. "We girls have lore among ourselves, you know. We go armored in each other."

"Whereas *you* go armored in failure," Anna said, smiling, "unless you can be willing to change your armor. If you can no longer do something well, don't do it any longer. Give yourself to your new life completely, Bill."

"That's *us*," said Elizabeth, "we're your new life. Serving us as we come up to court, one by one by one."

"Never yore," a raven said. "Forever more."

And I could say nothing at all, just gaze at them in horror: the stupid silly bitches, the clasped hands, the unthinkable future.

Fun With Hieroglyphics

Margaret Ball

After thirty minutes of staring at a blank screen, I was finally inspired by the distinctive death-rattle sound of Norah's old Chevy coughing itself to a halt at the curb outside – not to words, but at least to action. I grabbed the mouse and clicked on the spreadsheet window I'd left minimized in the bottom left-hand corner of the screen. The resulting display of Dennis's and my finances was not a cheerful sight, but it was better than letting Norah look at the opening pages of my new book.

All 0,000 words and 0 K of it.

"Riva?" Norah called through the screen door as she came in with someone trailing her. "Is Jason ready yet? Oh, this is my friend Stephanie. She's a tech writer at Xycorp, that's why she looks like a grownup."

"How many times do I have to tell you, I'm *not* a 'tech writer'? My title is manager of hard-copy composition and distribution resources," Stephanie corrected Norah. A faint line showed between her two perfectly arched, perfectly shaped brows. Her mouth was painted a clear, bright red mouth-shape and her eyes were outlined with curving, dark brown eye-shapes that matched her hair. At least, I assumed it was hair. It didn't stick to her forehead or creep across her cheeks or cling to the back of her neck the way everybody else's hair did in Austin's spring humidity and heat.

"Whatever," Norah agreed cheerfully. She sank down in a wicker chair that creaked under her plump form. "How's the book coming, Riva?" She turned to Stephanie. "Riva's another writer, did I tell you? But she never comes to Austin Writers League meetings—that's where I met Steph," she interpolated in my direction before looking back at Stephanie. "Her Salla and my Jason are working on some kind of truly dumb school project together."

"Theoretically," I agreed, happy to drop the subject of my nonexistent second book. "They *said* they needed to do some research at the library. I dropped them off about an hour ago. They were going to take the bus home. But if I know them, they haven't started their research yet; they're still kvetching about the dumb project. Sorry, Norah. I'll bring Jason home when they show up."

"Well, it *is* dumb," Norah said. "Develop a 3-D diorama in an empty oatmeal box, illustrating the building of the Pyramids."

"It does seem more like third-grade work than eighth-grade," I agreed. "But they've also got the option of staging a one-act play dramatizing some incident of Egyptian history."

Norah groaned. "Twenty-two eighth-grade girls playing twenty-two versions of Cleopatra and the asp."

"Never happen," I said. "With Gene Kruzak teaching the Ancient History module, they'll never even have *heard* of Cleopatra. They probably think she's a charm you find at the bottom of the oatmeal box."

"Your Salla knows about Cleopatra," Norah said. "I'll bet."

"Salla's too strong a feminist to play that part. If they do a play, she'll probably rewrite Egyptian history to have Cleopatra recruiting an army and conquering Rome."

If I hadn't said that, would it have saved us all from what happened? The Paper-Pushers don't believe in the power of words, for all they use so many of them. My people know better. Words—especially mathemagical equantations—call spirits out of the air. And other things.

However, at the time I didn't feel any *frisson* of warning. The cold chills were caused by Norah's renewing her inquiries about how the book was coming. She'd been too good a friend, for too long, for me to actually lie to her. I did sort of wish the intimidatingly competent Stephanie hadn't been there too, though, listening to my confession of failure with those perfectly shaped brows rising in perfect half-moon crescents above her eyes.

"Everything else I've written . . ." I concluded, then glanced at Stephanie. "Er, Stephanie, you don't read science fiction, do you?"

Stephanie gave me a patronizing smile. "In my position, I'm afraid it's all I can do to keep up with the current psychological and technical literature."

"Right. Well. *You* know, Norah, I'm not so good at making up plots. That first book was just about stuff that happened right here in Austin. And the stories I've been selling to anthologies are all based on things that happened . . . in my homeland," I said, bearing Stephanie's presence in mind. "Now my editor says she wants the new book to be set in this uni . . . I mean, country, not in Da . . . my homeland. And I haven't *done* anything to write about here, at least not since . . . that stuff in the first book." Stephanie didn't seem offended by all the elisions; in fact, she didn't even seem to be listening. She was tapping one foot and staring off as if she could see right through the wall to the pile of laundry in our bedroom. Still, there was no point in bringing up my—unusual—background with somebody who didn't already know about it.

"You know what, Riva," Stephanie said suddenly. So much for my theory that she'd spaced out ten minutes ago. "I've met a lot of women like you, and I think I can help you."

"You can?" Somehow Stephanie didn't seem like a good source for sword-and-sorcery adventure plots, but who knows? Maybe she too had a Past.

"Sure. You're one of the standard types," Stephanie said. "I bet you quit your job to raise the kid, right?"

"Well . . . Not exactly. I tried working part-time for a few years . . . "

"And it didn't work out! Exactly! It's just too hard for women to divide their attention between the career and the home."

Actually, what I'd found was that after I hit thirty-five, working as a swordswoman-for-hire was too hard, period, but Stephanie was not interruptible.

"Now your daughter is old enough that she really doesn't need you, except to drive her places, and you're at loose ends. The home-based businesses you may have tried didn't work out," Stephanie went on.

I couldn't contradict her about Salla, anyway. Since she turned thirteen Salla hardly said anything to me except, "Oh, Mooom!", "Will you drive me to the mall now?" and "How much longer are you gonna tie up the computer, I want to get on my chat room."

"What you need, Riva," Stephanie announced confidently, "is someone to help you reenter the professional world, get you started back in a career-track job. And I can do that for you."

"Um . . ." I didn't want to insult Stephanie, but she *really* didn't look like somebody who would have any contacts at all with my old employers—people like Zolkir the Terrible and Rodograunizzo the Revolting. Even if I'd wanted to get back into that business.

"Stephanie came to the Writers League tonight because she was recruiting tech writers for Xycorp," Norah put in.

"And *you*," Stephanie announced, looking straight at me, "are just the kind of person I'm looking for! Women who've been shunted out of the mainstream of professional work by our society's sexist attitude towards child-rearing, looking for a way back in . . . "

"Umm . . . I don't have much of a resume," I pointed out.

Stephanie waved her hand airily. "I can take care of all that. You *have* writing experience. And Norah's told me about your past life."

I glared at Norah.

"Any woman with the guts to do what you've already done – to leave your child's father and your homeland, to immigrate to the United States and start a new life from scratch – well, it's clear to me that you have what it takes to make it in the trenches of office politics."

And it was becoming clear to me that Norah hadn't told Stephanie *all* about my past life.

She leaned forward and took my hands. This close, the fervor in her eyes was almost hypnotic. "I need you, Riva. Xycorp needs you. This *society* needs you and women like you."

"Writers?"

"Strong women. Women who can roll with the punches and come up fighting."

Hmm. Maybe being a technical writer wouldn't be so boring after all. At least it seemed to call for skills I really had.

"Of course," Stephanie said, "you'll have to dress professionally at work."

I looked down at my jeans and T-shirt, visualized my old working outfit in its box under the bed. Somehow I had a feeling that a bronze chain mail corselet and thigh guards were not quite what Stephanie had in mind.

"What's wrong with these clothes?"

Stephanie and Norah looked at each other and there was one of Those Silences. You know the kind I mean: the kind where you realize that you've just revealed your total ignorance of the game and total unworthiness to play.

"I'm sure," Stephanie said finally, sounding considerably less sure than she had up to now, "that we can find something for you."

"Finding something" turned out to be somewhat more work than I had envisioned. Take shopping malls, for instance. I used to sneer at the ladies who got their exercise by walking up and down the length of an air-conditioned mall because they couldn't stand to work up an honest sweat. After Stephanie and I had been through Barton Springs Mall three times in one afternoon I had more respect for them. If nothing else, their feet were considerably tougher than mine, which ached from instep to heel, with separate factions of rebellious nerves lodged in each toe. As a member in good standing of the Bronze Bra Guild, with forty individual kills and several successful campaigns to my credit, I had too much pride to complain. I did reflect, however, that the Guild's training, which relied heavily on forced marches through the desert, running up mountains, and combat sparring, could reasonably be augmented by a few more endurance tests. In short, I had never trained for so many hours of walking on concrete floors. Of course, on Dazau we hadn't *had* concrete . . . .

By the time Stephanie pronounced herself satisfied with a gray suit that simultaneously concealed my chest and hobbled my knees, together with a set of undergarments that had been constructed by someone with bridge building and other major engineering feats on his mind, I was too tired to care about the funny-looking shoes that made me look as if I were walking on tiptoe. I couldn't tell if they fit anyway; my feet were going to hurt no matter *what* I wore. Ice packs seemed like a good choice.

All this may explain why for once I didn't mind when Salla staged her usual homecoming routine. This consisted of yelling, "I'M HOME!", slamming the front door, grabbing a handful of cookies and a Coke from the kitchen, and shutting herself in the cubbyhole we called a "study," where she could simultaneously watch TV, log on to a chat room with her friends, and talk on the phone. This was known as "doing homework." Some days I regretted the passing of the time when she'd wanted to tell me every detail of her day. Today, though, I was perfectly content to lie on the bed listening to my feet throbbing.

The longer Salla spent on the phone, the louder her voice got. That would have been okay with me, too, except that the walls of our house were made from something with all the sound-baffling qualities of a damp cardboard box. Thin cardboard. So I had the dubious pleasure of listening to one side of a conversation that seemed to consist entirely of, "No way!", "He *did*?" and "No *fucking* way, dude!"

"Salla," I called, "are you aware that I can hear every word you're saying?"

"That's okay, Mom," she yelled back, "I only reveal my innermost thoughts on the chat room. Right now I'm online with a nice old man in Copenhagen who likes little girls."

Well. I had to move sometime, if only to go to the

bathroom. I hobbled to the study and looked over Salla's shoulder. The chat-room log showed nothing but the usual string of banalities:

```
SoMch2dl4: blah
FadeSoSlow: oaky
SoMch2dl4: blah
SoMch2dl4: Do u know Y jess is so mad at
    mark?
FadeSoSlow: no
SoMch2dl4: i c
FadeSoSlow:so are you gonna do the fucking
    assignment?
SoMch2dl4: Yeah
SoMch2dl4: if I don't my parents will KILL me
SoMch2dl4: they are like totally paranoid about
    school
```

"You got that right, anyway," I told the back of her head, "but what happened to the dirty old man from Copenhagen? You enticed me in here under false pretenses."

Salla giggled. "Come on, Mom. You know I wouldn't be dumb enough to chat with anyone like that." She paused and pretended to think for a moment. "Unless, of course, he had *candy* . . . "

"So what's the 'fucking assignment'? And why aren't you doing it now?"

"Just a *minute*, Mom!" Salla typed, "got2go, my mom is hassling me," and logged off.

"It's that dumb thing for the ancient Egypt study unit, okay? You know, we gotta do a diorama in an oatmeal box, act in a dumb play, or . . . hell, where's the damn assignment sheet?" She rooted around in her backpack, tossing several empty juice boxes and a collection of ponytail holders onto the floor, and finally pulled out a crumpled sheet of paper. "Or find some other original and creative way of dramatizing ancient Egyptian life and making it real to your fellow students," she read with a sarcastic twist of her lip.

I hadn't seen this piece of paper before, and the decorative markings around the edges made the hairs on the back of my neck rise. I took it from her. "*Where did you get this?*"

Salla sighed again, more elaborately. "From Mr. Kruzak, where else?"

"But these *symbols* . . . " An old phrase from my apprenticeship to the wizard Mikhalleviko came to my mind. "Sacred carvings."

"Mom. They're just old Egyptian writing. Hieroglyphs. Nothing to get bent out of shape about. I got a cheat sheet off the Net that says what they stand for and how to pronounce them. See, this one means 'star' or the sound 'sba,' and this one means . . . " Salla's eyes drifted to the top of her cheat sheet and she looked confused. "And it says right at the top of the page that the word 'hieroglyph,' literally means 'sacred carvings.' How'd you know that?"

"I've . . . seen them before. Some of them, anyway. On Dazau they're . . . a wizard told me once that they were extremely potent magical symbols from the Old Tongue, only most of them had been lost and nobody knew exactly how to pronounce the ones that are left, so it was dangerous trying to invoke them; you never knew quite what you were going to get." Some of the results Mikhalleviko had gotten while experimenting with Sacred Carvings Magic were enough to wake me up screaming in the middle of the night fifteen years later.

"Way coool," Salla said. "Too bad Dazau magic doesn't work here."

"Thank goodness." I took a deep breath, tried to calm my fluttering nerves, and remembered just how much my feet hurt. "So what are you going to do for your project?"

Salla's three-cornered grin should have warned me,

but I was thinking about those peculiar shoes and wondering whether I'd actually be able to stand up on them. "Something original and creative, of course. That's ten points extra."

"Like what?"

"When I figure it out, I'll tell you." Salla sat back in her chair and stared at me with that opaque look she'd developed around her thirteenth birthday. It meant, "Go away, don't bother me, information will be dispensed on a strict need-to-know basis."

So I did. I needed to rest up before tomorrow, anyway. Stephanie had scheduled me a six-hour appointment at Hair Apparent. I had no idea how anybody could spend six whole hours cutting hair, but I figured I was about to find out. What I didn't realize was that I shouldn't have been worried about the remodeling of Riva – I should have been thinking about Salla home alone with the computer for several hours. We'd had Call Trans-Forwarding and a link to Furo Fykrou via Virtual Service Provider for years, ever since I'd been a commuter mom with an address on the Planet of the Paper-Pushers and a day job as swordswoman for Duke Zolkir; and I *knew* Salla had figured out how to access all that stuff.

I also knew, or thought I knew, that Salla was too smart to get herself in trouble messing with Dazau magic, after her last experience. You'd think having to be rescued from involuntary apprenticeship to Furo Fykrou would make her at least a little wary of doing deals with a wizard. But no . . . she was thirteen now, and all those exploding hormones were short-circuiting her brain function. At least, that was my friend Norah's way of explaining what happened to teenagers.

I didn't actually see this chat room log until it was all over, but you probably need to know about it now:

SoMch2dl4: helo? FF r u there?
FF2dazau1: is this riva?

SoMch2dl4: no its salla don't logoff I wanta maka deal

JosieLou2: hi this is jess

JosieLou2: what r u wearing 2 the dance fri?

SoMch2dl4: the grey skirt the long one and a cami top

FF2dazaul: u wanna deal or talk to yr little friend? Ima busy wizard.

JosieLou2: way cool ima get a new dress

SoMch2dl4: ever hear of sacred carvings?

JosieLou2: isnt that the new rap group

SoMch2dl4: I wuz talkin 2 FF, jess

SoMch2dl4: allo?

FF2dazaul: so what about SC?

SoMch2dl4: nuthin much, only I got a complete set here. With pronunciation guide!

FF2dazaul: ok, scan them in and ill see if theres anything I cn use

SoMch2dl4: you gotta be kidding I want payment up front

FF2dazaul: how do I know you really got them?

SoMch2dl4: u trns enuf power to invok 1 carving, maybe 2.

SoMch2dl4: if it works you know I got the good stuff

SoMch2dl4: if it doesn't work no loss

FF2dazaul: xcept u wastin my time

SoMch2dl4: wheres yr spirit of adventure?

That happened Tuesday, while I was being chopped, tinted, lacquered, sprayed and waxed in Hair Apparent.

"*Waxed?*"

"Relax, Riva," Stephanie told me, "she's not going to take your eyebrows off, just shape them."

I've been wounded in battle; I wasn't going to fuss over a little thing like having tiny hairs pulled out of my face. Although I will say this for battle as opposed to eyebrow waxing, at least you're allowed to defend yourself. However, when Stephanie started making noises about my bikini line, I pointed out quickly that when I wore the suit she'd picked out, plus panty hose and all the other junk designed to mold me into an acceptable shape, nobody was going to have any opportunity to inspect *that* hair.

These Paper-Pushers people have no sense of decency. There are limits to everything.

When the hairdresser got through with me, I stared into the mirror she held up and wondered where Riva Konneva had gotten to. Instead of a proud member of the Bronze Bra Guild, long hair falling loose and unconstrained (as a challenge to the enemy: you're never going to get close enough to me to grab my hair or anything else, so don't even think about it!) I saw a sleek, smooth woman who looked like a dark-skinned copy of Stephanie: close-cropped shining helmet of hair that clearly wouldn't dare lift a strand in any breeze, perfectly arched lines of brows, and a lost look in the dark eyes under the freshly waxed brows.

"Great!" I said, too heartily, to conceal my confusion, and reached for my purse. "Gosh, that was quick, too; I thought you said this would take all day, Steph, and it's only been three hours." Three interminable hours. Three hours that would have been more pleasantly spent staked out on an anthill. But who's complaining. After all, Stephanie was doing me a *favor*; showing me how to present myself in the World of the Paper-Pushers, a skill I'd never quite mastered on my own. If I wanted to work here instead of on Dazau—

"Where do you think you're going?" Stephanie and the hairdresser said simultaneously as I reached for a hip pocket I no longer had. Oops. No jeans. Pencil-slim gray skirt that not only hobbled my knees, but wouldn't hang right if you dared put anything in the token pockets. Where was that purse?

"Well, I thought—"

"Sit," Stephanie said, sounding as if she were talking to a recalcitrant dog. "*Sit*. The cosmetologist is going to show you how to do your face."

I sat.

Did you realize some people can spend *two hours* putting on eye makeup alone?

"I won't have time to do this every day and work too," I pointed out to Stephanie. "Oh, you won't need to," she assured me. "You'll learn how to do the makeup real fast, and then all you'll have to do is get up a couple of hours early to wash and blow-dry your hair."

I took a deep breath and thought about those predawn training runs – up Black Saddle Peak and down again – when I was an apprentice in the BBG. I hadn't given up then, even though the downhill jog had been really punishing for a nursing mother who hadn't been issued her bronze bra yet. I certainly wasn't going to wimp out just because Paper-Pushers' apprenticeship rituals were harder than I'd expected.

I will admit, though, that for the second day in a row I reached home and collapsed without much energy for bugging Salla about her homework. Dennis was working late that night, meeting with a series of parents who couldn't understand why their darlings were flunking Algebra II. If Salla wanted to spend the evening in a chat room, munching on pizza, that was fine with me.

"As long as you give me a piece of the pizza," I stipulated. "From the side *without* anchovies."

She forked over the pizza and assured me that her Egyptian Studies project was practically done, and I left it at that. I was in bed before Dennis got home, with the alarm set for five so I could get up and do the required maintenance on my Paper-Pushers' costume, so I didn't get the benefit of his comments on my new look. And Salla, of course, hadn't noticed. When she's doing her chat room / telephone / television multicommunications thing, I could strip stark naked and paint myself with green stripes and she wouldn't notice.

From comments I'd heard from other people who had real Paper-Pushers' jobs, I kind of expected the first few days to consist of thinking up lies to put on interminable forms and waiting for somebody to tell me what to do. Stephanie had other plans.

"Drop those in your cubicle, you can fill them out at home in your spare time," she snapped when I found my way to the Composition and Distribution Center clutching my inch-thick stack of green, white, yellow and pink forms.

I looked out over a maze of chin-high cardboard partitions. It looked like a large-scale version of something Salla had built for torturing white mice in a Science Fair project last year. The inmates of the cubicles looked kind of like the mice after Salla got through changing the maze structure on them for the fortieth time. Dazed. Uncomprehending. Quiet. And with a little light of madness in the eyes . . .

"This one's yours." Stephanie indicated a closet-sized space near her own desk, took the papers from my hands and dropped them on a desk that was already covered with manuals and diskettes. "And that's your first project. I'll bring you up to speed after the meeting."

"Um, don't I have to have an interview? I mean, I haven't actually been *hired* yet." I didn't think. The people in Personnel had been rather like Stephanie: so brisk and efficient that they didn't have time to tell you what was going on.

"A formality," Stephanie assured me. "We're des— I mean, we're in an aggressively up-hiring mode at the moment. Come on, you're late. The monthly

Vision Statement Meeting is about to start and I want you to sit in, get you up to speed on Xycorp's philosophy. Don't worry, you won't have to say anything, just listen."

That *sounded* easy enough. I made a mental note of another Paper-Pushers' translation. Did "Aggressively up-hiring mode" translate to "Desperate, as in you can hold us up for an extra sack of gold zolkys," or just "Desperate, as in we don't really care what you know as long as you have a measurable pulse?" Probably the latter, I concluded as I followed Stephanie down long tunnels glowing with the eerie blue-tinged lights that Paper-Pushers favored for indoor spaces. That might be something to worry about. Back home, the second version of "desperate" amounted to sending untrained recruits out as sword-fodder while saving the skilled fighters for the second wave of the attack. What exactly did it mean here? Maybe I'd find out in the meeting.

Ha.

Within half an hour I was completely lost and unable to translate anything anybody said. It was a hallucinatory experience. The conference room *looked* real enough, with an expensive oval mahogany table, padded swivel chairs, and a computer console built into each place at the table. The *people* looked reasonably real and competent—for Paper-Pushers, anyway; Duke Zolkir could have taken out the entire roomful with no help from his Guild swordswomen, but Paper-Pushers didn't go in for that kind of battle. They fought with words instead—and the words that eddied and swirled around that table like happysmoke were so slippery I couldn't begin to get a grasp on them.

At the beginning I figured out a few things. "Vision Statement" didn't mean that they cared whether I or anybody else could see farther than six inches without glasses; it meant that they had to come up with some words describing what they were trying to do at this branch of the company. That sounded good to me; I could have used some explanation. "Write software to do stuff, write manuals describing how to use it to do stuff, sell it to people who want to do stuff," was all I'd gotten out of Stephanie's description of Xycorp.

But the words! "Leverage" was a favorite. I thought this had something to do with getting a stick under something you wanted to move and applying force to the other end of the stick. But these people planned to "leverage" information, services, resources, catalysts, solutions . . . Somebody wanted to make sure that the planning process proceeded proactively; me, I wanted him to say those four words twenty-five times quickly without stuttering. Somebody else insisted that the vision statement must include the words "high payoff," "low risk," and "return on investment." A third somebody insisted that the core paradigm was a matter of principle-centered market-driven infrastructures.

Oh, well, Stephanie *had* introduced me as a new hire who was just there to listen and get up to speed. After half an hour I figured I'd done enough of the listening part. People were starting to shout at each other; I sat back and fingered the computer console. Maybe I could do the "get up to speed" part now, find out through the computer just what this company actually did.

Wrong again. I didn't have the passwords to access any company files. Salla wouldn't have let a little thing like that stop her, but I didn't know how to circumvent the password system. Besides, it might be a bad idea to hack into the company's system while sitting in my very first official business meeting. But I needed to do *something* to take my mind off the spiky shoes, the engineer-constructed underwear, and the suspicion that my oily skin was slowly infiltrating the perfect mask of makeup Stephanie had instructed me to apply. Ah, an Internet connection! Never mind the company passwords; I gave it the key words for my home system and quietly logged on while two guys in suits yelled at each other about "innovative paradigms," and "mission-critical services." Perhaps I could look up Xycorp on the Net and at least find out what their software was supposed to do.

As soon as the screen flashed on my personal home page I was poised to hit the "Search" button. But my hands froze over the keyboard as a scrolling banner unrolled in the "Local News" section of the screen, where I normally kept track of weather and school holidays and good movies coming up.

"Terror at Colton Middle School," the banner announced in flashing red and yellow letters that made my stomach turn over. I skimmed the few words below. There wasn't much. A report of armed men disrupting an eighth-grade Social Studies class, police being called to the scene, need to proceed slowly for fear of creating a hostage situation, the lack of any statement from the teacher, Eugene Kruzak . . .

Gene Kruzak.

Eighth-grade social studies.

Salla's class.

And Salla had been planning to do something "creative and original," with Sacred Carvings . . . .

I switched into Instant Messenger and activated the trans-world chat mode, holding my breath until the purple screen with the scrolled edges came up. So my passwords worked fine on this system. So far, so good. Now if only Furo Fykrou was on line . . . I sent an emergency alert to ff2dazau1@zolkir.org and prayed that the beeping would annoy him enough to get an immediate answer.

Some jerk at the head of the table was yammering about the need for a value-added encirclement strategy.

"Too complicated," somebody else said.

"Well, why don't we just ask the tech writers—I mean, the Composition and Distribution Department—about that?"

I had a feeling that everybody was staring at me. Why not Stephanie? Where *was* Stephanie? She must have taken a bathroom break. I tried to remember the last words. Encirclement strategy.

"Well, uh . . . I always thought it was desirable to locate the enemy before attempting to surround them," I said, almost at random.

The guy at the head of the table stared and then laughed loudly. After a moment, everybody else did so too.

"Ah! You've been reading Sun Tzu, haven't you? *The Art of War?*"

That last phrase, at least, I recognized.

"I . . . have studied the art of war, yes, sir," I said.

"See?" he lectured the others. "I *told* everybody you need to read that book. It's a classic. See, even the *tech writers* can quote it! By God, it's time we brought some fresh blood into this place! If anybody here could read anything but memos . . ."

I tuned him out as the screen cleared to a normal . . . well, more or less normal . . . chat mode.

FF2dazaul: ok salla you satisfied with yr results?

RivaK: This is Riva, not Salla, and I am NOT happy, Furo! You've been sneaking around behind my back getting Salla in trouble again, haven't you?

FF2dazaul: hey it was her idea

RivaK: Any more following Salla's ideas without checking with me and I'll get Dennis to turn you into a sand-lizard. He can do it, you know. He's a professional. They know more

> mathemagics on Paper-Pushers than you've
> ever . . .
> FF2dazaul: ok,ok,ok, keep cool. How was I to
> know the Sacred Carving she picked out to
> test was the dragon's tooth?
> RivaK: You know Salla, don't you? Now you're
> going to fix it. And fast!

I instructed him to invoke some 4-d equantations
that would get me over to Colton Middle School a little
bit faster than fast – like about half an hour ago, before
the cops showed up and this whole mess got on the
Internet. And on the way, I wanted a stop at home,
to change into my *real* working outfit. I couldn't do
any good in a gray hobble-skirt and bound feet.

> FF2dazaul: that's heavy magic you know. Gonna
> cost.
> RivaK: Wrong. Your payment is I *don't* have
> Dennis turn you into a sand-lizard, and maybe
> in five or six years I forgive you.
> FF2dazaul: Works for me.

Wizards are arrogant, tough, mean-minded bastards,
but they're no match for an infuriated mother. Especially one with a paid-up membership in the Bronze
Bra Guild and a husband who just happens to be a
mathemagical genius.

"Sorry to leave you, guys," I said as I stood up,
"but there's an emergency over at my kid's school. I
gotta run."

I had instructed Furo Fykrou to activate the transfer from the women's room around the corner from
the conference chamber. Didn't want to make these
people nervous by having them see me vanish into
thin air.

Stephanie was just leaving the women's room as
I got there. She smiled weakly and said something

about coffee and long meetings; I nodded and pushed through the door without really listening. Oh, hell, there was some girl playing with her eye makeup in front of the mirror. And no way to tell FF to delay the . . .

I think she screamed as I was leaving, but I'm not sure. I hope they don't insist on her taking a drug test or anything.

I'd asked for just enough time at the house to make a quick change from suit and pantyhose into something I could really work in. With my arms and legs free and mail protecting vital parts, with my sword Sasulau hanging in her scabbard by my side, I found I could already think better. While I was changing, some other things had occurred to me that might come in handy. I grabbed my cell phone, a roll of aluminum foil, the last two clean white sheets in the laundry hamper, and a can of shoe polish. No time for more—the air was quivering around me already in preparation for the second transfer. I bundled everything into a pillowcase just before my stomach turned inside out and upside down.

I *hate* time-transfers.

There was no time to throw up as the dingy brown halls of Colton Middle School came into focus around me, though. I tossed the pillowcase full of gear behind me with my left hand while my right drew Sasulau. She came out singing blood and death; I came up crouching, weight balanced, ready to spin, turn, thrust wherever was necessary—

—and found my path to the enemy blocked by kids and teachers. Encirclement strategy, my left boob! I couldn't even get *at* the tall, mean-looking, half-naked men who were jabbering in the doorway to a classroom. There were teachers diving for cover, wannabe gangsta students trying to act tough, and some idiot drowning out all our words with panicky calls for help on the loudspeaker.

"Move it," I suggested to the kid in front of me, the one who was turning pale green under his dreads and threads while his buddies urged him on.

He didn't seem to hear me, so I repeated the suggestion with a gentle hint from Sasulau. Didn't even tear his jeans, but he gasped, did a leap like a hooked fish, and subsided gently onto the floor. I stepped over him and encouraged a couple of other people to move aside. At least these kids didn't faint— good, the floor wouldn't be *too* littered when I got to where I really needed to move.

The warriors were bunched up in the doorway. Bad planning; only one of them was free to move against me. That one gave me a nasty grin and lowered a javelin about three times the length of Sasulau, waggling the pointed head suggestively between my stomach and groin.

While he was enjoying himself and waiting for me to shriek and faint, I went under the javelin and planted Sasulau in his thigh. She slid in nice and clean between the overlapping metal scales of his half-armor, protested with a high whine when I drew her out before she could go all the way through. I didn't want to kill the guy, just get his attention.

I had to break two of their javelins, flip a bow-man over my shoulder and slightly wound a couple of swordsmen before they figured out that they were no longer dealing with Paper-Pushovers, but it was no big deal; the idiots kept trying to defend the doorway one at a time. No training in palace fighting, clearly.

"Throw down your weapons and get over in that corner!" I snapped as soon as they began looking appropriately worried. I wasn't sure the Sacred Carvings had given them modern-day language comprehension, but my gestures made it clear enough.

Most of the Social Studies class had gone under their desks, fortunately, so they weren't in the way.

I didn't see Gene Kruzak anywhere, but Salla popped out from cover behind the computer table as soon as she heard my voice.

"Okay, what are they, and how can I talk to them?" I demanded. I hoped I would get some points with her for not rushing across the room and hugging her like a little kid. I wanted to. I wanted to drag her out of there and to hell with the rest of the school. But she'd stirred up some adult-sized trouble here; she had better help me clean it up like an adult. *Later* I'd hold on to her for, oh, seven or eight hours, or days, or whatever it took to get my heart rate down to normal.

"I—I think they're Nubian mercenaries," Salla stammered. "Or maybe Libyan. Later than Sixth Dynasty, because the costumes and weapons indicate—"

She was starting to get into Lecture Mom mode already; I cut her off with a chopping motion of Sasulau. "Never mind the ancient history; what do they *speak*? I need to make a deal with these guys."

Fortunately, it turned out that the Sacred Carvings magic worked just like modern mathemagical transfer equantations, implanting an ability to use and understand the dominant language of the culture you were landed in. Less fortunately, it seemed that the magic had picked up the dominant language as being that of Colton Middle School: teen-speak. I had to get Salla and the kid with dreadlocks to translate for me. Fortunately the deal I had to offer wasn't complicated: passage to a nice, big, rich planet with a climate very much like their home, with plenty of work for good mercenaries.

"Not," I added, "that you people seem all that skilled to me, but I expect you'll shape up pretty fast." Those that lived. These guys had probably been tough once upon a time, but it appeared—luckily for me— that Salla had called up some kind of elite palace

guard detail that hadn't had to do any real fighting
for some years. We don't waste a lot of time on
ceremonial processions or palace guard detail on
Dazau. They'd probably enjoy the chance to get some
real work for a change, once they adjusted.

All I had to do then was activate Call Trans-
Forwarding on my cell phone and alert Furo Fykrou
to pick up his new employees.

"But what am I going to *do* with a mercenary
army?" he whined. "I'm a wizard of peace, not a
duke."

"Rent them out to Zolkir," I suggested. "Take a
percentage of the rental and give them the rest as
salary."

"Umm." He sounded happier already. "Four parts
for me, one for them. Or do you think that's too
generous? Maybe five for me . . ."

While he was happy, I persuaded him to activate
the transfer, and just in time too; there were sirens
wailing in the distance.

I heaved a sigh of relief as the dark, scarred men
quivered, became columns of darkness, disappeared.
I didn't have a clue how to reverse Sacred Carvings
magic so as to send them home again, and neither
did anybody on Dazau—Sacred Carvings had been
a lost art for so long – but I was pretty sure they'd
be happy serving Duke Zolkir. And Furo Fykrou
probably wouldn't cheat them any worse than their
previous employers had.

There was just a little cleanup work to be done,
quickly, before the cops arrived. I tore up the sheets,
tossed one strip to Jason and Salla and had them mop
up the blood on the floor, while I collected the
wannabe eighth-grade gangstas and used the rest of
the sheets, the aluminum foil, and the boot polish
on them. Since their leader was still pale and shaky
from his faint, and I hadn't had time to clean the
blood off Sasulau yet, they were cooperative. Quite.

The hardest part was persuading Gene Kruzak to come out from under his desk at the front of the classroom. But when he finally emerged, he blinked at the line of eighth-grade boys in torn-sheet loincloths and aluminum-foil armor, with their hair matted into shape with shoe polish, and agreed that yes, Salla had come up with a striking demonstration of Seventh Dynasty mercenary soldiers, and yes, it was a pity that some people who didn't understand how he liked to dramatize history for the kids had misunderstood and panicked, and no, of course he hadn't been worried for a moment.

I gather that this story did *not* amuse the cops when they finally got there, expecting full-scale gang warfare in the halls. I wouldn't know firsthand; Salla had insisted that I hide in the bathroom before anybody else saw me, pointing out that a six-foot warrior woman in bronze chain mail would probably make the police seriously nervous. "I could say I dressed up to help out with your project?" I suggested.

"*Please*, Mom," Salla said. Her lower lip was quivering. "I can deal with it from here. And if anybody else sees you, I'll just *die!*"

That should have warned me, but it didn't. I paced up and down in the eighth-grade girls' bathroom and listened while Salla and Gene Kruzak convinced everybody that the whole kerfuffle had been a false alarm. The police were relatively easy to convince; they were happy not to have to deal with a gang war, and even happier not to have any bodies to take away, so they didn't give the principal too much of a hard time about stupid hysterical phone calls to 911.

Everybody, in fact, was happy . . . . Except Salla, as I discovered when she came in to release me. "Honestly, mo-ther!" she started on me before the swinging door had closed. "How could you *embarrass* me like that?"

"Huh?"

"*Look* at you!" She was close to tears. "Coming to school in that ridiculous outfit. It's indecent. Your *boobs* are showing through the chain mail. And all my *friends* saw you!"

"You'd rather all your friends got chopped up by Nubian mercenaries?" I asked in what I thought was a neutral tone.

"Oh, don't patronize me," Salla wailed, "you just don't *understand*! Haven't you got any decent clothes with you? In the car?"

Car.

I hadn't thought about how we were going to get home.

"Uh, actually, I guess I'll have to ride the bus with you," I told her.

"In *that* outfit? You can't! I'll walk home! I'm never going to be able to show my face in this school again, and it's ALL YOUR FAULT . . . ."

Let's skip the rest of the scene, okay? Anybody who's raised a teenage daughter knows how it went, and the rest of you, believe me, will be happier not knowing the gory details. Suffice it to say that I waited in the bathroom, semi-decently concealed in a stall, until Dennis dismissed his own classes and was free to drive us both home.

Where I discovered, on checking my email, that Salla wasn't the only one who was less than thrilled with my recent actions.

Oh, Furo Fykrou was happy enough. He'd already been able to rent my little gift out to Count Bukklivannizi for a border war, in return for so many zolkys that he'd actually, in a moment of unwizardly generosity, credited my account with ten percent of the rental as a sort of finder's fee.

But Stephanie was another matter. Her email reiterated, several times over, that she was disappointed in me. Very, very disappointed. After all her efforts to help me reenter the career track, how could I blow it all by acting so unprofessionally as to take off from work just for some little problem my kid was having at school? Needless to say, Xycorp was not going to hire me now. They had concluded I wouldn't be a good fit with the corporate culture.

I wrote back that I thought Xycorp was quite right, and in any case I wouldn't be looking for work in the near future, because I'd had an idea for another story.

Troll By Jury

Esther M. Friesner

"I don't know why she's going through with this if
she doesn't want to," Garth Justi's-son said as he and
his two companions picked their way along the bank
of the Iron River that misty morning. "If you don't
want to do something, don't do it, that's what I always
say. Life is simple."

"For the simple-minded, maybe." Garth's wife, Zoli
of the Brazen Shield, was all grouches and grizzles.
The erstwhile member of the Swordsisters' Union was
in one of her none-too-affable moods.

"You sound even less enthusiastic to be attending
this event than Ethelberthina," Garth observed. *"She's*
got to be there because it's her Maiden Morn—a girl
turns thirteen just once, if she's lucky—but *you* didn't
have to come."

"Ethelberthina asked us to be there," Zoli shot
back. "D'you think I'd do this for anyone else? Poor
kid, she needs us. Otherwise she'll be surrounded by

relatives. *Her* relatives." Even the hardened ex-swordswoman shuddered at the thought.

"You know, I wonder why she *is* doing this." Garth rubbed his chin thoughtfully. "It's plain she'd rather die. When I was a lad, a girl *had* to celebrate her Maiden Morn or there'd be talk, but times have changed; folk here in Overford think it's old-fashioned. Skip it nowadays and no one blinks an eye, let alone gossips about it, and you know how we Overfordians love to gossip. Do you think someone's forcing her?"

"Who's got that sort of power?"

"If she were an ordinary girl, I'd say everyone and the miller's donkey," Garth replied. "But seeing as it's her—"

"Indeed." Dean Porfirio, head of the Overford Academy and the third member of the wandering party, gave a fond smile. "I've always said that Ethelberthina Eyebright is a most exceptional child."

"A twelve-year-old who counts a couple of retired sellswords and a wizard as her best friends? Yes, I'd call that exceptional, all right." Zoli adjusted the set of her armored bodice and spat into the reeds.

"The *richest* twelve-year-old in Overford and half the dukedom 'round," the wizard added.

"Maybe she's doing it because someone promised her a nice Maiden Morn present," Garth conjectured.

Zoli stopped, spun around, and hollered in his face: "Would you *listen* to yourself? She can buy her *own* presents! There's no reason she has to endure this stupid Midden Morn nonsense if—"

"*Maiden* Morn," Dean Porfirio corrected her, steepling his fingertips and nodding in that sage manner that so many wizards affected. Even while matching Garth and Zoli stride for stride, he still managed to convey the impression that he was back in his office, sunk deep in a comfortable armchair, delivering an instructive speech to wayward students.

"A singular, local custom whose origins are lost in the mists of antiquity."

"Like us," Zoli grumbled. It was that legendarily darkest of all hours, the one that came just before the dawn, and nature had decided to add to the travellers' problems by casting a thick blanket of fog across their path. "We never should've agreed to call for you this morning. A wizard ought to be able to get himself out of bed and off to his appointments. I know the path from our house to the Iron River blindfolded, but from Overford Academy it's another story." She scowled at Dean Porfirio. "The only way we're going to find the river now is if we fall into it."

"We can't be late," Garth said. He sounded worried. "We've got to find the toll bridge, or at least the ford. The ritual's going to be held on the *town* side, and if we're not there soon, we won't be able to see a thing!"

"What's there to see?" Zoli wanted to know.

"Ah, I can answer that!" Dean Porfirio said. "First, the girl herself wades into the river and as soon as she sees the sunrise touch the water, she recites the Prayer for a Prosperous Husband. Then—"

"Prayer for a *what*?" Even through the fog it was possible to tell that Zoli was looking at the wizard as if he'd broken out in a rash of parsnips.

"Prosperous Husband. That's the whole point of having a Maiden Morn, letting a girl send out the word that she's officially on the marriage market. Then, as soon as she finishes reciting the poem—"

Zoli stopped spang dead in the middle of the path and slapped her forehead. "So *that's* it!" she exclaimed. "*That's* why Ethelberthina's gone crabbier than an ogre with the itch: It's that stupid poem!"

"Doesn't want a prosperous husband?" Dean Porfirio inquired mildly.

"Doesn't *need* a prosperous husband, nor any other

kind," Zoli said. "What a question! You know the girl as well as I—more to the point, you know her father. From the moment she was born, Mayor Eyebright was her first, best, and only example of a prosperous husband."

Dean Porfirio's brow darkened. "That bloated sack of lizard droppings had me assaulted and left for dead in an alley, once. And Ethelberthina still talks about how he kept trying to get his hands on her trust fund. Hmph! No wonder the child doesn't want to advertise for a husband, even if it is no more than an empty ritual: She must think they're all like her father."

"Even me?" Garth asked in a surprisingly small voice for one who had single-handedly destroyed his share of dark legions, demon hordes, and effete high priests in his salad days.

"Of course not you." Zoli patted her husband's cheek. "It's not that Ethelberthina *never* wants a husband, it's just that she thinks it's stupid to make folks think that's *all* she wants."

"Unlike her sisters," Garth remarked. Everyone nodded. Ethelberthina's elder sisters, Mauve and Demystria, were famous in Overford song and story as being two of the most husband-hungry maidens ever to flutter a fan, drop a hankie, or bat a set of eyelashes at anything midway male. Recently Demystria had succeeded in her quest, using all her wiles and three bottles of Old Dragonbreath Reserve to extract a promise of marriage from a blacksmith's apprentice. Her whoop of joy shattered forty-eight neighborhood windows and her mother's best mirror.

"Ethelberthina's sisters would look quite natural in a pasture, chewing cud," said Zoli. "They take after their mother: No brains, but a baby-maker that works overtime. What's she up to? Seven kids?"

"Eight, and a ninth in progress." Dean Porfirio

made a few mystical gestures and created a white-hot ball of light that immediately vaporized the surrounding fog for the radius of a good spear-cast. "Ah, *there* we are." He smiled up at the overhanging bulk of the toll bridge.

Zoli uttered a meaty curse. "Oh, wonderful. We've blundered right *under* the hideous thing. Now we'll have to climb back up the bank to cross on it."

"Don't bother; we're too late already," said Garth, pointing. The remaining mist had decided to move on before Dean Porfirio sizzled it into oblivion; the view across the Iron River was clear. From their vantage point on the Academy side, Ethelberthina's three friends saw the crowd of guests massed on the farther shore. Ethelberthina herself was already knee-deep, a crown of rosebuds perched at a tipsy angle on her head, her brand-new birthday dress kilted up between her legs but the long sky-blue cloak on her shoulders trailing heavily in the water. A plump, usually chipper child, she currently wore an expression popularized by dispirited captives everywhere. Behind her there hovered a large, obviously pregnant woman whose radiant smile more than made up for Ethelberthina's dejection.

"Stand up straight, dear!" the lady chirped. "You'll get your gown wet otherwise."

"Ah, Goodwife Eyebright," Dean Porfirio murmured. "But I don't see her husband anywhere."

"You wouldn't; this isn't about him," Garth said. "When he's not the center of attention, he stays away."

"Now are you certain you know all the words of the Prayer, darling?" Goodwife Eyebright went on.

"Yes, Mother." Ethelberthina sounded weary.

"You're sure? You wouldn't want to humiliate me in front of all our relatives. I don't mind working and slaving to give birth to you, and to make you a lovely home, and to cook and sew and clean up after you with not one word of gratitude. A mother doesn't expect gratitude. But if you wouldn't mind too much, my precious, could you possibly avoid embarrassing me?"

"*Yes*, Mother."

"Don't you use that tone of voice to me, young lady! I *gave* you a choice: I said you didn't *have* to do this. I told you that it didn't matter to me if my life became a living hell because all the neighbors would talk about how your sisters had their Maiden Morns but *you* didn't. A mother doesn't mind a little living hell. *You* agreed to this, *I* never forced you, *you* were the one who—" She began to weep without once slacking the pace of her ongoing rant until Ethelberthina loudly reassured her mother that yes, she would recite the Prayer letter-perfect and no, she did not deserve such a devoted parent, wicked and ungrateful child that she was. Goodwife Eyebright's tears dried up faster than a used-ox merchant's guarantees.

Garth looked at Zoli. "Well, that explains that."

"I'll say," said Zoli. "Poor child never had a chance. Who ever thought of motherhood as a deadly weapon?" It was a concept of startling novelty to a woman whose best defense had always been killing the other person first. "We should be over there, standing by her in her hour of need, giving her a little moral support. And we would be, too, if a certain wizard I could mention wasn't such a baby." She gave Dean Porfirio a significant look.

"You could always swim across," the wizard responded coldly.

"Dressed like *this*?" Zoli clanged a fist against her iron breastplate.

"It's not every woman who can bear four children and still fit into her wedding-day garb, eh, Dean?" Garth preened as if the credit were all his.

"Impressive," said a rough and rumbly voice that did not belong to Dean Porfirio. It came from just

under the bridge and was followed by the sound of
stone grating against stone as a squat, blocky shape
came half-walking, half-rolling into view.

"Ah, good morning, Bursar Tailings," said Dean
Porfirio.

"Morning is never good to my kind," the troll
replied. "Not unless it's cloudy with a chance of
showers. Sunlight tends to turn our skin to stone and
work its way inward from there."

"It's nearly sunrise," Garth said. "What are you
doing out-of-doors at this hour?"

"Ethnic weakness," the bursar of Overford Academy replied in a voice that might be called gravelly
and mean it. Like most trolls, he was short and not
much bigger than a nail keg, with huge feet, a jut-
ting jaw, and tusks. Unlike the normal run of his
kinfolk, his flint-colored hair was neither shaggy nor
unkempt, but carefully groomed and slicked back into
a short braid. His complexion was granite gray, with
a light stippling of acne or chisel marks. "Every so
often, we trolls just *have* to spend a stretch of time
under a bridge. If a billygoat or two goes tripping-
trapping over it, so much the better. It's instinct, like
the salmon swimming upstream to spawn, or the
swallows returning to Swallow Combackington, or
mothers trying to force their children into marriage."
He nodded meaningly in the direction of
Ethelberthina's massed relatives. "Charming old custom, a Maiden Morn. Especially if you've got no other
hope of bringing your daughter to heel. Well, I'll just
be on my way now and—"

Dean Porfirio drew his wand and tapped the bursar
lightly on one shoulder. Magic was the only way to
stop a determined troll in his tracks; otherwise a man
might as well try to impede the progress of a runaway boulder. "Just a moment, old man," the wizard
said. "I'm confused, and I don't like it. What's this
about a forced marriage?"

"Holy schist, do you mean you're the only person in town who *doesn't* know?" The troll was genuinely shocked.

"He's one of three," Garth said.

"Then free my feet and we can go back to the Academy for a nice hot cup of tar and I'll tell you all about it."

Zoli squatted and gave the troll her finest this-will-hurt-much-more-if-you-move look. "Save time; tell us now."

"I *have* no time! You know what'll happen if I'm caught out after sunrise."

Dean Porfirio clicked his tongue. "You won't turn to stone—not all at once—and nothing at all will happen to you if I lend you my cloak. Don't fuss over trifles."

"That's all *you* know about it," the bursar said. "When I was a young troll, my friends and I used to play Dare Daylight, seeing who could stand the sun longest. Look at my skin, why don't you!" He held out one overlong arm for inspection. It resembled the surface of a badly baked clay pot, all flakes and cracks. "My internal petrification's just *this* short of fatal. I'm living on quarried time. One more major dose of sunlight will do me in."

"That wasn't very smart of you."

"Show me the young creature, troll or human, who doesn't think he's immortal, that the rules don't apply to *him*," the bursar countered.

"Looks like you'd best talk fast, then," Zoli suggested.

The troll scowled at her so hard that rock dust trickled down his nose. "Very well, I'll make it short and sweet. Unlike *some* retired swordsisters I could mention. This very morn marks the day of Goodwife Eyebright's revenge."

"Took her long enough. Good for her! How'd she kill him?"

"Not *him*. It's not her husband she wants snaggled. Everyone in Overford with half a brain knows that Goodwife Eyebright's greatest grudge stands against her youngest daughter."

"Half a brain . . . that sums up most of this town," Zoli mused.

Garth jabbed her to silence with his elbow. "Why would any sane mother resent her own child?" he asked. "And such a bright one, too!"

"I'll paint you a picture," said the troll. "All that Ethelberthina's ma could ever do with her life was marry and breed. Many a woman's happy keeping house, but only when it was her choice to go that road, not her last resort. Like you, ma'am." He rolled his eyes at Zoli.

"I see," the former swordsister said. "Goodwife Eyebright *had* to marry so she wants her daughters to do the same. The thought of Ethelberthina having opportunities *she* never had riles her."

"Quite so." The troll nodded. "That's where this Maiden Morn claptrap comes in. You see, there's one bit of the ceremony not too many folk know of: The Answered Prayer."

"What's that?"

"It's rather charming, really." A faint smile touched the troll's wide mouth. "If there's a man among the witnesses who's eager to marry the girl, all he needs do to lay claim to her is wait until the *very instant* she utters the last word of the Prayer for a Prosperous Husband, then dash up and winkle himself under her arm or her cloak or her skirt or something and declare his devotion. He's got to time it just right, because if he misses the last word by three heartbeats, he's out of luck. But if he's nimble and determined . . . poof! Instant betrothal."

"Impossible. Such nonsense can't be binding."

"Oh, it is, but only because Duke Janifer's never

taken the time to remove the Maiden Morn regulations from the law scrolls. It's such an old-fashioned custom, I doubt he even knows they're still— Uh-oh. What's that?" The bursar's eyes grew great with sudden fear.

What *that* was, was the sound of Ethelberthina beginning to recite the Prayer for a Prosperous Husband. Garth gasped. "Sunrise! Quick, Porfirio, toss your cloak over the bursar!"

"Yes, at once, I—" The wizard reached for the clasp of his cloak. A sickly green came over his face as he realized he hadn't bothered to put one on. Neither had Garth or Zoli.

"For the love of mica, set me free! I'll run back under the bridge!" the troll bellowed.

"Of course, of course!" Dean Porfirio hastened to draw his wand once more. Unfortunately, in his agitated state the wizard went all butterfingers. He jerked the wand from his belt, promptly lost hold of it, and watched in horror as it flew off to sink beneath the current of the Iron River.

"Here, Zoli, we can shift him under the bridge," Garth said. "You take his head, I'll take his feet, and—"

"Look there!" Zoli wasn't listening. Her eyes were wide, her face pale, her hand shaking as she gestured across the river to where Ethelberthina stood performing the most hangdog recitation imaginable of the Prayer for a Prosperous Husband. The girl's apathy was beyond the power of mortal man to measure. Horse thieves had gone to the gallows with more eagerness, hemorrhoid sufferers had greeted a recurrence of their affliction with more zest. If youthful exuberance had a direct opposite, Ethelberthina Eyebright was its personification.

In other words, she was putting so much effort into behaving churlishly, just to show her mother what was what, that she failed to notice the scrawny, oily-pelted young man who was slinking down to the water's edge, a look of intense concentration on his sallow face. Only once did he pause and cast a questioning look over one shoulder. A brawny, stern-faced woman in the crowd jerked her chin at him brusquely, silently urging him on.

"That's Ludlow Pennywhistle," Garth observed.

"Oh no, it couldn't be." Dean Porfirio shook his head rapidly. "Not even the most vengeance-crazed creature alive would willingly bind her child to a malicious good-for-nothing like Ludlow. He's a beast, a coward, and a scoundrel. I had him in my Introductory Invocation class. We had to expel him for demoralizing the demons. He must be in his twenties by now, and I hear he does nothing with his days but loaf about the taverns until they boot him out for toughing up the barmaids."

"Maybe Goodwife Eyebright doesn't realize what she's doing to her daughter," Garth offered.

Bursar Tailings had another opinion: "Maybe she does. She's a Pennywhistle by birth, you know; Ludlow's ma is her second cousin. This way she gets to shackle Ethelberthina with a husband, break her spirit, and keep the girl's money in the family at the same time."

"But that— that's not to be stood for!" Zoli sputtered. "It's atrocious! It's cruel! It's— it's— it's got to be stopped!" Her hand dropped to her belt and found only belt. "Damn it, Garth, why didn't you remind me to wear my dagger?" she shouted.

"And risk having you throw it at someone? Darling, I know you too well: In situations like these you tend to over—"

Across the water, Ethelberthina let the last word of the Prayer for a Prosperous Husband fall from her tongue as though it were a slime-smeared toad. The instant he heard it, Ludlow's lips twisted into a gloating look as he leaped from the riverbank. The girl turned in time to see him but too late to do anything about it, for her cloak was so sodden it weighted her to the spot. Instantly she knew whose hand was behind her plight. She raised her fists to the heavens and wailed in helpless rage, "*Motherrr!*"

Zoli threw the troll.

"—react," said Garth.

Duke Janifer slowly paced the width of the great hall for the twenty-third time. Before him stood a row of plaintiffs, defendants, and witnesses in one of the biggest lawsuit pileups he had ever been called upon to judge. It was all that his men-at-arms could do to hold back the throng that had come to gawk at and gabble over the proceedings. Most of Overford and half of the Academy was there. They filled the hall, overflowed into the passageway beyond, and all but dangled from the rafters.

"Now let me see if I've got this straight," he said. "*You're* charging *her* with assault with a deadly weapon?" He pointed first at Ludlow, then at Zoli. Ludlow nodded and tugged his forelock deferentially. His fingers came away dripping sheep fat.

"And *you* are charging her with reckless endangerment of your person?" This was directed at Bursar Tailings.

"*Potentially fatal* reckless endangerment," the troll corrected. "That's worse."

"I should say so. Now *you* are charging her with creating a disturbance?" He gave Goodwife Eyebright an inquiring look.

"It was the best I could do, Your Gracious Eminence." Ethelberthina's mother made cow eyes at the duke. "That's what my dear husband told me to do. He said it's the closest we could come to finding a legal term to describe the way that hussy broke up our Ethelberthina's lovely Maiden Morn. I'm just a weak, ignorant woman with very little knowledge of things that don't concern me. I always say we ought to leave law and such confusing stuff to the men who've got the brains for it. Like yourself, Your Unspeakable Wiseness."

"Of course you are." Duke Janifer was not really listening. He continued to pace the hall. Unlike his forefathers, he never sat upon the intricately carved and gilded Siege of Justice when hearing a case. Some said it was because he was a true friend of the people and disliked setting himself too far above his subjects. Others, including his old nurse Wylalie, said it was because he was a fidget, born with that condition commonly referred to as "shrews in your trews."

The duke paused in his peregrinations, coming to a halt before Ethelberthina. The girl stood between Ludlow and Bursar Tailings, with a look on her face even stonier than the troll's calcified countenance. "You're a little young to be in court, my dear," Duke Janifer said kindly. "I take it you're a witness in your mother's case?"

"The Netherrealm I am!" Ethelberthina snapped. Her mother clapped a hand to her bounteous bosom and gasped loudly. "I'm here as a complainant. I wish to file suit against Goodwife Eyebright for Conspiracy to Coerce Matrimony, which you'll find in the Scrolls of Sardor, Volume 23, Section 5, Column B, Paragraph 16, first tried before Duke Merriam the Bizarre in the case of Vila Grubneck vs. Rittana, the Landlord's Beautiful Daughter. Oh, and I also want a divorce."

Duke Janifer stared at the girl, an unreadable expression on his face. "Er, yes," he said. It was something many grownups found themselves replying to Ethelberthina because they simply *could* not think of anything else to say.

"Actually, I believe the correct term is an *unfasting*, since Bursar Tailings and I have only entered into a state of betrothal rather than an actual marriage. I suppose we could ignore it, but I don't want some silly little legality messing up my life at a future time when I might actually *want* to wed."

"Er, yes," said the duke again. "And Bursar Tailings would be—?"

"Me, Your Grace," said the troll.

The duke peered at the bursar of Overford Academy as if hoping to thus convert him into something other than a troll. "How old are you, my good fellow?" he finally asked.

"Two hundred eighty-seven come next Sandpit Day," the troll replied.

"And the girl is—?"

"Thirteen!" Ethelberthina stamped her foot. "As if you had to ask! I just had my Maiden Morn, remember? Which is how this whole muddle got started, and it's all her fault." She thrust a finger at her mother. "Oh. And hers." She pointed again, but no one was at the other end of her finger.

Garth clicked his tongue. "Zoli, my dear," he called into the vast spaces of the duke's great hall. "Come back, please. We can't settle most of these cases without you."

"Keep your codpiece on, I'm coming." Zoli's voice arose from where she had wandered off to enjoy a long, satisfying, mother-daughter visit with her Lily, the lass who had outshone so many of her male counterparts while at Overford Academy and risen to the enviable post of Duke Janifer's senior resident alchemist. The two ladies were snugged up in a cozy niche below one of the lancet windows, chatting and sharing the contents of a brimming fruit bowl.

By this time the duke was entirely flustered. "How can one woman be responsible for so much chaos?"

"I say she practices," said Dean Porfirio. Like Garth, he was in the duke's court solely in the capacity of witness. "But her husband here assures me it's purely a natural talent."

Something whizzed through the air and hit the wizard at the back of the head, knocking his conical cap off. "My Garth never said any such thing about me," Zoli announced, hefting a second peach. "He knows better." She sauntered back to the ranks of her accusers while Dean Porfirio recovered his hat and plucked bits of fruit out of his hair.

"*Did* you disrupt this girl's Maiden Morn?" Janifer quizzed her.

"Yes," Zoli admitted freely. "You'd've done the same, in the circumstances." She explained the details of Goodwife Eyebright's plot against Ethelberthina.

The good duke was appalled, but compelled to press on with his examination: "Then you admit to assaulting Ludlow Pennywhistle with the flung body of Bursar Tailings?"

"Sometimes I don't know my own strength." Zoli giggled. "Sometimes I do."

"And did you thereby recklessly endanger the life of this troll?"

"I wouldn't say *that*. I recked plenty. I knew Ethelberthina wouldn't let him come to harm. She knows what sunlight does to trolls, so she swept her cloak over him the instant he hit the water. None of us *had* cloaks who *claimed* we did." She gave the wizard a nasty look.

"Yes, but when she threw her cloak over him, that betrothed them, according to the laws governing Maiden Morns."

"What do you want, law or justice? If I *hadn't* tossed the troll, then by the same laws, she'd be hogtied to *that* piece of work instead." She nodded at Ludlow. "The troll's a better deal."

"But it's not *legal* for trolls and humans to marry!" the duke exclaimed.

"Well, they're not married; they're only betrothed." Zoli shrugged. "You're the duke; *un*betroth them."

"I don't have that authority."

"But you *do* have the authority to bother me with all of these silly lawsuits, don't you?" Zoli challenged. "Is *this* what we pay our taxes for? Especially Ethelberthina."

The duke's moustache began to twitch in an unsettling manner. "You . . . pay . . . taxes, child?" he asked the girl.

"Ever since the Swordsisters' Union bought up most of my stock of Mama Ethina's Elixir of Equality," she replied. "It turns dragon-scale armor so brittle that it shatters on contact with a feather."

"*Nothing* can do that to dragon-scale armor!" the duke objected. "That's why the king's men all wear it."

"Nothing *could*," Lily said, stepping forward, her alchemist's robes rustling softly over the stones. "But now something *can*; something Ethelberthina invented, and *that's* why she's independently wealthy." She patted the girl on one shoulder and added, "It's not turning lead into gold, but close. Fellow alchemist, I salute you."

"Fellow alchemist, do you have anything that might shatter my stupid betrothal?" Ethelberthina asked.

Lily smiled. She was a beautiful young woman, with her mother's dark coloring and her father's home-loving nature. When she first entered Duke Janifer's service, many court gossips hissed that he had not hired her for her brains. The whispers stopped when Lily demonstrated that she had also inherited her mother's elementary yet effective way of dealing with rumormongers.

"As a matter of fact," she said, "I do. And it will settle all of these silly lawsuits besides."

"*Will* it?" Duke Janifer gazed at Lily in awe. "Huzzah! Tell us what it is, I beg you!"

"Nothing fancy; just trial by combat. Oh! To the

death. It must be to the death. You can't get anything *really* settled unless someone dies."

The hall fell silent, including the spectators.

The sound of Zoli's sword rasping from its sheath
broke the quiet. "Suits me," she said amiably.

"It would." Bursar Tailings huffed like an over-
weight dragon. "Me fight a retired swordsister?
Might as well ram a chisel through my throat and
save time."

"Do we *have* to?" Ludlow whined.

"Not if you drop the charges," Lily said. "No
charges, no case; no case, no need for any sort of
trial."

"Good enough for me," said the troll. "Consider
'em dropped."

"Me, too," Ludlow said eagerly.

"After what she did to us?" Goodwife Eyebright
snapped. Her hand, grown strong and swift in the
ministering of domestic justice to her helpless brood,
shot out and grabbed him by the ear. "If it weren't
for her and her prodigal troll-flinging, we'd both have
what we wanted by now."

"I don't care." Ludlow squealed and squirmed.
"What good's a dowry if I'm dead? You want your kid
married off so bad, *you* fight the tin-plated bitch!"

"All right," said Goodwife Eyebright. "I will."

"Did I miss anything?" Garth Justi's-son asked Dean
Porfirio as he sidled along the row of benches ringing the duke's arena. Normally the sand-covered
enclosure was reserved for riding exhibitions, but
today it had been hastily judged the best site for the
upcoming trial-at-arms.

"Not a thing." The wizard reached into a paper
cone filled with salted nuts and munched primly. It
was amazing how fast word of the combat had spread,
fetching still more people to the ducal palace grounds.
With the crowds came hucksters of every stripe. They

seemed to swarm out of the ground, like maggots in meat, which coincidentally was what some of them were selling.

"Sorry I took so long," Garth muttered, sitting down. "I had to teach Ludlow some manners. He *might* be walking normally by next Market Day, if he finds an ice pack. No whelp calls my Zoli a bitch and gets away with it."

The wizard stuck the paper poke under Garth's nose. "Nuts?"

"Fair enough, she *is* that. But only a little, and I think our Lily caught it from her. Trial by combat to the death, no less! What *was* going through that girl's head?"

"Probably the notion that she could save you a lot of legal woes. She believed they'd *all* drop their cases because no one would be fool enough to fight Zoli." The wizard ate some more nuts. "Never underestimate fools."

In the center of the sand-strewn ring, Duke Janifer stood between the two combatants and nervously asked, "Ladies, are you certain you wouldn't like to reconsider?"

"*I* would," Zoli said. "It's not combat, it's bloody murder. I've eaten seafood that had more hope of killing me than *this* idiot." She gestured scornfully at Goodwife Eyebright. "Plus, she looks ready to drop her calf any second now. One needless death on my hands is bad enough, but two?"

"*Will* you withdraw?" Duke Janifer turned to Goodwife Eyebright, entreating her with his eyes. "Pleeease?"

Ethelberthina's mother stood herself up a bit taller and held the sword she'd been given as though it were a carpet beater. "I'd sooner die."

"I was afraid you'd say that." The duke sighed, shrugged, and tossed a bright orange kerchief high into the air. As he dashed from the arena he called back over one shoulder, "When it hits the ground, start fighting!"

The audience gasped and held its breath. Zoli went into her preferred fighting stance, grim and silent, eyes fixed on the floating kerchief. Goodwife Eyebright, on the other hand, began jabbering the instant the bit of cloth left the duke's hand.

"My gracious, aren't you in a hurry? I'm sure it's not going to take you long to kill me, but don't you worry about that. Nor about the poor, innocent, unborn babe I'm carrying that never did anyone a bit of harm. Nor about all my poor little lambkins that'll be left orphaned and helpless, oh no, don't you give any of them a second thought! Mayor Eyebright will probably remarry quick enough, and then they'll have a stepmother, and who knows what she'll be like? But don't you fret over it, you've done your duty, you don't have to bother your head about whether they'll be decently clothed and fed and who'll tuck them into their cold, lonesome little beds of a winter's night with not even the comfort of a loving mother's kiss on their tiny, tear-stained faces, no. Don't you concern yourself over their bitter tears or their heartbreaking sobs or their—"

"Gnut save us, what's the wretch doing?" Garth exclaimed.

"What she does best." Dean Porfirio sounded glum. "What she did to force Ethelberthina to undergo a Maiden Morn. And it's working again. Just look at Zoli now."

It was true: Under Goodwife Eyebright's verbal barrage, Zoli's sword drooped by degrees, leaving a hole in her defensive posture fit to drive an oxcart through. Her shoulders trembled and, as Goodwife Eyebright expanded upon the tragic fate awaiting her soon-to-be-motherless babies, she sniffled. Just as the orange cloth touched the ground, she burst into tears, dropped her blade completely and pounced on the kerchief in order to wipe her streaming nose and eyes.

Goodwife Eyebright had been a homemaker long enough to recognize something ripe for the plucking. While Zoli howled her heart out, the mayor's wife swung her own sword back, ready to strike. It was not an elegant attack, but with Zoli thus disabled, elegance was unnecessary. The blade swept straight for the former swordsister's head.

A second blade shot out and blocked Goodwife Eyebright's swing with a clang. Panting hard, holding the hilt of Zoli's discarded weapon with both hands, Ethelberthina glowered at her mother.

"Drop the charges," she ordered. "*And* the sword."

"Young lady, you go to your room," her mother said. "This is no place for a child."

"Says you." Ethelberthina lifted her chin impudently. "I've had my Maiden Morn rite: I'm not a child any more."

"Then this is no place for *you*," Goodwife Eyebright countered. "This case concerns only me and that Zoli person." She nodded at the crumpled swordswoman who was still blubbering on the sand, occasionally wailing something about the poor, comfortless little orphans.

"And my case concerns you and *me*. Or have you forgotten? I've simply decided to move it ahead on the duke's docket."

Goodwife Eyebright laughed in a condescending manner. "You can't be serious, darling. *You* fight *me* to the death? You'd kill your own mother? Not that you haven't tried to do that ever since the day you were born. But *I* don't mind. A good mother doesn't care if her child—who has been given *every advantage* at *great personal sacrifice*—turns out to be a little viper. I love you anyway."

"Oh, I wasn't planning on killing you." The girl dropped her sword, and grabbed hold of her mother's forearm. With a few quick twists and turns, Ethelberthina had herself under the startled woman's defenses with the edge of the blade pressed to her own small throat. Glancing up, she grinned and said, "Whenever you're ready, Mother."

Goodwife Eyebright tried to wriggle her sword away from her daughter's neck, but in vain. "Ethelberthina, what are you doing and stop it!"

"Not until you do. Drop the charges against Zoli or I swear I'll make you cut my throat. Know what that means?"

"It means you are a very inconsiderate child," the goodwife replied stiffly.

"It also means that you will have to go into strict mourning for two years. That's the minimum acceptable period for the loss of a grown daughter. *Strict* mourning," she repeated. "*No* celebrations of any kind."

"No . . . what?"

"No celebrations," Ethelberthina said. "Oh, like, just for an instance say . . . weddings?" Her smile was a caution to the ungodly.

A cry more bestial than human shot skyward from the crowd. Demystria and Mauve Eyebright burst into the arena, their hair streaming wildly, their faces contorted into masks of mindless terror. Only the thought of what a collision might do to the sword at Ethelberthina's throat stopped them from throwing themselves at their mother's knees. Instead they pitched facefirst to the sand, pounding it with fists and feet while they yowled with grief.

"Do what she says, Mummy!" they begged in unison. "Drop the sword! Drop the charges! Let her go!"

"Girls, girls," the goodwife chided. "If your sister wants me to cut her throat, that's her choice, isn't it? Besides, it's just come to me that if she dies—not that I'm encouraging that sort of thing, mind you—then all of her money goes to her closest living relative. I do believe that should be me. Then Mummy will be able to give you the biggest, splashiest, most expensive weddings that Overford has ever seen."

"And how am I supposed to get married with no groom?" Mauve demanded. "There's no courting allowed during strict mourning! By the time I'm free of it, I'll be *ooold!*"

"That can't be helped; you should have planned ahead, like your sister. *She* knew what to do to get a man!" Goodwife Eyebright beamed at Demystria. "Well, at least *you* shall have the finest wedding ever, and you'll have two whole years to plan—"

"I can't wait two years to get married." Demystria sat back on her haunches and gave her mother a hard, eloquent look. "I want—I *need* to get married. *Now.*"

There were times when Goodwife Eyebright could be as quick on the uptake as Ethelberthina. Her eyes locked with Demystria's, her face lost some color, but she never flinched. All she said was: "Oh."

The sword fell from her fingers to the sand.

"Thank you, Mummy dear." Ethelberthina made a perfect curtsey that was a thumbed nose in thin disguise.

It was a lovely wedding, the talk of Overford. The Eyebrights hired the entire Crusty Boar tavern to host the festivities. Garth Justi's-son helped break up six knife fights, and that was just counting the ones that broke out before the happy couple cut the bridal cake. He had to: Five of them involved Zoli.

Dean Porfirio finally called upon his magic to compel the retired swordswoman to take a Time Out. One moment she was arguing hotly with Mayor Eyebright, the next she was °poofed° into a locked storage room. Her curses shook plaster from the walls and dust from the thatch.

"Calm yourself, m'lady; we're in for the duration," came a familiar voice in the dark. Bursar Tailings passed her a tankard of ale drawn from one of the many barrels around them.

"Why're *you* locked up?" Zoli asked, sipping the brew.

"I'm here at my own request, to avoid accidental exposure to sunlight. Nothing spoils a good wedding like an unintended fatality, I told them."

Zoli lifted one eyebrow. "This wedding *began* at *sundown.*"

"I know." The troll chuckled. "Most of the ale's in here and so am I, with no Eyebrights to say me nay. Not the sharpest bunch of pickaxes in the mineshaft, are they?"

"Except for your betrothed," Zoli teased.

"Oh, that's all off." The troll waved his hand cavalierly. "As a troll I can't wed a human, and it seems that since I was designated a deadly weapon in Ludlow Pennywhistle's suit, I can't be betrothed to a human either. It's against the law."

"*What* law? Since when has anyone bothered to *enact* a law against marrying weapons? Who'd even think of *doing* something like that?"

A ball of parchment sailed out of the dark recesses of the storeroom and hit Zoli in mid-breastplate. The retired swordsister uncrumpled it, read it, and blushed.

"An *imperial* law, for your consideration, which is still on the books of this and all other lands once ruled by the Talligar Empire," said Ethelberthina, emerging from the shadows, a cup of sparkling quince juice in her hands. "Rushed into effect more than forty years ago by a certain warrior queen whose only daughter announced she'd sooner marry her sword than any man."

Zoli's blushes deepened. "I was young and idealistic! I didn't know any better! I hadn't met Garth yet! You have no idea how bossy my mother could be! And it was only *thirty* years ago; closer to twenty." Noting the badly concealed smirks of her listeners, she nimbly switched the subject. "What are you doing in here, Ethelberthina? Your sister's wedding is out *there*."

"It's rude to answer your own questions," the girl responded pleasantly. Lifting her cup, she proposed a toast: "To other people's weddings! I'm not losing a sister, I'm gaining closet space." She drained her drink to the dregs.

"You know," the troll murmured, "she really *is* an exceptional child."

"Since she's had her Maiden Morn, she's an exceptional *adult*," Zoli corrected him. "And as such, she'd best be thinking about her future."

"Don't *you* start in on me about marriage," Ethelberthina spoke up.

"Me? Never. But you will be wanting something to do with your life. You can't sell any more of Mama Ethina's Elixir—your stock's as good as all gone—so what *will* you do?"

Ethelberthina tapped her lips with a fingertip thoughtfully. "Well, I'm not exactly the physical type to enter the Swordsisters' Union, much as I'd like to, and I don't fancy further dabblings in alchemy—too stinky. What I *would* like is power: Great honking heaps of unmitigated power, the ability to make people fear me, to cringe before me, and most especially to never, *ever* think they can bully me and get away with it. Not even Mummy. So I suppose what I'd truly *like* to be is—"

"—a wizard?" Zoli suggested.

"—a bursar?" The troll tried to be helpful.

"—a priestess?"

"—a queen?"

"—a lawyer," said the girl.

And the shrieks which burst from the storeroom of the Crusty Boar caused Goodwife Eyebright to go into labor, so that Ethelberthina did not lose a sister that day after all.

Looking for
Rhonda Honda

William Sanders

The minute she clanked into the office I knew she
was trouble.

Okay, she didn't clank, not really; body armor hasn't
clanked since before I was born. But people like her
always seem as if they *ought* to clank, or at least jingle
a little. Maybe it's the attitude they all seem to wear
with it.

She said, "You're Johnny Noir?"

I sat back in the creaking old swivel chair and
looked at her. That wasn't hard work at all. She had
pale skin and nice small features, maybe a little on
the sharp side. Short-cropped reddish-brown hair
showed beneath her squared-off black beret. She was
a little on the short side, but what there was of her,
under that snug-tailored black one-piece suit, looked
pretty good. Of course it was hard to tell, with so

much of her upper body concealed by that damned bulky vest.

Which was silly, since nobody really needs to wear that kind of heavy protective gear any more—you can buy a vest off the rack, now, capable of stopping anything short of an antitank projectile, and light and thin enough that your own tailor couldn't spot it— but then that wouldn't send the message: *My job is so important, people try to kill me to stop me from doing it.*

I couldn't guess her age. Who can, nowadays? She looked somewhere in her middle twenties, but for all I knew she was old enough to be my grandmother. For all I knew she could *be* my grandmother; the old dear had been talking lately about getting a new morph job.

I said, "Yes, I'm Johnny Noir. And you're not, are you?"

She ignored that. So much for dry humor; it wasn't my best subject at detective school. She was looking around the office with an expression that might have indicated either scorn or routine professional paranoia. I couldn't really tell with those wraparound mirror shades hiding her eyes.

She finished her inspection and looked at me again. "My name is immaterial," she said in a dry flat voice. "You can call me Margo."

She didn't offer her hand. I had a feeling that wasn't all she wasn't going to offer. I said, "Well, Ms. Immaterial—uh, Margo—what can I do for you?"

"We need you to find somebody," she said.

"We?" I looked past her but I didn't see anybody else.

Her mouth pulled tight at the corners. "I . . . represent the interested persons," she said reluctantly. "Please don't ask questions. You'll be told everything you need to know."

She took a quick step forward and leaned across

my desk. For a second I thought she was warming
to the Noir charm after all, but she was merely
reaching for the battered old phone. She picked it
up, jabbed quickly at the buttons, and handed it to
me. I held it up to my ear just as a familiar voice
said, "Noir?"

"Chief." I caught myself sitting up a little straighter.

"Listen closely, Noir." The Chief's voice was high
and hoarse, with an edge like a cheap steak knife.
About the same as usual, in other words. "Somebody
is going to tell you what she wants you to do. Do
it."

I said carefully, "I see."

"The hell you do. You got no idea at *all*—Christ,
I don't know how far up this comes from. The person in your office right now? She's not really there.
Anything she says to you, you never heard. Whatever
you wind up doing for the people she works for, it
never happened. Am I getting through, Noir?"

I said, "Is this an order?"

There was a moment of silence, broken only by
the Chief's wheezy breath. "Of course not, stupid,"
he said finally. "How can I order you to do something that's never going to happen, for people who
don't exist? Especially when I'm not even talking to
you right now."

He hung up. "Yes, *sir*," I said to the dead phone.

Margo was undoing the front of her bulletproof
vest. Hope sprang to life again, but she was just
getting something out of an inside pocket. "Here,"
she said.

She reached across my desk again, this time holding a disk which she popped into the ancient computer with a gesture that sneered. She tapped a few
keys, her fingers moving faster than I could follow,
and the page I'd been working on disappeared, to be
replaced by a head-and-shoulders portrait of a blond-
haired woman.

"This," Margo said, "is the person we want you to find."

The face that looked back at me was pretty, maybe even beautiful if you liked that tanned-SoCal-goddess look. There was a time when I would have said she was in her late teens or early twenties. Now, I wouldn't even bother trying to guess.

"She have a name?" I queried.

"Immaterial," Margo said immediately.

"Related, are you?"

Margo grimaced. "I know, but I'm serious. Her birth name really *is* immaterial, because she's not using it now."

She reached out and touched the keys again, and the picture changed to a full-length shot of what appeared to be the same woman, standing next to a purple-and-black motorcycle. She was dressed in elaborate protective gear: full snug-fitting leathers, high-topped racing boots, lace-on plastic knee and elbow guards, even a shiny perforated breastplate, all of it neatly color coordinated to match the bike. Other figures, similarly dressed, stood around in the background, or sat on other bikes.

Jesus, I thought. A roadgrrl.

"According to our information," Margo went on, "she is now known as Rhonda Honda."

Marvelous. Now it was beginning to add up. You get these cases all the time: somebody's darling daughter runs off to join a roadgrrl gang, and the distressed family wants her back. Or now and then it's somebody's darling wife; that happens too.

Damn unusual, though, for somebody like me to catch a case like this. Not if the people concerned could afford anything better . . . I said, "You know, you'd do better to take this to one of the big private agencies, like Herod Foxxe or Gabriel Mallet—they've got the staff and the facilities, I'm just a—"

"No." She was shaking her head. "We've already

tried that. It's been six months now since she disappeared, and it took a private agency most of that time to find out the little we know now. You're familiar with the Peter Pick Agency?"

I nodded, repressing a couple of adjectives and a noun that came to mind. Margo said, "Their man was able to determine that she'd joined up with these bikers—"

"Roadgrrls."

"Roadgirls?" She did a kind of double take. "I'm not—"

"Roadgrrls." I pronounced it carefully for her, trying not to grin. She probably didn't know it, but she'd given her age away with that one word. Nice clean morph job, but this babe had to be at least as old as me.

"Bikers," I told her, "are a lot of overage punks who hang around cheap bars and pool halls—or nursing homes, now—and trade lies about how tough they were in the old days. Roadkids are a whole different breed."

"Yes." She nodded vigorously. "You know about these things, Noir. You worked undercover among the outlaw clubs for almost a year, when you were with the state police. Still got your own bike, don't you?" Christ, somebody knew *way* too much about me. "You can get close to these people, talk their language. That's why we picked you."

She gestured at the photo on the screen. "That was taken by the Peter Pick op just before he lost her. Supposed to be a good man, but he let her slip away. Somewhere near Salinas, as I recall. His report's on that disk."

I studied the picture. "Just what did you have in mind, if I do find her? If you want strongarm stuff, go back to Peter Pick."

"No, no." She scaled a white card across the desk at me. It bore a hand-printed phone number. "Just call that number when you find her. Any time, day or night. We'll take it from there."

As I stowed the card in my wallet she said, "Noir— this really is important. More important than you can imagine."

"I'll give it my best."

"Of course you will." This time she actually smiled. "After all, you're a Public Investigator."

At home, that evening, I put dinner in the microwave and fired up my computer—an old Micromac, still better than what I had at work—and checked my messages. The only new one was from my ex-wife, asking why the current alimony payment was late, and threatening various actions, including coming down and unscrewing my head, if it got any later.

I groaned and hit the reply button. *Dear Blanche,* I typed, knowing that would piss her off. Or "him," I'm supposed to say, but screw it, gendermorph be damned, I'll start going along with that the day she/ he quits grabbing half my pay.... *As you undoubtedly know,* I wrote, *the city is broke right now. I haven't been paid for a month. You'll get yours if and when I get mine.*

I sent it off and turned off the mail, not wanting to read the reply. For God's sake, I wouldn't mind so much, but Blanche, or rather Mad Marvin, makes more from a single pro wrestling match than I make in a month.

The microwave dinged. I got my dinner out and brought it back to the little desk, balancing the hot box on my lap and eating it while reading the online news. Not that I really gave a damn, but it was a distraction from the tasteless soysteak.

Not much of the news was new. The President was still undergoing treatment for undisclosed medical problems; the First Lady had issued another statement promising he'd be back on the job any day. I wondered why anybody gave a damn. After all, the Presidency had been an almost wholly ceremonial office for over a decade. But the public took a keen interest in the First Family and their problems; like the old British royal family, they had prestige—and money, and therefore power—all out of proportion to their legal status.

Here at home, the mayor and the city council continued to argue over whose idea it had been to invest the entire municipal treasury in Indian government bonds, two weeks before the Pakistanis nuked New Delhi into an ashtray. An Alaskan nationalist militia, a militant Kwakiutl splinter faction, and an animal-rights group had all claimed credit for last week's sinking of a Japanese fishing vessel with no survivors. The Dow-Jones showed Blood-Crip stock up and Mafia down.

Dinner finished, I poured myself a shot of bourbon for dessert, dug out Margo's disk, and pulled up the Pick op's report.

It was a very neat, professional report. Unfortunately it didn't really contain much information. The subject had definitely been identified as the person now known as Rhonda Honda. She was now riding with, and probably a member of, a motorcycle gang known as the Devil Dolls. That was all, though the Pick guy tried to pad it out to make it sound more substantial.

I punched up the full-length photo again and sat back and looked at it, remembering Margo saying "bikers." She'd better not make that mistake around any real bikers, or roadkids either, or she might find herself needing that bulletproof for real. That's one thing the two groups do have in common, besides motorcycles and attitude: they hate each other, enough to get severely physical with outsiders who confuse them.

Actually the difference is mainly one of styles and

generations. Your classic biker is a traditionalist: raggedy-assed denim, heavy boots, wind-in-the-armpits vests covered with faded patches, with the rawhide-faced old mamas favoring fringed leather bras and lots of body piercings.

Roadgrrls, on the other hand, go in for the armored look: bright-colored high-tech protective gear, the kind of thing you might see on a dirt-bike racer or a hockey player. Their male counterparts prefer snug-fitting racing leathers and everybody wears spaceman-looking full-face helmets.

Even more important, while any real biker would walk before he'd ride any bike but a Harley—preferably one made before the Xiang-BMW takeover—no roadkid would be caught dead on anything that slow and old-fashioned. Their tastes run to hot Japanese and European sportbikes, preferably customized beyond recognition. This one appeared to have herself a new Honda Kamikaze.

The bourbon glass was empty. I poured myself another one. "Here's looking for you, kid," I said to the picture on the screen.

Mike Donne said, "You know, Noir, I wonder about you sometimes."

We were sitting in his office at the Gabriel Mallet Agency. It was a lot bigger than mine; it was nearly as big as my apartment. He had on a light gray suit that had to have cost as much as I made in a month. I didn't care about the office, but I did envy him that suit. The last good suit I had, a nice Italian silk job, got ruined a year or so back by some paint-spraying animal-rights activists protesting the exploitation of silkworms.

I wouldn't have minded a morph job like his, either. He looked younger than he had when we were on the force together, a decade and a half ago. Any morph work I could afford would probably leave me looking worse than ever. Go to some cut-rate clinic, get some alcoholic doctor who switches my dick with my nose, no thanks.

Donne said, "When are you going to give it up, Noir? You're too good a detective to spend the rest of your life in a cheesy little office and a crappy old apartment."

I said, "I'm a public cop, Mike. It's what I do."

He made a disgusted face. "It's what nobody does anymore, and you damn well know it. I'm not even talking about anything new—as long as we both been alive, anybody who really wanted something guarded went to a private security outfit, or if they wanted somebody caught they hired a bounty hunter. Hell, they had private contractors running jails, clear back last century. We're just seeing the logical development of trends."

He snorted. "Haven't you been paying attention to what's going on? The city's broke, the state's in receivership, and the United States is a geographical expression. The President is a figurehead and lately he doesn't even bother showing up to make speeches and wave at parades. Face it, Noir, the public sector has had it. Why should cops be exempt?"

Donne shook his head. "It's the twenty-twenties, Noir. It's the day of the corporation. Forget the old days," he added angrily. "I was there too, remember? But it's *over.*"

He sounded really pissed off. Probably I made him uncomfortable. Most of the corporate ops despise public detectives, regarding us as low-rent losers or worse; Donne was one of the few who'd even talk to me.

"All the same," he went on, "you're right, this business with the missing babe smells funny. I'll check into it. Kid down in the basement owes me a couple of favors, he can hack into anything."

"Thanks," I said, getting up.

"No sweat. Call me this evening at home, I'll let you know if I've turned up anything. Be careful," he said as I started for the door. "These people sound like bad news."

"There's some other kind?" I said. "Like you say, this is the twenties."

"Devil Dolls," Crazy Norm said, "yeah, sure, new club. They split off from Hell's Belles last year."

He glanced furtively over his shoulder as he spoke. It was midafternoon and the bar was half empty, nobody close enough to overhear us, but Crazy Norm had to have his little drama.

"I've done business with them," he added. Crazy Norm was one of the biggest hot-bike-parts dealers on the Coast. "Don't really know much about them, though. Why?"

I pulled out the photo of Rhonda Honda, which I had printed out last night. "Sorry," he said after a glance. "Never seen her with the Dolls or anywhere else."

Up at the bar one of the customers groaned. The television set at the end of the bar was showing a talking-head of the First Lady. "Our next guest," she was saying, "is the well-known—"

"Loudmouthed bitch," another customer said. "Hey, Ray, shut her off."

There was a chorus of agreement. The bartender reached over and the voice ceased. The picture, though, remained, and as the camera pulled back to a waist-up shot there were appreciative murmurs and whistles. The First Lady's talk show might be unpopular with this crowd, but her latest morph job had been spectacularly successful, and she was visibly not wearing a bra.

"What you oughta do," Crazy Norm said, "try Coyote Bay. Big rally and swap meet this weekend, all the clubs will be there. Better watch your ass if you do go," he added. "One wrong move around those roadgrrls, you could wind up getting a free gendermorph job, know what I'm saying?"

I thanked him for his concern and stood up to go. As I left, the guys at the bar were still trading remarks about the First Lady's new knockers.

I called Donne as soon as I got home. "Noir," he said, sounding relieved. "Glad you called. Listen, I—"

He paused. "Huh," he said after a moment. "Thought I heard something . . . anyway," he continued, "it was no sweat getting into Peter Pick's files. Turns out we've been hacking their confidential records, and all the other major agencies', for years. Been a very valuable resource."

"I can imagine."

"Yeah. But what you can't imagine is what I turned up today. Your little friend in the bulletproof? You'll never guess who she works for." His voice dropped. "Two words. Fur—"

Modern silencers are very efficient; with a good one, properly fitted, there is no sound at all. What can't be silenced, however, is the sound a bullet makes hitting human flesh and bone. It's not loud, but it's very distinctive. Even over a telephone.

Donne stopped speaking. Then he said again, in a very weak voice, *"Fur—"*

A clatter in my ear said he'd dropped the phone. There was a heavy thud, as of something heavy hitting the floor. Something about the size and weight of a medium-sized private detective.

The phone clicked off. A moment later I was standing there listening to a dial tone.

The sun was going down out over the Pacific when I pulled into the storage park where I kept the bike. I was keeping it in a rented lockup partly because things like motorcycles tend to walk away where I live, and partly to keep my ex from grabbing it for back alimony. I swung the metal door open and stepped inside. The big black Suzuki looked like a space ship in the dim light. Reddish sunlight winked off chrome.

Everything looked okay. It should; I'd spent enough money and sweat keeping it that way. The Suzuki GSX1300 Hayabusa was the fastest street bike made during the last century, and there weren't many left. It was easily the most valuable thing I owned.

I pushed it out onto the concrete drive and climbed aboard. I'd already changed into my old black racing leathers, back at the house. I stuck the key in the ignition and pulled full choke and thumbed the button. The starter whined and then the engine burst into full heavy-metal song. A little while later I was sitting at an Interstate Corporation tollbooth, counting out money under the supercilious single eye of the robot attendant.

I didn't try to get very far that night. All I wanted right now was to get clear of the city. Whoever had hit Mike Donne might or might not be looking for me, but I wasn't hanging around to find out. Or waiting till the body was found and the Mallet people cranked up their we-avenge-our-own machinery. They'd want to ask me some questions, and they wouldn't be nice about it, especially if they didn't like the answers. My badge wouldn't mean a thing, either; the giant conglomerate that owned the Mallet Agency could buy and sell the city, PD and all, out of petty cash.

And I didn't even have a gun. The Department's insurance company had made us stop carrying them.

Up beyond Obispo I got off the payslab and found a cheap motel. I didn't get much sleep. Mostly I lay there in the dark muttering, "Fur?"

❖   ❖   ❖

Coyote Bay might once have been an actual functioning town; now it was nothing but a collection of dilapidated buildings, most of them empty and boarded up, strung along the ruined old coastal highway, between rusting railroad tracks and a narrow strip of beach.

But by the time I pulled in off the toll road, around noon the next day, Coyote Bay had become quite a bustling place. Roadkids were everywhere, riding slowly up and down the sand-blown street, sitting on parked bikes, or just wandering about on foot. The air reverberated with the crackling blare of high-revving engines and non-stock exhausts.

Here and there, dubious-looking characters sat or stood next to folding tables or parked pickup trucks, displaying various odds and ends—motorcycle parts and accessories, weapons, drugs, even lingerie, most of it either illegal or, almost certainly, hot—for sale or trade.

I stopped the Suzuki in front of an abandoned motel and stood for a few minutes studying the crowd. It was a warm day, and lots of the guys had peeled off their leathers and were walking around in T-shirts and shorts. The roadgrrls, though, weren't about to lose their cherished look for anything so trivial as comfort; their bright-colored outfits definitely added something to the scene.

It was quite a gathering; I recognized clubs from all up and down the Coast: Vampires, Roadkill, Black Widows—you don't want to hear about *their* admission requirements—even a big contingent of Road Goths in their distinctive outfits, faces painted white and bits of tattered black lace trailing from beneath flat-black armor. A couple of shaven-headed young grrls strolled past, holding hands and leading a Dalmatian puppy on a leash; the spiky lettering on their breastplates read VENICE BYKEDYKES.

Finding the Devil Dolls was simple enough. From

the minute I put the sidestand down, the old Suzuki began collecting a fascinated little crowd; as I'd hoped, riding in on a classic bike was enough to get me at least temporary acceptance, even though a blind man could have spotted me for an outsider. I sat there and answered technical questions for a few minutes, while jocks and grrls gathered around and goggled; then I asked my question.

"The Dolls?" A husky roadjock in skin-tight pink leathers stepped from the crowd, everybody moving hurriedly out of his way; the Oscar Wilde Motor Corps are easily the most dangerous gang in the state and their members get the kind of total respect the old Angels used to. "Sure, they're here. Camping down at the south end of the beach. What do you want with *them?*" His plucked eyebrows went up about an inch. "No accounting for *tastes,* I suppose...."

"Camping" was an overstatement; the Dolls, like most of the other groups present, had merely picked themselves an area and occupied it. A couple of plastic tarps had been set up as sunshades, and a few sleeping bags and blanket rolls lay scattered about on the sand. Roughly in the middle of the area were the blackened remains of a big driftwood fire. That was just about it.

I stopped the Suzuki at the edge of the weed-cracked concrete parking lot that bordered on the beach. Down here, the sand had piled up into a line of low dunes dotted with scrubby bushes.

A few yards away, a line of shiny parked sportbikes gleamed in the sun. I gave them a brief scan, but there were at least a dozen or so that might have been the one in the photo; evidently purple and black were the Devil Dolls' club colors.

Out on the beach and among the dunes, roadgrrls wandered about, drinking beer and passing joints and talking, or lay stretched out on blankets in the sun. Here, on their own staked-out turf, several of them had felt secure enough to shed their silly plastic protective gear in favor of cutoff shorts and T-shirts, or bikinis—with or without tops—or, in a couple of cases, nothing at all.

Believe it or not, though, that wasn't what got my attention.

Nearby, a grrl stood leaning against the half-demolished metal guardrail that separated the parking lot from the beach. Her back was to me and I couldn't see her face, but everything else set off recognition signals: long blond hair, purple-and-black armor—

Maybe this was going to be easier than I'd expected.

I shut off the engine and said, "Excuse me," and she turned to face me and so much for *that*. Nose too big, mouth too wide, eyebrows too heavy; not even close.

I said, "Sorry, my mistake. I was looking for Rhonda Honda."

"Nah, man." Flat drawn-out *a*'s, Boston girl a long way from home. "My name's Vonda. That's Rhonda Honda ovah yondah."

I started to ask her to say that again. Then I was afraid she would. Shaking my own head, feeling a desire to hit it sharply a couple of times, I looked where Vonda was pointing.

And sure enough, there she was, the grrl from the picture. I wondered why I hadn't spotted her before. She stood out like a racing greyhound in a pack of mutts, and not just because she was a good six inches taller than the rest. Easily half of the other roadgrrls on the beach had that same leggy-blonde look, but it was as if somebody had been practicing and then finally got it right.

She was walking along between a couple of other

Dolls, a redhead and another blonde, and swigging a can of beer. I watched her for a moment, trying to decide on my next move. Truthfully, I hadn't thought things out beyond this point.

As it turned out she was the one who saved me from overloading my brain any further. Suddenly she glanced my way and her face broke into a blinding smile. "Oh, hey," she cried, "check it out!" And came running across the sand toward me, shoulder guards clacking, while the others turned to stare.

It wasn't, of course, my smoldering good looks that had pushed her button; her eyes were fixed on the Suzuki. "Wow," she breathed as she stopped beside the front wheel, and hunkered down for a better look at the engine. "It's beautiful—"

The other Dolls were moving in now, bunching up in a semicircle behind her, looking at the bike and then, with considerably less admiration, at me. "Who's this asshole?" somebody asked, not bothering to lower her voice.

The one named Vonda said, "He was askin' about Rhonda."

It was a nasty moment. I could feel them all tensing, practically crouching to spring. Various sharp shiny implements began to appear, amid a clicking and clattering of flick blades and butterfly handles. My insides felt very loose. For all the superficial fun-in-the-sun look of the scene, this was a bad spot for anybody—particularly male—who didn't belong. These were no Girl Scouts; they weren't into sitting around the campfire singing old songs and roasting wienies—but one wrong step and they'd be roasting mine.

I said to Rhonda, "Can we go somewhere and talk?"

A big, seriously mean-looking brunette said, "No way, man. What the fuck you think—"

Rhonda was getting up. "It's all right, Donna." She

tilted her head toward the nearby road. "Want to go for a ride? I'd like to see what that thing will do."

A few minutes later we were roaring off down the old coastal highway, Rhonda in the lead. Right away it was clear she knew what she was doing. She laid the purple-and-black bike over till her knees almost scraped the crumbling concrete, and she blasted out of the turns like a rocket. Keeping up with her took all my concentration; the road had become a very narrow place and the horizon kept tilting at unreasonable angles.

Not that we were going flat-out by any means; like every other public road in the state, this one was too gnarled and potholed for real balls-to-the-wall riding. But we were going damn fast, all the same, engines shrieking like buggered banshees; and then as she led the way into a long blind turn I picked up a change in the note of her exhaust, and her shoulders hunched as if bracing for something. Without pausing to think about it I downshifted fast and rolled off the throttle and clamped down hard on the brakes.

Rhonda's Honda was already sliding to a smoking, fishtailing stop. The Suzuki's greater weight took me on past her and for a sickening moment I thought it was all over, but then the brakes took hold and the big bike stopped dead.

Just beyond the front tire, the pavement ended in a jagged break, clear across the roadway. Thirty or forty feet away, the other half of the earthquake-shattered bridge hung over a deep rocky gorge. I could have spat over the handlebars into the gap.

Rhonda Honda pulled off her helmet and grinned at me. She tossed her head, making that long blonde hair flare and bounce for a moment. "All *right*," she said.

I stared at her, momentarily speechless. Had she just tried to kill me? Or was this merely her idea of a good laugh? Her face gave nothing away; her smile was innocent as an upper-middle-class baby's.

She said, "So why were you looking for me?"

I returned her grin, trying to look much cooler than I felt. "There was a guy asking around about you," I told her. "Down in the city, a couple weeks ago."

"And you thought you'd get a reward for finding me?" The smile went away very fast.

"Nah." I shrugged. "He didn't say anything about a reward. But he had this picture and, well, you looked cute, okay? I just wanted to meet you."

It sounded phony as hell to me, and I only tried it because I couldn't think of anything else. But after a second her face cleared and she said, "Why, that's sweet. I'm flattered."

She laughed. "Only I'm afraid you had a long ride for nothing. See, I've got . . . a girlfriend, you know? Donna. You kind of met her, back there."

"Oh." I managed to look disappointed. "Sorry."

"That's all right." She started her engine. "Come on. I'll ride back with you."

I spent the rest of the day skulking about Coyote Bay, trying to figure out what to do now. I still had the number Margo had given me, but I wasn't ready to call in yet. Not until I had some answers, and right now I wasn't even sure what the questions were.

As the setting sun began to turn the ocean red, I wandered over to where a couple of locals had set up an outdoor grill and were serving greasy soyburgers at extortionate prices. I bought one, handing a fifty across the counter and getting a dirty look and a handful of small bills back. I walked away, munching on the burger and counting my change. I wouldn't have been surprised to find I'd been shorted, but it was all there.

I fanned the bills out, idly, and looked at them, thinking how little they bought compared to when I

was younger. Now, I wondered why they even bothered printing anything smaller than fives. Even the
new Richard Nixon three-dollar notes were barely
worth carrying. Dead Presidents, it seemed, weren't
what they used to be. Just like live ones—

I stopped, feeling the world miss a shift.

"No," I said out loud.

"You see," I told Rhonda Honda, "this old friend
of mine died yesterday."

We were down at the end of the beach, in between
a couple of dunes. It was dark now. Behind me, on
the other side of the dune, I could hear occasional
shouts and laughter: the Devil Dolls, settling in for
the evening's partying.

They hadn't been happy to see me again; the one
called Donna had made some very detailed threats,
in fact, before Rhonda got her pacified. I hoped she
stayed that way. Things were intense enough as it was.

Rhonda turned to face me. She'd shed most of her
roadgrrl outfit now, all but her shoulder and shin
guards, with shorts and a bikini top. Her flawless skin
shone silver in the starlight.

"Yeah. He died trying to tell me something. *Fur*,"
I said, turning the helmet in my hands. "That was
what I heard. Didn't make any sense. A shipment of
hot furs? Animal-rights terrorists? What?"

I wished now I hadn't waited till dark. I'd have
liked a better look at her facial expression.

"But he wasn't saying *fur*, was he? I didn't get it
till just a little while ago . . . *First Family*," I said,
"that's what he was trying to say, wasn't it? That's who's
looking for Rhonda Honda, and doing everything
necessary—including killing people—to make sure the
whole thing stays secret."

She took a step backward. Even in the deep
shadow between the dunes I could see the whites of
her eyes.

"So I ask myself, what's the story? Runaway First Family offspring? We haven't seen the President's daughter in the news lately, have we? But then we haven't had a White House sex scandal in a long time, either. Another young intern who couldn't resist the Presidential charm? Maybe even carrying a little addition of her own to the Family—"

From the darkness Margo's voice said, "You ask too many questions, Noir. I warned you about that."

She came walking around the dune, stepping carefully in the loose sand. In that black outfit she was almost invisible, but the starlight was enough to pick up the flash of her teeth. And the gun in her hand.

"Margo." Rhonda Honda's voice carried tones of an old familiarity. "I should have known he was one of yours."

"Mine?" Margo laughed shortly. "Just temporary help, that's all." She looked at me. "Bad help, too. You were supposed to call in when you found her. Not take her for starlight walks and pour out your pathetic heart."

She gave a contemptuous snort. "Of course we weren't stupid enough to depend on your following orders. Your Chief warned us you weren't a team player." Her left hand came up, holding a small shiny object between thumb and fingertips. "So I put this little tracker on your bike. That's not much of a lock on that storage shed, Noir."

Rhonda Honda said, "I'm not going with you. You can't make me."

"Sure you are." Margo's voice was almost warm. "And sure I can. Don't be silly."

She tossed the beeper aside and made a quick gesture. Half a dozen bulky, dark-suited forms materialized from the back of the dune.

"I've brought some help," Margo told Rhonda, "in case they're needed. But I hope you're not going to be difficult. It's over, you know that. And if you make a fuss," she added, "call for help or anything silly like that, you'll just cause a lot of your new friends to get hurt."

One of the men behind her said, "Want me to go get the car?"

Margo shook her head. "Too conspicuous, with all these damned motorbikes around. No, we'll all just go for a nice quiet little walk."

"Bring this guy along too?"

"Oh, yes." Margo gave me a bright smile. "Noir's a loose end. A *talkative* loose end. Can't have that."

"You can't do this," Rhonda Honda protested.

"Oh, stop snivelling," Margo said impatiently. "We can do anything we want, you of all people know that. Now then—"

That was when Donna came charging out of the dark, knees and elbows, plastic armor clattering, screaming like a whole ward full of madwomen. God knows how long she'd been there, or what she was doing there in the first place. Maybe she'd followed Rhonda and me out of jealous suspicion.

Margo half-turned, the pistol coming up in her hand. I threw the helmet at her, a clumsy under-handed pitch that missed by a foot but was still good enough to throw her aim off; the gun muzzle flashed—no sound—and then Donna hit her like a first-string offensive blocking back taking out a dangerous tackle. You could have heard the impact a block away.

The pistol flew from Margo's hand as she went down, and I fielded it in time to snap a shot at the nearest man in black, who was hauling out some sort of machine pistol. He went down and I threw a couple more slugs at his buddies, who were scattering out among the dunes. Something popped past my ear, though I didn't hear any bang. These people must have gotten a quantity deal on silencers.

By now there was plenty of racket coming from

behind me; the Devil Dolls had finally realized something was going on. There were high-pitched shouts and curses and a man's voice cried, "Oh, *shit*, look out—" On the ground at my feet, Margo and Donna were rolling over and over, grappling and punching. Neither of them seemed to be doing much damage; they were both too well armored for serious catfighting.

I emptied the pistol in the general direction of the bad guys, threw it away, and grabbed Rhonda Honda by the wrist. "Come on," I told her. "Time to get out of here."

We ran around the dune and almost collided with a trio of Devil Dolls going the other way; one had a length of chain, one carried what looked like a machete, and the third—who appeared to be entirely naked—was brandishing a big chunk of driftwood. They paid us no mind; they were in a hurry to get in on the fun.

The Suzuki still stood where I'd left it. I mounted up and hit the button, hearing Rhonda's Honda come alive behind me.

A mile or so east of Coyote Bay I pulled over and cut the engine. She eased to a stop beside me and we looked at each other. "Well," she said. "Thanks, whoever you are."

She glanced up the road, in the direction of the payslab. "Riding south?"

I nodded. She said, "Then I guess this is where we—"

I said, "I'm not playing the sap for you, Mr. President."

For a second she went absolutely rigid. Then she sort of sagged, all over. "God," she said in a totally different voice. "You knew?"

"I just figured it out. Too much heavy action for a simple First Family runaway or another Presidential bedroom scandal. Who'd go to all that trouble—let alone kill—to keep the lid on something that ordinary?"

I looked her up and down. "Nice morph job. Only six months?"

She shrugged. "I always was a quick healer."

"You've got to go back," I said. "Back to Washington, back to the job and the Family. I won't give you any speeches about how it's your duty. It's just the only way you'll be safe."

"I'm not letting them change me back," she said flatly. "No matter what."

"Who said you had to? I'm no student of history," I said, "but even I could list a lot of antics your predecessors got up to, every bit as outrageous as this, and the public loved it. And they'll love this."

I looked her over again. "Of course you're going to have to lose the ensemble, and the rest of the roadgrrl bit. I mean, there are limits. How'd you get into that, anyway?"

"I figured it was the last place anybody would look for me. And I rode bikes a lot when I was younger, only quit because they said it was bad for my image. . . . What about the First Lady?"

"What about her? She can discover she's always liked girls—that'll work, everybody likes lesbian celebrities. If she can't handle it you can dump her. She's not very popular, you know."

"That's true. The last poll showed she was hurting my ratings." Rhonda rubbed her face thoughtfully. "You really think I can get away with it?"

"Getting away with it," I said, "is the American way."

I never saw her again. At least not in person; like everybody else I watched her coming-out press conference, and I followed the news long enough to satisfy myself that I'd been right. The public ate it up; the Presidential ratings hit an all-time high. And when the First Lady revealed that she had always preferred to lead when she danced, her own popularity went up too.

Me? I went back to L.A., back to the job and the life. I thought I might catch some trouble, but nobody bothered me. Nobody even said anything to me about the whole business. After all, none of it had ever happened.

You can sweep anything under the rug if you've got a big enough broom.

A couple of weeks later my ex showed up and tried to kill me. But that's another story.

The Case of Prince Charming

Robin Wayne Bailey

Her fierce gaze lent the sun its blaze
　　As she rode out of the west
With a heart full of pride, and a sword by her side
　　And chain mail on her breast.

She didn't complain of the chafing pain;
　　She never let out a whimper;
She didn't flinch, nor give an inch,
　　But that gal was quick to temper!

Now since days of old her story's been told
　　In poesy, fiction, and song
By children dear both far and near—
　　Yet everyone got it wrong!

Name's Rose. Bad Rose in some villages. I move around a lot; that's best in my line of work. Get in, get out, solve the problem, do the job, move on. This wasn't always my life, but it beats swabbing floors in some dark forest shack for a bunch of leering dwarves, and with every monk and nun from here to Shrewsbury making names for themselves at this game, I figured I'd try it. I'm good at poking my nose in, asking questions.

I'd gone a while between hires. My purse was flatter than a wedding singer when I passed through the woodlands of Sardeenia. Without warning, six horsemen emerged from the trees, armed and armored identically. Red tabards with gold baldrics covered the steel plate under which they sweated and stank. On each baldric was emblazoned a small gray fish.

Bringing Asta, my piebald mount, to a halt, I put a hand to the hilt of my sword and straightened in the saddle. "Fashion statement?" I asked, sneering. A good sneer can hide a lot of uncertainty; I practice mine. "Or are you just really fond of each other?"

A seventh figure rode up beside the others. A little skunk of a man in black robes with white ruffles at collar and cuffs. A seal of office on a red ribbon hung around his squat neck. I guess it was supposed to impress someone.

He sniffed a pinch of snuff. "Your own armor—" he said with a sneer as practiced as my own, "—what there is of it. A fashion statement, too? That *barbarian princess* look is so stale."

"It's practical," I answered. "It's cool in this heat." I sat up straighter and adjusted the leather strap over my right sun-reddened shoulder. "And when I walk into a fight, my opponent ogles my chest for three or four seconds before he notices my sword. By that time, I'm wearing his testicles for earrings."

He had a voice like a barrel of oil and a manner twice as slick. "I see I've found the right woman." He made a bow from his saddle. "I am Lord Parfum, advisor to His Majesty Leonardo, who, hearing a rumor that you were traveling through Sardeenia, sent me to find you, Rose."

Leonardo. The Lion-King, himself. "He has a job for me? A thief to catch? A murder to solve? Some mystery beyond the talents of his constables?"

Parfum demurred. "He has dinner."

My stomach growled.

That was five days ago.

I fingered the purse on my belt, which jingled half full of fish-shaped gold sardeenmars. Leonardo had a job for me, all right, but I'd earned these coins the hard way. Two days and nights of feasting, and his hands had been busier under the table than the palace mice. My thighs were bruised and mottled from his insistant pawing.

His gold was good, though, and it wasn't as if I hadn't fended off such advances before. Especially from employers.

Asta shifted restlessly. I steadied him with a pat on the withers. From the edge of the woods, I observed the gates of an ancient castle. Its walls were burned blacker than a new bride's biscuits, yet they stood stout and formidable.

Quiet, too. The old stones kept their secrets. Nothing moved on the parapets, no sentries, no pennants stirring in the breeze, not even birds.

On the bank of the moat, charred ribcages stuck up like driftwood, a legbone here, a skull there. Scattered among those, a few rusted tools—rakes and hoes mostly—stark testimony to the evil of the queen who dwelled inside.

If she had a name, no one used it. Leonardo, whose sister-in-law she was, called her the "Evil Queen," or sometimes the "Old Witch," though his voice dropped when he spoke of her, and he tended to look over his shoulder a lot.

I brushed a hand through a shock of tangled black hair that had strayed over my shoulder. I wanted a bath, but I guided Asta in a slow circle around the castle, careful to keep out of sight beneath the surrounding trees.

I disliked kidnapping cases; I disliked magic even more. Sorcerers, wizards, witches—all river rats as far as I was concerned, best left to the night. But Leonardo had paid me well and promised more, enough for an office and a secretary if I ever chose to settle somewhere. I liked the idea of a secretary; some masculine piece of candy to lounge across my desk, who'd taunt me with his efficiencies on slow, hot days. Someone to take a little shorthand, or even a little longhand.

A low branch slapped me across the face. I dismissed my fantasies and brought my mind back to business.

The Old Witch—all right, Leonardo hadn't really said "witch"—had poisoned his brother Clarence and seized control of neighboring Anchovia, crushing all opposition with her black arts. "But I have a nephew," Leonardo had continued as he squeezed my thigh. "Clarence's son, the rightful sovereign of Anchovia. He hasn't been seen since Clarence's murder."

I'd lifted his hand from my leg and pressed it firmly into a bowl of mashed potatoes. Lord Parfum had sniggered, then quickly raised his napkin to hide his grin. An uncomfortable silence had filled the dining hall as Leonardo stiffly wiped his hand on the tablecloth's hem. When he leaned close again, I had the creepy feeling he had enjoyed that.

He'd resumed the conversation as if nothing had

happened, describing his nephew: nineteen, fair of face, blue eyes, hair black as his mother's heart. Leonardo had winked then. "And a manner that can charm the skin off a snake. He's known as Prince Charming."

From the far side of the table, Lord Parfum had murmured, "The prince takes after his uncle." He'd smiled slyly, showing perfect teeth like the boards in a white picket fence. "If you could bottle and sell whatever that boy's got, you'd make a fortune."

I could learn nothing more from the outside of the castle. I turned Asta and followed a narrow stream to the village a half mile away. It wasn't much of a village. It lay nestled in a valley among the wooded hills, nearly abandoned now. The cottages on the outskirts were aged and deteriorated. Shops and businesses were ill-kempt or empty. Mud and filth had long buried the paving stones of Main Street.

I remembered those charred bones outside the castle walls. Perhaps the populace had decided living next to a wicked witch wasn't such a great idea.

The inn looked a little better. A sign hung on rusty chains above its door, and a pale stick figure over faded black letters proclaimed the inn's name: THE THIN MAN. I draped Asta's reins over a post and tugged my saddlebags from behind the saddle.

An old woman, her face as rough and rutted as the street outside, glared at me over a bucket of water and a mop as I entered. She eyeballed my armor and sword, then resumed her work. "Ye looks like trouble," she grumbled. "I don't needs no trouble in my place."

"Trouble is my business," I answered. Moving carefully around the wet edge of her floor, I lay a gold sardeenmar on a counter. "I need a room, a bite to eat, and some wine if you have it. A bath, too."

She leaned on her mop and licked her lips as she looked at the small, gleaming fish. Her tongue painted a smile where a frown had been. "Well now, milady," she said with newfound cheerfulness, "yer business don't be any business o' mine. An' I gots a fine room with a sunset view freshly made up."

I held up a second coin. "Can someone stable my horse?"

She snatched the sardeenmar from my fingers and swept up the other in the same motion. "Done an' done," she answered. "We gots a stable out back, an' feed's no extra charge." She winked. An ornery glint sparkled in her eye. "I can even digs out a spare sweater for ye. Come evening ye might gets a bit chilly in that outfit."

It had been a long day. I was tired from the saddle and itchy with scratches from brush and tree limbs. My manners and my patience melted. "Most men think the less I wear the hotter I am. Not that you'd understand that."

She barked a laugh. "Now I know how ye makes so much money." She parked the mop in the bucket of water and beckoned as she led the way across the room and down a corridor. "All yer tartin' won't earn ye much here, milady. We don't gots but one real man in this town, an' he be locked up in the castle."

That caught my attention. "Prince Charming?"

She glowered over her shoulder, a look that on a younger woman I might have construed as jealousy. "Aye, every woman what's left in this dunghill town pines for that beautiful boy," she admitted, "an' all their husbands be sulkin'." She pushed open a door. "I'll fetch ye a bite to eat now. The bath'll be a basin bowl an' a pitcher o' water. I'd heat it up for ye, but seein' as how ye're so hot already . . ."

I sighed and offered another goldfish as I entered the room.

" . . . Seein' as how ye're so generous with yer riches," she corrected, "I'll heat it nice an' hot." She backed out with a mocking bow, closing the door, muttering as she went, "An' if'n ye scald yer pretty pink opportunities it's no fault o' mine!"

The room, as promised, was meticulously clean. A polished little oak chair stood by the door. Dropping my saddlebags, I sat and wearily began pulling off my boots. For a moment, the place reminded me of the domestic life I'd left behind. The floor gleamed in sunlight that came through the open-shuttered window. A dainty oak table and another chair occupied the center of the room. On the table, a vase of fresh flowers rested on a crocheted doily.

The bed made me gasp. It was piled with feather mattresses, pillows, and covered with elaborate piece-quilts.

I fumbled with my belt, let sword and purse fall to the floor, armor next. Forgetting all else, I stretched naked on that plushness. With no intention to sleep, I closed my eyes. For an instant, I heard singing saucers and dancing teacups—a strangely recurrent nightmare—then even that melted away.

"Let me die in such a bed!" I breathed.

"I can arrange that."

A gloved hand settled over my mouth. I opened my eyes. The bare edge of a dagger teased my breast. My uninvited visitor added, "But it would be such a waste."

I lay still, irritatingly aware of my sword belt out of reach on the floor and the open window through which my guest had come. His eyes gazed into mine as he slid the dagger over my belly.

"Bad Rose," he murmured. "You don't look so bad to me. Not bad at all."

A grin spread over his weather-beaten face. As faces went, it wasn't unpleasant; the smattering of dark whiskers and the broad mustache gave it character. A falconer, I assumed, for on the shoulder of his laced jerkin, a black bird was embroidered, and I recognized it—a Maltese falcon.

I made myself as provocatively comfortable as I could under his dagger point. Maybe I could lull him into carelessness. "Such a big blade," I purred, "must take a tight sheath."

A clatter sounded at the door; an ancient foot kicked it open. The falconer shot a look over his shoulder. With a folded towel on one arm and a pan of steaming water between her hands, the landlady entered. She stopped; a look spread over her face that might have heated the water another ten degrees.

The startled falconer leaped from the bed. Taking advantage of his inattention, I planted a foot on his conveniently turned, not to mention well-shaped, rump and shoved.

"Rape!" screamed the landlady. She threw the pan's scalding contents.

The falconer's scream rivaled hers for shrillness. He clutched his face, then his clothes as the water penetrated to his skin. He danced around in pain. The landlady had at him with the empty pan, beating him about the head and shoulders, while crouched at the foot of the bed, I watched in amusement until he batted her aside with an enraged gesture.

Half-blinded, he lurched toward the window, overturning a chair, stumbling against the table.

I dived for his legs, wrapping my arms around handsomely muscled calves. Even in the midst of combat such things should be appreciated; there had to be a reason to call it *close combat*. He fell with a crash. I snatched up his dagger, grabbed a handful of his nicely textured black hair, and jerked his head back.

At the touch of steel against his throat, his groans stopped. I sat on his spine, his arms pinned under my knees, suddenly enjoying myself. "Now this is my idea of a provocative posture!"

"Rutters!" screamed the landlady. She ran at me, her face contorted, the pan raised high.

Before she could strike, I turned the blade toward her. She stopped in mid-charge. "Don't make me kick your saggy baggy butt out of here, old mother," I warned.

She lowered the pan; her shoulders drooped; she turned and slunk toward the door. "I never gets to play," she grumbled. "Why don't they ever invites me to play in their sick games?"

"Don't forget my dinner!" I called after her.

The falconer shifted uncomfortably, his garments still steaming. I rapped his head with the flat of the dagger, and he grew still once more. "Isn't this nice?" I chirped pleasantly.

He gave a low groan. "Nice," he agreed uncertainly. "Are you going to cut my throat or not? If not, let go of the hair, please. I couldn't attract a nice piece like you with a bald spot."

"Sassy," I purred. Moving the dagger point to the back of his neck, I let go of his hair and reached between his legs. He gave a shiver and groaned an entirely new note.

"On the other hand, I hear some women like bald men," he hissed through clenched teeth.

I gave him a couple of gentle squeezes. He twitched and squirmed as much as he dared. "Not that I object to company," I said conversationally, "but I usually prefer to dress for my guests. What must you think of me?"

His voice turned husky. "My opinion is going up by the minute." And to my surprise, I noticed, so it was. I let go of the grip I had between his legs and slapped his rump sharply.

"Yes!" he moaned. He raised his head from the floor; his eyes were closed. "Spank me!"

I drove my fist between his shoulder blades. "What kind of girl do you think I am?"

"Punish me!" he begged. "I've been bad!"

I'd heard of men who craved abuse. Living with a bunch of dwarves in the woods, I'd heard of just about everything. And who was I to judge? Ripping free his jerkin's leather lacing, I draped it over his neck like a horse's reins and bounced jauntily on his back.

It was time to get down to serious business, though. I dealt his rump a sharp slap. "You didn't just happen by my window," I said, slapping him harder. "You knew my name—who sent you?"

"You can't make me tell!" he challenged. I knew he wanted to prolong the fun.

He arched his back, an invitation, and I grabbed him between the legs again. The landlady surely heard the sound he made. "No, no!" He shook his head furiously. One arm slipped from beneath my pinning knee, but he made no effort to throw me off.

"Who?" I shouted. I jerked on the lacing. The landlady must have heard me, too. In fact, by the shuffling and the shadow at the bottom of my door, the nosy crone was in the hallway listening. "Give it to me," I ordered. "Give me what I want!"

I lashed him with the thin leather, snapping it on cheeks and shoulders. My thighs squeezed his ribs. His feet drummed the floor; his vertebrae popped noisily, I rode him so hard. "No!" he cried. "You'll never make me betray my queen!"

I frowned. I stood up.

He rolled onto his back, disappointment flooding his eyes. "What's wrong?"

Careful not to slip on the wet floor, I righted the overturned chair, centered the flower vase, and lay the dagger on the table. "I don't like easy men," I answered without looking at him. A breeze from the the window reminded me I was naked. I pulled the sheet from the bed, wrapped it around myself, then picked up my sheathed sword.

When I turned around, the disheveled falconer

stood holding the dagger limply in his hand. The lacing dangled from his neck. "Maybe I lied," he said half-heartedly. "Maybe I have more information."

I shook my head. "Just leave the way you came." With the tip of the sword's sheath I nudged him toward the window.

He backed up reluctantly. "She saw you spying on the castle," he said as he sheathed his smaller weapon and tried to straighten his clothes. "You'll never get in. The place is impregnable."

"Tell her I'm coming to see her."

His expression brightened. "You're into that, too?"

I leaned on the sword. With an awkward cry, he tumbled backward over the sill and out the window. I heard frantic scrambling in the bushes as I closed and locked the shutters.

With a sigh, I placed my sword on the table and tiptoed to the door. I jerked it open. The landlady, on her knees at the keyhole, looked up. Sweat beaded her forehead. She might have been startled, but not a hint of embarrassment showed on her face unless it was hidden somewhere in all those wrinkles. Without rising, she lifted a platter. "Ye like chicken?"

I sighed again. "I prefer aged beef," I answered, sure the sarcasm wasn't wasted. But I took the chicken. "Wine, please."

"Looks at all that water on my floor! I'll have to mop it! Ye mights have wrecked my room! I grows roses outside that window, ye knows! Is that my good sheet?"

I closed the door and sat down to eat. At least the old bag had been thoughtful enough to include a few bits of cooked turnip and leeks on the side. I'll give her this, too, none of it tasted bad.

Night fell like a broken curtain, like the hopes of jilted lovers, like a black bird shot from the sky. As similes went, I didn't like that last one. It reminded me of the falconer. He really wasn't a bad sort. Maybe I'd been too rough on him.

While I polished my armor and contemplated nightfall, the landlady returned. Not bothering to knock, she pushed the door open with her mop, which she carried under one arm as if it was a lance. No matter that the floor had dried by itself an hour ago. She also carried a small oil lamp, which she sat on the table. Wordlessly, she cleared away the cold chicken bones and exited again.

I leaned back in the chair and put my bare feet up on the table, my sword in my lap.

The door opened swiftly. "Ye better not scuffs my furniture, ye better not!" Then she was gone again.

Night fell like an old woman's breasts after the age of fifty.

I wondered why I'd bothered to reopen the shutters. Night was only depressing me. At least the lamp's steady flame offered some cheer. I fetched my saddlebag from under the bed and withdrew the scrolled map Leonardo had given me in Sardeenia. King Clarence, he'd said, had given it to him just before Clarence's untimely demise.

It revealed a secret, forgotten way into the castle.

After studying the scroll's markings, I returned it to my saddlebag, shoved that back under the bed, and dressed for work.

One thing I could say for my armor; I didn't need a squire to assist me, although I'm sure I could have found one without too much advertising or for too much money. When all the hooks were fastened and both breasts in place, I stamped into my boots. Lastly, I buckled on my sword.

I could almost hear theme music, I looked so good.

No sign of the landlady in the hallway. Still, I tiptoed to the front of the inn. There I exchanged my small lamp for a bailed oil lantern hanging conveniently on a peg. As I reached for the doorknob, she popped up from behind a counter. "I knew'd it!" she cackled. "I knew'd ye'd be walkin' the streets. So I left thats fer ye!" She winked. "Good huntin', dearie! Sure ye don't want that sweater?"

I growled at her. "I'll bring you back a carcass to gnaw, you old buzzard." In truth, she was beginning to grow on me.

The lantern cast a yellowish circle of light as I walked quietly to the end of town. There I turned toward the stream and followed its bank into the woods. Darkness and I were old friends. I loved the forest at night, and the tree branches waved as if I'd just come home.

After a time I found an old church—the Church in the Wild Wood, later known as the Church in the Dell, but in any case long abandoned. If not for a bit of moonlight, I might have missed it altogether, it was so overgrown with moss and vines, and the trees had grown up close around it. With the lantern high, I strode into the weeds. The windows were empty of the stained glass they had once contained, but the doors stood like patient, if aged, sentries. I pushed one back and stepped inside.

Birds or bats—I couldn't tell which—filled the blackness with an urgent fluttering. The stone floor was slick with droppings. I crept down the long aisle between the wooden pews, trying to be silent for no reason. The place had long since been stripped of anything valuable, and I was quite alone.

Three stairs led up to the altar, which was a huge rectangle of weighty marble. Like the floor, droppings covered it. Birds and bats respected nothing. Shining the lantern around, I recalled Leonardo's map and its instructions. On the wall behind the altar hung three tall wooden crosses, the middle one slightly higher than the outer ones. Like everything else, they were covered in droppings.

I couldn't help frowning as I moved to the

rightmost cross and leaned against its filthy bottom. A fine white powder of dried birdshit cascaded down onto my head and shoulders. I leaped away, sputtering in disgust.

According to my light, the cross hadn't budged so much as an inch.

I cringed inside; I was going to get very dirty. Sometimes it came with the job. I set my lantern on the altar, and this time planted my shoulder against the foot of the same cross. Another powdery shower rewarded me. Cursing under my breath even if it was a church, I strained harder.

Old gears gave a metallic screech. The rightmost cross shifted suddenly. I nearly toppled. My screech rivaled the gears as ancient birdshit accumulated along the cross's horizontal arms rained down. I sprang away, shaking my hair, brushing my arms. The stuff had gotten into everything, even my boots!

When I looked up, however, the cross's tip had moved to touch the center cross.

Halfway done. I wondered if all the goldfish in Sardeenia were worth this degradation. The leftmost cross remained to be shifted. Why, oh why, hadn't I brought a raincoat, or a cloak, or accepted the old woman's offered sweater?

Leonardo was going to pay me double for this!

Trying not to breathe the chalkish air, I returned to work. The leftmost cross proved more stubborn than the rightmost; my delicate shoulder was going to bruise. But like the first, it eventually lurched into position and all three came together in a point.

A complaining rumble filled the church; a vibration shivered through the floor. My lantern's flame trembled and quivered. I lunged to save it, suddenly fearful of the dark.

The altar stone grated and scraped. It might have been a pit into hell, so black was the hole exposed by its shifting. Licking the powder that caked my lips,

I gathered my courage and crept forward with my light.

Steps led down into that hole.

One by one, I took them, nervously at first, then more surely, twelve in all. By the time I reached the bottom and a stony cavern floor, I exhaled with relief. At least, there weren't thirteen, not that I was superstitious. I gave a little laugh and wiped my brow, surprised to find a few beads of sweat. I raised my hand to the light and found white paint on my fingers.

Then I spat, nearly gagged. My lips! I'd licked them! I wiped at my mouth. It was no use. Birdshit all over me!

There was nothing to do but finish the job, get into the castle, and try to discover the fate of Prince Charming. I'd come this far; no turning back.

The map had been simple. Whenever the cavern forked, I took the left turn and made good time with my lantern to light the way. Only a few bats quickened my heart, and once a deep crack in the cavern floor. I leaped it easily.

Then, a sound whispered past my ear. I froze. The sound—a voice!—came again.

"Here comes Peter Cottontail,
    hopping down the bunny trail;
    grab him, squeeze him, make him wail,
    gut him with my fingernail,
    suck his blood and sweet entrails!"

I paused to consider. That wasn't the way I'd learned that song. Goldfish or no goldfish, I wondered if I should go on. Again, the voice.

"Now I lay me down to sleep
    under the earth so cold and deep;
    Death is long, and life is cheap;

Shiver, quiver, wail and weep,
Oh, shiver, quiver, wail and weep!"

Someone was trying to frighten me. Well, Bad Rose didn't frighten easily. Besides, I hated bad poetry.

"Oh yeah?" I shouted. "Here's one for you, buddy! Roses are red and violets are blue—your momma's a slut, and your daddy's one, too!"

A pause, followed by a gasp, then a fleshy sound as of a hand striking a cheek in surpise. "Oh my gawd! You're a girl!"

A figure moved out of the darkness and sashayed to the edge of my light, manlike, but dressed in out-of-date flared trousers and a pink shirt with ruffles at the neck and the lapels. Gold chains encircled its gray-skinned throat and sparkled in a thatch of withering chest hair. Jewelry dangled from its wrists. Rings flashed.

A stronger iron chain entrapped one of its ankles. Heavy links trailed back into the gloom.

"An old troll," I muttered.

Astonished eyes looked me up and down. "Why honey!" The scary whisper was gone, replaced by an almost breathless drawl. "When I smelled human, I assumed somebody upstairs had finally remembered to feed me! They treat me like a dog you know, all leashed up and everything!" It shook the ankle chain and made a face. "Not that they treat me at all these days, or trick me, either!" It laughed. "It's been forever since I've seen anyone! Now here you are and so welcome, let me tell you!" It flapped its wrists until I could feel the wind passing. "Don't you be nervous, either—everyone knows I wouldn't eat a girl!"

I wasn't so sure, so I stood my ground. "What are you doing down here?"

It tilted its head. "Why, honey, old King Clarence imprisoned me here to guard his tunnel!" It leaned forward conspiratorially and cupped one hand to the side of its mouth. "As if his tunnel hadn't already been breached, and more than once, if you know what I mean!—the stories I could tell!"

My mind began to race. I only knew trolls by their reputations. I needed to get by, but I wasn't inclined to hurt the poor creature if it wasn't here by choice. I edged a step closer to show I wasn't afraid. "Would you mind . . ."

I'd been a fool, suckered by its most powerful weapon—its amusing charm. It had yet more length of chain, enough to reach me. It lunged. Powerful arms encircled me. The lantern fell from my grip.

In complete darkness, I felt its breath like a cheap cologne on my face. "You said you wouldn't eat a girl!" I shouted angrily.

"I might keep one around for company," it answered. "I've been so lonely. And later, who knows—it's been ages between snacks!"

I didn't want to hurt it, but it wasn't giving me a choice. "This is no way to make friends!" I warned.

I didn't have enough freedom to draw my sword, but I could raise it a couple of inches from the scabbard. A bright blue light surged around us. The troll squealed, cast me aside, and scurried back into darkness. "Dwarf light!" it cried. "Horrid, hurtful dwarf light! Your blade—a dwarf forged it!"

It was my turn to laugh as I strode forward. "Not one, but seven dwarves! All your charms can't stand against its magic!"

It shivered as it cringed on its knees and pressed its head against the ground. Then it wept like any frightened child.

> "Star light, star bright!
> Horrid, nasty, dirty light!
> Sears the skin, and stings the sight!
> I wish I may, I wish I might
> Beg mercy from this snow white knight!"

An improvement over his last versification, I thought, and his last line genuinely surprised me. I raised my arm. In the sword's blue dwarf light, the powdered birdshit that covered me sparkled and glowed! "I really am snow white!"

Call me a woman. A man would have simply killed the creature, but my heart went out to it. I offered a bargain. "If I sever your chain," I said, "will you promise not to eat me?"

It lifted its head and peered with one eye between two fingers. "You'd do that?" it said. "For me? I'd be your friend for life—your best friend!"

I shook my head. "I don't need a dog."

It fingered its lip, suddenly thoughtful. "Well, I do have relatives I haven't seen in ages! And you're not really my type. It's a deal!"

I raised the sword high over my head. The troll covered its eyes as I brought the blade down on the iron chain. Sparks fountained as dwarf magic sliced through iron. The links shattered.

The old troll squealed with delight. It lingered long enough to clap its hands and cry, "Thank you, thank you!" Then, leaping upward, it jackknifed and plunged headfirst into the earth.

Life was just one adventure after another in my occupation. I brushed my toe at the ruined lantern, then continued on with my sword's light to guide me.

Not far beyond I encountered another set of stone steps. Eager for fresh air, I mounted them two at a time and found myself on a narrow landing. A rather loud ticking made me nervous. Raising the sword higher, I discovered a network of intermeshed gears.

I sheathed my sword. When my eyes had adjusted to the darkness again, I put a hand experimentally on the wall directly ahead and pushed. With little effort, it gave way. I stepped through the wooden casement of a giant grandfather's clock.

I found myself in a vast hall. Aside from the clock,

there was little furniture, only a large table laden with platters of fruit, a pitcher, a bottle. Certain I was alone, I started forward, thirsty for a drink.

Halfway across the room, I noticed the glass coffin.

It lay on a dais that someone had draped with red velvet. A pair of braziers stood on either end of it, providing a reddish light. The glass construct glittered. Forgetting food or drink, I crept toward it, drawn by the handsome youth laid with ceremonial splendor within.

For moments, I looked down at him. No glass lid or other barrier separated us. My heart pounded. His hair, black as night and gleaming; skin flawlessly fair; lips redder, more inviting than ripe cherries!

Beyond a doubt, I had found Prince Charming. Alas, he was dead!

I couldn't help myself. Tears welled in my eyes. Never had I seen such beauty—such sleeping beauty—in man or woman. I bent over the coffin's side and brushed my lips upon his.

Behind me, a feminine voice screamed. "Stop! Don't . . . !"

I spun around. A woman stood frozen, halfway down a gracefully curving staircase, her eyes wide, frightened. She had her own graceful curves. Not even the stern black dress and cloak she wore could conceal her striking loveliness. Had I been a man, my tongue would have unfurled from my mouth and written *mercy*! on the floor. *This was the Evil Queen?*

"Don't stop," said a deeper voice. Before I could speak a hand caught my arm and spun me about again. I looked into sea-blue eyes. Prince Charming, now sitting up awake, cupped one hand on the back of my head, drew me close, shoved his tongue so far down my throat my tonsils started packing to vacate.

I couldn't—didn't want to—resist. When he finally pushed me away, it was as if gravity had ended. I reached for him again, his witch-mother completely forgotten, but he put out a hand. "I'm thirsty," he said, climbing out of the coffin and stretching long unused limbs. "Find my slippers, and bring me a beer at once."

I had no will to resist. His command rang in my brain; nothing mattered but to please him. I whirled, wondering where in this huge place a prince might keep his slippers. I ran to the table like a common serving wench. I could get his beer first, then look for the slippers.

His mother beat me to the table. Snatching up an apple, she offered it to him. "You must be hungry after your long sleep," she urged.

He brushed her hand aside; the apple rolled across the floor. "Oh, Mother!" His voice dripped scorn. "The old poisoned apple trick again!"

My heart pounded. There was no beer on the table, no beverage at all but a pitcher of water and a brown bottle of liquor. I snatched it up. *Hammett & Chandler Old Brandy.* A good brand! I ran back to him, throwing myself at his feet.

"Good dog." He patted my head, then took the bottle, raised it to his lips, and swigged. He gave a loud sigh of pleasure, belched, and smiled. Then the smile vanished. He glared at his mother. "Bitch . . . !" He barely got the word out. The bottle slipped from his hand, shattering. He sank to the floor. I tried to catch him, but his weight proved too much.

Pinned beneath him, I struggled to make sense of what had happened. A veil seemed to lift from my brain. "What the . . . !" I thrust him off and sprang to my feet. "You've poisoned him!"

The Evil Queen dug a slippered toe into her son's ribs. "He's only sleeping," she answered with a weary sigh. "He thought it was just the apple, but everything on that table is enchanted—just in case he ever woke when I wasn't around."

I protested. "Why?"

She looked at me as if I were an addled school-girl. "Didn't you feel it?" she said. "Did you really want to fetch his slippers? Did you want to get his beer?" She shook her head, her eyes heavy with sadness. "He has an affect on women. We do anything he says. It's a power, his *charm*, and he has no compunction against using it. He's raised every skirt in the kingdom." She laughed bitterly, and with a startling display of strength, lifted him back into the coffin. "He had this trick with a glass slipper; you wouldn't believe how many foolish young girls fell for it!"

She offered her hand. "My name's Glenda," she said. "I so seldom have company."

I took a step back, eyeing her with suspicion. "You're an evil witch!" I said ungraciously. "I saw the charred bones outside your walls!"

She shrugged. "Peasants and torches," she replied. "They drink a little courage, storm the castle, start waving fire around. The local women went crazy the first time I put Bobo to sleep."

I glanced at the coffin and the beautiful boy within. *Bobo?*

Glenda shrugged again. "Okay, there was oil in the moat instead of water, but a woman alone has to protect herself. When Clarence ran off with that damned Blair Witch . . ."

I interrupted. "Leonardo told me you murdered him!"

It was her turn to regard me suspiciously. "His brother put you up to this?"

"No, I put her up to it!" Lord Parfum stepped through the clock, his face triumphant. His entourage of six soldiers followed with drawn swords. His lips curled in a snarl. "Where's the Prince Charming?"

I drew my own sword and stood protectively before the coffin. No one seemed impressed by its dwarf light. But Glenda fled across the vast chamber, her cloak spreading out like birds' wings. She flung her arms across a previously unnoticed liquor cabinet. "You'll never get it!" she challenged. A desperate fear filled her voice. "I'll blast you into ashes if you try!"

Lord Parfum sent his men forward. "You silly bat! We know the Blair babe stole, not only your man, but most of your power, too." He gestured smugly at me. "We only needed her to clear any traps in Clarence's so-called secret tunnel."

I looked from Parfum to Glenda to Bobo, and jerked my gaze away from Bobo as I felt the urge to kiss him awake again. "If you didn't want Leonardo's nephew," I muttered, "what the heck *are* you after?"

He chuckled. "I told you over dinner; if you could bottle and sell whatever that brat has, you could make a fortune." A glint of insanity shone suddenly in his rodent eyes. "Bobo found a way to do that! He comes from a sorcerous family, after all. Locked in that cabinet over there is a whole case of the little stud's private brew—Old Prince Charming." He laughed. "Women will never resist me again!"

"You, or any man!" Glenda cried. "Bobo's brew is too strong! If one bottle is uncorked, the fumes will turn women everywhere into subservient weaklings!"

Parfum nodded. "Sounds good to me." His men agreed as they flung Glenda aside and threw open the cabinet doors. Neatly racked, twenty-four glass bottles gleamed in the braziers' light.

It didn't sound so good to me. I ran at Parfum, my blade upraised, but the little skunk dodged and slashed at my ribs with a small dagger. I danced away, unhurt. Two of his men hurried to his defense. I engaged them both, fighting furiously, while by the liquor cabinet, another soldier withdrew a bottle.

A new player—the falconer!—ran out of the shadows. "I'll take that!" he said, seizing the potion. He kicked the soldier away and positioned himself before the cabinet, his sword ready. He faced four opponents—I faced only three!

A bolt of lightning erupted from Glenda's outstretched hand. A pile of ashes smoked at the falconer's feet. Now he faced only three. "Most, but not all my power!" she shouted.

Parfum turned pale. Blinded by the sudden flash, two of the falconer's opponents stumbled back; he ran them through as I dispatched one of my own. "I hate it when a plan falls apart!" Parfum raged. His dagger whisked through the air, missing me by inches. His remaining two soldiers, on the other hand, knocked me flat as they retreated for the tunnel.

Parfum was not quite ready to give up. He seized the brandy bottle and flung that at the advancing falconer. Next, he grabbed up the apple Bobo had knocked from Glenda's hand. He prepared to hurl it.

But clearly his plan was ruined. With a growl, he ran to the tunnel's entrance at the old clock. There, he paused. "You can't guard that stuff forever!" he shouted. "There's no way to dispose of it! You'll hear from me again!" He flung the apple straight for the cabinet and the exposed bottles. Glenda shot out a hand, neatly intercepting it, as Parfum raced into the tunnel.

A choked gurgle came from that blackness, a crunch, the sound of swallowing. A moment later, the old troll stepped from the dark, its stomach distended, a grin on its face. With one long fingernail, it picked its teeth. "Oh, you won't be hearing from him," he assured.

The falconer helped me to my feet, and the troll shielded its eyes while I sheathed my sword. Glenda, after closing the cabinet, crept uncertainly forward. I read her expression. "You didn't know about the troll?"

"Clarence kept a lot of secrets." Her ruby lips turned upward in a frown, but plainly it wasn't the troll that bothered her. "I can't figure how they even knew about the Prince Charming."

"My fault." The falconer knelt at his queen's feet. "Leonardo and Parfum hold my sister hostage. They forced me to spy on you. Had I known they plotted the subjugation of women, I would never have cooperated. Subservience is *my* role."

The old troll gave a purr of interest, but I waved it sternly back. It responded with an injured look. "I had no place else to go," it explained unasked. "This is home. Call me a prodigal!"

Glenda sighed and beckoned her falconer to rise. "I can't punish you," she said. His shoulders sagged. "Not with your sister in danger."

"I think I have my next case," I said. "And Leonardo's own gold will fund it." I eyed the cabinet. "But can you continue to guard that stuff alone?"

Her frown deepened. "I can't dump it in the ground, can't pour it in the water supply, can't expose it to the air—it's too toxic!"

The troll performed a little tap dance and clapped its hands. "Let me help!" it offered. "Anybody who tries to open that cabinet is mine, and I'll clean up the bones, too!"

Glenda considered, then nodded. She really had little choice, and the troll had experience as a guard.

An hour later, with the falconer's belongings in a bag, we said a long good-bye at the front door. The sun was coming up, and I wanted a bath in the village before we hit the road again.

As Glenda and the troll waved behind us, the falconer whispered, "Do you think they'll work out?"

"An evil queen and an old troll under the same roof?" I answered. "What do you think?"

Incognito, Ergo Sum

Karen Everson

"Mistress Irene! Mistress Irene!" Andromeda charged into the stableyard, droplets of fresh blood spattering from the flapping skirts of her mail tunic. The Persian ambassador's entourage scattered like chickens as she plunged through them, waving her arms. "The Empress just bit the head off a live goat!"

Irene waved back, then noticed that the Persian ambassador had quietly fainted into the clean straw on the stable floor. She sighed and handed the halter rope of the ambassador's Berber mare to the Hippolyta. "Please revive the ambassador," Irene said, "and explain to him that the Empress, in this instance, is a griffin." The real Empress, Irene thought as she hurried to meet her apprentice, would never bite the head off a goat—not when she had ambassadors and imperial officers available.

Irene reached and passed her blood-splashed apprentice without stopping, heading for the griffin's aerie. Andi managed a skidding about-face, adding a patina of dust to her bloody armor, and scrambled to reach Irene's side. Andi's legs were twice as long as Irene's—but it was almost always Andi trotting to keep up. "Sorry about the ambassador, Mistress."

"He'll be fine," Irene said dismissively. "He's new. You might want to *try* to remember to call the Golden Empress 'Goldie,' though, just to avoid this sort of confusion."

Andi colored. "Should I go back and apologize?"

"Certainly not! We've a superfluity of Persian ambassadors, but only one griffin."

Irene's pace carried them quickly through the small garden that buffered the Aerie and disguised the feeding pens. Irene shouldered through the antechamber door, Andi on her heels.

A half dozen goats cowered in the near corner of the aerie, too terrified even to bleat. Irene didn't blame them. Goldie's tawny feathers were crimson with blood. She gripped the corpse with one forefoot, probing the torn belly with her hooked beak.

"I brought her several goats to choose from," Andi whispered, bending so that she was closer to Irene's ear, "but she grabbed the Judas, the female in estrus I used to make the males more biddable."

Suddenly the griffin stilled. She made a soft croaking sound, then lifted her head, a mass of pink flesh in her beak. As Andi and Irene watched anxiously, she choked down the organs, her twitching wings stretched to their full sixteen-foot span.

"What's that she's eating?" Andi whispered.

Irene squinted and whispered back. "Ovaries. And a uterus, I think." Irene thumped a fist against her thigh. "The Fading *is* connected to a breeding cycle. Her humors are unbalanced!"

Goldie stood for a moment, eyes closed, making the same soft croaking. Her wings slowed and mantled, and she looked down at the dead beast beneath her talons as though surprised to see it there.

After a moment, she settled to her haunches and began to feed normally.

"Good girl, oh, good, my beauty," Irene murmured. Tears slid silently down her face. Six months ago, Goldie's amber plumage had been sleek and glossy, her eyes bright with intelligence and curiosity. Now she was thin beneath her dull and brittle feathers, her dark eyes haunted. Irene leaned against the aerie's arabesque of iron bars, watching the Golden Empress feed.

Irene felt Andi's hand squeeze her shoulder. "She took milk this morning too, Mistress," Andi said, "Warm from the cow, just as Master Kerides suggested."

"Wonderful," Irene said. She straightened, wiping her damp face on the purple breast scarf that marked her as one of the Empress Theodora's officers. Andi plucked the scarf out of her hand and substituted a handkerchief.

Irene blew her nose. "As long as she's eating there's hope. Kerides has kept Windwing alive for a full year since her Fading began." She fisted her hands against the bars of the aerie. "Goldie *has* to live long enough for you to complete your apprenticeship, so that you, not Tulius, take my place."

Andi's face twisted. "Theodora has known you all your life. I can't believe she'd have you killed."

Irene turned resigned eyes to her apprentice. "The Golden Empress is Princess Helena's signet beast, the augury of her future reign. In my arrogant youth, I swore I'd keep the griffin alive. If Goldie dies, I won't live to see the next dawn."

"We'll heal Goldie," Andi said. "You won't die."

Irene stared at the feeding griffin. "Well, not today, anyway." Her hands relaxed. "Rescue the leftovers, will you? Then get changed. We have to go to the menagerie."

Andi paled. "For how long?"

Irene rubbed at her eyes. "That depends on how many animals from yesterday's 'performance' are still alive."

A long stone ramp led to the catacomb of cells and cages that ran beneath the hippodrome. The walls distorted the cries of the captive animals, so that the stones themselves seemed to wail, and in that stygian closeness the smell of blood and sweat and rotting waste was almost stifling.

"Honoring us with a visit, Irene?"

Irene turned. "Good-day, Tulius."

Tulius was tall and darkly handsome, and Irene had seen him be charming when he had something to gain by it. It made his easy cruelty all the more grotesque. Irene nodded toward the first corridor of cages. "We'll see the animals now, thank you."

Tulius made an ironic bow. "Certainly. We lost half the hyenas, and two of the lions, but there're others that may do for the arena again if you want to patch them up."

"Which lions?" Andi demanded. "You didn't fight Leda? What did you do with her cubs?"

"Did you miss the show? Too bad! I loosed the hyenas on the cubs, then set the lions on the hyenas. It was inspired."

Andi's eyes blazed. Irene set a hand on her shoulder. "Which lions did you lose?"

"The big male—a shame about that—and the mother. The hyenas got one cub, but the two surviving lionesses drove off what was left of the pack before they got the other." He made a face, mockingly tragic. "Of course, I had to have it destroyed anyway. Too young to live without its mother. Well, enjoy your rounds, ladies. I'm sure you can find your own way." He threw a ring of keys at Irene. Managing not to flinch, she snatched them out of the air before they struck her in the face.

This was the man who wanted her place, wanted control of her animals, of her people, of *Andi*. If my Golden Empress dies, Irene thought, before the princess's Varangians come for me, perhaps I will come for you.

Tulius turned on his heel and went whistling up the corridor toward the arena. Andi stared after him, her eyes speaking hate. Irene touched her arm. "Andi. There's nothing you can do for the dead ones. Let's go see what we can do for the living."

"They're all dead," Andi said bitterly. "Just some of them are still breathing."

Irene gave a small crooked smile. "You could say the same of me. Or of anyone." Irene took Andi's hand, squeezed it. "We all cheat death one breath at a time."

Andi squared her shoulders. "Let's go cheat like hell."

A weak or sickly beast did not make a good show, so Tulius's captives at least had clean water and adequate food. But their quarters were cramped, and they lived in a miasma of fear and filth where even a minor wound could turn deadly.

One of the surviving lionesses had a shallow gash in her flank, which only needed to be cleansed and stitched.

The second lioness was not so simple. Though the bone of her injured leg was miraculously unbroken, the flesh was deeply torn, in places hanging in strips like meat cut for smoking. Serious infection had already set in, angry-looking purple streaks running into the undamaged flesh of hock and thigh.

Irene shook her head. "The poison's entering her blood. It might be kindest just to cut her throat."

"No!" Andi protested. Irene looked at her sharply and the younger woman reddened. "We can give her a chance."

Irene squatted back on her haunches. "Talk."

"I have a new medicine," Andi said, "supposed to fight this kind of infection. The Varangian who told me of it swore by it."

"Varangians swear by a lot of things," Irene said doubtfully. "False gods. Their swords. Beer." She nodded. "Try it."

Andi flashed a smile, put flame to her blade and began to excise the wound. She scraped some of the deadly ooze into one of Irene's costly glass jars.

"What will you do with that?" Irene asked.

"If I can get the poison to grow outside the flesh, perhaps in a dish of fresh blood, then I could try our medicines in turn, to see which best destroys it."

Irene nodded approval, watchful as Andi packed the wound with a grey paste. "What's in your Varangian's goo?"

Andi colored, but began to pull the tattered flesh together with small neat stitches. "Biscuit mold and spider webs."

Irene smiled wearily. "Well, I've heard worse."

By the time they finished their rounds in the maze of cells, they were sick-hearted and weary. Irene sank to the thin straw that littered the passage, her back against the wall. Her head ached from working by lamp and torchlight, her fingers were cramped from wielding knife and needle and her hands raw from repeated washing. She closed her burning eyes for a moment, feeling vaguely guilty as Andi cleansed their instruments and emptied basins into the narrow gutters.

"Mistress?" Andi said. "What's this end cell for?"

"It's called the Dragon Cage," Irene answered, without opening her eyes. "Large exotics were confined there, back when rare beasts like dragons were actually exhibited and killed in the arena. It hasn't been used for years."

"It's in use now," Andi said grimly. Irene's eyes popped open and she sat up. Andi had her ear pressed shamelessly against the rough cedar door. "This lock is new, and I can hear something moving inside."

"That bastard!" Irene spat, anger and alarm banishing fatigue. She scrambled up, fumbling for the ring of keys. The lock answered to none of them.

Irene withdrew in frustration. "Damn. We can't get in."

Andi bent and rummaged in the satchel, emerging with a farrier's hammer and horseshoe pry. "Bugger that," she said flatly. She planted the wedge of the pry against the lip of the door hasp and struck down hard with the farrier's hammer, once, twice. The hasp plate tore away from the wood and the whole lock assembly swung free.

Both women pushed through the doorway into a small antechamber. Irene lifted the lantern to illuminate the barred cell beyond.

Andi gasped. "Mistress Irene. *What is it?*"

"I have no idea," Irene said softly.

The creature was a lithe darkness against the grey stone, eyes shining an eerie green in the light. It was built like a lion the size of a *Kilbanophoros* steed, with a sleek scaled head atop a powerful, graceful neck that reminded Irene of horses. Then it arched its back like an enormous cat, and a series of bladelike scales rose like a clattering phalanx of spears along its spine. Lamplight spilled over scales and claws scratched on stone as the creature wheeled to face them head-on. It tried to shriek, but only a faint and angry hissing escaped its beaked and muzzled jaws.

"I see you found my prize," Tulius said from behind them.

"And I so wanted to surprise you."

Irene turned furiously. "This is an exotic, Tulius! It belongs in the Imperial Mews, not in the arena!"

"Oh, yes?" Tulius's posture was confident, his eyes and voice amused. "Now, *Mistress*, I have a long, long list, written in your own hand, of creatures you may take from me in the Empress's name." His voice went low with sudden hatred. "I know that list as well as you, you dwarfish bitch, and that creature *is not on it*. Therefore, it is *mine*."

The Black Beast lunged at Tulius, crashing against the bars of the cage. Talons snagged on iron and scraped parallel grooves in the stone floor.

Tulius laughed, an honestly joyous, happy sound. "A prince of the Vandals comes to the City, and I promised the Empress a fitting entertainment for her barbarian guest. My Black Beast will kill until the sands are red, and he will die magnificently." He grinned and leaned over Irene's small frame, his predator breath hot in her face. "I and my Black Beast will be remembered when you are a long-forgotten joke, *Mistress* Irene."

"The Empress takes no pleasure in such things!"

"But the prince *does*," Tulius said with confidence. "And your precious Empress values a treaty with his father more than the life of this beast."

"Left to your care, the beast might not live to see the arena," Andi said. Irene and Tulius turned. Andi knelt beside the bars of the cage, the beast scant inches away on the other side of the bars. Its chest scales rattled as it struggled for breath. "At least take the muzzle off it. It's overheated. It needs to pant, like a dog or a lion. It also has untreated wounds." Andi addressed Irene. "It must have been caught with wire snares. There are lacerations, one high on the right hind leg, another just above the wrist joint of the left fore. They're underneath the lap of the scales, so I only saw them when the beast leaped at the bars."

"Any sick animal is under my jurisdiction," Irene reminded Tulius sharply.

Tulius laughed. "The Black Beast isn't sick. You want to take its muzzle off, they're your hands." With easy arrogance he took a key from a cord around his neck and handed it to Andi. "Bandage him up while you're at it, if it will make you happy. But the Empress knows about the beast—and she has said I may use it in the arena."

"I can't believe that," Irene said, stricken. "I'll go to Theodora myself. She won't—she can't—let something so rare and beautiful be destroyed."

Tulius grinned. "Ask her." He tossed Irene a salute and sauntered out of the chamber.

The Black Beast raised its head to watch him go, rumbling with impotent hate.

Andi fetched their satchel. She took something from it, then slowly knelt before the bars again, her eyes locked with the beast's baleful glare. Slowly, the muted growl died. From amidst the scales, graceful ears lifted. Andi held her right hand motionless, cupped just before her chin.

"Shhhh," she whispered. The creature arched its graceful neck toward her. At the base of the muzzled beak, nostrils flared wide to take in her scent.

Andi's lips puffed. The soporific powder smoked through the bars, drawn deep into the beast's throat and lungs.

The long neck swayed as the beast drew back; the heavy, beaked head sank down onto the armored breast. In a little bit, it slumped onto its side, unconscious.

Irene set her hand on Andi's shoulder. "Well done."

Andi turned her eyes to Irene's, and Irene saw in them a reflection of her own despair. She turned her eyes away, and, taking the key, opened the door of the cage.

Irene hoped she'd be allowed to see the Empress before she'd sweat-soaked all three layers of her court clothes. Her costly cotton tunica was more forgiving than silk, but the wide-sleeved underdress was amber-colored samite, her overdress russet silk trimmed in shades of yellow and amber. Her cap and superhumeral, the wide formal collar, matched the underdress and were trimmed in seed pearls and amber drops.

She felt like a courtesan's bed-curtain.

One of Theodora's secretaries, a small, slim eunuch named, inappropriately, Herakles, came out of the Blue Chamber. "The Empress will see you now, Mistress Irene," he said, "but be quick. She's tired, and she has much more to do before she will consent to rest."

Irene nodded. Wishing she could calm her fluttering stomach, she drew a deep breath and followed Herakles into the Blue Chamber.

The Empress Theodora VI was seated in a highbacked chair behind an elegantly simple wooden table. On a stool beside her mother sat the seventeen-year-old Princess Helena, frowning over a wax tablet as she nibbled an apple slice. A platter of cold chicken and fruit and a water jug were wedged in between piles of documents. A half-dozen secretaries worked at low desks or glided to and from the table and racks that held maps, books, and parchments. A high window admitted air without making enough of a breeze to trouble the papers.

Irene prostrated herself, awkward in her unaccustomed clothes, then moved forward to kneel on one of the cushions scattered before the table, to wait for the Empress to acknowledge her.

Helena noticed her first. "Mistress Irene! I'm sorry I've been too busy here to come to the aerie. How is my Goldie?"

Irene felt relief that she could honestly give a good report. "She is better, Highness. She fed well yesterday."

The Empress put her signature to the paper before her and handed it off to a secretary. Helena hastened to move the platter of food beneath her mother's fingers before she could select another document. Theodora spared a smile for her daughter, and took a piece of food without looking. "Mistress Irene," Theodora acknowledged. She inclined her head. "You may sit." She ate a bite of chicken while Irene settled more comfortably. "I assume you are here about Tulius's Black Beast."

Irene's heart sank. "Yes, my Empress. Tulius means to have it torn apart in the arena." She looked up at the woman she had served all her adult life and found herself pleading. "My lady, please—it is unique, perhaps the only one of its kind. It is—it is beautiful, perhaps intelligent as well. You can't allow it to simply be destroyed."

"One does not say 'can't' to one's Empress, Irene," Theodora said sharply. Irene quailed, and the Empress went on more gently. "I understand. You are as passionate in your calling as I am in mine. But my concerns are larger than yours. I have intelligence that this Vandal princeling has a barbarian's taste for a bloody show, and I have need to please him." She made a face. "As little as I like it, his people control trade routes that we need. I learn from my ancestress: treaties are better than war. I'm sorry, but unless circumstances change, the beast belongs to Tulius." The Empress took another document and turned her eyes to it. "You may go."

Irene made obeisance and got slowly to her feet. As she turned to go, the Empress's voice caught her. "Oh, and Mistress Irene, a word of advice." Irene froze. "If I were you, I would concentrate my attention on the creatures already in your care."

The Empress's pen dipped, tapped, and began to write. Irene was dismissed.

"She said, 'Unless circumstances change, the beast belongs to Tulius.' I'm so sorry, Andi."

Andi knelt beside Irene's bed and carefully folded Irene's cold fingers around a cup of mulled wine. "It's not your fault, Mistress." The younger woman stayed kneeling by the bed, one hard, thin arm curved loosely around Irene's waist.

Irene forced herself to drink the hot sweet wine, feeling its heat begin to melt her cramped muscles. "I feel my life's work slipping away from me," she said. "I thought I'd made a sanctuary, a place where animals could be cared for and studied. Now a fabulous, unknown beast is going to be torn to pieces *to please a Vandal!*" She lifted a hand to her eyes. "If Tulius gets the Mews, it will be as if I'd never lived."

"Don't say that!" Andi snapped. "Even if the worst happens, if Goldie dies and some Varangian knifes you in your bed and Tulius takes over here, you've *still* saved scores of animals from the arena, advanced our knowledge tenfold! And you've taught me, much more than healing. I swear to you, Irene—Tulius isn't going to win." For the first time, Andi put her arms around Irene and hugged her.

Irene hugged back, drawing a fierce comfort from the press of Andi's body, warm and hard even through the quilted tunic. "Thank you," she whispered.

Andi drew back, gestured at the cup. "I'll make you more wine. I'll go to the menagerie, check on the animals and change the bandages, while you stay here and rest."

"No," Irene shook her head. "No, Tulius may have won this battle—but I'm damned if I'll let him see me surrender the war." She straightened her shoulders, wiped eyes with the back of her hand, and sniffed. She grinned a little. "You're fragrant. What were you doing while I groveled?"

"Oiling Goldie. For bug repellent, this stuff isn't too bad. You aren't going to make me change, are you?"

"No. I rather like rosemary and cedar with base

notes of griffin." Irene rose and went to ready their horses while Andi checked their supplies.

To Irene's relief, Tulius was about other business, and they were able to make their rounds without disturbance. The lioness with the shallow wound was moving easily, and willingly accepted a treat of drugged meat. Andi's special patient, recipient of the "Varangian goo," was awake and alert, though she had yet to take solid food. Sedating her, they found her wound much better, the swelling and fever reduced. Encouraged by the success, they went to see the Black Beast.

The antechamber door was open, the key to the Black Beast's cell hanging from the inside handle of the door. Irene felt a twinge of anger, knowing this easy access was Tulius's taunt, daring her to defy Theodora.

The Black Beast lifted its head at their entrance, making a soft, curious honk. It rose to its feet and came to the bars, surveying them with large dark eyes. "It's much calmer today," Irene said.

"Tulius isn't here," Andi said. "It remembers us." She knelt by the bars, crooning. "Don't you remember me, Beastie?"

The Black Beast took a step backward, yanking back its head and squeezing its nostrils shut. Irene laughed. "It remembers you all right." Realization touched her, leaving grief where wonder should have been. "Andi, it's intelligent. On some level, it understands what's happening to it." She reached out, gently touching the bars of the cage. "Oh, Beastie, I'm sorry."

The Black Beast looked at Irene, then at Andi. Andi held her hands up, flat, to show that they were empty. The beast came closer, almost mincing, and flared its nostrils wide. It snuffled all around Andi through the bars, even extending a leathery grey tongue to taste her hands. It made a soft croaking noise and *puffed*, all its scales standing out from its body so that it looked like a quadruped pinecone. Irene, standing to one side, noticed something else. "Andi, you have an admirer."

Andi leaned over and peeked between the Black Beast's legs, then shook her head at the beast. "Trust me, boy, I'm not your type." She did take advantage of the beast's interest by giving him a drugged treat.

The beast gave her an accusing look just before his double eyelids slowly shuttered closed. "I'll change his bandages," Andi offered. Irene just nodded, deep in thought. There was something about the Black Beast, about the way it had responded to Andi, that was teasing at her mind, something terribly important, but the harder she tried to grasp it, the more elusive it became. Andi had to tap her on the shoulder to tell her it was time to leave.

Outside the torchlit gloom of the menagerie, a purple dusk was falling, nightjars stitching the sky with their cries. All the way home, Irene's thoughts went in circles like puppies chasing their tails.

They were on their way back to their quarters from the stable when the dovecote boy caught up to them, his face pale by the light of his lantern. "Mistress Irene. A pigeon came while you were gone. One of the big red ones."

"One of Kerides'," Irene said, hope in her voice. "Do you have the message capsule, Thomas?"

The boy looked down. "I'm sorry, Mistress." He reached out and pressed something into Irene's hand. "This is all there was."

The bit of black ribbon lay in Irene's palm like a snippet of night. "Windwing and Kerides are dead," Irene said, and turned her face to the darkness.

She clawed her way out of sleep, pushing and hitting at the hands that gripped her shoulders. The hands retreated and Irene sat up, aching and sick and dizzy, a flood of lantern light blinding her eyes. She threw her arm up to shield her face.

"Get that damned light off me," she snapped. The light withdrew. Irene squinted, saw the creased face of Anna, one of the gate guards, looking anxiously down at her.

"Mistress Irene, I'm sorry," the woman said. "Your quarters were empty, and the Master of the Menagerie has sent for you in all urgency." She frowned. "He said you would know why."

Irene staggered to her feet. She was in the antechamber of Goldie's aerie, one of Goldie's winter blankets and an empty wine jug tumbled at her feet. Memory came flooding back, and with it a heartache far worse than the ache in her head and body. Windwing and Kerides were dead. She looked over at the hulk of her griffin, was surprised to see her awake, the great eyes reflecting green in the faint rays of lantern light.

"You did well to find me at all, Anna," Irene told the guard, grateful she hadn't gotten drunk enough to try to sleep with Goldie.

Irene went to the water cistern and dunked her head. The cold water revived her. "I have a guess what Tulius wants," she said, mopping her face with the tail of her purple scarf. "Andi wasn't in our quarters?"

Anna, mute with shock, shook her head.

"I'll find Andi," Irene said. "You have horses readied, for yourself and a companion as well. I want an escort."

Irene ran into the courtyard. The night told its hour on her skin. In perhaps two hours the birds would begin their pre-dawn chorus. Except for the guards, the Imperial compound slept.

Irene had a good idea where to find her painfully modest apprentice.

A single lantern glowed in an interior room of the

baths. Irene swept in like a thunder squall. "Andi!
Out and dressed! Now!"

Andi had been soaking, half asleep in the warm
water. The apprentice gasped, floundered wildly for
a towel and missed.

"Come on, girl," Irene said sharply. "You haven't
got anything I haven't seen in the mirror." She
stepped forward, grabbing up the towel. Andi rose
from the bath and faced her.

Irene stared. "I take that back."

"Here," she said. She snapped the towel at Andi's
offending anatomy. Andi gasped and made a frantic
grab and Irene tossed him the rest of the towel. "We'll
discuss *that* later," she said. "Get dressed. We're
needed at the menagerie."

Andi scrambled into his tunic—high-necked to
cover the Adam's apple in his throat, extra padding
to suggest small breasts where none existed. As Andi
yanked the garment into place, Irene grasped him by
the arm. "What did you do to the Black Beast?"

Andi met her eyes. "I poisoned him."

The Black Beast lay on his side, panting, tongue
rolling swollen and grey from the gaping beak. The
glossy scales were dulled, and rustled like a fall of
dry leaves with the creature's labored breathing. His
injured hind leg was swollen and hot, the bandage
crusted yellow.

"What did you do to my Beast?" Tulius raged,
following them into the cell. Irene spun on her heel.
Her calloused palm struck out, with all her considerable strength behind it. Tulius staggered back,
wheezing as he tried to pull air back into his dia-
phragm. "Shut up!" Irene shouted, stalking after him,
stiffened fingers jabbing repeatedly at his chest. "The
Empress said the Black Beast was yours—*unless the
circumstances changed*. Well, for now, they *have*
changed. The Black Beast is sick, and sick animals

are *mine*." She snapped her head towards Anna and Catullus, waiting just outside the door. "Get a transport wagon. This animal is too ill to remain here. We're moving it to the Imperial Mews. And while you're at it," she added, indicating Tulius with a thrust of her chin, "get that . . . person . . . out of here so we can work."

Tulius, still wheezing, turned an even darker red, but was not prepared to argue with the two armed and determined palace guards. Catullus hustled Tulius away, and Anna pulled the cedar door closed, leaving Irene and Andi alone with the Beast.

Irene checked the beast, sedated him to damp his pain. "You realize you could have killed this animal."

"It was going to die in the arena," Andi said, cutting away the bandage. "I thought I could keep him sick long enough for the barbarian prince to come and go. Then maybe the Empress would intervene."

Irene nodded begrudgingly. "All right. It makes sense, in a twisted sort of way. But if you ever do anything like this again, I'll geld you myself."

Andi colored, but his hands continued to move, baring the wound, purging the poisoned flesh. "My father, my teachers—they all said, Irene is the best there is—perhaps the best that's ever been. I *had* to work with you, to be able to see, to study, creatures like Goldie. I *knew* I was good enough. But everyone said that only women and eunuchs get positions at the palace." He glanced at her. "You know that's true."

"True enough," Irene admitted. She stroked the beast, its neck warm beneath her hand. The scales had a pattern of striations running out from a central vein, giving them a silky feel. In the oblique lantern light, they looked like feathers.

The puppy-thoughts in Irene's head suddenly caught their tails. *Are his scales specialized feathers, or her feathers specialized scales?*

The Black Beast had not reacted to Andi, but to Goldie's scent on Andi's flesh. His vocalizations had played upon her memory because they were echoes of Goldie's. In size, in the shape of body, beak and talons, the Black Beast was Goldie's mate, yet his lack of wings had deceived her—until now.

"I didn't even want to *pretend* to be a eunuch," Andi said. "So I pretended to be a woman." He smeared Beastie's wound with Varangian goo. "It wasn't that hard. Except I had to shave a lot."

"Don't worry," Irene whispered. She stroked the beast, shaking. "When this animal is healthy again, you'll be so indispensable that no one will care whether you're a whole man or a bearded lady." She laughed. "There's adequate precedence for both."

There was a soft knock. Anna eased the door open. "Mistress Irene, the wagon is ready."

Irene stood. "I want this animal taken directly to the griffin's aerie. We'll bed it in the antechamber."

"The aerie?" Andi asked, startled.

Irene felt the grin stretching her face. "Don't you see it, Andi? You aren't the only gentleman who's been traveling incognito. This Black Beast is a male griffin—*and griffins are on the list*."

"We think the sexes are highly specialized," Irene explained to the Princess Helena. "The female hunts, but it is the male, with his scales and superior strength, who guards the nesting site. Lions have a similar arrangement."

"Certain fish, also," Andi put in. "And the sea horse, Your Highness. The male guards the eggs and young."

"Ah," Helena said, graciously inclining her head. "Androcles, is it not? Your Mistress tells me We have you to thank for the Dark Emperor's survival, and the Dark Emperor for the return of Goldie's health." She smiled. "I am very grateful."

Andi bowed.

The Princess turned her eyes back to the aerie, where the two griffins lounged side by side in the warm sand, necks twined as human lovers twine arms. Andi, dismissed, went back to work.

"A whole man for an apprentice," the Princess mused, loud enough for Andi to overhear. "Very daring, Irene."

Irene startled. "How did you know . . . ?"

The Princess smirked. "How did I know he wasn't a eunuch? How does a mare know a stallion from a gelding? Honestly, Irene, if you have to ask that, you've been celibate too long." Helena cast an appraising eye on Andi, not bothering to be subtle about it. Irene felt a flush creeping up her neck.

"He has very good bones," Helena observed, "but he's awfully thin, and he works hard. I suppose he must be exhausted by the end of the day." She lifted a sympathetic brow. "Really, my dear, don't you want me to send you one of my Varangians?"

The Princess Helena completely misinterpreted Andi's laughter, but that, Irene thought, was probably just as well.

Chain of Command

Leslie What &
Nina Kiriki Hoffman

"Mom," Kayla said in that tone teenagers use when they're practicing for the time they will put you in the nursing home. "You're not going to wear THAT, are you?"

I forced myself to smile, making sure I showed teeth. I'd had my canines lengthened and my incisors filed to subtle points. Remember, I told myself. I'm the mom. I'm Alpha. Wolf Woman. A CEO of Earth Muthas, a militant woman-owned multinational. Only my teenage daughter was powerful enough to make me forget this.

I was wearing mail and a leather thong and copper breastplate because I had a focus group to lead in half an hour and there wasn't time between now and then to change from civvies. I held the keys in my mouth for a second while I tightened my belt.

All I had to do was drop off Kayla at her friend Tiffany's; from there they would walk to their cheerleader meeting at the high school. I could hide in the Jeep; no one need see me.

Kayla was five foot seven and growing fast enough that I expected her to surpass me during the coming year, when she would be a junior. Her hair was bronze from a bottle, though on her, it looked feminine. She preferred a fruity-smelling department store perfume called Flower Power to my musky Marker, the flagship product for my company. Her scent made my eyes water, but I decided against saying anything. "Choose your issues," our family counselor had warned.

I had chosen.

So had Kayla.

The issue was not about scent.

Kayla did not want to come with me to this weekend's Women Warriors retreat, starting tomorrow, where one hundred women would gather to trap trespassing trolls, celebrate our strength, hunt our own dinners and leave nature's scavengers to do dishes when they picked the carcasses clean. Instead, my daughter wanted to stay in town with Tiffany and shop for makeup and high heels. Kayla was a pacifist. I was a warrior, an awkward situation for us both.

"You look good," I said, thinking that if her pleated skirt had been cut from leather instead of polyester and if her tank top had been chain mail instead of spandex, she could have passed. Her arms and long legs were muscled and tan, not from fighting, but from cheering the football team. It stunned me that someone who existed on tofu and fruit could grow the body of an Amazon.

She made a face. "I can't believe you're going to wear that. This is SO embarrassing."

"Are you all packed?" I asked. The counselor had

recommended changing subjects to diffuse tense situations.

"Let's talk about packing later," she said, meaning she hadn't started. "We gotta go."

I had prearranged for Bear Woman to get the focus group sharpening knives if I ran late, so I wasn't in any hurry. "Pack," I said, settling into a power pose on the floor. I crouched on my haunches as if ready to spring, fingers poised an inch above my boar-tusk knife handle. I had killed the boar myself while on safari in Peru.

"Mom!" Kayla screamed.

I forced myself not to smile. "Go upstairs and pack," I said. Alpha power surged through me in a premenopausal electrical storm. I unsheathed my knife and lazily carved my initials into the pecan floor.

Kayla stood by, defeated. "Oh, all right!" she said at last. She turned and ran to her room.

Only then did I notice I wasn't breathing. I gasped, both with surprise and the need for air. I had won the battle. The war wasn't scheduled to start until tomorrow.

Kayla's suitcase was big enough to hold a gray whale, which, incidentally, she tried periodically to save. She had packed a month's worth of clothing, makeup, and reading material—nearly all relating to Ricky Martin, her latest pop star heartthrob. She was bringing her own cooler filled with Rainier cherries, mangos, and a chewy vegan concoction called tempeh that Kayla liked to chop and season with sunflower seeds and roll up in whole wheat tortillas.

My cooler held a case of chocolate truffles, a few bottles of my favorite white zinfandel, barbecue sauce, spices, and pork casings to make sausages, in case there were any leftovers from the kill. Okay, so we were militant, but I was born in the Midwest, and when you were from Iowa, you never threw away anything you could can, freeze, or over-winter in the cellar.

The retreat was near the Washington/Oregon border, a three-hour drive by highway, a little over two hours if you knew how to get there off-road, which I did. I ignored Kayla's whining and refused to take the Jeep out of four-wheel drive until we had crossed a shallow ravine called Starving Woman Creek. The creek was empty year-round, except for an occasional flash flood. Tomorrow, if things went well, we planned to fill it with a river of animal blood when we hosted our full moon Earth Mutha ceremony.

"Mom," Kayla said, "you're not really going to trap trolls, are you?"

"It doesn't hurt them," I said, for the umpteenth time. "We just trap them in cages to transport back to the Idaho wilds." I had no sympathy for the hairy beasts. They weren't even native to the area and had been brought to the Northwest by Idaho farmers looking for cheap help to harvest their potato crop.

"Goddess, Mother!" she said, using that I-can't-wait-till-you're-in-the-nursing-home voice. "I suppose you think it was okay for the government to intern Japanese Americans during World War II."

"Not a good analogy," I said. "This is way different. Trolls aren't even human. They behave like pigs. They steal our supplies, trash our site, and urinate on our bedding. That's why they're called trolls, for Goddess' sake."

"Now you're going to pretend like I don't know what I'm talking about so you don't have to listen," Kayla said. "You and your friends are bigger thugs than the trolls."

"I'm sorry, dear, but the trolls are too much of a nuisance to ignore. We tried living in peace with them, but this really is an 'Us or Them' kind of issue, and I'm sorry you don't understand that." How quickly our discussions degenerated into variations of Because I Told You So!

"It's people like you who make us have wars," Kayla proclaimed.

I stared at my difficult daughter. She had shed her sweater to reveal the "I heart Trolls" shirt she knew I detested.

"I want peace as much as you do," I said. "We just disagree on the best way to get it."

"I'll say." Kayla liked to have the last word. I decided to let it pass.

She bent to dig around on the floor and came up with a crinkled paper sack. "Want some teriyaki seaweed jerky?" she asked.

"No, thank you," I said. "Could you pass me the dried buffalo strips?"

"Sorry, but I don't touch dead things. Get it yourself." She arranged her earphones, turned on her CD player, and mouthed the words to Ricky Martin's latest hit.

The counselor had suggested that when I was angry I count to ten before speaking. I counted to fifty. That helped a lot. Despite our differences, all I wanted was a nice mother-daughter weekend together. Outdoors, communing with nature. Getting in touch with the warrior within. While Kayla ate her trendy vegan diet, the rest of us would dig roots, pick berries, hunt animals. We would come together for dessert. We had two diet rules: 1) Unlimited chocolates and 2) Everyone eats what they kill. Rule one built community. Rule two protected our offspring when patience ran thin.

Kayla didn't believe me, but I was trying. As a concession to civilization and my easily grossed-out teen, I'd brought plenty of dental floss so she wouldn't have to see her mother with sinew hanging from her teeth. Still, I had my limits; Kayla would have to learn to accept them.

She flipped down the mirror to apply lipstick. I heard the unmistakable sound of a mister as she sprayed herself with yet more Flower Power. My eyes watered. Then she did her nails. I rolled down the window and tried to focus on nature, which was harder than it should have been, despite our being a hundred miles from the nearest town.

Finally, we arrived at the retreat. A narrow gravel road led up a hill to the grassy meadow in the forest where we would sleep a dozen to a teepee. Twelve teepees were already set up, their tanned hide walls stitched together with gut and painted with the stories of our exploits over the years. There were many images of women spearing animals. One picture story depicted the time Mavis shot a man with her crossbow. He should have known better than to wear brown in the woods the weekend of our retreat.

In the center of the circle of teepees was a fire circle. Gladys Badger Woman was already hauling wood in for the fire we'd need during the drumming we'd be doing later tonight. She had mighty thews and a big axe.

Other SUVs and ATVs were parked beside teepees while women offloaded weaponry, toilet paper, and auxiliary mail. The air was alive with jingling, jangling, clanking, and greetings.

Our meetings would be held in the lodge, a river-rock building just a short hike up the trail. To the left of the lodge, a flagstone deck held a stone altar and overlooked dry Starving Woman Creek. Other communal buildings were tucked further into the forest beyond the lodge.

I parked beside the executive teepee to unload;

Kayla scampered out to explore the rock cave in the nearby woods.

Three years ago, she'd been enthusiastic about coming on a Women Warriors retreat with me. She'd had the time of her life here. No whining then about what to save and what not to eat. I had a Polaroid of her in the bottom drawer of my desk at work. In the picture, she held up a half-cooked rabbit on a spit, and her mouth was smeared with animal fat. She wore the biggest smile I'd ever seen on her face.

You'd never catch her smiling at me like that now.

"First workshop starts in three hours," I called after her.

"Oh goody, arts and crafts. I can hardly wait."

"Force yourself," I said.

There were ten girls enrolled in the Teen Warriors program. The applied arts class was held in a lean-to constructed of sharpened bones and animal hides that opened to the front. It was a rustic look that practically screamed Don't Mess With Me! I thought it attractive enough that I had instructed our PR division to make postcards with an inscription reading "Wish you were here."

Kayla seemed determined to corrupt the others with her pacifist nonsense. It only took one wrong-headed person to ruin things for everyone else. So why did that one have to be related to me?

"I'll be back to check up on things," I whispered to Lanyard Lana, our arts group leader, and left to make sure the bow-stringing class was running smoothly. All the materials were in place for the mask-making workshop tomorrow. Another group had already speared a twelve-point buck and were gutting it in preparation for roasting over the coals for dinner. Everything looked well under control. I headed for the galley at the back of the lodge and watched Cookie stir her huge black cauldron. I smelled vegetable broth and frowned. Had Kayla somehow gotten to Cookie? "Need any help?" I asked, on the lookout for any white cubes that might be tofu.

She grinned. "One troll," she said. "That's all I ask. Enough for a decent broth, and the rest of them can go back to Idaho."

Trolls were a protected species. "Sorry," I said. "But I'll be glad to skin you a rabbit."

"Not the same," Cookie said with a sigh. "Goddess, I miss the good old days when you could kill anything you wanted."

I shrugged. "You gotta change with the times," I said, and waved good-bye.

I decided to drop by the sign-up desk. There was one problem with a credit check, but otherwise everything was in order. I checked on supplies. We had enough ammo and plastic wrap to last a year. The troll traps were set and my border guards were alert and on patrol.

Back at the lean-to, the girls were constructing chain mail from soda can pop tops, a very clever project, I thought, with proprietary pride. Then I saw Kayla's innovation. Instead of aluminum, her chain mail was made from paper gum wrappers.

She looked up, saw me, and got an impish grin. Before I could protest, she pulled a lighter and her perfume mister from her pocket. She coated her mail with Flower Power. "To peace," she said, and lit it on fire. The whole thing burnt to ashes within seconds.

I could barely see through my allergic tears.

"Kewl!" said one of the younger girls. "Can we burn ours, too?"

"I'd like a word with you, Kayla Marie," I said, and

took my daughter's hand to pull her outside. I forgot how to count to ten and was well into my lecture when I heard Cookie's monstrous laugh, followed by a child's horrified scream.

"Got one!" Cookie cackled.

"Oh no!" Kayla screamed, breaking away from my grasp. She ran up the hill, toward Cookie. "Murderers!"

I didn't have to see to know we had trapped our first troll.

I was sound asleep when I heard the camp guards sound the ram's horn. I heard booted footsteps approaching my teepee, and barely managed to rouse myself before a woman in a plated copper tunic thrust her torch before my face and said, "You'd better come out. When we did the bed check, we found a few irregularities."

"What type of irregularities?" I asked, stifling a yawn.

"Well," she said, keeping her cool. "The troll has been sprung, and, uhm . . ."

"Go ahead," I prompted. "Tell me." How bad could it be?

"I'm really sorry to report," she said with an expression so flat I could have used it as a mouse pad, "we think your daughter did it. She and the troll are missing."

I jumped up from my bed of skins and pulled on my light mail nightie and some sandals. I preferred sleeping au nature; because of the chafing factor. I lit a torch and rushed out to search the Jeep first, then climbed up to the tree house, then checked the arts and crafts lean-to. Empty.

I decided to look for her in the cave and headed down the pathway into the forest. The guard stomped along behind me. A breeze wavered our torches, but other than an occasional owl call and the mutter of leaves and pine needles in the trees above, the night was quiet.

The cave was too low for me to stand up straight in it. I crouched over and shone my light in the crevices as I explored. Mud caked on the knees of my nightie. The guard waited at the cave entrance, maybe to spare me embarrassment.

I caught sight of the tip of Kayla's eco-green sleeping bag, peeking out from under a rock overhang. I made my way toward her and crouched down until I could see beneath the overhang.

It was Kayla, all right—her Flower Power scent brought tears to my eyes—but there was something else, something dank, sour, and wild. I saw then that there were two bumps covered by the sleeping bag. One of them moved and I saw a hairy tuft and agate black eyes as a horrid little troll lifted its head and stared into my light.

My daughter was sleeping with the enemy.

I reacted instinctively and went for my weapon. For a wild moment, I wasn't sure who I wanted to slice up more, and I did my best to convince myself this was all something much more innocent than it appeared.

My hand groped for my knife, but I didn't have a knife sheath on my chain-mail nightie, which was strictly for trips to the latrine. All I had on my hip was an entrenching tool. I unhooked it and shook it in the air, making an unrecognizable screeching sound and knocking down a few nearby stalactites.

Kayla's head popped up beside the troll's. "Oh, Mother," she groaned, and covered her head again.

I stopped shrieking.

"Wolf?" the guard called from the cave entrance.

I recognized Gladys Badger Woman's voice. "Wolf Woman? You okay in there? What's going on?"

I got a good grip on my entrenching tool and counted off breaths, breathing in for four counts, holding for four counts, and breathing out for four counts. My torch hissed softly and spread a layer of carbon on the ceiling of the cave.

"Never mind," I called. "I'm fine."

The troll stared at me with the jail-yard stare of a hundred boys trying to psych out their girlfriends' mothers, that look that says, "You don't know what she does when you're not around, and you can't stop her." Reflected flames flickered in its black eyes.

My inner warrior was all set to deal with the situation. Let Kayla wake up with hot troll blood splattering all over her. Let her see that she was never too far away either physically or emotionally to escape my protection. How dare this hairy little slug think he was good enough for my daughter?

"What's that noise?" Kayla asked sleepily.

I tasted blood and realized that I'd bitten my lower lip with one of my surgically enhanced canines, an occupational hazard. I also realized I was growling.

I dug a small hole in the damp clay floor with the entrenching tool and stuck the torch in it, then crept toward the sleeping bag and the waking troll on my hands and knees. We had not broken our staring contest since its head rose from the sleeping bag. I wanted my hands around its neck in the worst way.

I knew if I hurt the damned thing Kayla would never forgive me. She was still mad that I'd stomped a spider in the house three weeks ago.

The closer I got, the worse its stench grew, though nothing could match the stunning strength of Flower Power. The troll's b.o. was almost refreshing next to Kayla's perfume. In fact, it startled me to realize I found it rather intriguing. I did my best to put any thoughts of intrigue out of my mind as I prepared myself for battle.

The troll sat up.

It was short and dense. Its head was shaped like an eggplant, with the tuft of dark, dread-locked hair rising from the stem end, its small agate eyes under a shelf of brow in the middle, and its broad, thin-lipped mouth across the big round part at the bottom. Ears like flyswatters stuck out on either side of its head. Its neck was invisible. Its shoulders were impressive under all the stinky, filthy hair. Even its muscles had muscles. It crossed its arms over its broad chest and dared me to come closer by flicking an agile, snake-split tongue at me.

My growl grew louder. I crept forward, right across my daughter's sleeping bag, until the troll and I were almost nose to nose. If you could call that little button a nose.

"Grrrr!"

It smiled and licked my nose like a grateful puppy. Disarmed by its friendliness, I didn't react for a second when it copped a feel. Not easy to do through mail, even light mail.

If it did that to me, what had it done to my daughter? Kayla's tender heart or not, nobody touched *me* without an invitation! Choose your issues, the counselor had said. Protected species or not, the beast was about to become troll sausage. I jumped on the troll, calling on my totem wolf to give me strength.

"Mother!" Kayla screamed. "Stop that this instant! Leave Sticky alone!"

There was something intoxicating about wrestling with the troll. The narrow confines of the cave forced us totally into each other's personal space. I found myself straining to breathe in its scent, and began to wonder if it exuded some sort of pheromone that interfered with my warrior abilities.

Pretty soon I had lost track of my original goal of killing it and concentrated solely on the pleasure inherent in roughhousing. It was pinching me, hard enough to hurt, and I pinched it back and felt proud to hear it gasp at my strength. Then it licked me with that tickly tongue, and now I gasped because I realized I was getting slightly more excited than was appropriate for a woman who thought she was being licked by a dog.

The troll was a worthy opponent, one of the few I had wrestled with recently who possessed a strength equal to mine. I couldn't help but be impressed by his power. In some ways, we were equals. We rolled around without letting go of each other. We smashed into walls and rocks and each other. He tickled my armpits with a stocky finger. I laughed. I couldn't stop.

I had my arms around the troll and he had his arms and legs around me and his mouth so close to my ear I felt his hot breath moisten my skin when I heard Kayla scream, "Mother!" in a tone of absolute shock.

It had been a long time since I'd startled *that* tone out of her.

The troll pressed his broad mouth against mine and licked my lips. The taste was not at all unpleasant. He hugged me one last time, then rolled off me and vanished down a narrow tunnel into the darkness.

I sighed. He was gone, yet his spicy taste lingered on my lips and his strong scent filled the cave like a pleasant memory. I wondered if I could work up a scent based on the troll's b.o. for the company. Would I name it "Attract" or "Repel"?

"Mother, how could you?" Kayla demanded.

I sat up. "I didn't kill it. I didn't even hurt it much."

"You terrified him!"

"I don't think so." I patted kinks out of my mail. The troll had really strong fingers. "Roll up that sleeping bag and get back where you belong, young lady."

"It's not fair," she said, and sniffled. She shoved ineffectually at her sleeping bag.

"Life's not fair. Actions have consequences. Your actions in particular are going to have some big consequences. Deal with it." I had a worry I didn't even want to bring into the light. After fighting with the troll, I knew he was male, horny, and well-equipped. What if Kayla's actions had the consequence of making me a grandmother to a half-troll child?

I blinked at her—my innocent baby. Hah! She was no more innocent than I was at that age. I remembered my mother's vague warnings when Ned and I were fooling around in the back seat of his Chevy. At the time I thought she didn't know what we were really doing.

Now I saw that she must have known, she just didn't know how to effectively deal with it. But Kayla and I had gone through counseling, so I knew better. At least, that was the theory. I decided to pretend nothing had happened, just like my mother.

I wanted to ground Kayla for letting that troll loose and sneaking off with it. She knew the camp's rules. Nobody stole someone else's catch.

Grounding, however, did not work on Kayla. Obedience to authority, mine in particular, was one of her issues.

I was tired of flashing my knife and my teeth to get her to do what I told her.

Maybe I should just lock her up in a troll cage.

She glanced up and caught me staring at her. "Mom," she whimpered, and my heart melted.

My head was still solid, though. "You're grounded," I said. It never worked, but what else could I do? "You're so grounded we're leaving for home at first light. No shopping or malls for a month! No TV for a week!" Any longer without TV and she would drive me crazy.

"Mom," she said again. I guess she realized I was serious. She snapped the sleeping bag over, flicked it so it rolled up, and stuffed it into a stuff sack. She *did* remember everything I'd taught her on our first camp-out.

Then she glared at me. "I hope you know, this is war. I challenge you!" She shook her head and looked down at me. "I'll never forgive you," she whispered.

"For what?"

"Stealing my boyfriend." She turned and crawled out of the cave, never glancing back.

When I woke up the next morning, I had the most beautiful collection of bruises I'd ever acquired, even in a lifetime of mock and real battles. Troll-pinching-mail-pinching-skin equaled bruises shaped like purple-black roses, mostly concentrated on my butt. I dressed in my everyday warrior woman wear, mail hauberk, stainless steel cuirass, and chausses, my mail stockings, which covered all my troll marks but the three hickeys on my neck.

Despite the already stifling heat, I unpacked my coif-de-mailles and put it on my head. It covered my head and shoulders, leaving only my face bare. My hair instantly dampened with sweat. It was going to be one of those days. I swallowed a salt tablet and chugged some water.

I pulled on my boots and loaded up on armaments. I really wanted to kill something. Preferably something big.

I stepped out of the teepee into the heat of the sun, and flashing light temporarily blinded me. Shading my eyes, I took another look.

A tall woman stood there in mail so shiny I knew it had never been fought in. She wore a helmet with a gray whale rampant for a crest.

I sniffled. Her birthday suit, the one I gave her when she turned fifteen. My daughter had finally put it on.

She raised her visor. The look in her eyes chilled me.

"Well," she said. "I hope you're happy now."

By all rights I should have been. She was armed and ready to fight. It was everything I had hoped for when we began this trip. Her upper lip curled into a snarl and her nostrils flared as she sniffed at the air. My daughter the warrior was ready to assert her final challenge to my authority.

The girls from the Teen Warrior program danced around screaming, "Fight! Fight! Fight! Fight! Fight!"

Cookie bent down to draw a circle in the dirt with her cooking spoon. Gladys Badger Woman, who was our warrior parliamentarian, cautioned, "No holds barred. Just remember our two rules."

I wanted to say, Stop. It's just a troll! He's not worth fighting over. But I couldn't bring myself to say the words. I tried to hold my head up. I faltered, just for a split-second, but probably long enough for her to see me show weakness. I gathered my thoughts and prayed to the Goddess for guidance. My strength returned. "Prepare to lick my boots," I said to Kayla.

"In your dreams," Kayla said. She started toward me, a full-fledged warrior.

In her cold expression, I saw enough of myself to be afraid.

Teenagers. What are you going to do?

The Thief & the Roller Derby Queen:

An essay on the importance of formal education

Eric Flint

The problem, in a nutshell, was that he had a lousy formal education. It didn't help, of course, that he suffered from delusions of grandeur. But if he'd stayed in school, he would have taken enough tests to realize that he was a dunce.

Being a dunce is okay, but you have to know your limitations. If you choose thieving as a profession, shoot for hubcaps instead of the Crown Jewels. For sure, don't try to steal from Satan. But that's exactly what he did.

Why did he do it? Well, partly because he was an

egomaniacal dunce. But, mostly, he did it because of his girlfriend.

So it's time to introduce her: Loretta Minisci. Twenty-two years old; five feet, ten inches tall; raven-black hair; brown eyes; beautiful; shapely; and possessed of an all-consuming passion to become the greatest witch who ever lived. *Her* problem, in a nutshell, is that while she was incredibly bright she didn't have any higher education either. And despite what you may have heard, it really takes a lot of book learning to be a great witch—much less the greatest witch who ever lived.

So, she was frustrated. Her spells never seemed to work quite the way they should (when they worked at all). And she couldn't use a lot of spells, because the really good spells are written in arcane languages, bizarre runes, and the like. You really need a Ph.D. to work through that kind of stuff, and she was a high-school dropout.

The worst of it, from Loretta's point of view, was that she wasn't able to summon demons. She tried, once, but the affair went badly. She followed all the instructions in the grimmoire, including the part about being naked while you do the incantation. That last was a piece of cake, for her, because she made her living as an exotic dancer in between roller derby matches. But because her education wasn't up to snuff, she didn't quite understand what a pentacle is. Stumbling through the words in the grimmoire, Loretta made the word out to be *tentacle*.

So there she was, when the demon materialized, surrounded by a pile of fried calimari.

"That stuff's like rubber," complained the demon. Then, ogling Loretta: "But what a babe!"

Things didn't go as badly as they might, because Loretta was used to fending off the advances of lustful males. And even though she wasn't wearing her roller derby pads, she still had a mean knee and a really vicious elbow smash. But it was sticky for a while, and she was always afraid to summon demons thereafter.

But what kind of great witch can't summon demons?

She brooded about the problem for several weeks. Then she decided that what she needed was a piece of brimstone. It's not clear where she got that idea. It's not in the literature, that's for sure. But Loretta had a tendency to invent her own recipes, which was one of the reasons her boyfriend insisted on eating out. (The other reason is that he felt a great thief should eat in fine restaurants, even if he couldn't read the menu.)

Now, mind you, fooling with recipes is no big deal when it comes to cooking. But it's really not a good idea when you're dealing with the underworld.

Loretta was just as stubborn as she was smart and good-looking. Once she got something in her head, that was that. Right off she started pestering her boyfriend to go to Hell with her and steal a piece of brimstone. She didn't actually know what brimstone was, but she remembered from her Sunday school days (which were a long way back) that there was lots of it in Hell.

The thief refused, at first, so Loretta withheld her affections (as they say). Eventually, he gave in. Loretta thought it was because he was terminally horny, but the truth is that the more he thought about the job, the more it appealed to his vanity. He liked to call himself the Cat, but his friends called him the Pussy (which, among his crowd, didn't have the same connotation at all).

"I'll show 'em," he muttered to himself. And he went to Loretta and agreed to do the job. "*Provided* you can get us into Hell."

"That's easy!" she exclaimed.

And it was. Any half-educated witch can get into Hell. The trick, of course, is getting back out.

Even then, she botched it. Loretta still hadn't figured out what a pentacle was, so when they arrived in Hell they were surrounded by fried calimari. Naturally, the smell drew every imp within range, because imps love seafood and there's a real shortage of it in the Pit of Damnation.

That's probably what saved them, for the moment, because the imps were so busy gobbling down the calimari that they didn't think to grab the trespassers until Loretta and the thief were on the lam.

Still, things looked bad.

Loretta and the thief were trying to make their escape across a field of ice. The thief was grousing and complaining the whole time because he'd dressed for what he thought Hell would be like, and sneakers and a bathing suit just didn't cut it. Loretta didn't hear him, however, because after the first five seconds she had skidded completely out of sight. *She'd* come to Hell in her roller derby outfit. (Damn what the book said; she wasn't about to deal with demons stark naked again.) And while the knee and elbow pads kept her from getting too badly scraped up, her roller skates were completely useless. Although, as it happens, they're probably all that saved her.

But we'll get to that in a moment. First, let's reexamine the moral of the tale.

The problem? *Lack of formal education.* Both Loretta and her boyfriend had gotten their ideas about Hell from watching TV evangelists late at night when there wasn't anything else on the tube. And the truth of it is that televangelists have the silliest ideas about Hell, as well as everything else. That doesn't hurt *them*, of course, since they always go to Heaven because God likes them even if they are a lot of con artists. (He's willing to forgive a pious scam. And it's not even a scam, anyway, because God favors faith a long way over brains so even the jerks who send in their money get to Heaven.)

But it was tough on Loretta and the thief. If they'd read Dante's *Inferno*, of course, they'd have known that Hell was a frigid wasteland.

Again: *lack of formal education*. Because if you trace it all back, you find that the preachers from whom they'd gotten their ideas were a poorly educated bunch themselves. Their ideas of Hell they'd gotten from the only book they'd ever read, which is the Bible. And while the Holy Book was accurate enough at the time it was written, you've got to stay abreast of the literature in your field. Satan does. Once the Devil read Dante's description of Hell in the *Inferno* he redecorated the whole place. Calls it Renaissance Chric.

Loretta got out okay due to blind luck. As it happens, the ice fields of Hell are almost frictionless. That's because the coefficient of— Never mind. No point going into the physics here. (The kind of people who'd buy a book like this—I haven't even seen the cover yet, but I'll guarantee it's covered with half-nekkid women wearing S&M gear—wouldn't follow it anyway.) (Oh, sure. Tell me it'll be on the coffee table when the guests arrive. Along with your leather-bound copy of Kant's *Critique of Pure Reason*.)

Like I said, frictionless. Two great roller-derby-queen-type strides into it and she was off her skates— *wham!*—right on her ass, sailing across Hell. Loretta steered herself as best she could, using her knee and elbow pads, but within five minutes she reached the Wall. (Yes, Hell has a boundary. It's flexible, of course. Depends, any given day or night, on the precise equation between damned souls and saved souls but, again, we'll skip the math. See reasoning above.)

She hit the Wall feetfirst. Anybody else would have broken their ankles. But Loretta was a roller derby queen, and she knew just how to handle collisions.

Next thing you know, she was skating up the Wall making her getaway. (Gravity works differently in Hell. Just trust me.) The Wall is infinite, of course, but she was saved by divine intervention. Once she got high enough to be noticed, an angel came and took her back home. Sports fan, he claimed, even though Loretta thought he was a regular in the club where she did her dancing, hiding his face at one of the back tables along with all the televangelists. Maybe not.

For the thief, on the other hand, things didn't go as well. At first, he was full of confidence. He always liked to brag to his friends that he'd never been caught. His friends always said that was because he never managed to actually steal much of anything. And it was true that he was better at the getaway part of the job than he was at the actual getting. (Which, when you think about it, kind of defeats the whole purpose of being a thief in the first place, but he was never smart enough to figure that out.)

The thief took one look at Loretta flying off and decided to try a different route. So he plunged into a snowdrift. Bright guy, like I said.

Soon enough, the thief was floundering around in the snow, freezing his ass off. He didn't get far, of course. After they finished gorging themselves on the calimari, the imps set off in hot pursuit. They had no trouble tracking him. They didn't even bother following his footsteps, they just followed the smell of suntan lotion. Imps know exactly what sun block smells like, because all surfers go to Hell.

(Yes, *all* of them. It's not that God has anything in particular against the sport. It's just that He hates the music of the Beach Boys, and He tends to over-react.)

(Hey, it's true, He does. Read the Bible. A little hanky-panky in Sodom and Gomorrah? BRONZE AGE HIROSHIMA. Eat the wrong fruit? LIVE BY THE SWEAT OF YOUR BROW, CHILDREN

BORN IN SORROW, PMS—the whole nine yards. Violate the building code? ALL LANGUAGES CAST INTO CONFUSION; MILLENNIA OF TRIBAL WARFARE. Eat shellfish? LOCUSTS. Jaywalk? SEVEN LEAN YEARS. Don't recycle? PLAGUE. Do this, ETERNAL DAMNATION; do that, ETERNAL DAMNATION. Strict is one thing. That Guy's into leather.)

Back to the story.

After they caught him, the imps straightaway hauled him up before the Prince of Darkness. The whole thing moved way faster than the thief expected, being, as he was, accustomed to the pace of the criminal justice system. Naturally, the dummy tried to cop a plea. (This is what's called "unclear on the concept.") The devils immediately convulsed with laughter.

"Wrong court, chump!" they howled.

The Prince of Darkness wasn't at all what the thief expected. No horns, no cloven hooves, no barbed tail. Just an ordinary-looking fellow, middle-aged, dressed in a navy blue Brooks Brothers suit. With a red power tie, naturally. He was sitting in an executive swivel chair on a raised mound in the very center of Hell, eating lunch off a TV tray. Around him, as far as the eye could see, stretched a horde of sinners squatting naked on the ice.

No, Satan didn't look like much, but the thief wasn't fooled for a minute. He wasn't bright, but he'd kicked around a lot. The Devil's lunch was the first tip-off. What you call a *real* power lunch: Satan was tearing the leg from a roasted baby and devouring it like a wolf.

"Unbaptised toddler." He burped. "My favorite."

That was bad enough. Then the thief spotted the tasseled Gucci loafers and the Rolex and knew he was really in deep trouble.

"I want a lawyer!" he cried. "Is there a lawyer anywhere around?"

Satan's minions started howling again. Two thirds of the horde of sinners scrambled to their feet. In less than a minute, a gigantic brawl erupted on the field of ice, millions of naked attorneys battling each other over the fee.

Eventually a wizened old character fought his way through the mob.

"Corporate lawyers," he sneered. "Punks."

"I'll take your case," he announced, extending his hand. "I'm Clarence Darrow."

Ignorant as he was, the thief had heard of Clarence Darrow. (Defense lawyers were of interest to him, given his profession.)

"But—you're famous! What are you doing here? You're supposed to be a good guy."

Darrow shrugged. "God's got a different opinion. At first I thought it was because of the Scopes trial. But then I found out it was really the Leopold and Loeb case that ticked Him off. The Lord views the insanity plea as a Personal affront, seeing as how He made man in His own image."

Clarence Darrow really was a great defense lawyer. Right off he entered a plea of not guilty on grounds of mental incapacity, arguing that only a moron would think of going to Hell to steal brimstone. Satan immediately agreed with him, but pointed out that Hell was the assigned eternity for imbeciles.

"It's not fair," admitted the Lord of Flies, "but I don't set the rules. God does. And you know how He feels about retards."

So then Darrow changed the plea to not guilty on the grounds that there was no crime involved anyway, seeing as how there wasn't any brimstone in Hell to steal in the first place. "It's like charging a man in a desert with trying to steal water," he argued.

This led to a long wrangle. The Devil responded that intent is as important as action in assessing a crime. That developed into a discussion of the metaphysical priority of mind vs. matter, which Darrow would have lost in a minute if he were in Heaven where (it goes without saying) Mind comes a long way before Matter. But he was a canny old lawyer, and he knew that Satan placed great store in things of the flesh.

Eventually, the Devil admitted the plea. The thief started to breathe easy, but not for long, because Satan right away charged him with trespassing.

"That's just a misdemeanor!" squealed the thief, before Darrow could shut him up.

"You dummy," growled the lawyer.

Sure enough, the Prince of Darkness and all his satanic subordinates were glaring at the thief like—well, like devils. "A *misdemeanor!*" bellowed Satan. He shredded what was left of the two-month-old sinner and hurled the hideous gobbets at the thief.

"Let me give you a taste of the punishment reserved for trespassers," he snarled.

The next instant the thief found himself transported into a realm of Hell that is so horrible and gruesome that even Dante couldn't bring himself to describe it. At the time, the thief thought it was for an eternity, but when he was hauled back Satan glanced at his Rolex and said: "How'd you like *that* thirty seconds?"

The thief was shaking all over. Tight-lipped, Darrow leaned over and whispered in his ear: "They're real big on the territorial imperative down here, stupe. From now on, keep your mouth shut and let me do the talking."

That said, Darrow went right back on the offensive, entering a plea of not guilty on the grounds that there were no signs posted informing the unwary traveler that Hell was private property.

The Devil spluttered. "What are you talking about, you lousy shyster? I don't need signs—everybody knows I own this place!"

Bingo. Jackpot. *Clarence Darrow for the defense!*

Because, naturally, as soon as God heard the Devil say that (He hears everything, of course) He blew His stack and intervened. Which was exactly what Darrow had counted on—winning on appeal to a Higher Court.

A great Presence manifested Itself.

NO YOU DON'T, BUM. I OWN THIS PLACE. I MADE IT, DIDN'T I? YOU JUST COLLECT THE RENT. (You can't put quotation marks around God's dialogue. He's unlimitable. First offense gets a rain of toads.)

Satan tried to squawk about jurisdiction, but that's really a flimsy argument when you're dealing with the Lord Almighty, Creator of the Universe. The Devil's usually a lot smarter than that, but he was caught off guard. In the end he irritated God so much that the Lord Above changed the terms of the lease.

FROM NOW ON, BUM, YOU DON'T GET THE UNBAPTISED BABES. (And that's how Limbo got created, in case you ever wondered.)

Satan gibbered with rage, which is an absolutely terrifying thing to see unless you happen to be God. After the display had gone on for a while, God got impatient.

ARE YOU FINISHED? IF NOT, I'LL CREATE A BIB TO CATCH THE DROOL.

Satan clamped his jaws shut.

THAT'S BETTER. NOW. WHAT'S THIS ALL ABOUT, ANYWAY?

God already knew what it was all about, of course. He's omniscient. But He gets some kind of weird kick out of acting dumb. (Always been like that. Remember the time, early on, when He was wandering through the Garden of Eden? Silly. A full-grown Supreme Being, acting like a Kid playing tag: "Yoohoo! Adam, where are you?")

Before the Devil could open his mouth, Darrow started talking. It was a great closing argument, too.

Then God announced His decision. He found in favor of the defendant on the grounds that while he was guiltier than sin the whole thing tickled the Lord's fancy. But the thief didn't get off scot-free, because God sentenced him to ten years in Purgatory before he would be released back to earth.

"What for?" whined the thief.

BECAUSE YOU'RE AN IDIOT.

Then God smote the Devil with a bolt of lightning. Contempt of court.

Finally, He glowered at Darrow. (Actually, God's immaterial. It was more that the whole Universe took on a sense of all-pervading GLOWER, aimed at Darrow.)

YOU RAT. YOU LOUSE.

The old man was a plucky character, you've got to hand it to him. "What did I do—besides win another defense case?"

THAT'S THE WHOLE POINT, DARROW. AS YOU WELL KNOW. MAN IS GUILTY OF ORIGINAL SIN, SO HOW CAN HE BE INNOCENT? YOUR WHOLE LIFE WAS AN AFFRONT TO ME, AND YOU'RE *STILL* DOING IT!

Darrow sneered. "So damn me to Hell, then."

God was silent. After all, what could He say? It's the ultimate problem in penal science, when you think about it. How do you punish a lifer who's already dead?

In the end, of course, Darrow caught it from the Devil after God left. Satan was purely furious about the whole affair.

"You're promoted," snarled the Prince of Darkness, and he gave Darrow the premier spot in Hell, on the ninth level. Satan even added a fourth mouth to his clone (which, contrary to Dante, isn't actually the Devil himself) so that Clarence Darrow could join Cassius, Brutus and Judas Iscariot as a chewee.

But Darrow wasn't fazed. Right away he introduced himself to his neighbors.

"Boy, am I glad to see you," said Judas.

"It was temporary insanity!" cried Cassius. "Caused by eating junk food. Shakespeare's my witness. He said himself I had 'a lean and hungry look.'"

"I had a warped childhood," whined Brutus. "Too much privilege."

As for the thief, he had ten years to think over the course of his life. Ten *long* years, because Purgatory is a doctor's waiting room. And he never got any time off for good behavior because he screwed up. (Tried to steal a six-year-old copy of *Sports Illustrated*. Wasn't even the swimsuit issue.)

But eventually, he served the time, and was materialized back in Loretta's cellar.

And found that the cellar was now the TV room of a very large and muscular truck driver who immediately beat him to a pulp. Partly for trespassing, but mostly because he materialized in front of the TV set in the last ten seconds of the Super Bowl with the go-ahead field goal on its way. The truck driver had four friends with him, too. Raiders fans.

A few days later, when the thief got out of the hospital, he went looking for Loretta. It took him weeks, but eventually he tracked her down to a very fancy house in a very nice part of town.

His tongue was practically hanging out as he rang the doorbell. Ten years' abstinence, you understand.

Loretta was there, all right. She even opened the door wearing her roller derby queen gear, all the way down to the knee and elbow pads. That had him salivating immediately. He'd always loved that outfit! I've got to tell the truth, now that we're getting to the end of the story. That thief was a warped, depraved, degenerate, kinky sicko. The only books he ever bought had covers just like this one.

Alas. She wasn't Loretta Minisci, stripper, would-be witch, anymore. She was still a roller derby queen—*the* roller derby queen, in fact—but she was also Mrs. Loretta White, Ph.D. (Harvard—*summa cum laude, Phi Beta Kappa*, the whole shot). It turns out that a week after she got back from Hell she met a chemist at the supermarket and while they were chatting in the cashier's line he explained to her that brimstone was just another word for sulfur, which, (hey, what do you know?) he happened to have a lot of in his laboratory and before they even got there she'd fallen in love with the mousy little guy and one thing led to another and ten years later she'd not only earned her Ph.D. in chemistry but had been able to apply her talent for witchcraft to revolutionize the entire science, and, no, she'd love to talk (*How have you been, anyway? Still stealing?*) but she had to catch a plane for the Olympics where she was going to win the gold medal—she'd gotten the sport internationally recognized just last year, *isn't that great?*—before she had to catch another plane to Stockholm to accept the Nobel Prize. *Bye.*

The thief went berserk at that point and tried to force his affections upon her (as they say). But that's really not the best seduction technique to use on a roller derby queen. A few knees and elbows later, Loretta was off to catch her plane and the thief went back into the hospital for a few more days.

Things went downhill from there.

He started thieving again, but the truth is that it's a young man's game and he was over the hill. Ten years out of practice, too. So he got caught. Hubcaps, believe it or not. He tried to steal them off a slow-moving car in the inaugural parade—yeah; Limo One. Sent up for three years. (Would have been way more—assassination attempts get twenty, easy—except the psychiatrist informed the court that the thief didn't know the names of any presidents since Abraham Lincoln led the war of independence against George Washington III.)

After he got out, he lasted on the streets for six weeks before he was sent back to prison. Stealing hubcaps, again. In the pits, at the Daytona 500. Five years. No time off for good behavior because they caught him trying to steal—never mind. You wouldn't believe it.

The next time he got caught he was a three-time loser and so they sent him up for life in the toughest prison in the state. He survived six, count 'em, six hours. After finding himself with two cellmates wearing "Aryan Nation" tattoos and reading weird books about women in armor, he got into a religious discussion in which he explained that he had met Satan personally and could assure them that the Devil was a white man.

So there he was, back again, a thief in Hell.

"I want Darrow!" he cried.

But the Devil just laughed at him. "Not this time, chump. You've already been convicted. No trial. No rights. No appeals. And I've been waiting for this day to come."

Satan rubbed his hands together with glee. It sounded like a rattlesnake. "Boy," snickered the Lord of Flies, "have I got plans for you."

And he did, too. Grotesque plans. Horrible plans. Indescribable plans. The worst thing you could imagine.

He made the thief listen to one performance of Wagner's *Parsifal* (which, of course, lasts for eternity).

It all goes to show the importance in the modern world of getting a formal education.

Although, now that I think about it, maybe it wouldn't have made much difference in the thief's case. Ignorance can be fixed. Stupid is forever.

The Right Bitch

Doranna Durgin

Sabre whooped with enthusiasm, barreling through the woods' thick undergrowth, his nose full of *magicsmell* and his ears full of Taliya's distant encouragement, with his brain too hot on trail to think. So hot he almost missed the answering trail cry to the south, a slightly clearer voice than his own and closing in fast. It made no sense; he didn't care. Not with the quarry so close, his sweaty, unwashed *humansmell* strong with forbidden magic.

But suddenly the trail doubled, adding more *humansmell* to the *magicsmell*, and Sabre understood. *Two smugglers*, joining forces, both being trailed.

Sabre called out, wild and strong. Confident.

The second dog sounded again, nearly in his ear, and charged onto his trail, cutting him off. He got a glimpse of flying black ears, smelled the blood of bramble-torn skin, and then saw nothing but dog butt, right in his face.

Bitch-butt.

Shiba, he realized instantly, checking his speed so he wouldn't plow right into her. Shiba, whom his linewoman mentioned far too often, and with far too much attention to the discriminating nature of her nose. And when *would* everyone forget about that vaunted critter episode?

She might have a nose, but she couldn't match his speed. "Oowh! Oowh!" he bellowed, demanding and impatient, finally—and rudely—shoving her aside to fly by at top speed.

Show-off speed.

The kind of speed to run him straight into trouble. Into—

Sabre yelped as a whip lashed across his head, popping a welt on one sensitive ear; he flung himself aside, yipping like a pup as the lash landed again. "Git on, you cur!" the man jeered, and Sabre tumbled down, rolling aside, hearing Shiba gone wise and silent—*in retreat*—leaving him to—

"Watch out!" the other human cried, too late for his partner to respond to the black and silver blur heading his way. Shiba uttered not a sound as the lash fell across her back, but leapt up to grab the stout leather whip handle, as intent on it as on any trail-prey. Beyond her, the other human took flight again.

"Shiba—call!" commanded her lineman—not so far away, now—and Shiba barked *treed* for him, dropping the whip.

"Sabre! Call!" Taliya shouted as Sabre climbed to his feet and shook off, sending bits of leaves and dirt and grit flying. He managed a half-hearted bark and ruefully pawed his stinging ear.

Shiba made enough noise for both of them. He got his first good look at her, then, as the linemen approached from their separate directions. Beautiful, she was—well-muscled, long-limbed, a graceful neck and lovely arch to her tail. Where Sabre was heavily marked with black—his blueing so thick it looked mottled instead of ticked, his head and chest heavy and masculine—Shiba stood a sturdy but clean-lined bitch, her back and head glossy black, her ticking so perfectly distributed that it appeared silver-blue from even a short distance.

Sabre felt an immediate and intense dislike.

And she was the one standing on tree, backing the man against a stout oak, while Sabre stood spraddle-legged and dazed as the linemen arrived, more or less simultaneously. *She* wore bramble-guard, a leather chest plate and canvas body jacket. *She* probably hadn't even felt the whip.

Sabre gave a small sneeze of frustration and pawed his head again. He never wore bramble-guard . . . because he could never stop himself from chewing it to bits.

"There should be two," Taliya said breathlessly, leaving Shiba's man to handle the magic smuggler as she kicked the whip well out of reach and dropped to her knees beside Sabre. Her long, tawny braid fell over her shoulder to brush the top of his head. "There, now, son. Got you a good one, didn't he?"

Despite himself, desperately wishing Shiba's sharp brown gaze pointed elsewhere, Sabre whined in response. *Hurts.* And when Taliya soothed him, he wagged his tail in silly submissive little jerks and whined again. Couldn't help it. Never could, where Taliya was concerned.

Shiba looked away as though embarrassed for the both of them.

"Well, there's only the one," Shiba's man—Tallon, that was his name—said, sounding frustrated. "The other must've gotten away. Sons of bitches, taking a *whip* to him—"

Taliya looked up from Sabre, who'd managed to insinuate himself into her lap, even though she was kneeling and had no real lap of which to speak. "How'd you train her for that? These dogs don't have an aggressive hair on their bodies, not when it comes to people."

Tallon shook his head, still pensively looking off in the direction in which the smuggler had escaped. "Didn't train her. Ever since the critter-based magic smuggling ring last fall, she's been impossible to keep off dangling things—laundry, ropes, hair, you name it. She's got a real grudge against the ugly things—and you know the way their tails hang down when they're treed. I don't hang my socks out to dry where she can reach them anymore."

The other side had concocted their scheme knowing that the linehounds were trained off critter trail, and had used the critters to carry minor magics and amulets, hoping to confuse the hounds. Only pups took a second sniff at critter trail—and any adult dog caught chasing them was retired. It had nearly happened to Shiba, Sabre knew.

"They all hate the critters," Taliya said mildly, which was true enough—no polite linehound would even think their true name, but used only the nickname commonly applied by humans.

"Shiba more than most, these days." He looked after the escapee and shook his head. "*Damn.*"

Taliya nodded at Shiba. "Is she sound? Send her on."

Tallon shook his head. "We've near reached the border already. I won't send her into that alone."

But she would have gone. Even Sabre could see that. And he would have joined her. That's what they did, the linehounds—patrolled the border between Ours and Theirs, sniffing out magic smugglers who wanted to contaminate Ours *with* Theirs.

"Smart man," said the captive, derisive despite the newly applied restraints. "You be smarter, you'll give up on those damn curs right now. They do you no good, soon enough."

Tallon silenced the man with an intense look; Taliya

swapped her appraisal from Shiba to her lineman, impressed. Sabre lifted his nose to the subtle scent of new magic, a strange, rich *magicsmell* he'd not encountered before. He couldn't sort it out.

He looked at Shiba, but she'd rediscovered the whip and snatched it up to administer a kill-the-rat death shake. The tolerant affection on Tallon's face gave Sabre a funny itchy feeling—except he couldn't quite figure out where the itch was, only that it was subtle and as invasive as a tick creeping across belly flesh.

Whipped. Embarrassed. Itchy.

More than a good linehound could take. Sabre hid his aching head under Taliya's arm.

Rumors flew. Sabre heard them when Taliya brushed him down—curried him, actually, massaging him while bringing the dirt up on his short, slick coat.

"Something big going on," Taliya told him, knocking the brush clean against the side of their well-appointed log cabin. The line cabins ran along the border between Theirs and Ours, all more or less identical dwellings—if you didn't count the personal touches the linemen added.

Taliya had added plenty. Nice curtains—even if there was no one in these woods to close them against—a special platform for Sabre's food bowl, a niche below the raised porch for his cool summer-time bed. He slept in the cabin with her, anyway.

Sabre applied a hind foot just behind his ear, still looking for that itch, not concerned with Taliya's gossip; the sound of her voice was enough. He paused, examining his foot—yep, still his—noted the continuing presence of the itch, and tried again, this time on his cheek, careful not to poke himself in the eye.

"Something they think will put us out of business, Sabre-old-boy."

Sabre-old-boy. One of his favorites. He stopped scratching again to pant happily at her. Early morning summer sunshine, just been brushed, about to go on patrol . . . Yes. *Happy*. He nibbled absently at his shoulder. And at some point he became aware of Tallon's approach, Shiba with him . . .

Not important. Maybe if he pretended they weren't there, his morning would stay just between him and Taliya. So he nibbled, even catching wind of the strange human with them, and didn't warn Taliya—though he was sorry when she jumped at Tallon's words, and even sorrier at her look of reproach.

"Looks like it's time for a dip," Tallon said.

As if Sabre had *fleas*.

"Grmph," Sabre said, a half-hearted grumble of greeting, making it clear they weren't worth barking at. Not even the strange man . . . he'd had magic on him once, but no more, and besides, his hands were tied behind his back. And Shiba . . . she went without bramble-guards today, and her coat shone in the sun, deep glossy black.

He still didn't like her.

"Just did one," Taliya said easily, as if no flea-born insult had passed. She even looked downright glad to see Tallon. "Been out on patrol already?"

"Had a tip yesterday—caught this one just after dawn. We were close, so . . ."

"Let me get some water for Shiba," Taliya said, picking up Sabre's dish.

Sabre's dish. "Grmph," he said, but no one seemed to be listening. And worse, he detected the strange new *magicsmell*. Shiba smelled it; she must. There— her nose twitched; she had the same puzzled look in her eye that Sabre felt on his own wrinkling brow. But she said nothing, merely took a polite drink from the water Taliya presented and stood by Tallon's side as Taliya gave him cellar-cooled tea and one of her own breakfast biscuits. And finally came to the point.

"What's this one been up to?" she asked, jerking a thumb at the sullen prisoner.

"He ditched the contraband before we reached him," Tallon said. "It doesn't matter. The point is more, what *will* he be up to? My source said he's a minor player—but he's got information. I thought you might be interested."

Taliya grinned, a surprisingly predatory expression. Sabre stopped sniffing the air to give her his full attention. Maybe the morning had lost its *happy*, but it had certainly turned interesting.

"Not telling you nothing," the prisoner grumbled, though no one had, strictly, asked. "Don't lay a hand on me, rules say you can't."

Taliya smiled beatifically; a slow grin spread across Tallon's face at the sight. "*I'm* not going to touch you," she said. "Except for this." And with two fingers on his shoulder, she guided him down. With a suspicious glance at Tallon, the man went to his knees, backed up against the house and with Tallon at his side to keep him there. "You just wait there," she said. "Tallon and I are going to discuss the dogs."

"We are?"

"We are. Sabre, son, come here."

Sabre complied immediately, for she had her *good dog* voice on. He didn't like standing so close to the man, but Taliya positioned herself so he had little choice. "Thatta boy," she said. "Tallon, you haven't been properly introduced to Sabre. He's the fastest thing on trail you'd ever hope to see." Ooh, that was definitely the *good boy* voice. Sabre's tail waved with pleasure. "In fact," she said, her voice going positively gooey, "he's the *best* linehound I ever hope to be with. He's *such* a good boy."

Oh, joyful! Sabre's tail whipped the air, impeded only by something soft and yielding and inconsequential. He ignored the strangled noises behind him; all that mattered was Taliya. His linewoman, cooing at him, admiring him, praising him . . . oh, delight! His tail exploded into frenzied activity.

"I'll talk! I'll talk! Just get that dog away from me!"

Startled from his Taliya-worship, Sabre glanced back to discover the man had turned a strange shade of pale green and was all hunched over, hands still tied behind him. He gave the distinct impression that he was trying to cover his groin with his elbows.

Somehow, he nearly succeeded.

Taliya gave him a partial reprieve. "Sit, Sabre," she said, and Sabre plunked his bottom down, his tail sweeping back and forth across the earth. She put her hands on her hips and cocked her head at the man. "Talk, then. Make it good. I still haven't said hello to Shiba."

"No, no*no*—have mercy! I'll tell you what I know! It's not much—"

"Just talk," Tallon growled, but Sabre thought he hid a smile.

"All I know . . . it's gonna happen soon. They've got a way to smuggle in a receiver spell, and once it's in, they'll trigger the other half from over the border. It'll make a safe corridor, one the dogs can't detect—they'll be able to bring magic right through."

Taliya and Tallon exchanged a glance. "How're they going to get the first spell through?" Tallon said. "How are they so sure they'll get it past the dogs?"

"I don't know," the man said, but he'd turned sullen, and wouldn't look either of them in the eye. Or at the dogs, for that matter Shiba had inched closer, scenting the air, eyes glinting with intensity, watching Taliya, following the swaying path of Taliya's long, thick braid against her lower back.

And Sabre scented it too, that strange magic again, the one that swirled around so close to imperceptible, not attached to any one person or thing. Although . . .

He turned a suspicious eye on Tallon.

Tallon was in no position to notice. "Taliya," he said, one firm hand keeping the man on his knees, "what was it you were saying about Sabre? What an excellent linehound he is?"

"Skunk!" the man squealed.

Tallon tightened his grip. "Watch your mouth!"

"No, skunk, skunk!" Desperately trying to protect himself with his elbows, the man did a strange twisting dance on his knees and babbled away. "They've got a skunk! Two skunks! Enhanced ones! They'll dump 'em right in front of the dogs, damn curs won't be able to sniff an outhouse in a sweet spring meadow." He jerked his head at Shiba. "Her, especially. After she broke up the [critter]-smuggling ring last season, they know they'll never get by her nose with *this*."

Crude! He'd said the true-name for *critter* right there in front of Taliya! Sabre, increasingly irritated by both the untraceable *magicsmell* and his undefined itch, went so far as to growl.

"Softly, son," Taliya said, though she, too, had a gleam in her eye.

Shiba moved forward, her head low, her expression intent. The kind of expression that meant a linehound had scented prey, and scented it so close that nothing mattered but the nose and the prey; not even the linemen could deter a dog so focused. And Sabre, agitated, lifted his nose to the new *magicsmell* and felt himself slipping into that same state; he growled again, despite himself.

"Sabre!" Taliya said sharply, turning to point a warning finger at him . . . turning suddenly enough that her braid swung briefly out from her body, then thumped gently against her back.

Too much for Shiba. She leapt, belling *trail* and

treed in a strange combination of voice and bearing straight down on Taliya.

Astonished Taliya, standing there with her arms akimbo and her jaw dropped, crouching slightly as though to run and no time to do it . . .

Too much for Sabre—*Magicsmell! Trail-cry!*—who bounded right over the top of Shiba, bearing straight down on Tallon.

Astonished Tallon, standing there with his arms akimbo and his jaw dropped, crouching slightly as though to run and no time to do it.

Magicsmell! Magicsmell! Oowh! Treetreetree! The trail-haze slowly lifted from Sabre's mind, allowing a slow trickle of input from his surroundings.

Bellowing humans made up the biggest part of it. Tallon, bellowing at Shiba—as best he could with Sabre perched on his chest and bawling in his face—his head twisted aside, his eyes squinched shut, one hand cupped protectively over that soft spot halfway down his body and the other ineffectually shoving at Sabre's broad chest.

Taliya, bellowing at Sabre—as best she could with her hands clamped firmly around her long braid, bent at the waist in a futile attempt to get more leverage than Shiba, whose jaws clamped firmly around the thick rope of hair.

"Get off!" they finally managed, more or less in unison. "*Bad dogs!*"

Uh-oh.

No more *happy*.

How and when the prisoner escaped, no one was quite sure.

How and when Taliya and Tallon came up with the idea to work together, Sabre couldn't imagine.

How and when they come up with the idea to work each *other's* dogs, he didn't *want* to know.

Maybe it had something to do with events when

they'd tried to team up. *Disgrace* was a word that came to mind. Definitely not *happy*. But who could blame a linehound for being a linehound? With *magicsmell* all around them, what were they supposed to do? Not his fault that the smell led him unerringly to Tallon. Not Shiba's that Taliya somehow did the same to her. Sent out to patrol in sweeps, the linehounds inevitably ended up back with the linemen, barking a subdued and chagrined *treed*, until both humans were flushed and embarrassed and frustrated. At that, the strange *magicsmell* seemed to fade, and Shiba—*critterspawn*, but she *did* have a fine nose—picked up the scent of familiar magic, leading Sabre along until the trail came clear to him.

They had worked it slowly, carefully—and had to, because the smugglers were on horseback, and had taken wild leaps from one place to another, traveled some distance up a deeply running creek, and wound their trail around in overlapping circles. Together, they closed on the smuggler, running side by side, picking up speed—

Together, they had run into the skunk.

"God and goddess," Tallon said now, his eyes watering visibly as he dumped another container of stewed tomatoes over Shiba's back, there in the side yard of his little cabin. "There's got to be a better way to handle this. We're lucky the smugglers spooked back to the other side of the border." He took a rough scrub brush to Shiba's back, smearing tomato into her coat—most unpleasantly, to judge by how flat she'd plastered her ears to her skull.

Critter, he didn't have to judge it by anything. Taliya did the same to him, rubbing sticky smelly tomato into his face, between his paws, along the velvet length of his ears, doing nothing for the itch that ever plagued him . . .

Not happy.

"They'll be back," Tallon persisted, "and we can't take the chance that they'll get through this time."

"No," Taliya said, dumping a big cold bucket of water over Sabre, a gleam coming into her eye. "We can't."

That might have been it, right there—the beginning of the idea. Not that Taliya had had a chance to say so just then, not after dumping another bucket over him, not after Tallon did likewise to Shiba, leaving the two hounds with their heads scrunched down between their shoulders, water streaming off their ears, dripping off their tails, running off their brows and sheeting across their flews.

They exchanged a glance, the dogs did, knowing the humans were engaged in developing some important Human Thoughts. Sabre felt a sudden kinship with Shiba the too-perfect, an admiration for the sly way she lowered and cocked her head, a sudden desire to emulate . . . humans distracted . . . wait till they lean closer . . . wait . . . wait . . . .

Shake off!

Yes, maybe that had done it. And this partner-swapping was meant to be some sort of punishment.

It seemed entirely likely to Sabre. He'd somehow gotten *used* to patrolling with Shiba. He missed her. And now he missed Taliya, even though he knew that the linewoman and Shiba weren't far behind. Shiba was probably harnessed and leashed, just as he was, probably even wearing her bramble-guard.

Humiliation.

And why did Tallon call ahead to him, constant encouragements, using Shiba's name?

Humiliation.

Until he struck the scent of magic, and forgot his woes in the thick glory of it. He forgot Shiba, he forgot Taliya . . . he even forgot about the skunk. He loped swiftly through the woods, nose to ground, thoughts consumed by *magicsmell, humansmell, horsesmell.* Vaguely, he heard Shiba backing him, but the rough frustration in her voice meant that she remained harnessed.

The scent was his, and he took it. *Gloryglory magicsmell!* He poured on the speed, glorying in that too, in his strength and confidence and certainty that these smugglers had no chance to escape—

Skunk! He literally tripped over the creature, staked right in the scent trail on a short chain. *Skunk!*

Mad skunk.

Mad skunk lifting its tail.

Sabre's eyes snapped shut, his trail cry cut short into gagging and sneezing. His sinuses instantly swelled; his nose began to run. He heard the skunk stamp its front feet imperiously—*again*—and flung himself blindly away from the creature—no seconds for him, no, no! He threw himself on the ground, rolling and whimpering and rubbing his face against the leaves and dirt in a frantic effort to relieve the sting.

At last, someone snagged his collar and dragged him away from the skunk. *Taliya!* He threw himself into her lap and met not her rangy curves, but unfamiliar angles of muscle and bone. *Tallon. Not his.* But as Sabre gathered himself to dive for the ground again, Tallon caught him up by the jowls and held him firmly, rubbing a wet cloth over his eyes and nose. Cool, soothing, something herbal . . . Sabre stopped struggling, if not whining. "Sorry, son," Tallon told him, tossing the cloth away and digging out a fresh one, soaked in tomato juice. "It was the only way." He scrubbed at Sabre's face, borderline harsh, and then brought out yet another cloth. This one he used more gently, wiping away the juice, smoothing Sabre's fur back into place with a petting motion, even wiping along his gums and jowls.

When he was through, Sabre blinked up at him, panting, able to breathe and see again. He gave a tentative wag of his tail and Tallon smiled at him. "Good boy."

Oooh. A *good boy*!

Not far—though definitely upwind—Taliya called to them. Not her human voice, but two short yipping barks. Tallon answered in kind, locating them, and in only a few moments, Shiba took up the trail cry.

Sabre understood, then.

They'd used him, used his speed . . . made the smugglers think Shiba was on their trail so they'd deploy their second skunk . . . and now Shiba had circled round him, her nose protected and intact, and taken up the trail.

He felt a strange twitch of pride. They'd not get past her. He barked, trying to back her even from here, and whined his most beseeching whine at Tallon. It rarely worked on Taliya; she was inured to it. But Tallon . . . Sabre could see him softening. He didn't need his nose to back Shiba, he needed only his legs, and he still had those. He still had his speed; he could catch up to her without trouble. He whined again, wagging just the tip of his tail, and widened his eyes in hopeful attention.

"God and goddess," Tallon muttered. "How *does* she resist you?"

Sabre knew permission when he heard it. He sprang to his feet, dug in his claws, and sprayed dirt and leaves into Tallon's face with his takeoff. Tongue lolling, eyes squeezed into slits against the undergrowth, he ran flat-out through the woods, his body stretching, coiling, exploding, barely heeding the obstacles in his way. He knew he was on trail again by the deep hoofprints before him, signs of the horse being pushed to speed in these tight woods.

And then Shiba was just ahead—first just her belling voice in his ears, and then her butt in his face. *Bitch-butt*.

Sabre was glad to see it.

He hung back, trusting her nose, until he saw the flash of movement through the trees. Then his bark roughened, grew choppy; he found a place to pass her and did, surging into his powerful speed. In moments he was barking *treed*, leaping up against the side of the horse to reach the magic carried on the man who rode it.

"[Critter]-spawn!" the man spat as the horse faltered; he jerked on the reins, fighting the creature while Sabre leapt at them again and again, knocking them both off balance, delaying them, not even considering that the man might turn the horse against him until one hard hoof landed on his front leg, briefly trapping him . . . snapping the limb in a clean break.

Sabre didn't even feel it, not with his quarry so close; he didn't need all four legs to throw himself at the man, and the injury barely slowed him. But it stole his agility, and the man easily kicked him aside; Sabre's strong tail was the next to break, and by then he was beginning to feel his hurts, hesitating—

The man was not. He drove the horse onward, kicking it into compliance, aiming it at Sabre . . .

Shiba. Bellowing all the while, she bounded into the fray from behind and with one mighty leap latched onto the horse's tail midway up its length. The animal froze—an instant only, and then it hunched its back and kicked out, but she was too high up, too close, for the kick to do anything but knock her aside; she was back on the tail in an instant, worrying it, growling, fierce in her trail fury. And all the while the man hammered his heels into the horse, yanking its head around, still trying to aim for Sabre, who'd taken up barking a steady *treed* for Tallon and Taliya, right in the animal's face.

And then he shook out the whip. He lashed at Shiba, the kind of feeble strike that would barely affect her through the bramble-guard, and which hit the horse right along with her.

Too much for any horse, even a good one—which this was not. It launched into a bucking protest, dislodging both Shiba and the smuggler.

Shiba landed on her feet. The smuggler, not as agile, rolled to a dazed stop on his stomach. Unlucky for him that he had clipped his long, scruffy hair at the back of his head. Unlucky. Just as he made the effort to prop himself up on his elbows, Shiba landed on his back, audibly driving the air from his lungs as she latched on to the trailing tail of hair. She braced her feet on his back and *pulled*. His head came up, the skin of his face stretched back and a squeak of protest in his throat. Sabre hobbled forward, stuck his nose in the man's face, and bellowed *treed* as loud as he could.

Which is exactly how Taliya and Tallon found them.

Sabre shifted his awkwardly splinted leg and woofed to let Taliya know they had visitors. Tallon and Shiba, as of course had been the case every day since Tallon had carried Sabre back to this cabin— with the help of a sling made from the smuggler's shirt, for no man carries a densely boned, muscle-packed linehound far without help, not even a line-man trying to impress a linewoman. And once the smuggler was secured, and Sabre's hurts tended, Taliya seemed quite impressed indeed.

Now she came out of the cabin, raising a hand in greeting as Tallon and Shiba broke through the trees surrounding their cabin. Tallon went to Sabre first— *wise man*—offering a treat of dried meat; Sabre accepted it delicately between his front teeth and swallowed it whole.

He was learning to wag his bottom instead of his broken tail.

Shiba sniffed Sabre's toes—*still his*—and sat nearby while Tallon went to greet Taliya. He seemed to have some sort of treat for her, too, although it didn't smell like dried meat. Nothing important, then. Sabre would have ignored them altogether if the strange *magicsmell* hadn't filled the air. He'd finally realized the truth of it the day before—when this same thing had happened yet again.

The magic wasn't Tallon. It wasn't Taliya. It was something that happened when the two of them came together, and he was critter-bedamned if he could understand why.

But it did make Taliya *happy*. And it made her *not happy* when Sabre fussed about it, and especially when he jumped on Tallon, so though it tore at his linehound sense of duty, he was willing to ignore the *magicsmell*. For her.

Shiba seemed to have come to the same conclusion. Though her eyes glinted and her nose flared at the scent of it, she turned her back on the humans— why did they lean so close to one another, anyway?— and sniffed Sabre's toes again, her long, graceful ears brushing his feet.

Ooh, that itch again. *Where*—he nibbled his side—*not there*—and lifted a hind foot to his ear— *not there*—and tried desperately to reach the spot under his splinted front leg—*no, not there*—and then noticed that Shiba had engaged herself in the same sort of frustrated exercise. She twisted herself around, trying to reach the loose skin directly over her spine, that glossy black fur twitching with her efforts . . .

Mesmerized, Sabre gave up on his own scratching and reached over to nibble the spot for her. To his utter astonishment, his own vague prickling sensations instantly vanished. Shiba regarded him in momentary surprise, then—still twisted around—she solemnly cleaned his face with her tongue.

It seemed he'd finally found the right bitch to scratch.

Foxy Boxer Gal Fights Giant Monster King!

Pierce Askegren

"So this is Japan," Jenna Ferguson said. "Everything's so different." She took another bite from her Big Mac, chewed the two all-beef patties, special sauce, cheese, pickles, onions and sesame seed bun, then swallowed.

Teruhisha smiled. They were seated beneath the sign of the golden arches and looking out through spotless windows at busy downtown Tokyo. Some of the local residents, mostly men, were looking back in, and Jenna knew they were looking at her.

That was understandable; even sitting down, Jenna stood out.

She was a redhead, with fair skin and green eyes, and a great body that put her a full head taller than most men. Right now, she was eating her second sandwich and watching Teruhisha work on his meal, which had been something of a surprise. Jenna had never seen rice on a McDonald's menu before.

"I am so pleased you are enjoying yourself, then," Teruhisha said, positively beaming. He spoke American that was almost perfect, with only the faintest accent. Sometimes he used words that Jenna didn't understand, but that was okay; it happened in America, too. "Later, if you like, I will tell you more of our city," Teruhisha continued. "Over dinner, perhaps?"

Jenna ate a French fry. Eating was a good way to paper over awkward gaps in a conversation and calories weren't a problem for her. A minimum of three hours a day working out, with free weights and Nautilus, with the jumping rope and the heavy bag, and she burned off the food as fast as she could eat it.

Jenna had arrived in Japan a week before, and Teruhisha Kitahara had been her almost constant companion. Connected somehow to the Japanese government, Teruhisha had met her at a reception and done his best to make his presence known ever since. He had cheerfully served as a combination tour guide, escort, and translator. Jenna knew that he wanted to serve her in other ways, too, but she didn't think that was going to happen.

"I am very glad you have decided to stay in our city, after the match," Teruhisha continued, as if Jenna had replied.

"Not much else to do," Jenna said, suddenly sad. She ate another French fry.

Four days before, she had come here to defend her title. Instead, she had lost the Lady Prizefighter Amazon Class World Championship to an unpleasant bit of baggage from California, a peroxide blonde with more plastic parts than a Barbie doll. The match had been heavily publicized, globally televised, so viewers on five continents had seen her go down in defeat. The day after *that*, her manager had decided that he liked blonde winners better than redheaded losers. Moving swiftly, he had renegotiated his contract—and his marriage to Jenna.

Now, there didn't seem to be any real reason to hurry home.

"That may be so," Teruhisha said, cheerful and oblivious. "But there is so much for you here! Why, in Tokyo alone—"

Jenna sighed. Tokyo's charms were beginning to wear a little thin, actually. Her best time had been spent in the Ginza, shopping and spending much of her consolation purse in an attempt to console herself. Even that hadn't been entirely successful; apparently, no dress shop in all of Japan had anything that would fit, and a mere mention of her shoe size made shop girls roll their almond eyes in something like horror. Teruhisha had tried to help, but what he really wanted to do was show her parks and shrines and monuments, scattered through the city like chocolate chips in a cookie.

Before she could even try to change the subject, however, something else did. It was a low, wailing shriek, a siren howl from outdoors so penetrating that Jenna's teeth (all of them her own) began to hurt.

Teruhisha turned pale. From a pocket, he pulled what looked like a cell phone. He spoke into it, gesturing curtly at Jenna for silence, and then paused and spoke some more.

The sirens still wailed. Looking past Teruhisha, Jenna could see that her audience was gone now, and the sidewalks almost empty. Men weren't staring at her anymore, and Teruhisha had been rude.

It was like the world was coming to an end, or something.

He came up swiftly through his lightless world,

through blackness that first was absolute and impenetrable, but which soon gave way to mere darkness, then gloom, then something like dawn, as the sun's rays penetrated the depths and found the monster's eyes. Then, at last, the blue-green waters of Tokyo Harbor parted to reveal the cloud-flecked, inverted blue bowl that was the roof of the world.

Beneath that arched roof stretched the familiar skyline of the hated city. The monster paused and gazed briefly at Tokyo through hooded eyes, as if taking its measure. Then the moment passed and he moved forward, continuing inexorably toward his traditional goal.

Only seconds passed before he was sighted, first by the passengers of a tour boat negotiating the harbor. Crowded and noisy and clumsy, the fragile vessel rocked violently in the thrashing turbulence of the monster's wake. As it pitched and yawed, he could hear screams of terror and recognition—the same thing, really—coming from its deck. Interspersed among them were more than a few calls of the name that had been given him by the soft ones, the crawling little humans who sought to share his world with him. He took no note of any of their bleating, nor of the more anguished cries as the tour boat capsized and began to sink. Such chatter was beneath his notice.

Approaching the city, however, he heard something more to his liking—the throbbing shriek of a familiar siren, growing louder as he lumbered towards the shore. It was a familiar wail, one that he had heard before. He had no idea what it meant to the humans, or why they sounded it, and he did not care.

For Reptilla, King of the Monsters, it was the promise of battle.

"We must go immediately," Teruhisha said, but he

still took time to gather up the litter from their meal
and deposit it in the appropriate waste receptacle.
Their fellow diners had already done the same.

"Go?" Jenna said, and blinked. This was a very
different Teruhisha Kitahara than the one who had
been her recent companion. He was more decisive
and emphatic, and Jenna wasn't sure she liked the
change. "Where are we going?"

"You must return to your hotel," Teruhisha said.
"A shelter is there. You are a guest in my country
and you must be protected!" He gestured with the
device he held. "I have my orders to proceed to
Mobile Defender Park."

The odd name was familiar. Jenna remembered an
earlier stop on her tour of the city, a flower-filled
expanse, incongruously large, with a near-abstract
metal sculpture in its center.

"My hotel?" she asked. "That's miles from here!"

"I will find you a cab."

"I don't *think* so," Jenna said, irritated. Losing a
title, a manager, a husband, and an accommodating
escort, all in a mere four days, was a bit much. She
pointed angrily at the sidewalks and street outside.
Already, they were deserted. "Do you see any cabs
out there?"

This time, Teruhisha blinked, then nodded again.
After a long pause, he spoke again. "You must come
with me, then. There is space for an assistant or
passenger. You will be in less danger. But we must
move swiftly!"

"What is it? What's happening?"

"The city is under attack," Teruhisha said. "Reptilla
has been sighted!"

"Reptilla?" Jenna smiled. "They haven't made a
Reptilla movie since I was a little girl!"

Teruhisha stared at her. "No movies, because
Reptilla has not attacked in years," he said. "Until
today!"

"Oh, come on," Jenna said, "You can't really expect me to believe—"

Her words broke off as Teruhisha's right hand, half the size of hers, grabbed her left wrist and tugged, hard. Mainly because she was too surprised to resist, Jenna found herself being pulled towards Teruhisha's car, a powder-blue Nissan parked in front of the restaurant.

"We must go now!" he said. "Time is short!"

As if to lend emphasis to his words, the sidewalk beneath Jenna's feet trembled and shook.

Reptilla climbed out of the harbor waters.

Reptilla *kept* climbing out of the harbor waters.

He was larger by far than any living thing had a right to be, a living mountain of muscle and bone and meat, all sheathed in armorlike scales. He was so big that it took him long moments to tear himself from the harbor's wet embrace and right himself on the land. Hundreds of feet stretched between his snout and the tip of his finned tail, and water was still cascading from the contours of his enormous body as he hauled the last of himself up and into the day.

In the minutes since he had first raised his head from the depths, most of the humans had found places to hide. If Reptilla noticed, he did not care. It was not the humans that drew him, or even the city where they lived, but some primal drive deep in his reptile brain. Here, the whispered prodding of instinct promised, there would be battle, and for Reptilla, the need for battle was sometimes as strong as the need for food or drink or air. The city was to be his battleground, but he scarcely took notice of those who lived there.

The reverse was not true, of course.

High-explosive, high-caliber cannon shells split the air as they threw themselves at Reptilla. They came roaring out of paired gun emplacements hidden within the warehouses that crowded Tokyo Harbor, heavy artillery that had waited long years since last seeing use.

The monster screamed his anger as the barrage found him and smashed into the scales of his armored skin. His eyes glowed red and the bulldozer jaw of his mouth dropped open.

Fire spewed forth.

Steel melted.

Brick burned.

Almost instantly, the first of the hidden gun emplacements was gone, now merely mounded wreckage painting the sky black with greasy smoke. The second fell less swiftly but no less decisively as the monster turned and lashed out at it with his tail, using the prehensile appendage like a massive club.

Reptilla roared again, this time in triumph. Then, slowly, as his echoing cries faded, another sound made itself known—the roar of jet engines.

A half-dozen fighter jets appeared in the sky.

Reptilla ignored them and strode forward.

The earth shook with each step he took.

Jenna's ex had been a maniac behind the wheel, but he had nothing on Teruhisha. The nice little guy who had waited so patiently while she compared consumer electronics and tried to figure out exchange rates was gone. Now, the man who had taken his place clenched the wheel with white-knuckled fingers and tried very hard to push the accelerator through the floor. In no time at all, they were doing nearly forty-three miles an hour, unheard of in downtown Tokyo.

It was a good thing the streets were empty, Jenna thought, and then she thought to ask why.

"Evacuation," Teruhisha said. He was calmer now than he had been at the restaurant, but it was a lethal calm, and he spoke with the voice of a man accustomed to command. "The sirens have sounded.

The populace knows what they mean and where to go. It is a well-established procedure."

"Where are *we* going, then?" Jenna asked.

"Mobile Defender Park," Teruhisha repeated. "We were there earlier."

"Why?"

"I thought that you might like to see it. It is very beautiful, really. The chrysanthemums—"

"No, not then—now," Jenna interrupted. "Why are we going there now?"

"The Mobile Defender is the city's final defense, built after Reptilla's last attack. The perimeter defenses will delay the monster, but if they do not stop him, I must man the Mobile Defender to ensure that Tokyo is saved." Teruhisha held up the device he had spoken into earlier. "This is the key," he said proudly. "It is my month to carry it."

"But, even if Reptilla *is* real—"

Teruhisha took his eyes from the road just long enough to shoot her an irritated glance.

"Okay, okay," Jenna amended. "He's real. But why would you put a weapon downtown?" She had seen decommissioned tanks and airplanes at parks in America, but nothing that worked.

At least, she didn't *think* they worked.

"The Mobile Defender is mobile," Teruhisha said, "but it must be accessible." He spoke as if he were saying the most reasonable thing in the world.

"But aren't you afraid someone will steal it? Or vandalize it?"

"Who would interfere with something so vital to the land's well-being?" Teruhisha asked. "Surely no one in America would do such a thing?"

Jenna wasn't sure how to respond to that.

That was when she heard thunder in the distance. A moment later, the road bed they were riding on shook like pudding. "Shock waves? What's happening?" she asked. "Are they bombing?"

Teruhisha shook his head. "Air-to-surface missiles are more likely," he said. He paused for a moment as he negotiated a turn without slowing, making the Nissan's little tires squeal. "But I do not think they will stop him," he continued. "They never do."

Three missiles came roaring towards Reptilla. Two missed, slamming into evacuated office buildings and exploding.

The third found its target.

It smashed into Reptilla's back and detonated. The monster howled as blood spurted, green in the afternoon sun. Moving with a speed that belied his great bulk, he spun in time to dodge a second volley. These, launched on a different trajectory, raced past him and into the city beyond, but Reptilla scarcely noticed. Instead, his attention was drawn by the plane that had launched them. Even now, that plane was wheeling to fire anew.

Too slowly, too late.

Reptilla's maw opened again. Nuclear fire spewed forth. Incandescent, searing, hotter than the surface of the sun, it burned a path through the unresisting air and found the steel skin of a fighter jet.

More explosions, more thunder.

Reptilla ignored them, like he ignored the hot wind that suddenly swept over him, and continued on his way.

Jenna was beginning to credit Teruhisha's wild tale. The city was empty, and the road they followed now shook and trembled so much that the little car was hard-pressed to remain in its lane. Worse, the tremors had become regular enough to take on a distinct cadence, one that Jenna found disturbingly familiar.

Slow and measured, it was nonetheless the rhythm of footsteps.

Impossibly huge, impossibly heavy footsteps.

"Only a few blocks more," Teruhisha said. "See?" He pointed at a storefront. "That is where you bought the T-shirts."

Jenna nodded. They were in familiar territory, all right. Even so, however, she knew that this street would never again be the same. Already, jagged cracks had opened in the pavement and display windows were spider-webbed with silver fractures.

Teruhisha seemed to read her thoughts. "Collateral damage," he said, a sound of agreement in his voice. "It is always thus, whenever Reptilla strikes. Oh! My poor city!"

"It—it looks like a war zone."

Teruhisha nodded. "It will be worse, before the day is done. But we will rebuild, as we always do." He looked suddenly bleak. "As we have, so many times before."

Something raced by overhead, something white and moving fast—a stray missile from the battle that raged somewhere behind them, Jenna realized. It buried itself in the facade of an internationally famous telecommunications firm's headquarters, creating a cloud of concrete shrapnel, much of which rained down in the Nissan's path.

Teruhisha said something in Japanese, something short and sharp and harsh, a word that Jenna suspected he would never have voiced before a woman who could understand it. He snapped the wheel to the left, hard, and then to the right, trying to dodge the chunks of flaming, falling stone.

"Brace yourself!" he said. "We—"

A fiery mass, small and heavy, struck the hood. The car flipped, tumbled, rolled. The world spun around Jenna. When it stopped, she hung sideways in her seat, held there by the harness Teruhisha had insisted that she buckle.

The car was on its side.

She shook her head to clear it, then struggled free

and inspected herself for damage. A few cuts, a few aches were all she found, but no broken bones.

Teruhisha had not been quite so lucky.

Like Jenna, her companion hung in the nylon web of his seat belt and shoulder harness. Unlike her, he was motionless, his eyes closed. Jenna peeled back one lid and inspected the blank orb beneath. She breathed a sigh of relief as she realized that he was unconscious but basically unharmed. Aspirin and rest, lots of each, were all he needed, most likely.

Jenna wasn't a doctor, but she knew a lot about being knocked unconscious.

She paused a moment, thinking. They were only blocks from their goal, and God knew how far from her hotel. She shrugged, her decision made. It made more sense to go forward than back.

She pulled Teruhisha free and slung him over her shoulder—he didn't weigh much more than her gym bag, really—and began walking.

Behind her, she knew, Reptilla was walking, too.

Technically, it wasn't the Army whose forces lay next in Reptilla's path; technically, Japan had no army, only heavily armed defense forces.

Reptilla didn't know the difference.

Had he known, he would not have cared.

He gazed for a moment at the low vehicles that swarmed towards him on tractor treads, bearing mounted cannons that did him even less harm than the missiles. He scarcely noticed the shells that struck him, or the clinging incendiary gel that splashed across his body and burned. Instead, moving without pause, he strode forward, stepping on some of the tanks and over the rest, nearly oblivious to the difference. Instinct drove him forward, uncaring, unmindful.

Mobile Defender Park was a square of green bordered by steel and glass office towers. In turn, the park's gardens and rolling expanses of close-cropped clover served as a setting for the squat assembly of steel cylinders and slabs at its center. Earlier, Jenna had assumed that the asymmetrical structure was some kind of abstract monument, but now she was willing to believe it was something more.

At least, she hoped it was.

Teruhisha's "key" in her free hand, she approached the Mobile Defender. As she neared it, a door, hidden until now, slid open. All second thoughts fled as she entered. Despite the bizarre circumstances, she felt a serene certainty now, one she knew well.

It was the calm before the storm, the tranquillity that always came just before stepping into the ring. She didn't know why she felt this way now, but she welcomed the familiar sensation.

Right now, in a city suddenly gone mad, in a world where Saturday matinees had supposedly come to life, familiar was good.

Beyond the monument doorway was a place like an airplane's cockpit—two padded seats, one front and center, one behind and to the side. Curved control arrays waited before both, but the larger, more complex one was in front of what Jenna knew instinctively to be the command chair. She took that seat for herself, after strapping Teruhisha into the other for safekeeping.

As she sat, the place came to life. The lamps overhead dimmed and the wall before her erupted in light and color, resolving itself quickly into an image that matched the view outside. The wall was a giant view screen, Jenna realized. Overlaying the picture it presented were what had to be instrument readings—luminous meters and gauges and neatly glowing legends. It was like a giant Nintendo display, but all in Japanese. Jenna made a frustrated sound.

She couldn't read Japanese.

She was so preoccupied with the screen that she

took little notice as padded grips reached out from the armrests, wrapped themselves around her hands. Equivalent devices grew from the floor and found her feet, then floorboards slid back to reveal a small treadmill. Jointed armatures linked her limbs to the control panel. Abruptly, resonating throughout the structure came the rhythmic rumble of hidden engines, so low in pitch that she felt rather than heard them, and then—

Something else.

The sound that metal surfaces made as they slid along each other, found new configurations and locked into place, and then moved together. The rumbling chatter that gears made when they met, and the sighing whisper of hydraulics. The rumbling *ka-chunk!* of powered systems engaging.

The world jerked, shifted, moved. The image in the view screen lurched, the instrument readings remaining in place as the vista beyond them scrolled by. Jenna's ears popped, as if she were on an airplane or in an express elevator. Then, when stability came again, Jenna took a deep breath and peered again at the outside world through the giant view screen.

But from a much greater height.

A moment before, looking straight ahead, she had stared at a hotel's lobby entrance. Now, she was looking at its twelfth floor—and at what was reflected in the building's mirrored glass facade.

At a humanoid figure, at least one hundred and twenty feet tall, with a barrel chest and broad shoulders, with oversized gloves and boots, and with a stern steel mask where its face should have been. At what the Mobile Defender had become, now that it had *unfolded* itself. At red and silver armor, at heavy slabs of metal shaped into a figure approximating that of a man—a very large, very armored man.

Or, at the moment, a woman.

Jenna smiled, as sudden understanding swept over her.

She had finally found something in her size.

She raised one hand, moving the grip with it, and watched as the reflected figure raised its matching one. She stamped one foot; her counterpart did the same, bringing a red metal boot down hard enough to send tremors through the surrounding ground. She took a step on the treadmill and curled the fingers of her right hand, and the armored figure moved forward, even as it formed a perfect fist.

Jenna's smile grew wider and became an expression of absolute delight. "Yes!" she whispered, and the single word hung in the control room's cool air. It all made sense, in a crazy kind of way.

Apparently, she hadn't fought her last match in Japan.

At least, not just yet.

Twenty-three minutes had passed since Reptilla erupted from the waters. In that time, besides the hidden gun emplacements, the fighter jets and the tanks, he had destroyed half a dozen buildings and trampled several smaller structures, leaving a trail of destruction that led more-or-less directly to Tokyo's center. All of this he had accomplished even as he sought an opponent worthy of his might.

As the twenty-fourth minute passed, and as he strode into Mobile Defender Park, a red steel fist slammed into his jaw. As much from surprise as pain, Reptilla gave a howl and tumbled backwards.

Inside the Mobile Defender, Jenna laughed exultantly—a luxury she could not allow herself in regulation matches—and pressed the attack. From behind her, she heard a sound like a sigh, and realized that Teruhisha had regained consciousness, or was about to. That was good but, at the moment, not especially important.

Only winning was.

Jenna's fists came up; so did those of the giant robot armor she wore. Metal knuckles pounded into Reptilla's chest and shoulders. The volley of blows was enough to stun the brute, enough to make him stumble and stagger back. Had there been ropes, Reptilla would have been on them now; instead, he slammed into a nearby office tower. Glass shattered and metal girders snapped, and the building trembled as the ragged plates studding Reptilla's spine sawed into it. Again, the monster shrieked in protest, but this time, there was a puzzled sound in his roar, a sound of confusion.

Jenna had heard that sound before. Most males made that cry, or something like it, the first time they met women stronger than they were.

She drew back her fists to strike again, and then—

Reptilla's left foot came up, a four-clawed appendage something like a bird's, but many, many times larger. Even from his awkward position, he could bring it up much further, proportionately, than could any human being. The three lead claws dug into what would have been the Mobile Defender's collarbone, while the fourth, opposed one, found the suit's abdomen. Alarm systems shrieked and several of the cryptic displays on the view screen turned red.

Reptilla's new tactic was one Jenna had never run across in any other match, regulation or not. Quickly, she moved to counter it. Her fists unclenched, became spread-fingered hands again, reached for Reptilla's ankle. Feedback systems in the controlling gauntlets told her when she found her goal, and it felt as though her actual hands were closing on the bony joint.

Jenna squeezed, hard.

Reptilla yelped, and drummed his foreclaws on the building behind him. Jenna felt disgust. This was more like pro wrestling than her chosen sport, but she wouldn't relent.

Neither would Reptilla.

His grip on her chest armor tightened, and more status displays turned red. Resonating through the Mobile Defender's body, she heard metal tear.

Her armor was giving way.

She squeezed harder. Another five seconds passed, another three—

A new display came to life, an electric-blue status bar that extended itself swiftly across her screen, an indicator that Jenna could not understand.

"Disengage," Teruhisha said, his voice a slur from somewhere behind her. "He will burn us, or the armor will rupture."

"Teruhisha! You're awake!" Jenna was so happy to hear his voice that she paid no attention to his words, and kept squeezing.

Reptilla's bulldozer jaw opened.

"Disengage," Teruhisha repeated, more forcefully this time. "Let go of him!" He was ordering her now.

Jenna didn't like taking orders.

She ignored him, "felt" bones grind beneath her fingers. Reptilla's grip loosened even as hers tightened.

Teruhisha said something in Japanese, something that sounded like a curse.

Fire sprayed from Reptilla's mouth and, simultaneously, blue-white arcs of electricity surged from the Mobile Defender's fingertips. Now it was Jenna's turn to shriek as the monster tore itself free, and her turn to stagger back, dodging the flaming attack. The bright lance of nuclear fire spraying from Reptilla's maw streaked past her right shoulder, while the monster convulsed spastically.

"What was that?" Jenna demanded angrily. The blue-white status bar had disappeared now. "I had him, dammit! What did you do?"

"Lightning attack," Teruhisha said, from his control panel. He sounded preoccupied. "It hurt him, and broke your grip. The armor could not withstand such a close strike!"

"Whatever it was, don't do it again!" she snapped. Sweat shone on her brow, and she was breathing heavily, as much from exertion as fury. "Once I'm in the ring, no one tells me what to do! *No one!*"

"You cannot be serious," Teruhisha said. "You—"

Typical male.

"Help if you want, but no back-seat driving," she snapped. "This is my fight now!"

"You don't have the training, you don't—"

"I said, *no back-seat driving,*" Jenna repeated, spinning to face him.

That was a mistake, because the Mobile Defender turned, too. The skyline scrolled raggedly past the view screen, and Jenna could no longer see Reptilla.

But he could see her.

Righting himself, the monster struck again. This time, he mimicked his foe's tactics, balling clawed forepaws into fists and pounding on the gigantic figure's torso. The world rocked crazily again as the punches shook the Mobile Defender.

"Oh, great," Jenna said. "This is just great!" She turned to face the monster again. "Now look what you've done," she called back to Teruhisha, still angry at the interruption, but focusing on Reptilla again. She was able to block his punches easily enough. The monster had the advantage in reach and struck with great power, but he had little finesse and no guard worth worrying about.

Ahead of her, the system displays, still in Japanese, changed. Behind her, Teruhisha spoke, using more compliant tones this time. "Cadmium charges on-line," he said, at once businesslike and obedient. "Fourteen seconds until launch capability."

"Is that good?" Jenna asked. There was too much

about the Mobile Defender that she didn't know; Teruhisha's help would be useful, provided he remembered who was in the command chair.

"Very good," Teruhisha said.

Jenna blocked another punch, and then her metal knuckles Reptilla's brow, cut it. Green blood streamed forth, obscuring the monster's vision. She socked him in the jaw, then grinned as his head snapped back and his guard, poor though it was, dropped. She drummed the Mobile Defender's fists into Reptilla's abdomen in a staccato rhythm.

Teruhisha continued. "Reptilla is a living nuclear reactor. Cadmium absorbs neutrons, can shut down his metabolism." He paused. "Missiles primed and ready to launch," he said. Then a panel on the Mobile Defender's left forearm opened, and Jenna saw what looked like five torpedoes, locked together in a metal rack. "To launch them, press—"

Jenna decided to throw him a crumb. "You can take care of that," she said. "Right?"

"On your command," Teruhisha said. He sounded a bit happier now.

"Where?" Jenna asked.

"Where?"

"Give me a target," Jenna said. "Where will they do the most good?" Reptilla had his second wind now and was giving as good as he got. Trying something new, she brought one metal foot down on Reptilla's bare one, then dodged as the monster almost toppled her with a lash of his tail. As she dodged, she hit him again, but the behemoth barely seemed to notice. Rage had lent him new strength.

Jenna knew that this was, quite possibly, her finest moment—but she also knew that it couldn't last forever. The system displays seemed to agree. Most of them were red now, and alarm buzzers were sounding.

"For maximum effect, you must have maximum

penetration," Teruhisha said. The words sounded incongruous, coming from such a gentleman.

Jenna nodded. "I'll tell you when," she said. Reptilla shuffled closer, reaching for her again. She dodged his blows as best she could, waiting for the opening she needed.

After a moment or two, it came.

Reptilla's claws came up, reaching for her. Her knee came up, too, smashing into the monster's crotch, right between where his hind legs joined his torso.

Jenna had grown up in New Jersey, after all.

Reptilla gasped. He dropped his attack, dropped to his knees, clutched himself, leaned forward. Not fire, but breath rushed from his lungs through his gaping mouth as he collapsed in agony.

Jenna grinned. She aimed her left fist at Reptilla's hanging jaw. "Now!" she said.

Trailing fire, the five missiles roared into Reptilla's open mouth and down his throat. They had scarcely passed from view when Jenna reached with metal-sheathed hands, grasped the mnster's jaw, and snapped it shut. She squeezed hard, sealing the monster's mouth.

There was a muffled rumble as the charges exploded. The monster convulsed, hard enough to tear him free even of the Mobile Defender's iron grip.

Reptilla stared at Jenna, as if baffled by what had been done to him, or confused by the lull in battle. He gathered himself together and stood erect once more. His jaw opened, but nothing came out. After a long moment, his eyes rolled back in their sockets, and then their green lids closed.

Reptilla fell.

He fell like a mountain might fall, or a redwood, with a certain majestic grace, but he fell nonetheless. The measureless tons of his mass impacted the park's trampled contours with a sound like thunder, and the earth for miles around shook.

Then, at last, all was still.

"Now what?" Jenna asked, panting. She considered the motionless monster at her feet—at the Mobile Defender's feet—and wondered fleetingly what had brought him here.

She wondered if there were more where he came from.

"He—he is defeated," Teruhisha said, from where he sat. "Perhaps even destroyed. Defeated, not driven off." There was a wondering sound in his voice. "This has never happened before, never. No one has ever—"

"He never faced a world champion before," Jenna said. She grinned. This almost made up for losing the title.

Almost.

A thought struck her. The control armatures had retracted now, so the Mobile Defender remained stationary as she turned to face Teruhisha. "Say," she asked, "what does a job like this pay, anyhow?"

Teruhisha didn't respond. He had donned a telephone headset and was speaking in urgent tones to someone. Jenna heard her name several times. After a minute or more of hurried conference, he broke the connection.

"What's the verdict?" she asked. "What do the judges say?"

"My superiors are quite pleased," he said. "You are the hero of the day. On behalf of the Emperor, and the government of Japan—"

Jenna interrupted. The details could wait. "We make a good team," she said. She could afford to be generous.

Teruhisha took a breath. "There is more," he said slowly, "if you have no other plans—"

Jenna almost laughed. He was persistent, she had

to admit. "Teruhisha, you big silly," she said, standing. "Not tonight. All I want right now is a shower and sleep. Maybe another time?"

Teruhisha shook his head. "That is not what I meant," he said, blushing. "At least, not now. I have been given new orders."

Jenna looked at him.

"To the north," Teruhisha said. "There has been a sighting." He paused again, then spoke slowly. "It appears to be a gigantic ape."

Jenna sat down again.

Hallah Iron-Thighs & the Change of Life

K.D. Wentworth

The Jamplit Mountains between Alowey and Damery were tall and forbidding, infested with nasty hulking bandits who hardly ever changed their socks or wrote home to their mothers. Gerta and I had done in eighteen already that morning, which wasn't even a record for a single day.

For the first time in our long partnership though, I hadn't kept up my end of the fighting. My mail was tight across the back and under my arms, making me much slower on the downswing. The score so far was Gerta, twelve; Hallah, six. I was in a seething, foul mood.

"It's just the Change of Life, Hallah." My sister-in-arms, Gerta, a good ten years younger, gazed blithely ahead at the winding mountain trail. She flicked a gnat off her wrist. "That's why it's best to die young. It happens to all of us eventually if we don't get our skulls smashed in glorious battle at an early age."

"Not to Hallah Iron-Thighs, eldest daughter of Marulla Big-Fist, it doesn't!" My bay mare, Corpsemaker, missed a step on the rock-strewn trail and I had to grab the saddle for support.

"So, when we get to Damery, we'll stop in at Benito's Hammer-and-Go and let his armorer add a few rings. It just means there's more of you to—"

I drew my sword with a great ringing hiss, irritated all the more at the way my mail pinched at the slightest move. "If you say it means there's just more of me to love, I'll slit you from nose to belly button!"

Our client, Perchis Dal, an anemic-looking hymnal merchant from far-off Brezia, cringed, then gazed longingly down into the green river valley below. His white donkey, resigned to his none-too-steady weight, merely bobbed its head and snorted. Not wanting to be left out, the three gray donkeys following behind laden with boxes of hymnals did the same.

Gerta tossed her head and her golden braids flew in the breeze. "What I was going to say is that there is more of you to *aim* at now, and so less chance of taking a mortal blow."

"Oh. That's okay, then." My brow furrowed. "I think."

I stared sourly at Gerta's perfect profile and firm figure. The serving lad, down at the Disappointed Sheep Tavern, had been making eyes at her last night, while I had only attracted the attentions of a smelly, no-good, toothless goat herder. I'd had to threaten to disembowel the latter in order to keep the idiot from hovering behind my back the whole evening.

"You always get crabby when you're too long in the saddle," Gerta said.

Overhead, a red-tailed hawk creeled and dove through the crystalline mountain air. I considered skewering it with an arrow for being so cheerful, then turned around in my saddle to glare at Gerta. "Are you implying that I'm getting *soft*?"

The hymnal merchant flinched, then kneed his donkey and trotted ahead of us around the next bend in the trail.

"I wouldn't do that, if I were you," I called after him. "This pass is dangerous. You never know when you're going to run into a bunch of low-down, dirty, skulking ban—"

"And just who are you calling 'dirty' there, ducks?" a familiar male voice called down from the rocks above. "Actually, I'm thinking the two of you could do with a bit of spit and polish your own selves."

"Lomo, you skunk!" Corspemaker's hooves clattered as I pulled her up.

"That's Lomo, King of the Bandits, to you," he said haughtily.

I leaped out of the saddle, my sword Esmeralda in hand. "I thought I split your thieving head open the last time you waylaid us!"

"That," he said loftily from his unseen perch, "was merely a clever ruse on my part."

"Rats and eels, I hate it when they won't stay dead!" Gerta joined me, her sword at the ready, head craning to check out the odds. "Hallah, you must be losing your touch." She stared up at the rugged gray cliff above us and shaded her eyes against the sun. "How many are there?"

A handful of small rocks cascaded down the cliff face and we lurched back, dangerously close to the edge of the sheer path. "Too many," I said, counting the visible tops of heads.

"Good!" As always, Gerta's blue eyes were joyously savage. "There is less glory in a fair fight!"

"Yeah, yeah." I tied up Corspemaker's reins and slapped her rump, urging the mare back the way we'd come. Gerta's gray gelding Slasher and the three pack donkeys followed. "I'll sneak back and climb up that depression just before the last bend. You guard his prissiness. I think he's cowering over there in those rocks."

"I'm not cowering!" Dal's voice rang out from around the turn. "I'm praying!"

"Praying?" Lomo called down the cliff side. His voice quivered with eagerness. "Is he a *priest*?"

"No!" I said crossly.

"But I have something to confess!"

"He's not a priest!" I reached for my bow.

He leaned closer to the edge and I could see his shock of dishevelled red hair decorated with pigeon feathers. "Are you sure?"

Now bandits, being depraved brutes, are often keen on priests, and they're never the least particular about what kind. They like the odd bit of prayer, when they can get it, just in case it might tip the scales in their favor someday, and they're absolutely potty about confession. Like kings and politicians, they have this peculiar notion they can do anything they want, as long as they're real sorry afterwards. "He's not a priest—he's just a stupid hymnal salesman!" I yelled back, trying to get a clear shot.

"Really?" Several more interested scruffy heads popped over the side of the cliff. "Does he know 'Nearer My Isis to Thee'?"

The merchant scurried back around the cliff on hands and knees, his face red as a throttled pig. I nudged his quivering body with my foot. "Well?"

He shook his head so hard, his flabby neck skin wobbled back and forth.

"No," I said, "he doesn't, so you might as well come down and have your heads properly lopped off while the light is still good."

"Yes!" Gerta chimed in with enthusiasm. "What fun is shedding blood if we can't see it?"

"How about 'Onward, Pagan Soldiers'?" a different

voice asked. "My mum used to sing that one over my cradle."

I cocked an eyebrow at Dal. He looked uncertain.

"Can you hum a few bars?" Gerta asked.

"Damnation!" I said, completely out of patience. "This isn't a sodding tea party, you know! Come down and fight!"

"Don't get huffy there, ducks," Lomo called down amiably. "I'll get around to killing you in a minute."

"You wish!" Cocky bastard! Now I remembered why I'd split his head open the first time. I motioned to Gerta to guard Dal, then sheathed Esmeralda and ran back down the trail to a slope that looked climbable. I found a fingerhold in the gray granite, and then a toehold, and set to work.

"What about 'The Old Rugged Rune'?" I heard Lomo ask. "That's always a real crowd-pleaser."

A few knobby roots protruded from the sheer cliff face here and there, and I used them when I could for handholds. My mail shirt strained across my chest as I climbed, so tight I couldn't get enough air.

Lomo's red-haired head appeared above me. He grinned. "What's the matter, ducks? Having a spot of trouble?"

"Just wait until I get my hands on you!" I wheezed, wishing I could stop long enough to loosen my mail. "I'll kill you so dead this time—"

"Oh, you always say that." He waggled a finger at me. "My goodness, have you put on a bit of weight? Maybe it's time you checked in at the Old Amazons' Home."

"You—are—" I said with great effort. Black dots were parading behind my eyes. "—a—dead—man!"

"You really should have sent Gerta, if you wanted some climbing done," he said reprovingly. "*She's* still in top trim, anyone can see that. While you, well—" He leaned over the side of the cliff. "My goodness, is that a gray hair?"

I lurched upwards, the black dots behind my eyes having gone volcano red. The next handhold in the rock crumbled beneath my weight and I made a frantic grab at a nearby root. It held for a second, then tore loose. I fell backwards, the useless thing still in my hand, Lomo's laughter ringing in my ears.

"I don't know what you want with that stupid root," Gerta was saying from the other side of the universe. "It doesn't look the least bit appetizing and it stinks."

Wasn't I dead? Anyone who hurt this much ought to be dead. I groaned and thought about opening my eyes. Not today, though. Maybe next week, or next year.

"They took everything," she said dejectedly. "Bashed me on the head with a rock the size of a castle, then stole Dal, his hymnals, *and* our swords. I can't even find the horses. We'll never live this down, once word gets around. That must be why they didn't bother to cut our throats. We'll be a laughing-stock for ten kingdoms."

I heard singing somewhere above us, echoing against the mountain side. Bad singing. Excruciatingly bad singing.

" 'On a hill faraway,' " off-key voices were screeching, " 'stood an old rugged rune—' "

I wondered if maybe I could pry open my eyes just long enough to find the side of the cliff and roll over the edge to make this torture stop. Unfortunately my eyes did open and the daylight seemed to explode inside my head, reminiscent of that time Gerta and I had drunk a whole month's profits in two hours.

I clutched my skull and decided even death would not help. Pain of this magnitude would no doubt follow me all the way to the Underworld. "How— long?" I croaked. My breath was a white cloud in the rapidly cooling air. I shivered and sat up.

Gerta squinted up at the sky. "It's almost dark."

She had a black eye and a knot on the side of her head the size of a roc's egg.

Hours, then. "Damnation!" I leaned forward and pressed my aching head to my knees.

The breeze shifted and the singing faded until I could no longer make out the words, at which point thinking became marginally possible. "I'm going to rip Lomo's toenails off and use them to dig out his liver!" I said hoarsely.

"That's the spirit," Gerta said weakly.

For some reason, my mail seemed even tighter than before, though that could have been because I now had a bruise on my back matching each and every ring. Every breath was an exercise in additional pain.

The wind shifted again and I heard enthusiastic strains of "'Come, come, come to the pyre in the *wild* wood! Oh, come to the pyre in the *dell*!'"

I pulled myself up against the rapidly chilling rock of the cliff. "Follow those voices!"

Gerta nodded soberly and we staggered off in what seemed the right direction. The trail twisted around the mountain like a drunken dragon, now rising, now descending. The voices that drew us on caterwauled like demented choirboys and as we drew near I made out the third verse of "Zeus Rest Ye Merry Gentlemen!"

"They are having entirely too much fun," Gerta whispered.

"Yeah." I sat back on my heels and tried to catch my breath. I ran a finger under the constricting collar of my mail. "Can mail shrink?"

"You're probably just adding muscle," she said soothingly, though I could see by her dubious expression she didn't mean it. "You've been so active lately."

"Right." It was full dark now and we could see the orange glow of a fire up on the cliffs above. The frost-ridden wind gusted down the cliffs and cut straight through me. I rubbed my hands together for warmth, then reached for Esmeralda. My chilled fingers closed on an empty scabbard. The thought of Lomo's dirty hands touching my lovely custom-made hilt with the exquisite embossed elephant's head made me see purple and puce.

"Sermon! Sermon!" the bandits were chanting. "We want a sermon!"

"But I'm not a priest!" Perchis Dal said abjectly. "I keep telling you that."

"Give us a sermon, my fine potted plant," Lomo said, "or we'll pluck out your nose hairs one at a time."

Gerta and I eased up the slope. Shadows cast in the firelight shifted on the rim as figures moved about and the stench of scorched donkey meat hung strongly in the air. "Dearly b-beloved," Dal said uncertainly, "y-you should always be good and—and—"

"Not fond of your nose hairs, are you?" Lomo said conversationally.

"andtrynottobebad!"

"Get to the confessing part!" someone cried. "That's our favorite!"

"S-some of you might have been a little bit bad," Dal continued reluctantly.

Someone sniffled, then broke into howling sobs.

"But if you confess to the almighties—"

"Which one?" Lomo demanded over a chorus of wails.

"How in the blazes should I know?" Dal's voice was aggrieved. "I keep telling you oafs that I'm not—"

There was the sound of a scuffle, then a shocked squawk. "Which almighty?" Lomo repeated.

"Any of them!" Dal squeaked in a voice at least two octaves higher than before. "I'm sure it's their very great pleasure to attend to whatever you fine gentlemen care to say!"

Gerta's hand slipped and she slid half a body length back down the slope. Above, I heard a familiar whicker—Corpsemaker! She must have gotten my scent. No doubt, the bandits had Gerta's Slasher too. Once we lopped off their mangy, lice-ridden heads, we'd recover our mounts and swords, and then deliver Dal and his hymnals to Damery as promised.

I tried to quicken my pace, but my mail was absolutely strangling me. Despite the impending battle, I realized I should have taken it off when I had the chance. I was gasping for air as I cleared the final foot of cliff.

A boulder shielded me from their view, but around it, a few yards off, I could make out at least thirty bandits. As always, they were a moth-eaten, vicious-looking lot. One, dressed in a dozen ragged castoffs, was kneeling before the hymnal merchant, who was holding his abused nose with both hands. Lomo stood with his back to us, surveying the scene.

"Great Isis, I'm really, really sorry!" the bandit, a scruffy, bald-headed rogue, wailed.

"A-about what?" Dal spoke through his hands, his face pale as watered cream.

"About killing that self-satisfied, stuck-up prig of a prime minister from Mazor last week and stealing all his gold."

"And you w-won't do it again?" Dal prompted.

The bandit wiped his eyes. "Well, of course, I'll do it again. Are you crazy?"

"Next!" Lomo called.

Gerta's head eased up over the side of the cliff and she crept up beside me, panting. "Now what?" she whispered, belly-down in the dirt. "Shall we charge them one at a time or together?"

My mail tightened another notch. This time, I actually felt it contract. My hand flew to the first buckle on the side seam.

"I could kill them all myself," Gerta said, "but it seems unsporting not to let you in on the fun."

Another sinner was brought before the hymnal merchant in the wavering circle of firelight. "A-and you?" Dal quavered.

This bandit was a withered old coot who looked vaguely familiar for some reason. Had I perhaps done a poor job of killing him at some point too like Lomo? "I ain't sorry about a bloomin' thing!" he declared.

Lomo cuffed him into the ashes at the edge of the fire. "You wanted to confess. Now get on with it!"

"My—mail!" I wheezed at Gerta, fingers wrenching vainly at the buckle. "Get it off!"

Her eyes widened. "Now?"

The bandit picked himself up and brushed at the new smudges on his ragged trousers. "Well, I suppose I could say I'm sorry about impersonating a goatherd last night so I could sprinkle your magic shrinking potion on Hallah Iron-Thighs' mail."

"That was very wicked of you!" Lomo said and then the two of them guffawed.

I recognized him now, as the scene before me was being rapidly blotted out by swirling darkness of impending unconsciousness due to lack of air. He was the smelly lout who kept hovering behind my back at the tavern. Magic, I thought weakly. Lomo had used one of his bandits to magick me, the rotten bastard! I could feel my veins bulging, my face turning purple. My fingers wrenched at the buckle, but it must have been jammed in the fall I'd taken earlier and wouldn't give.

"Hallah, they're going to hear you!" Gerta whispered disapprovingly.

"Yes, ducks." Lomo walked around the boulder. "You really should be more careful."

"Don't worry, Hallah!" Gerta sprang to her feet. "I'll save a few for you to kill!"

The first buckle finally gave and my mail popped

open down to the second buckle, giving me a bit more room to breathe, though not nearly enough.

Gerta charged, but her balance was off, courtesy no doubt of the lump on her head. Lomo thrust out his foot, then turned to me as she went down like a poleaxed buffalo. "What about you, ducks? Is there something you'd like to confess before we throw you into that convenient bottomless crevice over there? It's best to go out with a clean conscience, you know."

With a creak, the second buckle opened. I gulped air into my straining lungs. Gerta was sprawled on the ground at Perchis Dal's feet, a new lump on her head beside the earlier one, making a matched set. I was outnumbered thirty to one. Lomo had my horse and my sword. Even my trusty mail, veteran of years of fighting, had let me down. Maybe this *was* the Change of Life after all and I'd worked too long at this exhausting, dangerous business. Maybe it was time to hang up my—

"Can I go now?" Dal ducked his head. "You can keep the donkeys and hymnals."

Lomo whirled and shoved him to the ground beside Gerta's limp form. "Get on with the confessions!"

Dal's head hit Gerta's scabbard with a sharp crack. His eyes fluttered, then he sagged like a windless sail. The bandits surged forward, aghast. "Lomo, you killed our priest!" one of them cried. "Now, how are we going to confess?"

My fingers wrenched desperately at the last buckle and finally with a squeak, it gave. My mail split open along the side seam and I drew in a blessed full breath.

"You promised us hymns and sermons and confession!" A hulking brute seized Lomo's shirt and hauled him up onto his toes. "Otherwise, we'd never have followed you. Now, we've finally caught something at least close to a priest, after all these months, and you bash his blinkin' head in. I think we need us a new king!"

A chorus of assent went up on all sides. Lomo looked decidedly nervous.

"First, though," the tall brute said, "throw that meddling Iron-Thighs broad down the crevice. We was doing fine until she showed up!"

"Yeah!" They advanced on me, a reeking, unkempt mob, unsatisfied repentance blazing in their eyes.

I raised my chin, remembering whose daughter I was. No bunch of priest-deprived bandits was going to take me down! A true warrior is never without resources. If they wanted a sermon—

"Brethren!" I cried. "We find ourselves brought together by fate tonight, out here, underneath these brilliant and, I can assure you, all-seeing stars!"

They paused, slack-jawed.

"Some of you have not always led, shall we say, admirable lives," I said with as much authority as I could muster. "Of that I think we can be certain."

One of the worthless band whimpered.

"Down on your knees, dogs!" I crossed my arms and looked uncompromising. "It's time to make amends!"

Three of the closest knelt. "Wait a minute!" Lomo cried, still hanging by his shirt from the brute's fist. "She's not a priest!"

"You never take presents to your mothers, do you?" I tapped my foot.

Two more dropped to their knees. Their eyes looked suspiciously red. "This is stupid," Lomo broke in. "Don't lis—"

His captor rammed him facefirst to the ground, then knelt, folding his hands piously. Lomo sprawled limply and barely breathing in the fire's dancing shadows.

"You slurp your soup and eat with your mouths open! You curse and burp and never ever share!"

Five more knelt, openly sobbing.

Gerta stirred. I put my foot in the middle of her back to hold her in place. "Raise your eyes to the stars and confess all the nasty, dirty, rotten things you've ever done!"

The holdouts knelt along with the rest of my congregation and commenced airing their dirty laundry. It was a loud and most enthusiastic list. I eased my foot off Gerta's back. "Get up!" I whispered urgently. "We have to go!"

Her hand twitched.

"Now would be a real good time!" I said.

The confessing faltered and the bandits' feral eyes once again glittered at me in the firelight. I whirled back to them. "Do you call those sins?" I cried. "By all the powers above, you are a pathetic bunch! I thought you were men! My *grandmother* has committed worse crimes than that!"

They raised their eyes and went back to it with a vengeance. I shuddered at the transgressions mentioned; by all accounts, they had been a very naughty lot.

Gerta groaned, then hitched herself away from the fire, one agonizingly slow bit at a time. I reached down and slipped a hand through Dal's belt and dragged him out of the light. "Find the horses," I told Gerta. "I'll collect our swords."

She nodded groggily and lurched off into the darkness. I put my hands on my hips and strode through the crowd. One of the appropriated hymnals lay open close to the fire and I picked it up and examined the inside cover. Oh, ho! I thought. If we ever got back to the lowlands, both King Mytchell the Extremely Picky of Damery and King Bentley the Culinary of Alowey would find *this* very interesting! I shoved the volume into my belt.

Then I recognized Gerta's sword, Gut-Spiller, on the hip of a rugged blond fellow. "Slackers!" I cried.

"Put your backs into it!" I whacked the yellow-headed thief across the shoulders and sent him reeling, at the same time deftly filching the sword. My nose wrinkled as I turned away. By his pungent odor, he apparently hadn't bathed since birth.

"Do you think confession works if you mumble?" I said. "I can't *hear* you!" The noise level climbed another notch. "Straighten up, you lily-livered wuss!" I told another. "You look like a leaking sack of feed!" I spotted my sword, thrust through Lomo's belt. He was lying across it. Damnation! I worked my way around the babbling throng until I was looming over him. "Fall on your faces, worms! Beg forgiveness of the almighties!"

Most of them did, but several, including Lomo's attacker, hesitated. "What we got to do that for?" he asked, as all around him confessions were shouted into the dirt. "I never heard of no priest saying 'Fall on your face!'"

I could fight him, of course, but then I'd have to take on all thirty of them, not a practical choice at the moment. "Say," I said, dropping my voice into a honeyed lower register and leaning closer. "You are a *big* one, aren't you? I could go for a fine full-sized fellow like you."

The light in his eyes changed from petulance to vanity. He flexed his bicep and winked. "Yeah?"

"Yeah," I murmured throatily, then turned sideways and gave him a sharp elbow on the point of his jaw. He toppled like a felled hundred-year oak. "That's the spirit, brother!" I cried, then glared at the remaining two bandits. They hurriedly buried their faces in the dirt.

Keeping an eye on my parishioners, I rolled Lomo's unconscious body over, freed Esmeralda from his worn belt, then glanced around for Gerta. She signalled me from the other side of the camp. Fortunately, she'd found the strength to hoist the hymnal merchant over Slasher's saddle like a deer carcass. The confessions were growing ever more hoarse and insignificant. The bandits were now down to episodes of dog kicking and flower trampling; we were almost out of time.

"All right," I said, "enough confessing. It's time for a rousing chorus of—of—" I searched for an appropriate song.

"What about 'Oh Come All Ye Druids'?" one tear-stained bandit suggested timorously. "I always find that so uplifting."

"Splendid!" I hauled the newly confessed miscreant to his feet. "I'm appointing you choirmaster. Lead on!"

As off-key strains of the chosen song violated the clear mountain night air, I vaulted into Corpsemaker's saddle. Gerta mounted Slasher behind the merchant's body, then we gave the horses their heads so they could pick their way down the winding rock-strewn trail in the darkness.

Behind us, the abysmal singing went on for a long, long time.

"I thought you two were supposed to be the best!" Dal said the next day, as we began our descent into the kingdom of Damery. His swollen nose was still beet-red and he talked thickly as though he had a cold. "You lost all my stock and didn't kill a single bandit!"

I pulled out the battered hymnal I'd picked up the night before and opened the cover. I squinted, then held it out to him. "Funny, I don't see an Alowey tax stamp anywhere in this book." I pressed the volume to my chest. "Merchant Dal, have you perhaps been dealing with those renegade cut-rate monks down beyond the Brimford frontier? You know, the ones who don't believe in lawful taxes?"

"Of course not!" Dal averted his bloodshot eyes.

"That's good," I said. "Because we all know how King Mytchell the Extremely Picky feels about tax evaders running goods across his border. I believe the last twenty or so were boiled in apple vinegar and then fed to the royal swine."

Dal flushed and stared down at his knotted fingers. "You know, I've been thinking of emigrating across the channel to Doria. The weather is so much better there and the population is known for having perfect pitch, just the place for a hymnal salesman to get ahead."

"Really?" I said. According to Gerta, who'd been born across the channel, Doria was so far north, they thought summer was when it sleeted instead of snowed. "That does sound like a pleasant change."

"What about our fee?" Gerta asked glumly. Golden wisps of hair had escaped her braids, her black eye was swollen shut, and she didn't look nearly as valiant as usual. "No doubt you want a refund."

I leafed through the illicit hymnal, then hummed a few bars of that old standard, "Cairn of Ages, Cleft for Me."

"Keep your fee!" Dal squeaked. "You earned it! I wouldn't dream of asking for a refund!" He swallowed hard. "Can I, um, have my hymnal back?"

"Yeah." I tossed it to him. "I suppose it does have a certain sentimental value."

Dal tore the pages out as we rode and threw them surreptitiously along the trail behind us, but otherwise kept blessedly quiet for the rest of the journey.

Two nights later, we dumped Dal off at the infamous Inn of the Second Wart at the foot of the mountain and then ate freshly roasted piglet out underneath the dazzling sweep of stars.

"Surprising that someone would be so careless about marking their stock," Gerta was saying. "Are you sure that pig wasn't marked?"

Not after I whacked its ears off, I thought. "Not a mark anywhere," I said. I wiped pork grease off my hands, then picked up my poor magicked mail. It was now so small, it fit in the palm of my hand, no bigger than a doll's shirt and shrinking ever more quickly as time went by. At this rate, it would be flea-sized by morning. "I will have to order new mail when we get to town, but at least it won't be because I'm getting old."

Gerta turned over on her back and stared up at the sky. "I'm afraid you are in for a change, though. Surely you've heard that, once you've been magicked, you're much more sensitive to spells and potions and such."

"Don't be ridiculous," I said. "That's just an old wives' tale."

"No, I swear it's true," Gerta said earnestly. "It happened to my cousin, Ernelda. This lovesick dolt in the next village bought a cheap spell and cast it on her. As soon as the wedding was over and she regained her senses, she beat him to a pulp, but now she can't even pass one of those stupid street magicians without feeling obliged to turn cartwheels and sing charming little ditties."

"Gee," I said, "something to look forward to."

"Well," Gerta said as her blue eyes sagged shut, "it did turn out to be a nice source of extra income. People are always throwing coins at her feet these days. I expect you'll get used to it."

And that, I reflected, was the most depressing prospect of all.

About the Authors

For a guy no one's ever heard of, **Pierce Askegren** has written a fair amount of fiction, for most of which he's gotten paid. He co-wrote a three book series of Spider-Man novels with famous comics guys Fingeroth and Fein, and he wrote two more Marvel novels on his own. He also cranked out five short stories for various Marvel anthologies, and a novel based on the popular *Traveller* role-playing game. Sometime after the Earth cooled but before the continents moved apart, he wrote stories that nobody remembers for Warren comics magazines—*Creepy*, the original *Vampirella*, etc. These days, by day, he writes business proposals and such for government contractors, as well as accepting the occasional technical writing or editing assignment. Pierce lives in northern Virginia in a frighteningly cluttered apartment with about a zillion Godzilla figures to keep him company.

Robin Wayne Bailey is the author of twelve novels, including the *Brothers of the Dragon* series from Roc Books, *Shadowdance*, and most recently *Swords Against the Shadowland* from White Wolf Books. His short stories have appeared in numerous anthologies, including the popular *Thieves World* series, *Future Net, Space Opera* and others. He's been a planetarium lecturer, musician, and martial arts instructor. An avid collector of books and oldtime radio plays, his hobbies also include weight-lifting, bicycling, and soccer. He resides in Kansas City, Missouri, with his wife, Diana, and their cat, Topper. Stories like "A Case of Prince Charming" represent the more harmless manifestations of his twisted sense of humor. Ask the editor.

Margaret Ball lives in Austin, Texas, with her husband and two children. She has a B.A. in mathematics and a Ph.D. in linguistics from the University of Texas. After graduation, she taught at UCLA and then spent several years developing her fantasy writing skills by designing computer software and writing proposals for defense department contracts.

After obtaining a degree in wildlife illustration and environmental education, **Doranna Durgin** spent a number of years deep in the Appalachian Mountains. When she emerged, it was as a writer who found herself irrevocably tied to the natural world and its creatures (which would explain the skull collection and all those unusual home-tanned skins). Doranna has a handful of fantasy novels out and four more in production, along with a smattering of anthology stories. She lives with two irrepressible Cardigan Welsh Corgis, Carbon Unit (Kacey) & Jean-Luc Picardigan. And if that's not entirely too much information already, go to www.doranna.net for all the latest news.

Karen Everson is a Jane-of-Most-Trades, including writer, artist, owner of "Moongate Designs," Mommy, and belly-dancer, though not exclusively nor in that order. She has a Master's degree in mythology but has never let that stop her from putting her nose into Byzantine history or anything else she finds interesting. Her published writings include numerous essays and a novel, *The Last Voyage Of Odysseus* (available through "Moongate Designs" and shameless self-promotion). "Incognito, Ergo Sum" marks her return to fiction. She lives in Canton, Michigan, with husband, Mark, daughter, Caitlyn, and her faithful cat, Topaz (a.k.a. furball with an attitude).

Eric Flint is the author of six novels, several of them in collaboration with David Drake. Born in California in 1947, Flint received his BA and MA in history from UCLA. He spent most of his adult life working as a machinist until he began writing in 1993. He currently resides in northwest Indiana with his wife, Lucille.

Esther M. Friesner, editor and creator of the popular CHICKS anthology series, lives in suburban Connecticut. This gives her great inspiration to continue with her writing career (i.e. "If I stop doing this, I'll have to get a real estate license or open an antiques store. It's the Law."). She has had thirty-odd books published, some odder than others, and over a hundred short stories. Of the latter, two have won the Nebula Award. She would like to live long enough to find out if success, wealth beyond the dreams of avarice, and the adoration of millions will spoil her. She rather hopes it will.

Nina Kiriki Hoffman has been pursuing a writing career for eighteen years and has sold more than 150 stories, two short story collections, several novels (*The Thread That Binds the Bones, The Silent Strength of Stones*, both from Avon, *A Red Heart of Memories*, from Ace, and *Past the Size of Dreaming*, also from Ace, due out in January 2001), several novellas, and a collaborative young adult novel with Tad Williams (*Child of an Ancient City*, Atheneum, re-released in mass-market size from Tor). She also collaborated on a Star Trek novel with Kristine Kathryn Rusch and Dean Wesley Smith, *Star Trek Voyager 15: Echoes*. She frequently sells short stories to DAW and Bruce Coville anthologies, and recently to *F&SF* Magazine and elsewhere. Hoffman lives in Eugene, Oregon, with many dolls, cats, and a growing anime collection.

Nancy Kress is the author of seventeen books: three fantasy novels, six SF novels, two thrillers, three collections of short stories, one YA novel, and two books on writing fiction. She is perhaps best known for the "Sleepless" trilogy that began with *Beggars in Spain*. Kress's short fiction has appeared in all the usual places. Her work has won three Nebulas and a Hugo, and has been translated into Swedish, French, Italian, German, Spanish, Polish, Croatian, Lithuanian, Romanian, Japanese, and Russian. In addition to writing fiction and regularly teaching at various places, including Clarion, Kress is the monthly Fiction columnist for *Writer's Digest* magazine.

Elizabeth Moon is a native Texan who did not grow up on a ranch (she wishes), never owned an oil well (ditto), and wasn't a cheerleader with big hair (ditto, NOT). To compensate for these fundamental gaps in a Texas girlhood, she joined the Marines, programmed computers, got elected to public office, worked on a rural ambulance crew, and finally started finishing the stories she wrote. Her novel *Remnant Population* was a Hugo Nominee in 1997. Her most recent novel is *Change of Command*; a sequel, *Against the Odds*, will be published by Baen in December 2000.

Kent Patterson was a science fiction writer from Eugene, Oregon, who before his death in 1995 achieved a small degree of infamy for his quirky sense of humor. Stories like "The Wereyam" and "Soren Sorensen's One Man, All Tuba, All Danish Band vs. the Short ET's" placed him firmly in the wacky-short-story camp, but his classical literature background would occasionally burst through with poetry. "To His Iron-Clad Mistress" was one such explosion, which he said was inspired by the sight—nay, the *vision*—of Leslie What in a chain mail bikini.

Mother Berchte (Berchta, Berta, Percht) first stormed out of folklore and into **Steven Piziks**'s life ten years ago. His life hasn't been the same since. This is his third sale to the *Chicks in Chainmail* series and his second sale involving Mother Berchte. (She stomped through *Marion Zimmer Bradley's FANTASY Magazine* in 1997.) Berchte now glares at him from the top of his Yule tree, daring him to write about her again, while Nassirskaegi burps in the branches below. He teaches English and health in southeastern Michigan, where he lives with his wife, son, and harp.

William Sanders was born in 1942 in Arkansas. He has been at various times a soldier, preacher, logger, construction worker, encyclopedia salesman, pow-wow dancer, and sportswriter, besides publishing 16 books. His short fiction has appeared in numerous magazines and anthologies; his story "The Undiscovered" was nominated for Hugo, Nebula, and Sturgeon Awards, and won the Sidewise Award for

Alternate History. His latest novel, *The Ballad of Billy Badass and the Rose of Turkestan*, was published in 1999. He lives in Tahlequah, Oklahoma, in a little old rock house, with his cat, his computer, and his motorcycle.

Charles Sheffield has published forty books. He is a winner of Nebula, Hugo, John W. Campbell Memorial, and Sei-un awards, and has had best-sellers of both fact and fiction. The story in this collection is the eleventh involving lawyers Henry Carver and Waldo Burmeister. He says that they are depressingly easy to write.

K.D. Wentworth used to have a life, but can't find it anymore. This is because of things like teaching 4th grade, working on con committees, and writing. As for the latter, she has sold short fiction to such markets as *F&SF, Hitchcock's, Realms of Fantasy, Return to the Twilight Zone,* and *Chicks and Chained Males.* Her fourth novel, *Black/on/Black*, was published by Baen in February 1999, and a sequel is currently in the works. Her first three novels, *The Imperium Game, Moonspeaker,* and *House of Moons* will be reprinted by Hawk Publishing, Summer, 2000.

Leslie What has published over forty short stories and many nonfiction feature articles and columns. Her work has been featured in a variety of magazines, including *The Writer, Amazing Stories, Hysteria, Asimov's,* and *The MacGuffin*, as well as in several anthologies. She has recently completed a comic novel and is at work on another. With Nina Kiriki Hoffman, she is the co-director of the *Writers On Rugs* photography studio. About the story, she writes: " 'Chain of Command' is a complete fabrication, a fanciful collaboration between two like-minded pranksters, and any resemblance to real life has absolutely nothing to do with the fact that I'm the mother of two teen-agers."